John and Susi Belmont were holding hands and laughing as their auto moved slowly down the driveway. The spring day had ended and the mercury vapor lamps were easing on to mark the evening.

Up ahead, they saw a blue car parked between trees alongside the driveway, its nose pointing out to the road. Suddenly they saw a man jump from behind the blue car into the driveway. He raised an automatic with two hands and fired. A bullet struck John Belmont in the eye before he could even slam on his brakes. The car careened off the roadway, jumped a small curb and hit a tree with a crash that shattered its front windshiel

Susi, covered ned once before th the open window her brain.

'Jesus Christ, Nicky.' Joey DeSalle croaked hoarsely behind the wheel of the blue Corvette. 'What's going to happen now?' He sounded even younger than he was.

His big brother laughed. 'Grow up, Joey. Nothing's going to happen. There ain't nobody in this town big enough to touch us.'

The Temple Dogs

Warren Murphy
and Molly Cochran

HEADLINE

Typeset in 10/12¼ pt Times
by Colset Private Limited, Singapore

Printed and bound in Great Britain by
Collins, Glasgow

HEADLINE BOOK PUBLISHING PLC
Headline House,
79 Great Titchfield Street
London W1P 7FN

This book is dedicated to
Eiko Nishimoto Cochran.
For her memories
and her dreams.

Hontoni arigato gozaimashita

Prologue

Yikio, the Master of Kozen Temple, was famed throughout the land as a trainer of dogs. It was widely believed that his dogs were able to suckle human young and to howl the melodies of temple chants.

A royal visitor one day watched Yikio's majestic animals perform and was impressed until he saw five dirty, flea-ridden, unkempt mongrels sleeping under a tree.

'And are these your failures?' the Prince asked.

'No,' Yikio said. 'They are my greatest successes.' He went on to explain that the five dogs were especially trained to guard the temple. 'As the sun goes down, one dog goes to the east wall, another to the west, and to the north and to the south, and there they patrol for the evening, repelling all bandits and keeping all safe within.'

'But there are five dogs. Where guards the fifth?'

'He is the most savage of all,' Yikio said. 'He sits inside the front door of the temple.'

'But why?' asked the Prince.

'Because most houses are brought down from inside the walls.'

– Japanese folk tale

BOOK ONE

MILES

1

The white chrysanthemums arrived anonymously, as they always did.

The unknown sender had been so conscientious through the years that the Haverfords had counted on the flowers, reserving an entire wall of New York's elegant Inn on the Park at their daughter's wedding reception.

They weren't disappointed. The blossoms, as delicate looking as the Eurasian bride, filled the wall and spilled over into the adjoining rooms, suffusing the restaurant with their soft fragrance.

Susi Haverford, now Mrs John Belmont, wore a white silk Mary McFadden gown covered by a Japanese ceremonial kimono duster, bright red and worked heavily with hand-painted gold. Her clothing, like her face, reflected the mingling of two cultures, two races, and as she danced with her brother, Miles, the two Haverford offspring looked like exotic and beautiful visitors from another planet.

'Even more flowers than usual,' Susi said.

'Our secret admirer never fails,' Miles said with a grin. He remembered a truckload of flowers had arrived at his apartment in New Haven on the day he graduated from law school. And it had been that way since they were toddlers. Every birthday, every personal milestone, had been greeted with white chrysanthemums; but no one ever knew where they came from.

At first their mother Mickey had believed that her

5

husband was sending them, but he quickly disabused her of that idea. 'Tomfoolery,' he had grumbled. 'And a waste of good money.'

As Miles spun her around the dance floor, Susi was able to see the vast array of the floral arrangements. 'These must have cost thousands,' she said. 'But why chrysanthemums? Aren't chrysanthemums for funerals?'

'Depends on where you live,' Miles said with authority. 'In Japan, chrysanthemums are the symbol of love.'

Susi smiled. 'I'm glad your two semesters of Japanese Language and Culture weren't wasted.' She closed her eyes as they danced, and Miles noticed how little she had changed since childhood. She looked as Japanese as their mother, golden-skinned and delicate. The difference between them was that Susi accentuated her Asian features with her makeup and clothing, while their mother had spent a fortune on plastic surgery to eradicate hers.

'You look beautiful,' Miles said quietly.

'I'll miss you, Miles.' She lay her head on his chest.

'Hey, this isn't goodbye. You can count on me for dinner every Sunday. John does cook, doesn't he?'

'Dog,' Susi growled mockingly and hugged him more tightly. 'Dad says you might join his law firm?'

Miles sighed. 'I guess so. I've been dodging it as long as I could, but I guess Dullstein, Boringly, and Stultifiable are now calling. God, Susi. Brain death as a career. Even marriage sounds better.'

Susi reddened. 'You'd still have to work sometime, at something,' she said stiffly.

Miles smiled at his sister.

'I'm sorry,' she said. 'I must be an awful bore.'

He kissed her forehead. 'Forget it, sis.'

In the tradition of younger sisters everywhere, Susi was given to worrying about Miles. It seemed to her that everything – money, women, athletic skill, social grace – had always come too easily for him. He was an excellent piano player who didn't practice; a fine boxer who, like as not, in a tough bout would surrender before the bell and walk out of the ring; potentially a brilliant lawyer who had chosen instead to party his way through Yale, graduating somewhere near the middle of his class.

Miles's lack of drive bothered Susi more than it did either of his parents. Mickey Haverford had never objected to her son's academic mediocrity, since he excelled at all the things that really mattered: he was six feet tall, darkly handsome, and possessed of the sort of shallow charm that shows best at cocktail parties. Miles was the perfect tenth man at dinner, glib, self-assured and undemanding – either of others or of himself – and the ideal escort for his mother on the many occasions when her husband begged off some unmissable 'A'-list party or another, preferring to hide in the sanctum of his law office.

As for Miles's father, Curtis Haverford felt nothing but disappointment in the boy who had once held so much promise. Miles had won a Westinghouse Science Award at eleven. He had given a piano recital of Bach fugues at Julliard when he was thirteen. By sixteen, he had read every book in Curtis's library, including those on law. And he was going to follow his father into the profession.

But that was long ago, it seemed. Long before Miles had lost interest in his future.

'It's just that you could do something wonderful with your life, if you wanted,' Susi said gently. 'If there were something worth dedicating yourself to . . .'

'Oh, Susi.'

'I mean it, Miles. You're special. Meant for special things. I've always known that about you.'

With a gesture, Miles invited his father to cut in. Curtis shook his head. During the brief exchange, Mickey

Haverford eyed the dancing couple with disdain, then, turned away.

'Okay, I'll shut up,' Susi said.

'Good.' He laughed. 'Did you see Mother? She looks like somebody forced a dill pickle down her throat.'

'It's my kimono,' Susi said with a sigh. 'She hates it. She hates anything that reminds her that she's Japanese.'

Miles didn't answer. He knew it was true. Mickey Haverford had spent more than forty thousand dollars on cosmetic surgery to systematically westernize the Asian features of her face.

'That's why she likes you so much better than she does me,' Susi went on. 'You don't look Japanese at all.'

'You're paranoid,' Miles said.

'Oh, I don't really mind. Not anymore. And she's been a lot better since I decided to marry John. He's a good round-eyed WASP, the way she likes them.'

She laughed and he joined her, but Miles felt uncomfortable all the same.

Susi had spoken the truth. Their mother exercised an almost absolute racial denial. She knew nothing about her own origins, and expressed no desire to know.

Mickey Haverford had been adopted by a wealthy Yankee couple when she was a small child. English was her first language, French her second. She had been raised in Westchester County, confirmed in the First Presbyterian Church, educated at Brearley and Barnard, married to an American husband, and produced two American children. There was, in fact, nothing Japanese about her.

But Miles remembered the woman on Fifth Avenue.

It had happened when Miles was still a small child. He had been walking down the sidewalk with his mother when a demented looking old woman lurched toward them muttering, 'Jap! Dirty Jap!'

Mickey had pulled Miles away, walking quickly to escape

8

the old harridan, but the woman had followed them, shouting and pointing, her eyes huge and bulging almost comically. 'You killed my son, Jap . . .'

'What's she talking about, Mom?' Miles had asked, but Mickey only rushed him silently toward home.

It was only later, when Miles sat up in his bed listening to his mother weep in his father's arms, that he realized it hadn't been the first time she'd been humiliated by a stranger.

And later, the same slights had been inflicted on his sister. Susi would come home from school in tears because of some obscene schoolyard insult. Miles had tried to comfort her.

'Don't pay any attention to them, Susi. The big event of their day is picking their noses.' He had smiled as he spoke, but he could feel the anger inside him threatening to explode. Anger, and something else – something deeper and infinitely more shameful.

They've never bothered me, he thought, *because I pass*.

'Anyway, Granddad stood up for me,' Susi said, bringing Miles back to the present. 'He told Mother that he'd traveled twelve thousand miles to bring me an antique kimono from Tokyo so that I'd have something old at my wedding besides him, and by God, I was going to wear it.'

Miles laughed aloud. 'The old man's more Japanese than Mother will ever be.' He spun Susi around and waved toward the bar, where their grandfather, Matt Watterson, was singing 'Amapola' along with the band. Watterson saw them, hoisted a glass of champagne in salute, and kept singing.

At seventy-five, he was still a big, hulking man who had lost none of his wavy white hair and only a little of the stevedore physique that had earned him the nickname Shiro Ushi, or 'White Bull,' in Japan during his younger days. No one could have looked less like an expert in Oriental

9

antiquities than Matt Watterson, yet among the trade his name was as respected as his fortune.

As Susi and Miles watched, a change came over the old man. His mouth fell open and the glass in his hand dropped with a crash to the floor. Susi gasped, pulled free of Miles, and ran toward him.

'Granddad!' she shouted, reaching for him. But Watterson waved her away absently while he walked toward the door.

Seven men had just entered. They were a strange group. All of them were Japanese. Six of the men, identically dressed in blue suits, formed a double phalanx on either side of the seventh, a diminutive old man with thinning gray hair and slender, sensitive hands, which he kept folded in front of him.

The crowd parted for the small man and his entourage. Even the band faltered, and a murmur went up from the guests as Matt Watterson moved slowly and hesitantly forward.

'Sadimasa?' he said softly into the silence.

The small man turned to Watterson and bowed deeply. His wrinkled face struggled with emotion.

The two old men stood facing each other for a long moment as if they were both suspended in space, then Watterson rushed forward, and they embraced like lost brothers while the blue-suited Orientals formed a protective circle around them.

The music started up again. 'I thought he was having a heart attack,' Susi said, sidestepping the busboy who had come to clean up the broken glass from Watterson's spilled drink. 'Who is that man?'

Miles shrugged. 'Drinking buddy, probably.'

'Don't be stupid,' Susi snapped as the circle around the two old men broke and Watterson stepped out, his arm draped over the old man's shoulder like a bear's. 'Look at

Granddad's face. He's so happy he's *crying*. And what are all those other men doing with him? They look like some sort of praetorian guard.'

'Guess you can ask him yourself,' Miles said. 'They're coming this way.'

Watterson brought the man over to them and introduced him as Mr Nagoya. The old man bowed to the bride.

'And this must be your grandson,' Nagoya said, extending his hand to Miles.

Watterson's florid face flushed even deeper. 'Yes. Yes, it is,' he mumbled. 'Miles, Mr Nagoya is –'

The old man dismissed Watterson's words with a gesture. 'I am a person of no account, whose worthless life your grandfather once saved.'

Watterson's lips tightened, and Miles saw the big man's pale eyes shine with tears.

'During the war?' Miles asked politely.

Watterson nodded, then took Nagoya by the shoulder and led him away. 'C'mon, Sadimasa. I want you to meet Mickey. That's what we call Masako, my . . .'

'Daughter,' Nagoya finished for him.

Susi leaned over to Miles and whispered, 'I hope he's not going to call her Masako.' She giggled.

'Not if he knows what's good for him.' He took her arm. 'I'd better get you back to your husband,' he said. 'It looks like Big John needs his woman.'

Susi halted abruptly. 'Miles, look.' She pointed toward the wall of white chrysanthemums. 'It must be the light, or something.'

'What are you pointing at?'

'The arrangement. Look there, in the center. The flowers are making a picture, Miles. It's a . . .'

Then Miles saw it, and his breath caught.

The top flowers had been arranged into a circle, and within the circle was a cascade of petals resembling a wave.

11

A *wave*. He felt a cold shiver run down his spine.

'It's your imagination,' he said, leading her away before she could notice the sweat suddenly beaded on his face.

Nick DeSanto nearly drove off the road while tooting a line of cocaine.

'Righteous!' he shouted, the rolled-up dollar bill still hanging from his nose.

The girls in the car were screaming. 'Jesus, Nicky, take it easy, will you?' his younger brother Joey pleaded, shoving his blonde girlfriend off his lap.

'What, you suddenly Mr Safety? Who's in charge here, anyway?'

'You are, Nicky,' the girl in the front seat said placatingly. She reached for a cigarette with one hand and placed the other on Nick's crotch. He slapped it away.

'Hey, what's with you?' she shrilled. 'All day you been like this.'

'Shut up, will you?' Nick roared. He took the bill out of his nose and threw it out the window.

With a shrug Joey took another dollar from his wallet and gallantly passed it and a silver coke box to his girl.

It had been a rotten day, Joey thought philosophically, and it had started the night before. The two brothers had lost nearly three thousand dollars between them at Mongo Lewis's poker game, not to mention the five grand down the drain at Belmont because Jimmy Belcastro's hot tip turned out to be a washout.

Joey decided that Jimmy Belcastro had better start saying his Hail Marys now, because Nicky was going to put a big hole in his plumbing just as soon as the opportunity arose. He had planned to find Belcastro that afternoon and do the job right there in Jimmy's apartment, except that the girls started complaining about how they'd bought new dresses and wanted to go somewhere legit for a change instead of the Peyton Place, where all the guys hung out.

Nicky was as pissed off as he could be, and was going to belt his girl, Gloria, when she started in whining like that, but Joey said that a fancy dinner in a nice place like the Inn on the Park would make them all feel better.

Even though he was only nineteen years old – a dozen years younger than Nick – Joey was a voice of reason in the DeSanto family, the diplomat of the two brothers. Besides, he'd copped a new stolen credit card he wanted to use before the numbers showed up on the hot list.

Nicky skidded the royal blue Corvette to a halt in front of the restaurant, forcing the valet to leap out of the way.

'See that you keep an eye on it,' Nick said, tossing the keys to the young man.

The valet caught the keys. 'Are you with the party, sir?'

'What are you talking about?' Nick growled. 'Open the door for the lady.'

'I'm afraid the restaurant is closed today, sir. The restaurant has been booked for a private party. A wedding reception.'

'Get out of here.'

'Sir . . .'

Nick muscled his way past the young man to the front door.

'May I see your invitation, sir?' the doorman asked.

'Get out of my face.' He tried to shove the doorman aside, but the doorman grabbed his arm. Nick made a fist and leaned backward, aiming for the man's face, when the valet ran up to restrain him.

It was at this point that Joey DeSanto hurled himself from the Corvette to take down the valet. Nick's right hook landed square on the doorman's chin. All four of them crashed to the ground, grunting and cursing as the restaurant manager came out, followed by a small group of onlookers.

13

'I'm calling the police,' the manager shouted.

'The fuck you are,' said Nick DeSanto, rolling out of the grip of the doorman flat onto his stomach, where he reached inside his jacket and pulled out a .22 Beretta.

A woman in the crowd screamed. The manager dropped to the ground, hands in the air, and the few guests clustered around the doorway darted back inside. The doorman and the valet froze in their positions, eyeing Nick wildly.

'Nicky, Nicky,' Joey said, smiling, using his most conciliatory voice. 'It's a dumbshit restaurant, no big deal.' He stood up slowly, brushing his silk suit with his manicured hands. 'Come on. We'll go to '21. The girls'll love it. Whaddya say, Nicky?'

Nick Desanto didn't move a muscle. For an interminable moment he stayed on his stomach, eyes fixed on the restaurant manager's bald head, finger poised on the trigger of the small automatic. Then, with infinite slowness, he rose and walked over to the manager. The gun was still in his hands; his pace was that of an executioner.

'So you gonna call the police, huh, Pops?'

'No. No,' the manager said softly, emphasizing the point with quivering tosses of his sweating head.

'Do you know who my father is?' Nick touched the barrel of the gun to the manager's scalp. 'Look at me, you stupid fuck.'

The manager looked, jowls trembling.

'I asked you if you knew who my daddy was.'

The manager squinted, then opened his eyes wide. 'Oh, God. God.'

Joey DeSanto laughed. 'That's close, eh, Nicky? "God." That's good.'

'Shut up.' He pressed the gun deeper against the manager's head. 'We want a table.'

'Y – yes, sir,' the bald man whispered, nodding frantically.

'Hey, Nicky, we don't need this shit,' Joey said. 'The girls –'

'Shut *up*!' He kicked the manager on the side of his ample stomach. 'Get up.'

The manager complied.

'And you're going to clear out a room for us. The best room, got it?'

The manager nodded and began stumbling toward the crowd packed inside. Nick and Joey swaggered along behind him. But just as they reached the doorway, six Japanese men in blue suits spilled out of the reception room like two streams of running water.

Before the two brothers could do anything, they were carried bodily down the front steps of the restaurant building. The gun was out of Nick's hand, skittering along the driveway. Then both brothers were thrown roughly on top of the blue Corvette.

'I'll kill you!' Nick rasped as the car door opened and he was thrust inside, with Joey following. The girls in the car screamed as the two men landed on top of them, sending the silver cocaine box flying in a blizzard of white dust.

'Stupid bitch!' Nick shouted, grabbing at the swirling powder with two hands. He looked back at the restaurant, but the six men had already vanished back inside and the heavy front door was closing behind them.

'Oh, God, Nicky, I thought you were both dead,' Gloria said. 'When they stuffed you in here like that –'

'Just shut your fat flap, okay?'

'Hey, you don't have to get shitty about it –'

Nick punched her in the mouth, then gunned the accelerator and tore out of the parking area with a squeal of burning rubber.

About a half mile away, where Central Park gave way to city blocks, Nick slammed on the brakes. He looked at Gloria, who was weeping loudly. Her hair was disheveled, coated by a veil of cocaine. Her makeup ran down her cheeks in black streams. Blood and mucus poured from her nose.

'Get the fuck out of here,' he said, showing her the back of his hand.

Cowering and emitting little squeals of grief, she got out.

'Her too,' Nick said, jerking his thumb toward Joey's girl in the back seat. Joey shrugged at his date in explanation. She huffed out, slamming the door.

'Fatassed bimbo,' Nick said.

Joey came around to the front seat. 'Relax, Nicky, okay? She's just a little teed off. You want me to drive?'

'Get in,' Nick said stonily.

Joey got in with a sigh.

'Where's the rest of the blow?'

'I got it right here, Nicky.' Joey pulled a glassine envelope from beneath the passenger seat and sifted it expertly into the small silver box. 'I even got a nice new bill for you, see that?' He snapped a crisp dollar bill near the windshield. 'Hey, you want to go to the Hilton, maybe pick up some fancy gash?'

'We're going back.'

Joey smiled nervously as his brother took the car up to eighty. 'What, that dump again? Why don't we just forget it, Nicky. Pop'll send Frankie Lupone to talk to the guy. Fat Frank'll see to it that he's real sorry, believe me –'

'Damn gooks.'

They rode in silence for a moment. Joey had hoped his brother had been too angry to notice the race of the six men. Nick had hated gooks, ever since his best friend, Hands Aleutta, had died in Vietnam. Hands had taught Nick everything he knew about the business. It was Nick's father's business, the counterfeiting and numbers and dope, but Anthony DeSanto had raised his children strictly, never bringing a trace of the rackets home with him. It was

16

only through Hands Aleutta that Nick even got a glimpse into the powerful feifdom that his father controlled, and it was through Hands that Nick was arrested for the first time.

Hands had allowed Nick, who was fifteen, to ride along while he drove to Florida with some stolen automobile parts. But they had been caught, and Hands had pulled six months at Lewisburg.

Tony DeSanto got his son off without probation, but he was furious. Nick was restricted to the house for the next year, although during that time he devised a hundred ways to escape and return undetected. What worried him more was Hands's safety. On one of his outings he visited Lewisburg, where he found Hands pale and nervous.

'It's your old man,' he said. 'He's pissed off. He can have me killed.'

Nick laughed. 'What? My pop? He wouldn't kill anybody.'

'Shit, kid, your pop's so big he don't even have to wipe his own ass, you understand? He wants somebody done, poof, they are gone. Case closed. And I got you arrested, Nicky. I got Tony DeSanto's boy his first mugshot. Christ,' he said, running the big strangler's hands that had earned him his name through his hair. 'I'm dead.'

Three days before Hands was due for release, Nick visited him again and was greeted with new cheer. 'I got an idea, kid,' Hands said brightly. 'Your old man ain't going to get to me, because I got a plan.' The man's lips spread in a big, silly grin. A cigarette dangled out of the space left by a missing tooth. 'I'm going to join the frigging Army,' he said.

'Nobody joins the Army' was all Nick could finally think of to say.

It was true. No one in Nick DeSanto's family, none of his family's friends, none of his own friends that he met through Hands or their fathers, had ever been in military service. It was just not done. The affairs of government were the affairs of law, and the further one stayed away from the law, the better off he was.

But Hands was insistent. He was released, enlisted, and was killed in combat the fourth day after he arrived in Vietnam.

'Hands got shot down by gooks,' Nick said, snorting some coke as he steered the Corvette back into the park.

'I know, Nicky.'

'Probably some of the same gooks in there.'

The car slowed to a halt some hundred yards from the restaurant, obscured from view by some tall bushes.

'What are we doing here?' Joey asked.

Nick didn't answer. He took a pair of gloves from his visor, then reached over Joey's lap to the special shelf he'd had cut behind the glove compartment and pulled out a .38 Browning.

'Hey, Nicky –'

'It's clean.'

'What are you –'

'Change places with me.'

Susi Haverford Belmont and her new husband stood on the long, curving stairway to wave good-bye to the wedding guests. As she tossed the bouquet, she saw her brother standing behind the women, his arms folded across his chest, grinning.

'It's for you,' she mouthed. 'You're next.'

Miles shook his head, then blew her a kiss.

It was the last time he saw her alive.

The bridegroom's car, festooned with tin cans and tissue-paper flowers, pulled out slowly from the lot in front of the Inn on the Park. Because it was considered bad luck to watch the newlyweds drive away, no one had escorted them from the restaurant building.

John and Susi Belmont were holding hands and laughing as their auto moved slowly down the driveway. The spring day had ended and the mercury vapor lamps were easing on to mark the evening.

Up ahead, they saw a blue car parked between trees alongside the driveway, its nose pointing out to the road. Suddenly they saw a man jump from behind the blue car into the driveway. He raised an automatic with two hands and fired. A bullet struck John Belmont in the eye before he could even slam on his brakes. The car careened off the roadway, jumped a small curb, and hit a tree with a crash that shattered its front windshield.

Susi, covered with her husband's blood, screamed once before the second bullet whizzed through the open window on the driver's side and pierced her brain. She fell forward across her husband's dead body. The impact jammed his foot down onto the gas pedal and the car's motor began to race wildly, its rear wheels biting deeply into the freshly planted damp spring sod.

'Jesus Christ, Nicky!' Joey DeSanto croaked hoarsely behind the wheel of the blue Corvette.

For a wild moment Nick spun on his brother, aiming the .38 double handed at him through the windshield of the blue Corvette.

'Nicky – Nicky, no,' Joey whimpered, slowly raising his arms in the air. 'I'm your brother, Nicky.'

With a slump of his body, Nick broke his trancelike concentration.

A few shouts came now from the entryway to the Inn on the Park. Nicky DeSanto ran off the roadway, slid into the Corvette beside Joey, and tossed the gun out the window.

'Hurry up,' he growled. 'Get out of here.'

The Corvette squealed backward in a cloud, then

19

maneuvered behind some bushes. It had disappeared the way it had come before the first frantic wedding guests arrived at the scene.

Joey gripped the steering wheel with two white-knuckled hands. 'What's going to happen now, Nicky?' he asked. He sounded even younger than he was.

His big brother laughed. 'Grow up, Joey. Nothing's going to happen. There ain't nobody in this town big enough to touch us.'

When their bodies were found, John and Susi Belmont's hands were still entwined.

2

Five days after the funeral, Matt Watterson persuaded his daughter and son-in-law to take a trip to the Bahamas. There was nothing they could do at home, he reasoned, except grieve for their lost daughter, and there was time enough for that. During their absence, he and Miles quietly began to put Susi's things away.

'It'll be easier on your mother this way,' Watterson said.

Miles nodded numbly. He picked up a photograph of himself and Susi that she'd kept on the nightstand beside her bed. It was a picture from a Hallowe'en more than fifteen years before. Miles was dressed as a cowboy, and Susi as a clown. She had insisted on putting on her makeup herself, he remembered. It was one of the first of the battles royal between Susi and their mother, and it was plain to see from the paint smeared all over Susi's triumphant little moon face who the winner had been.

Miles stared at it, feeling a flood of memories of his sister washing over him in sickening waves, until the glass of the frame broke in his hands.

'Son,' Watterson said.

Miles threw the shattered photograph against the wall. 'What the hell are the police *doing?* It's been a week. They've got descriptions of those guys from a dozen people.'

'I know. I'm as frustrated as you are. But the law will come through, count on it.'

'The law,' Miles said.

21

Watterson picked up the photograph, dusting the broken glass off it. 'I took this picture,' he said quietly. Then he sat on the floor with his head in his hands.

The doorbell rang. 'Damn it,' Watterson said as Miles rose, 'tell them nobody's home.'

Miles came back a moment later. 'Granddad,' he said hesitantly, 'it's your friend, Mr Nagoya. I tried to tell him –'

'I'll see him.' The big man lumbered upright.

Watterson embraced the Japanese man in the doorway. As Miles excused himself to leave the two old men alone, he saw Nagoya wipe his eyes. For the first time Miles noticed that the small finger of his left hand had been severed at the knuckle.

'I have come to ask permission to say the prayers of mourning for your granddaughter,' he said brokenly.

Watterson took his hand. 'Sadimasa . . .'

The small Japanese pulled himself erect. 'We must both grieve, Shiro Ushi, in our own way. I have brought you some information.' He reached into his jacket pocket and pulled out a slip of paper.

'What is this?' Watterson asked, examining it.

'The names of the two men who came uninvited to the wedding reception. And their address. They are brothers.'

'How – how did you find this out?'

Nagoya lowered his expressionless face. 'It is not necessary to burden you with such trivial matters, Shiro Ushi-san. It is sufficient that you have the information.'

Watterson stared at him for a moment. 'You're never going to tell me anything about yourself, are you?' he asked.

'I owe you my life. All else is meaningless.'

Watterson glared at him for a moment longer, then begrudgingly smiled. 'All right, have it your way. Thanks. I'll give these names to the police.'

Nagoya inhaled sharply. 'I do not believe these men will bend easily to the law.'

'What the hell's that supposed to mean?'

'Nothing, my friend. I meant nothing. The police will do their best, I am sure. Please inform me of their findings.'

'Oh, you'll be in the thick of things. The detectives have been looking for you and your friends.'

Nagoya raised an eyebrow. 'For me?'

'They want to match your description of these two guys with Miles's and mine. Your men were the only ones who saw them up close.'

Nagoya hesitated. 'I am afraid that will not be possible,' he said apologetically. 'We leave for Tokyo this afternoon.'

'Now wait a minute. You can't go. Not now. Not just like that.'

'It is with deep regret that I leave, Shiro Ushi. But it is necessary.'

'The police –'

'They will not require our testimony.'

'Why not?'

'Because there will be no case against these men.'

'What?'

'The police will not arrest them. Their presence at the restaurant does not prove their guilt.'

'Then why would you give their names to me?' Watterson asked belligerently.

'Sometimes, Shiro Ushi, there are other ways.'

'What do you propose we do, blow these punks away ourselves?'

Nagoya didn't answer. But his eyes never left Watterson's.

'You must be crazy.'

The Japanese smiled gently. 'All men our age are entitled to a little madness, no?' He touched his friend's arm. 'I must go.'

23

'But you just . . .' Watterson stuck his hands into his pockets. 'I don't know if I can last another forty years,' he said.

'We shall meet again, my friend. If not in this life, then perhaps in the next. But I will not forget. I will never forget.'

Watterson turned away, blinking.

'I ask but one thing of you, Shiro Ushi.'

'What is it?' Watterson asked hoarsely.

'I hope that I am wrong about these men and about the ability of your police and your laws to bring them to justice. But if I am not, I beg you to get word to me.'

Watterson grunted. 'What are you going to do?'

'I beg you, Shiro Ushi.'

Watterson turned around slowly. Their eyes met again. The two men bowed. This time Watterson made sure that his bow was lower than that of the aged Japanese.

Miles watched out the window as two of Nagoya's blue-suited soldiers escorted him into a waiting black limousine. The others followed in another car.

'Who is he, Granddad?'

'I don't think I'll ever know for sure.' Watterson poured himself a glass of Irish whiskey and sat down heavily. 'I knew Nagoya in the late thirties. His family owned the biggest auction house for Japanese antiquities in Tokyo, sort of the Sotheby's of the Far East. But the war took care of all that. He lost everything.'

He pointed to a tall vase in a glass case in the corner of the room. 'Nagoya gave that to me in thirty-nine. Fourteenth century. It was from his family's personal collection. Even then, he knew it was the end and wanted to save it.'

'So he gave it away? It must be worth a fortune. He could have just asked you to store it for him.'

Watterson shook his head. 'A Japanese couldn't do

24

that,' he said. 'You see, he was entrusting its *ka* – its soul –
to me. Once that transfer is made, it can't be reversed. The
gift wasn't given lightly.'

'And you never saw him again?'

'Once. Right after the war. That was the last time, until
the day Susi was killed.' He swallowed the rest of his drink
in a gulp.

Miles was puzzled. 'But then . . . how did he know about
the wedding?'

'Oh, I kept in touch.' The old man stared out the window. 'It's a strange story. About five years after the war
ended, one of those gnomes of his came to my office with a
gift from Nagoya.' He gave his grandson a sly look. 'I've
still got it. Care to see?'

'Sure,' Miles said.

They went into the bedroom of the Haverfords' Manhattan apartment, which had been Watterson's home as well
since his wife had died. The room was spare and plain.
Aside from the vase, Watterson had chosen to bring along
none of the antiques and Oriental treasures that had filled
his big Victorian mansion in Westchester.

Inside his dresser drawer, beside the revolver he'd bought
after he got out of the service, was a plain white box nearly
six inches square. Watterson removed it and opened it carefully on his bed. There was another box inside, metal,
sealed with wax. He carefully peeled off the seal and
opened it.

A third box rested inside. It was covered with brilliantly
painted silk. On its corners were designs of elaborate gold
filigree in Chinese style. 'I don't know how Nagoya managed to get such a thing,' Watterson said. 'Gold in Japan in
1950 was practically nonexistent.'

Slowly Watterson lifted the lid.

Miles gasped. Lying in the center of the box, on a bed of
white silk, was the top joint of a man's little finger.

It took Miles a moment to find his voice. 'Nagoya's?'

Watterson nodded.

'But why?'

The old man held the box in his lap. 'He entrusted his *ka* to me. This was a token of his appreciation.'

'For taking his vase?' Miles whistled.

Watterson smiled. 'Not for the vase.' He put the box away. 'He said you saved his life.'

The old man grunted. 'Yes, I suppose I did.'

'Then the finger was for that,' Miles said, probing.

'The finger was a kind of down payment.' He closed the dresser drawer slowly. 'You see, the Japanese take things very seriously. When you save a man's life over there, he owes you a debt that money can't repay. He owes you his life. Literally. Nagoya was telling me that by sending me his finger.'

He sat back down on the bed. 'There was a message with it. Nagoya wanted me to write to him every month. He made me promise. He wanted me to fill him in on everything that went on with my family. Every month until the day I die.'

Miles laughed. 'He must have been a lonely guy.'

Watterson stared straight ahead. 'Yes. He lost his whole family in the war. He was probably lonely as hell.'

Miles cleared his throat, ashamed of his insensitivity. 'I'll bet you did it, too,' he said.

The old man nodded. 'Not that the son of a bitch ever wrote back.' His somber mood dissipated as quickly as it had come. 'Not a postcard. To this day, I don't even know where he lives. All I've got is a post office box at Ginza Station in Tokyo.' He chuckled. 'It got to be so maddening that on one of my trips to Japan I hired a private detective to help me find him. I came up empty.'

'But you kept writing? How did you know he was even still alive?'

26

'The flowers,' he said quietly.

Miles whirled around to face him. 'The wave! Inside the flowers. You saw it, too!'

'Always. In every arrangement. I didn't think you'd notice.'

'I didn't, until the last time. Granddad –'

'I can't tell you any more, son. Don't ask me to.'

'But the wave. It's the same –'

'You'll know everything someday. Just be patient.'

He put an arm around Miles's shoulder to usher him out the door. 'Listen, son. One thing I wanted to tell you.'

'What's that?'

'If anything ever happens to me, you let Nagoya know. I keep his address inside the drawer with the gun. Okay?'

'Sure. But what's going to happen to you?'

'Nothing,' the old man said. 'But remember Nagoya.'

Watterson gave the names of Nick and Joey DeSanto to the police. Within a week a detective named Halloran visited him with their findings.

'It wasn't them,' Halloran said.

'How do you know they didn't kill her?'

'Because they weren't there. Mr Watterson, the DeSanto boys are not the two men you saw at the restaurant.'

'What?' Watterson exploded. 'Damn it, my grandson and I identified their pictures at the station.'

'I'm sorry, sir. Both of them have an airtight alibi. Thirty witnesses swear they spent the whole day at a bar in Little Italy called the Peyton Place. There was some kind of birthday party or something.'

'That can't be. They were at the Inn on the Park, I tell you.'

'I have only your word for that, Mr Watterson, and your grandson's. Nobody else saw them.'

'What about Nagoya?' Watterson asked in desperation.

27

'What if I could get him and the six Japanese men who beat the DeSantos up –'

'You can do what you like, Mr Watterson, but frankly, I don't think it'll make much difference. The witnesses who matter don't happen to agree with you.'

'Which witnesses?'

'Let's see,' Halloran said. He looked through the papers in his lap. 'Okay, the doorman. You claim he was on the ground, fighting with the DeSantos –'

'Yes, yes.'

'Well, he claims they were never there. Ditto the valet. Also the manager.'

'You must be joking,' Watterson said. 'The *manager* doesn't remember them? They threatened to shoot him through the head.'

Halloran sighed. 'Yeah. Well.'

'Officer, they're not telling the truth.'

'Look, Mr Watterson. You want the truth, I'll tell you. The manager could be lying. The doorman and the valet, too. All those bums at the Peyton Place, everybody involved. But it's still their word against yours. All of them.'

'But why would they all lie? Who are these boys?'

'Mr Watterson –'

'Who are they?' the old man roared.

'They're Tony DeSanto's sons.'

'DeSanto, DeSanto . . . I think I've heard of him. Isn't he some kind of gangster?'

The detective laughed bitterly. 'Yeah, he's some kind of gangster. He's the head of the biggest mob organization in New York City. Believe me, if there was any way we could get at DeSanto through this incident, we'd do it.'

'So he's covered up for his boys,' Watterson said quietly. 'And I guess that means they can do anything they want, kill anybody they want. Is that what you're telling me?'

'Mr Watterson, I wish I could put them away for you. But my hands are tied. You see, even if we could break the restaurant manager's story – *and* the doorman's, *and* the valet's, *and* the gang's at the Peyton Place – it still wouldn't prove anything except that the DeSanto brothers came to the wedding reception and then left before the murder. It would be a long investigation, and we'd probably come up with nothing. It's been two weeks already, and all we've got is an unregistered gun with no fingerprints and an unshakable alibi.'

'So this investigation is over, is that what you're saying?'

'As far as Nick and Joey DeSanto are concerned,' Halloran said. He paused. 'For what it's worth, the decision to drop this wasn't mine.'

'They killed my granddaughter.'

There was a long silence. 'I'm sorry,' Halloran said softly.

3

The first thing Watterson did that evening was to send Miles out. 'Why don't you get lost for an evening?' he said. 'You've been hangdogging around here long enough.'

'I don't think so,' Miles said. 'I thought I'd stay home with you.'

'Who needs you?' He touched Miles's shoulder. 'The truth is, I want to spend some time alone.'

Miles uncurled his long frame from the sofa he'd been lying on. 'All right, I'll get out of your hair.' He was putting on his jacket when Watterson came up to him. 'Son,' he said awkwardly. 'I – I –'

'Yes, Granddad?'

'I want you to make something of your life.'

'That's sort of what I was going to talk to you about,' Miles said.

When the old man just looked at him, Miles said, 'I've decided to join Dad's law firm.'

'I thought you regarded that place as the seventh circle of Hades,' Watterson said, smiling.

Miles shrugged. 'It's something I ought to do.'

' "Ought to do"? Dammit, boy, that's the worst reason in the world for doing anything.'

'I don't know. I just thought with . . . with Susi gone, maybe I ought to start being more responsible. A better son.'

'Miles. I don't care if you go in that sappy law firm or

31

not. All I want is for you to do something important. Something that makes a difference. To you. Not to anybody else. Not to me or your father or your mother. Not even to your sister's memory. To you. Do you understand?'

Miles looked at the floor. 'What if nothing makes any difference?'

'Then your life's over before it starts,' Watterson said.

Miles tightened his jaw. 'I guess I'll be on my way.' He started out the door.

'Miles.'

'Yes?'

'I love you,' Watterson said softly.

Miles smiled. 'I love you too.'

The second thing Watterson did was to check his gun.

It was an old Smith & Wesson revolver that he'd kept in his office during the sixties and seventies. It was wrapped in a towel now, stored in the same drawer where he kept Nagoya's strange gift.

Watterson hefted it in his hand. He had never fired it except for a few practice sessions. The cold metal felt foreign and distasteful to him. Nagoya's words came back, spinning in his thoughts like wisps of cotton candy:

Sometimes, Shiro Ushi, there are other ways.

Watterson spun the empty barrel. If he killed the De Santos, he would go to jail for the rest of his life.

He put in one bullet.

It's your word against theirs, all of them . . .

Two bullets.

An airtight alibi. No further investigation.

Three, four, five.

These men will not bend easily to the law, my friend.

Six.

His granddaughter had been shot in the face with a bullet like these, and the men who killed her were going to go free.

He closed the barrel. Sometimes there were other ways.

The next thing Matt Watterson did was to write a note, which he sealed inside an envelope and placed inside his dresser drawer atop the plain white box that contained Nagoya's finger.

In the kitchen he wrote another note to Miles, placed it on the table there, put on a light jacket, and left.

The DeSanto home was a large brick Tudor mansion in the Park Slope area of Brooklyn. From the street, Watterson could see only a glimpse of the long, circular driveway behind the thick boxwood hedges and the forbidding black ironwork fence. In the driveway was a blue Corvette.

Watterson parked his car in front of the fence and waited. As the darkness deepened, the lights in the house were lit one by one. Occasionally he saw a shadow move inside. His legs were cramping. He checked his watch: ten o'clock. He had been waiting for six hours. Then the front door opened, and Watterson felt his heart pound. A shouted remark, a door slamming, then the blue Corvette pulled out of the driveway, through the black iron gates, into the street.

Panting to keep his breath, Watterson followed.

The car stopped in lower Manhattan, in the section known as Little Italy, in front of a dingy stucco building with a sign reading 'PEYTON PLACE' in neon script above the doorway. It was the sort of bar Watterson had seen in every American small town he had ever visited: plain no frills, nothing to attract tourists or casual visitors. It looked incongruous next to the gaily colored awnings and brightly lit windows of the Italian storefronts and restaurants. But what seemed even more out of place was the parking lot. It was filled with expensive cars, some of them with chauffeurs who stood around smoking or reading the newspapers.

Nick DeSanto didn't even bother to roll up the windows of the Corvette. He hopped out, shouting greetings to the drivers, who all waved to him. In front of the Peyton Place, he shook hands with a grotesquely fat man and spoke to him in Brooklynese-tinged Italian. When he opened the door of the bar, several voices called out to him.

He's at home here, Watterson thought, sweating.

Thirty witnesses swear . . .

And then, almost with a feeling of regret, he realized that he could not kill Nick DeSanto. Not without knowing for certain that he and his brother were guilty.

Detective Halloran had been right. Suppose the restaurant employees had been scared into changing their stories. Suppose all thirty witnesses were lying. It still proved nothing. It was the law.

The law. It was the only thing that separated men like himself from the killers who had destroyed his grand-daughter's life on her wedding day. If he pulled the trigger of that gun, would Matt Watterson be any better than any other murderer?

Despite all appearances, despite even Watterson's own gut feeling about them, Nick and Joey DeSanto may not have been guilty. He had to accept that. He had to obey the law.

But he had to see Nick DeSanto for himself.

He walked in behind Nick and sat at the bar. More than one pair of eyes looked him over. Watterson ordered Bushmill's.

The interior of the place was better than the outside suggested. It was spacious and cool, with a horseshoe-shaped bar near the door and a dozen tables in the rear, along with plush banquettes in the darkened corners. At the tables were a few couples, Watterson noticed, or rather, the female halves of couples. Most of the men were congregated at the bar while the women sat alone, fidgeting with

34

their drinks and adjusting their clothing and jewelry.

Every so often one of the men at the bar would peel off from the group and walk to the banquette in the farthest corner of the room, where a man sat alone. Although it was hard for Watterson to see the man well in the dim light, he appeared to be tall, with a head of slicked-back thinning gray hair.

He wore rings on both hands. As he spoke with his guests, diamonds glittered with every gesture. Watterson mused that among all the wealthy men he had known in his life, not one of them had worn diamonds.

There was a bottle of red wine on the table before the gray-haired man. As each visitor sat down, the man poured him a small glass. His own glass was full and remained virtually untouched.

A scene repeated itself again and again: the gray-haired man listened intently to his visitor for a few minutes and then he would speak, gesturing and flashing his diamonds. Then he would clap his hand on the shoulder of the man he was talking to, and the visitor – the supplicant – would nod and rise and hurry away. And the gray-haired man would take another empty glass from a tray on the table and place it in front of the empty spot.

Watterson thought he looked like an old-fashioned Boston ward heeler holding court for out-of-work constituents.

One of the men came back to the bar and sat within earshot.

'Well?' someone asked him. It was the fat man who had been outside.

'Nothing,' the other man said.

'Didn't you need nothing? Didn't you ask him for nothing?'

'I don't need nothing. I only come here because he gets sore if I don't.'

The fat man wheezed out a laugh.

'I'm serious, Frankie. You work for him, you got to go through this shit so's he can sit there like King Lancelot. Jeez.'

Frankie nodded, his huge cheeks billowing up around his eyes. 'Yeah. So what'd you say?'

'I told him I hit my wife.' He shrugged.

'Do you?'

'Get out. I hit my wife, she'd cut my balls off.'

Frankie's whalelike body rippled with laughter.

'Hey, I got to say something, don't I? So now he forgives me, and I ain't supposed to hit her no more.'

Fat Frank slapped the table, wheezing stentoriously.

Matt Watterson wondered what the man in the back banquette would have thought if he could have overheard this conversation, but his thoughts were interrupted as the fat man turned and looked at him. The laughter had faded from his eyes. 'What are you staring at?'

Watterson tried a smile. 'I didn't mean to stare.' He shifted slightly in his seat, turning away.

Frankie Lupone stood up, walked the few steps over to him, and knocked over his drink. 'Sorry,' he said. He was smiling, but his eyes were vicious.

Watterson wiped his hands with a cocktail napkin. 'That's all right,' he said quietly.

'That's my seat you're in.'

Watterson looked past him to the seat he had just vacated. 'What about the one you were sitting on?'

The fat man doodled in the spilled liquor on the bar with his finger. 'That one's mine, too.'

Watterson got up slowly.

'That's better.'

'You don't like strangers here, do you?'

'Now, why would you say that?' Frank laughed uproariously as the other men at the bar grinned.

'What's the problem here?' A handsome young man in a silk suit stepped between them. It was the first time Watterson had seen Nick DeSanto's face close up. He was much better looking, Watterson thought, than his mug shots.

Nick had the kind of clean face that juries trust and women find attractive. He wore his hair combed straight back. His eyes were soft, lazy, and smiling. He spoke with the authority of a man accustomed to getting what he wanted without having to ask for it.

'I saw you spill this gentleman's drink. What's the matter, Frank, you getting clumsy in your old age? Huh?' He slapped the fat man good-naturedly on his bulbous jowl.

Frank laughed again. 'My mistake.'

'I haven't see you here before,' Nick said, extending his hand. 'I own this place. My family does. Nick DeSanto.'

Watterson ignored the hand at first, but Nick persisted. His manner was so genial, so open, that finally Watterson took it.

'That's better,' Nick said. 'So. You just sightseeing, what?'

'I – I wanted to look at you,' Watterson said.

Nick tilted his head coquettishly to one side. 'So look.'

'Mr DeSanto, may we talk?' He looked over his shoulder at the fat man. 'Privately, if you don't mind.'

Nick shrugged and gestured toward the tables in the back.

'You a cop?' Nick asked casually as they sat down.

'No.'

'Then why are you packing?'

Embarrassed, Watterson touched the bulge in his jacket. 'I think I was planning to shoot you,' he said.

Nick laughed. 'Hope you changed your mind.'

Watterson nodded. 'I couldn't shoot a man in cold blood.' He looked into Nick's eyes. 'Could you?'

'Me? No way. I'm a lover, not a fighter.'

'I've lived in this country too long not to believe a man's innocent until proven guilty.'

'Good for you.' Nick put his arm around the older man, while with his other hand he gently extracted the gun and laid it on the table. 'Mind? Makes me a little uncomfortable. Now. Want to tell me why you were going to kill me?'

Watterson folded his hands, as if in prayer. He spoke earnestly. 'It's my granddaughter, Mr DeSanto. She was killed on her wedding day. Murdered.'

Nick's face was impassive.

'You were there. I thought –'

'Whoa, old-timer. I haven't been to no wedding since my own, and I'm sorry I ever went to that one.' He stood up, smiling. 'Sorry. You're talking to the wrong guy.'

'It was you, damn it,' Watterson said hoarsely. 'I saw you with my own eyes. You and your brother.'

With the swiftness of a snake Nick's hand lashed out and grabbed the collar of Watterson's shirt. 'I told you, I wasn't at no wedding. I got witnesses.'

Watterson's eyes narrowed. 'I didn't even tell you when it was.'

Nick's grip tightened. Watterson looked around wildly. Around him had materialized a dozen faces, all looking down at him with blank-eyed menace.

'You killed her,' he rasped.

Nick's eyes shifted toward the fat man, the one called Frank. Almost imperceptibly Frank nodded.

'Get him the fuck out of here,' Nick said. He released Watterson with such force that the old man's head struck the revolver lying on the table. A trickle of blood oozed from his forehead.

Watterson reached for the gun, but the fat man intercepted him. 'I don't think so,' he said. He examined the Smith & Wesson. 'Take a look at this,' he said. 'Must be thirty years old.'

'Take him out the back way,' Nick DeSanto said. He turned away and sauntered back to the bar.

'Let's go, pops,' Frank said. He twisted Watterson's arm

behind his back and half dragged him out the fire exit into an alleyway.

Three men followed him. As Watterson was pulled through the double metal doors, shouting and kicking, he could see sporadically between the shoulders of the men to the small crowd in the restaurant. Not one person so much as turned to look at him. The gray-haired man in the corner banquette was pouring wine for yet another supplicant.

'Help!' Watterson cried. 'Someone call the police!'

The gray-haired man did not even glance in his direction.

Puffing and wheezing, Fat Frank shoved Watterson against the brick wall of the building in the narrow alleyway, then stepped back and pulled a bag of peanuts out of his jacket pocket.

The three men with him didn't waste any time. One of them, a thin, rangy man in a cheap suit and pointed-toed shoes, slapped Watterson backhanded across his face. A big ring he wore tore a gash into the old man's cheek. He howled in pain, but the men were experts. A blow to his Adam's apple halted his screams before they could attract attention from anyone on the street.

A muscular young man wearing a tight yellow T-shirt jabbed him in the stomach. Watterson felt nauseous with the first punch; the second made him vomit. He wasn't allowed to bend over. While he threw up, someone smashed a fist into his nose. He heard the crack as the white-hot pain shot through his face.

He wanted to collapse, but they wouldn't let him. A shoe heel cracked against his kneecap. The pain was excruciating, but the only sound that came out of his mouth was a breathy croak. His nose was streaming blood. It was hard to breathe. Through his swollen eyes he could see the expressions on his assailants' faces. There was no malice in them, no emotion at all. They were beating him as if he were a side of beef, not a human being. They were going to kill him, he realized, and not one of them could care less.

Sometimes, Shiro Ushi, there are other ways.

Another jab to the ribs. They broke, but Watterson no longer felt anything.

Oh, Susi, he thought, *how I've let you down. He killed you, and I didn't even give him a fight.*

The law. The damn law.

There is no law here anymore.

Then there was another pain, one so great that it overwhelmed all his senses. It began in his arm, shooting upward like an arrow into his chest, where it exploded. Watterson gagged. His arms flailed so violently that he lifted the muscular man who was holding onto his shoulders off the ground. The men beat him harder, but he felt now as if he were watching them from outside himself. His eyes bulged.

His last sight was a glimpse of Fat Frank delicately picking peanuts out of the bag.

'Come on, come on,' Frank said impatiently. He dumped the rest of the bag's contents into his mouth and swallowed them without chewing. 'How long's this going to take?'

The muscular man holding Watterson's limp body let it slide to the street. 'I think he's dead, boss,' he said, prodding the body with his toe.

'Shit,' Frank said. 'What the hell's the matter with you?'

'We didn't hit him that hard, Frank,' the thin man said. 'Not enough to kill him, anyway.'

Frank wet his finger and ran it along the bottom of the bag, then sucked off the salt. 'Fuckups,' he said. With a sigh he took the old Smith & Wesson out of his belt and tossed it on top of the old man, along with the crumpled cellophane peanut bag. 'Get a car.'

Frank came back inside and whispered something to Nick at the bar. The young man rolled his eyes and dismissed him with a disgusted gesture. Then Nick walked to the back, where the gray-haired man was making pronouncements to his latest visitor.

'Beat it,' Nick said, tapping the visitor on the shoulder.

The gray-haired man shrugged, smiling sadly. 'Impatient youth, my friend,' he said in apology. 'My son needs my immediate attention, it seems.'

'Sure, Don DeSanto,' the visitor said, rising.

'I am well disposed to your proposal,' the Don said. 'It will benefit us all.'

'Talk some other time, okay?' Nick pushed the visitor away and slipped into his vacated seat.

Then Don's mild eyes suddenly glowed furiously. 'Who do you think you are?' he whispered. 'When I'm conducting business –'

Nick laughed. 'Business. Yeah. What kind of business is Ernie the Pimp pushing now, hookers in the subways?'

'Numbers,' the Don said quietly.

He didn't know how it had happened, but over the years he, like everyone else, had bent to the force of his son's personality. Nick DeSanto had an absolute sense of his own superiority. When confronted with it, other men – even strong men – found themselves doubting their wisdom and their manhood.

It had made Nick enemies, although no one would admit to harboring a hatred for Tony DeSanto's first son. The Don knew this, knew that when he was gone, Nick would bloody the streets proving his own power, but he was helpless to change him. And recently he felt any control he'd once had over the boy slipping away altogether.

Once, long ago, he had been able to dismiss Nick with a paternal smile. But things were different now. When Nick wanted to know something, you answered. Even if you were Don Anthony DeSanto.

So when Nick asked, 'What kind of numbers?' DeSanto replied: 'Ernie has made a contact through the unions. He's able now to push numbers at all the construction sites in the city.'

Nick considered a moment, then shook his head. 'Not a bad idea, but the wrong guy. Ernie's too stupid to make it work. And you know it, too. And still you keep sitting here like Marlon Brando blessing everybody. "It will benefit us all," ' he mimicked.

'Don't talk to me that way, Nicky. It may not be an important business venture, but the tradition of listening to the *soldati* when they come to speak is important. The Don must always listen. It is the way we have kept unity through the years. It is why I am the head of this organization.'

'Jesus, you're starting to believe your own bullshit,' Nick said. 'You're the head of this organization because you took it from old man Andalucci.' He lit a cigarette. 'Who knows, Pop,' he said with quiet malevolence. 'Maybe someday somebody's going to take it from you.'

DeSanto clenched his fists on the table. 'You got any idea who that will be?'

Nick raised his arms in an elaborate shrug. 'None at all, Don Padre.'

'What do you want?' DeSanto asked sullenly.

'Oh, yeah. I thought you might want to know we got a stiff in the alley.'

'What?'

'A stiff. D.E.A.D. Got it?'

'Who? The one making all the noise?'

'Yeah. I don't know who he was. Had something to do with that wedding in Central Park. He thought that Joey and I were involved. Pulled a gun on me and Fat Frank, so the boys busted him up. Must have had a bad heart. He didn't make it.'

Tony DeSanto took a long look at his son. 'Lying's so easy for you,' he said quietly.

'What are you giving me?' Nick stubbed out his cigarette.

42

'Some old hairball drops dead, and right away you start in with the accusations.'

'Don't you think I know you bribed thirty witnesses to swear you were here the day of those killings? Thirty witnesses who'd turn you in to the cops as soon as they had the chance?' He looked away in disgust. 'I covered for you,' DeSanto said. 'I got a judge to say he was here, too. To keep your stupid story from falling apart.'

Nick grinned. 'Attaboy, Pop.' He slapped his father on the shoulder.

DeSanto pushed his hand away. 'I didn't do it for you. I did it for Joey.'

Nick shrugged. 'Whatever you want.'

'I don't want Joey involved with any of your poison,' DeSanto said, trembling visibly. 'Do you hear me? Keep Joey out.'

'What Joey?' He looked around him in exaggerated innocence. 'You see Joey around here? Huh? I'm asking you.'

'Nicky –'

'Aaah, forget I even bothered.' He pushed himself away from the table and stood up. The glass of wine in front of him fell over, staining the tablecloth. 'Go back to pretending somebody still listens to you.'

When he was gone, Tony DeSanto sat quietly while a waiter changed the cloth and set up a new glass for the next visitor.

4

Usually Matt Watterson was an early riser, so when Miles came home the next morning and did not find the old man sitting at the kitchen table reading, he walked through the apartment to his grandfather's room and knocked on the door.

He wasn't there. On his bed was a towel and an open box of .38 cartridges.

In the kitchen Miles found the note Watterson had left. He read it through.

Miles,
Remember what I said: If anything happens to me,
    contact Nagoya.
Whatever it is, he will help. Nagoya will tell you the
    truth.

The truth? The truth about what?
'Granddad!' he shouted again, feeling afraid.

Matt Watterson's body was found two days later in a Newark dump site, covered with lime.

The police had no leads.

Numbly Miles called his parents' home. Again there was a funeral, a stream of detectives, a phone call from Halloran. Again there was no evidence on which to arrest the DeSanto brothers.

Contact Nagoya. He will tell you the truth. The words were engraved on Miles's mind. He had not shown the note to the police. He had never told his parents about it.

But why Nagoya? Watterson himself had seen the man only once in forty years.

Nothing made sense anymore. Miles's family had been ripped apart by people with so little conscience that they were capable of killing a young bride on her wedding day and an old man with a weak heart. All without reason. And without punishment.

Then Mickey Haverford was gone again. Her psychiatrist had recommended a health spa with all the amenities of a first-class hotel, where she would be physically pampered and protected from the more frightening aspects of her grief. Her daughter and the only father she had ever known had been murdered within two weeks of each other and their killers were still free. She had been waking up screaming in the night, depending on barbiturates to get back to sleep. At the spa, her doctor said, she would be watched carefully through the awful mental ordeal she was suffering, before her anguish could grow into even more serious problems.

Her husband agreed at once. He had no time to spare for her or anyone else these days. Curtis Haverford spent nearly every waking moment trying to find a way to bring the DeSanto boys to justice. When he found out that the family was Mafia, he thought surely he could build a case against them, but he had been wrong. The DeSantos were well protected from every angle. Even to allege that Anthony DeSanto was involved in illegal enterprises was to invite a slander suit.

During the weeks that followed the discovery of Matt Watterson's body, Haverford consulted with dozens of criminal lawyers all over the country. Every day their conclusion was the same: without evidence, the DeSantos had to be presumed innocent. And every night, long past midnight, Miles's father sat alone in the den with a bottle of bourbon on his desk. He no longer asked Miles about joining the law firm. His son's uselessness was an irritation he no longer needed.

We've fallen apart, Miles thought. Those men, those strangers, have destroyed us all.

Whatever it is, he will help.

Miles walked into the den and waited for his father to look up from his desk.

'What is it?' Curtis Haverford said as he wiped his nose with a balled-up handkerchief he kept beside the bourbon bottle.

'I was wondering, Dad. Is there anything I can do to help?'

His father laughed once, a hard, mirthless bark. He refilled his bourbon glass, sipped it, and looked at his son a long time before he answered: 'Don't you have anywhere to go?'

Miles put his hands in his pockets. 'Sure,' he said.

Alone in his room, Miles looked at his reflection in the mirror. It was the face of a coward, a fool. Miles Haverford, the rich boy who bought his way into law school. The boxer who always threw in the towel. The son so useless that with his family racked by tragedy, no one could think of anything Miles could do to help. His presence here made no difference. And if nothing made any difference . . .

. . . *Your life is over before it ever started*, Matt Watterson had told him.

He got a cardboard box and went into his grandfather's room. Nothing had been changed. The room looked as it had on the last day Miles had seen the old man alive. Miles sighed, feeling the terrible weight of death settle around his shoulders like a shroud.

47

He didn't want to be there. He had already gone through the agony of sorting through his sister's belongings after her death; to do it again, putting away the few treasures Matt Watterson owned, was almost too much for Miles to face. But he had to do it, he knew. The old man wouldn't have wanted anyone else rooting among his things.

He opened the dresser drawer and noticed the sealed envelope on top of the white box that had so shocked Miles when he saw its contents. The envelope was addressed simply: SADIMASA NAGOYA, BOX 1076, GINZA STATION, TOKYO, JAPAN.

If anything happens to me, contact Nagoya.

He stared at the envelope, turning it in his hands. So the old man had known Miles wouldn't have the gumption to honor his last request. He had written to Nagoya himself.

But what could he have said?

Sitting on the bed, Miles started to tear open the envelope, then stopped. He knew.

He owes me a life.

Miles felt his breath coming faster. He remembered Nagoya's six Japanese automatons and how they had taken care of the DeSantos like a couple of children. He remembered the quietly regal manner in which the old Japanese man had conducted himself. Whoever Nagoya was, he had power. And whatever power he had, he would use it to help Miles. He would have to. Watterson had kept possession of Nagoya's ka, his soul.

Miles quickly put the old man's room in order, then packed an overnight bag for himself.

'Dad, I've got to go,' he said in the doorway of his father's study.

Haverford looked up from his drink. 'Naturally. This place isn't exactly at the hub of the Manhattan social circle these days.'

Miles ignored the sarcasm. 'I'm just going to get lost for a while. Don't worry about me.'

His father smiled crookedly. 'Frankly, I've given up on that.'

'Yeah, well . . .'

'You know, maybe you were right about not wanting to be a lawyer,' Haverford said quietly, swirling his ice cubes in his glass. 'The law doesn't mean anything. Matt knew that. He knew the law wouldn't help.'

Your life is over before it ever started, Matt Watterson had said.

Then I don't have anything to lose, do I?

'I'd better go,' Miles said.

His father waved him away as if shooing off a fly.

5

What distinguished Tokyo from every other city Miles had ever visited was not its Orientalness. The Ginza, with its showy shops and chic women, could easily be mistaken for any other boulevard in any other world capital. What made it unique was its sound. The music of New York was its traffic, its blaring horns, the squeal and groan of pneumatic brakes, the ceaseless hum of idling engines. But here, on the busiest street in the world, all Miles could hear was the sound of conversation.

Everyone talked, from the businessmen looking through restaurant windows at wax replicas of food to the passengers on a passing bus watching a baseball game on a tiny television anchored near the driver. All around him people chattered in the rapid-fire Japanese which seemed so different from the language Miles had studied at Yale. Hearing them, he wished he'd paid more attention.

He walked along the crowded sidewalk in a daze, looking at the giant signs and picking out the few words of English he could find. One of them was 'MUSIC', although the translation was hardly necessary. Screeching rock music blared through the open doors of an enormous record emporium, where life-size posters of a pretty teenage girl with 'NOKKO' emblazoned on her minidress gazed down on passersby for half a block. Apparently Nokko had replaced Madonna as the queen of the teeny-bopper set here, but the music was just as ear-splitting. Some things never changed.

Two doors down from the record store was a small alcove with books in the windows. He waited outside, searching his memory for a few moments, then walked in. When a young male clerk with acne approached him, he said as slowly and distinctly as he could, '*Eigo ga dekimasuka?*' Do you speak English?

The clerk nodded.

'I guess I didn't have to ask you that in Japanese,' Miles said with a smile.

'Sorry?' The clerk raised an eyebrow. 'Not understanding.'

'Never mind,' Miles said. 'I need a book. An English-Japanese phrase book, please.'

'Ah.' The clerk picked up a small volume covered in plastic near the cash register. 'This very good.'

Miles nodded, and the clerk wrapped the phrase book carefully in colored paper. 'Many Americans buy this.' He looked at Miles more closely. 'At first, I think maybe you are Japanese.'

'I'm not,' Miles said curtly, and left.

It was the first time in his life anyone had said he looked Japanese, and Miles felt vaguely insulted. He was not the one children made fun of in school; he was not the one old ladies attacked for being the enemy. Miles was charmed, the beautiful one, the one with no obstacles before him.

The post office was just down the street, and the boxes were right out in front in the entryway. Miles checked the number he had carried in his wallet from Manhattan: 1076.

His plan was simple. It was 10 A.M. He would wait in front of the boxes until Nagoya opened number 1076, then speak with him. If Nagoya didn't come for a day or two, what did it matter? Miles had nothing but time anymore.

Within five minutes a slight man in a blue suit came to open the box.

'Hi,' Miles said affably, walking up to him with his hand extended. 'Miles Haverford.'

The little man, whose thin, lined face looked as though he had been born with too much skin, looked up quizzically. 'Hava . . . Fo?' he asked.

'Haverford,' Miles repeated, feeling foolish. 'Actually, I'd just like to see Mr Nagoya. That's his box, and . . .'

The Japanese man held out a small notebook and a pen. 'Hava . . . Fo.' He pantomimed writing, then forced the pen on Miles.

'You want me to write my name?'

'*Hai. Hai.*' He nodded enthusiastically.

Miles complied, printing his full name carefully, and handed the notebook back to the man.

'*Arigato*,' the Japanese said, bowing quickly. Then, without a backward glance at Miles, he closed the postal box and walked through the doors and onto the sidewalk.

'Wait, wait,' Miles said, running after him while he tore the paper off his phrase book. 'Hold on a minute!'

The man paid him no attention.

'You! Come back here!' He shoved past some people coming through the large glass doors. Ahead, the little man in the blue suit was already nearly half a block away. Miles ran after him up the crowded street.

Out of breath, he finally caught up with him at the corner and touched his shoulder. 'Excuse me –'

The man whirled around, his arm seeming to uncoil like a snake, and struck Miles in the chest.

Miles reeled backward, miraculously avoiding a collision with the astonished passers-by as he thudded against the window of the record store. The posters of the teenage singer quivered above him as he slid bonelessly to the sidewalk. An old woman bent over him, yammering excitedly in Japanese. Miles shook his head, still seeing stars, then gestured to her that he was all right.

53

Faraway, the small man in the blue suit melted into the crowd.

'Christ,' Miles muttered, pulling himself upright. 'Talk about touchy.'

He picked up the phrase book, which had fallen on the ground. Maybe his English had offended the man. 'Hello,' he mumbled belligerently. '*Ohio gozaimasu*.' He practiced the strange words a few times before searching for another phrase. 'I want to see Mr Nagoya. *Nagoya-san ni aitai des*.' He closed the book. 'Ohio . . . Ohio . . .'

'Ohio!' chimed two girls leaving the record store in unison. They looked like refugees from a Fifties drive-in, with pony tails and saddle shoes. Covering their mouths delicately, they giggled as they scampered past him, their long poodle skirts swirling.

The next morning Miles tried a new tactic. At the hotel, he asked a clerk to write his two new sentences in Japanese characters on a piece of paper. Then he taped the message to the front of box 1076 and waited, arms crossed, for the little man to come again.

Six hours later, he did. Without a glance at Miles, he removed the piece of paper, folded it neatly, and put it in his pocket before emptying the contents of the box.

Miles sighed, trying to keep his temper in check. 'Look, I've come a long way.' He switched to Japanese. He had memorized the lines carefully the night before. 'My name is Miles Haverford. I know Mr Nagoya, and I'd appreciate it if you'd take me to him.'

The man stared at him for a moment, then smiled and bowed. Awkwardly Miles bowed back. When he straightened himself up, the man was leaving.

'Okay, buddy,' Miles said, collaring the man. 'You've just exceeded my bullshit tolerance. Where's Nagoya?'

Suddenly his arms were no longer around the tiny man's shirt collar, but windmilling in the air as a barrage of blows crashed down on him. He tried to get into his fighter's stance, but his legs seemed to be knocked out from under him, and his hands were useless against the quick, darting jabs of the Japanese.

As a group of terrified onlookers scrambled for cover, the little man dragged Miles outside, across the full width of the sidewalk, and deposited him inside a black limousine.

Someone was waiting for him there. Another Japanese was on the backseat beside him. He held a gun pointed directly at Miles's face.

'You've got to be kidding,' he said weakly.

The little man who had fought him in the post office climbed in delicately on the other side of him. He said something to the driver. When the car was in motion, he took a long black scarf and a pair of handcuffs from his pocket.

'Now, wait a minute,' Miles said, trying to sound reasonable. 'Whoever you think I am, I'm not him, okay?'

There was no response.

'What I mean is, you guys are making a big mistake here.' He tried to force a wan chuckle. 'A real whopper, believe me –'

The man with the gun clicked off the safety.

Miles sighed and held out his wrists. 'Be my guest.'

Then the little fellow in the blue suit folded the black cloth into a long, thin rectangle. Miles swallowed, feeling sick. 'Let me guess. A blindfold?'

The man nodded. It was a quick, economical gesture, like the head movement of a chipmunk.

'Hey, you speak English!' Miles said in as hearty a voice as he could muster. The man nodded again, continuing to fold the cloth. 'Well, here's an idea. Why don't we park and talk about this?'

'No,' the man said.

He held up the blindfold. As he did, Miles saw a tattoo on

the underside of the man's wrist. A tattoo of a wave.

Miles gasped, lunging at the man's arm with his manacled hands. Immediately he was slapped down. The man with the gun reached over and got an arm around Miles's neck while the other tied on the blindfold.

'You don't understand!' Miles shouted. 'It's your *arm*. The tattoo on your arm, the wave.'

The small man said something in Japanese. The one with the gun answered.

'What the hell's going on?' Miles pleaded. 'Who are you?'

But there was no more talk from the two men. They rode the rest of the way in silence.

Nearly an hour later, Miles's blindfold and handcuffs were removed. The limo stopped in front of a ten-foot-high gate with acres of rolling lawn beyond it. Speaking softly, the driver said a few words in Japanese into a walkie-talkie, and the gate swung open. Dogs barked somewhere in the distance as the car drove inside the huge estate.

Miles looked around in wonder as the limousine rolled slowly past a field of raked sand through which a small, stone-lined creek meandered. Boulders grew out of the expanse like islands in a white sea. All of the elements of the strange garden were natural, yet the effect was one of absolute, controlled artifice. As they rode, a low, rambling mansion with the curved eaves of ancient Japanese temples came into view.

'Holy shit,' Miles muttered.

The small man beside him raised a finger to his lips. 'No talk.'

'What do you mean, "no talk"?' Miles exploded. 'You kidnap me, you blindfold me, you handcuff me, and then –'

He stopped when he felt the gun pressing against the other side of his head.

'No talk,' the little man repeated, smiling politely.

The car stopped in front of a circular driveway surrounding a stone pond filled with brightly colored carp. A young man wearing a cotton kimono slid open the polished bamboo doors and bowed to the men as they approached.

In the foyer, which was bare except for a low table on which a vase of lilies had been placed, the men removed their shoes and stepped into cloth *zori*. Miles winced as he dutifully jammed his size-twelve feet into the small thongs and allowed himself to be led through the austere, immaculate house.

Occasionally, he heard the sound of voices, men's and women's, from various parts of the house, but no one else came to greet them. The two Japanese escorted him silently to a small room with sliding doors and no windows, bowed, and left him.

'Hey, wait a minute,' he called after them. 'You can't just leave me here.' He hobbled after them.

The small man gently nudged him back into the room.

'But I don't even know where I am!'

'You here,' the Japanese said pleasantly, pointing to the floor. 'You stay.' He turned to leave.

'Oh, no, you don't.' Miles lit out after him. Then another door slid open, and a three-hundred-pound giant stepped out. His hair was cropped so short that his scalp showed. He was wearing a kimono the size of a pup tent. He crossed his arms over his chest and stepped in front of Miles.

'I stay,' Miles said.

The giant bowed.

Miles took off the murderous thongs and padded back toward the windowless room in his bare feet, but before he reached the door, the big Japanese touched his shoulder and gestured down the long hallway.

Miles thought about running, then sighed. 'Oh, what's the use,' he muttered.

He walked in front of the giant down the hallway until

the man opened another, heavier door. In the center of the large white-tiled room was a huge iron pot suspended by chains over burning coals. The pot was filled with water. Steam was pluming off the surface.

'Sweet Jesus, they're going to boil me and eat me,' Miles whispered. Panicking, he bolted down the hallway, but the big man grabbed him under both armpits and carried him back, legs flailing.

'Help!' Miles shouted. 'Over here! Somebody help!'

At the doorway the obese Japanese turned around, grunted, and flipped Miles over his head. He landed with a crash a few feet from the cooking pot. Miles saw stars. And then, through the miasma of steam and semi-consciousness, he saw other things. Dragons. Fuscia vines. The crossed eyes of a white-faced samurai warrior. A nipple. A navel.

Gradually he began to realize that he was looking at a human body almost entirely covered with tattoos.

The designs, executed in brilliant hues, extended over both shoulders of the young man who stood in front of him. They trailed down his arms nearly to the wrist, and covered his entire chest except for a strip down the middle, like a bolero. From the waist down, the man was wrapped in a white towel.

'I don't suppose you'd have a drink,' Miles said.

The tattooed man took off his jacket, then expertly unbuttoned his shirt. He got hold of the zipper of Miles's pants. 'What the hell are you doing?' Miles shouted, pushing him away. 'If you're looking for the Continental Baths, fella, you made a wrong turn at Albuquerque.'

'Ah, bath,' the young man said, smiling sweetly. He pointed to the iron cauldron.

'In that? No. Oh, no.' He shook his head emphatically while rebuttoning his shirt. 'Now if you'll excuse me –'

In a flash the man had him on the floor. The shirt came

off from behind, the buttons flying in the air like fireworks. Miles's head thumped on the tile floor as his trousers were whisked off his legs.

'Stop!' Miles shrieked, clutching his Jockey shorts.

The man stopped, looking as if he'd been slapped.

'Look,' Miles said in his most reasonable lawyer's voice. 'You don't look like a pervert.' He swallowed. 'At least your face doesn't. What I'm saying is, I know when I'm beat.' He shambled to his feet. 'You want me to take a bath, fine. But if I'm going to be boiled, at least allow me the dignity of a pair of underpants.'

The young man smiled and nodded, then yanked down his drawers.

Miles sighed. 'And they say the Japanese have no sense of humor,' he said.

Briskly the tattooed man soaped and scrubbed him, pouring buckets of scalding water over him. When he was finished, he patted his face with a warm towel.

'That's it?' Miles asked, smiling with relief. The water had been hot, but it was nothing like what was steaming in the cauldron in the middle of the room. 'Hey, that wasn't so bad. For a minute I thought I was going in there.' He pointed to the cannibal pot and laughed.

The tattooed man nodded. '*Hai*. Now bath.'

'I just had a bath!' Miles looked toward the door. Behind it he could see the giant's shadow standing with arms akimbo.

The tattooed man pushed him firmly toward the cauldron. On its surface floated a thick, circular piece of wood with a hole cut in the center. He pulled over a step stool, then demonstrated how to enter by hopping quickly from one foot to the other. He pressed the board down with his hands. As he did, water came up through the center hole and the board slowly lowered. 'Okay?' he asked with an eager grin.

Miles looked through the hole in the board to the bottom of the pot. It was glowing red hot. 'Go ahead and kill me,' he said. 'I'm leaving.'

He walked two steps before he felt himself being lifted bodily, then dropped, screaming, into the blistering water.

The board began to slide out from under his feet, revealing the red bottom of the iron pot. Immediately he squatted down to keep his balance, and felt his testicles roasting.

In the distance he saw the shadow of the big man outside the door receding. The coward probably couldn't stand to see someone boiled alive, Miles thought.

'*Hai. Hai,*' the tattooed man said encouragingly as Miles maintained his precarious balance on the wooden platform. Miles was beyond words.

After what seemed like an eternity, with his heart throbbing at a gallop, he was permitted to leave the pot and given a cotton robe to wear. The tattooed man bowed to him.

'It's too late for apologies,' Miles said indignantly.

Looking hurt, the young man turned away. On his back was one gigantic tattoo spreading from one shoulder to the other, showing a crested wave. Except for its size, it was an exact duplicate of the tattoo on the wrist of the man who had brought him from the post office.

'Wait,' he said breathlessly. 'Please.'

The tattooed man turned back to him, his face questioning. Hesitantly Miles touched the design, and the Japanese beamed.

'What is this?' he asked slowly.

The young man shrugged and shook his head. He didn't understand. Then, smiling, he took the American's hand, shook it, and led Miles to the door.

The fat Japanese man was waiting for him outside the bath chamber.

'You again,' Miles said.

The man bowed and touched his chest. 'Hiro,' he said.

Miles understood. 'Miles.' He indicated himself.

'My-o?'

Miles nodded and offered his hand. 'Hiro?'

'Hai.'

'I'm really tired of this,' he said wearily. 'How's about telling me what's going on here.'

Hiro smiled.

'Do you speak English?'

'Engrish?'

'English. Yes.'

'Engrish. No.' He led Miles back to the small room and gestured for him to enter.

'What about my clothes?' He plucked at his robe. 'Clothes.'

Hiro smiled, then bowed and slid closed the rice-paper door.

Miles sighed.

A thin futon had been unrolled in the center of the room. Near it stood a tray of food. There was a bowl of steaming rice, some marinated turnips, some pieces of raw fish decorated with cut paper, and a pot of tea. He ate it hungrily, then sat back on the futon. Through the paper door he could make out Hiro's hulking outline.

He was going to stay there all night, Miles realized. Not that he could get very far on an estate in the middle of nowhere wearing nothing but a bathrobe. But why had he been kidnapped? Who did these people think he was?

He lay back on the futon. Everything that had happened since he came to Tokyo had been bizarre, but the strangest thing of all, he thought, the one element that made no sense at all, was the tattoo. Both the man in the car and the bath attendant had had the same tattoo. The crested wave design was the same one he had seen in the arrangement of flowers at his sister's wedding. It had appeared, apparently, in *all*

61

the arrangements of all the white chrysanthemums through the years.

Slowly he pulled back the wide sleeve of his robe, revealing his own forearm. There too was a mark. A tattoo.

Of a crested wave.

It had never been explained to him. As far as he knew, his own parents had not understood it. When Miles was two days old, he had inexplicably disappeared from his bassinet in the hospital nursery. There was a furious search of the hospital, and the police were notified. But the next morning the baby was found, once again in the nursery. The infant had not been harmed in any way, except for one thing. Its arm had been tattooed.

Mickey Haverford had gone into shock at the sight of her child. A lawsuit was brought against the hospital, but was dropped because of the harmful publicity that might affect the child.

As time passed, Miles was simply told to keep the matter of his strange tattoo to himself. It was understood that as an adult, he would have it removed.

He examined his arm by the flickering light of a candle near his bed. *Granddad knew*, he thought. *All these years, he knew.*

Nagoya will tell you the truth.

And he knew with sudden certainty that no one had made a mistake. This was Sadimasa Nagoya's house.

Whoever Nagoya was.

6

When Miles awoke in the morning, he found his clothes, clean and pressed, inside the door. Only his shoes were still missing. The tight *zori* of the night before had been replaced by a larger pair. He checked through the pockets of his trousers quickly. He found his watch, a Rolex, wrapped neatly in tissue paper, and his wallet had been undisturbed. Inside it was the folded envelope that Matt Watterson had left with Nagoya's name on it. He put it under the sash of his kimono.

Hiro brought him a breakfast of rice and clear soup.

'Have you been there all night?' Miles asked.

With gestures Hiro urged him to eat. When the bowls were empty, the big man beckoned Miles to come out into the hallway.

He led Miles down a series of low-ceilinged paper corridors, past an indoor pond with a curved bridge crossing above it. Beyond it was a wall of sliding doors. Hiro stopped before the bridge and bowed once more to Miles.

'Nagoya?' Miles asked.

'*Hai*,' he said quietly, nodding toward the sliding doors.

Miles turned and walked softly across the bridge, then slid open the rice-paper panel of the door. The room was large and airy, scented with the fragrance of the tatami mats which covered the floor. Nagoya was kneeling on a cushion near the far wall. Before him was a roll of rice paper, a ceramic pot of murky dark liquid, and a block of solid black ink. In his hand he held a foot-long, thick-handled artist's brush with which he made a series of light but decisive strokes on the paper.

Miles had never understood the Japanese fascination with calligraphy. Even after his smattering of Japanese studies, he had not been able to fathom how anyone could devote his life to writing the letters of the alphabet.

He cleared his throat. Nagoya ignored him, making two more brush strokes with infinite slowness. Finally, after surveying his handiwork, he cleaned the brush and set it aside.

Gracefully the old man stood up, smoothing the folds of his formal black kimono, and gestured for Miles to enter.

'Why do I feel like I've been granted an audience with the pope?' Miles said.

The old man smiled. 'Please accept my apologies for your inconvenience.'

'Inconvenience? Is that what you call it?' Miles heard the edge in his voice, but did not bother to soften it. 'For your information, I was assaulted by your gang of thugs.'

'Assaulted!' Nagoya said in mock outrage. He peered at Miles shrewdly. 'You must be in superb condition to have recovered so quickly.'

'Well, "assaulted" may have been a little strong. But I was also kidnapped, handcuffed, held at gunpoint –'

Nagoya laughed. 'And tortured?'

'Yes. Boiled,' Miles said quietly while Nagoya guffawed. 'Frankly, I didn't think it was very funny.'

He smiled kindly. 'Forgive my laughter, honored guest,' Nagoya said. 'I am an old man. My associates, though overzealous, were only anxious not to disturb my sleep.'

'Is that so,' Miles said dryly. 'Gosh, I hope your sleep wasn't disturbed by my screaming when I got tossed into that cauldron you keep in the back room.'

'Ah, the bath. Alas, you are not the first to complain

64

about the facilities here. We do have modern conveniences in Japan, but some of us still prefer the old ways. They are simpler, and remind us of other times.'

Miles was about to speak, but the look on the old man's face dried up his words. Nagoya was looking into the distance of his own life, his papery skin as thin and fragile as the memories that kept him alive. Feeling like an intruder, Miles averted his eyes from him and looked around the room.

And he saw it again.

Above the door where he had entered was a painting: the black design of a crested wave.

'What is that?' he asked quietly. The question had sounded like a threat.

Nagoya looked over his shoulder at the painting. 'It is *sumie*, an ancient form of Japanese brush painting. It utilizes an economy of form, bringing out the design with only a few strokes.' He spoke softly, then knelt again on the brocaded pillow at his feet. From behind him he produced a small clay teapot. 'Would you care for tea, grandson of Shiro Ushi?'

'I demand to know what that design means.' Miles strongly felt his patience coming to an end. 'And you know perfectly well what I'm talking about.' He rolled up his sleeve and thrust his tattooed forearm in front of Nagoya's face.

The old man looked at it without interest. 'Very good tea. Black tea.'

'What in the hell is going on here?' Miles shouted.

Nagoya looked up. 'I am serving tea,' he said politely. 'And you are not in a position to demand anything. You may join me, or you may leave.'

With a sigh Miles sat down uncomfortably on the floor and accepted a cup. 'Thank you,' he said.

'That is better.' The old man smiled. 'You were born in

the year of the tiger, grandson of Shiro Ushi. When you were a small child, Matt Watterson used to write to me about his tiger cub who possessed such a loud roar.'

The mention of his grandfather pained Miles. 'Mr Nagoya,' he said hesitantly. 'I've got something to tell you. My grandfather . . .' He could not find the words to continue.

Nagoya put down his cup. 'Yes?' he asked softly. 'What is it you wish to say?'

Miles took a deep breath. 'My grandfather, Matt Watterson, is dead.'

Nagoya's face did not change expression, but his ancient eyes darkened and seemed to look inward. 'I am saddened by this news,' he said quietly. 'The White Bull was a fine man. A good friend.' His voice trembled and he broke off. After a moment he spoke again. 'Was his death a peaceful one?' he whispered.

Miles took a moment to answer. 'No, sir. He was murdered.'

He saw the old man's hands shake. 'He was beaten to death. The police don't know who did it. But I do. And I think you do, too.'

'The men who came to the wedding with guns?'

Miles nodded. 'The DeSantos were never arrested for my sister's murder. I think Granddad went to see them about it. And they killed him.'

The gnarled old hands clenched into fists.

'He left a note for me that day. It said to contact you. That you would help.'

Nagoya inhaled sharply. 'He said that?'

'Yes. And he left this for you.' He pulled out the envelope Matt Watterson had left for him, and handed it to Nagoya. 'I don't know what's inside it, sir. Granddad just left it for you.'

Nagoya tore open the envelope delicately, took out a single sheet of paper, and read it. Then it fell from his hands and fluttered to the floor. Miles saw that it had been written in Japanese. The old man's face was ashen.

'Are you all right, Mr Nagoya?' Miles asked, alarmed.

He looked up quickly. 'You do not read Japanese? Not at all?'

'No, sir. I studied a little in college, but I only know a few spoken words.'

Nagoya tucked the note into the sleeve of his kimono. 'What did your grandfather tell you about me?'

'Only that you were a mystery. He said he came to look for you once, but couldn't find any trace of you here in Tokyo.' He hesitated for a moment, working up his courage. 'And he said that you owed him a debt.'

The old man sat stock still, as if he had ceased to breathe. 'It is so,' he said. 'But more than a debt, grandson of Shiro Ushi. I owe him a life.'

Miles looked at his feet. 'Then excuse me, sir, but . . . that's why I'm here.'

The old eyes narrowed. 'You wish something from me?'

'I do.' Miles stood as straight and tall as he could. 'I want to get even with the men who killed my grandfather and my sister.'

Nagoya looked away. Then he unhurriedly picked up his tea and gestured for Miles to sit down. 'And how do you propose to do this?'

Miles hunkered down, barely able to contain his excitement. 'The DeSantos are a Mafia family, Mr Nagoya. The murderers are the sons of the head man, Tony DeSanto. They deserve the death penalty, but because of who they arc – what they are – they won't get it. The police won't even investigate them. Do you understand what I'm saying?'

'Quite clearly,' Nagoya said.

'I want to see them dead.'

'You wish for me to assassinate these men?'

Miles stopped short at the ludicrousness of the suggestion, 'No, sir. Not you. I – I'll kill them.'

The old man looked at him coldly. 'They are difficult words to speak, are they not? Tell me, have you ever killed a man before?'

'Of course not,' Miles said.

'Then perhaps you should reconsider the seriousness of your intentions.'

'I have considered.' He fidgeted uncomfortably. 'Believe me, Mr Nagoya, I'm not some kind of bloodthirsty maniac. But there's no other way. If I don't stop these men, no one will. I just don't really know how to do it.'

'That is because what you propose is an imbecility,' Nagoya snapped.

'But your men, I saw what they can do.'

'Oh? What can they do?'

Miles's jaw tightened with anger. 'For one thing, they can take a baby out of a hospital, tattoo him, and bring him back under the noses of the police without anyone seeing anything,' he said.

Nagoya sipped his tea in silence.

'All I'm asking for is a little protection, Mr Nagoya. Just long enough to get me close to the DeSantos. After that, I don't care what happens to me. Your men won't have to be responsible. But I have to do this for my grandfather, don't you see?'

'I see you are senselessly throwing your life away,' Nagoya said. 'These men may be no more than cheap killers, but their organization is large. And dangerous. Far too dangerous for an inexperienced schoolboy like you.' He put down his cup. 'I am sorry. What you ask is impossible.'

Miles stood up, shaking with humiliation. 'Excuse me for

bothering you,' he said quietly. 'I made a mistake.' He turned to leave. 'And so did my grandfather.'

He opened the sliding paper door so hard that it twisted off and crashed to the floor.

The old man drank his tea.

7

The young man keeping watch by the front door shouted to Miles as he stormed out.

'Sue me,' Miles said. He slammed the front door closed and started down the long driveway. It occurred to him that he had not the slightest idea where to go once he reached the front gates of the estate, but he didn't care. He wanted to get away from Nagoya, to forget that his grandfather had ever called this man friend. Besides, he thought bitterly, he would probably be shot before he ever reached the front gates, anyway. He didn't care about that either.

Within minutes he heard the soft purr of an automobile engine behind him. Like clockwork, he thought. The Japanese were nothing if not predictable. When he heard a car door slam, he turned in disgust to face Hiro.

'Look, I don't want to fight you, big guy. Frankly, I'd rather go on living. But whatever you try with me, it's not going to keep me here.'

Hiro bowed. 'No keep. I take back to Tokyo, *hai*? Okay?' He grinned and opened the passenger door.

Miles laughed. 'You speak better English than you let on.'

Hiro shrugged. 'Is better sometimes, no talk. You come.' He jerked his enormous head toward the car. 'Hiro no crash.' He offered his hand.

'You're okay, Hiro,' he said as he sat down.

As they inched along in the onerous traffic of the city,

Miles took a closer look at the big man. Hiro was no obese slug. He was built like a bull. And he was young – younger, perhaps, than Miles.

'Can I ask you a personal question, Hiro?'

'Maybe yes,' he said, smiling.

'What are you doing working as Nagoya's houseboy?'

Hiro stared at him blankly. 'Houseboy?'

Miles nodded. 'Aren't you Nagoya's servant?'

Hiro guffawed. He laughed so hard that he sat out a green light, setting off a symphony of blaring horns behind him, which didn't seem to affect him in the least. 'Hiro no houseboy,' he said at last. 'I study to be sumo. Wrestler, yes? Very strong. But Mr Nagoya give better job.'

'What kind of a job, Hiro? What do you do for him?'

'This, that.' He winked.

'But you live in his house, don't you?'

'Many live,' he said. 'Hiro too.'

'And you work there,' Miles persisted.

Hiro pulled smoothly up to the curb in front of Miles's hotel. 'American nose very long,' he said, then exploded into laughter again as he got out. He walked Miles through the revolving doors. 'You go home tonight?' he asked.

'I guess so,' Miles said, disquieted. 'There isn't much reason for me to stay here.'

'Good.' He patted Miles on the back. 'You go home. Make mama happy.' Then he waved good-bye and walked magisterially away.

Miles called the airlines. There were no available seats on any flight to New York until the next day.

'Great,' he muttered. He would have to spend another day in Tokyo. Another day the DeSantos spent alive and free.

He remembered the day of Susi's wedding. The music, his sister's laughter, the cryptic symbol of the wave on the arrangement of flowers, the appearance of the old Oriental with the missing fingertip, the six anonymous men who followed him like a miniature army . . .

Those men had fought like nothing Miles had ever seen before. And it had looked effortless.

Nagoya's men, he knew, were the key to everything. Who were they? Why did they stay with Nagoya?

Who was Nagoya?

What did it matter? Miles thought bitterly as he packed his few belongings. He remembered his grandfather's last message to him: *Contact Nagoya. He will help.*

That was a laugh. For all his money, for all the trained men he had at his disposal, Nagoya wasn't about to risk a hair on his head to catch Matt Watterson's killers. He should have saved himself a finger, Miles thought. Nagoya may have said he owed a life, but he wasn't going to pay up. Not for a dead man. That would be up to Miles, and Miles would have to do it alone.

He spent the day in his room, and went to bed early. By two he knew he wouldn't be able to sleep. Too much had gone on, too much he couldn't understand. And there was more, he knew, to come. Without Nagoya's men his move against the DeSantos would be a suicide mission.

I guess I am Japanese, after all, he thought wretchedly. *The kamikaze kid.*

If there were something else, anything . . . But there wasn't. Not without Nagoya.

His head pounding, Miles got out of bed and dressed. Tokyo was a bigger city than New York. Somewhere on its noisy streets would be something to fill his thoughts until morning.

He began walking on the well-lit Ginza, but with nothing special to see and nowhere to go, he began to wander along the narrow side streets. Some of the avenues turned into quiet residential neighborhoods where one could almost forget he was in the middle of a modern city; some led him into seamy dark alleys where people moved in shadows. They frighten him, these enclaves so unlike anything he had expected from the squeaky-clean atmosphere of daylight Tokyo.

Women in doorways called to him softly. Some, he saw, were no more than young girls whose breasts had barely begun to bud. Here was the only place in the city where Miles saw any variation in race. Here were dark-skinned girls with frizzy hair, and tall, lank women with European features. Some, he saw, even had freckles on their round Oriental faces, red hair above their almond-shaped eyes. They were the unwanted descendants of wars past.

Half breeds, Miles thought. *Like me.*

He ran from them until he saw lights and broad avenues again. But this was not the Ginza of elegant shops and theaters. Everywhere were bars lit by the garish lights of businesses that thrive only at night. Here was a city within a city, where the blare of tinny music and the voices of the night people drowned out Miles's disturbing thoughts.

The bustling streets were filled almost exclusively with men, from businessmen in suits to young Japanese toughs with strange neo-samurai haircuts, whose turf the street was. In front of a burlesque house, nearly naked women behind panes of dirty plate glass danced as a barker shouted to passers-by to enter. Miles was jostled toward the entrance.

He had not even noticed the pickpocket, but someone else had. A hand seemed to come out of nowhere beside him and crashed into the jaw of a teenager whose spiked hair was dyed a purple-red at the temples. Miles's alligator wallet spun in the air and landed at his feet. The punk groaned, turned to his assailant, then pulled out a switchblade, and was on his feet.

Two other young thugs ambled menacingly closer. One

snapped open a knife in his hand. The other pulled from his pocket a set of brass knuckles.

Miles could only stare, panic-stricken, as the man who had stopped the thief backed away slowly, then stopped. He assumed a karate fighting stance, his hands open in front of his body.

The punk tossed the knife from one hand to the other, swaggering toward the defenseless man. He said something in Japanese, his mouth curled into a sneer.

The other man did not answer as he began to move, circling, crouched low. His movements were like a cat's, lithe, graceful, sure. His face too was feline, and his eyes were strangely compelling, as resolute and cold as a panther's, almost glassy with concentration.

One of his fingers was missing.

He waited for the knife. When it came, he shot out his hand so fast that Miles could not even follow the movement. In what looked like a primitive and beautiful dance, his body seemed to stretch in all directions at once, knocking down both of the pickpocket's comrades. There was a scream, and then he stood up, the bloody switchblade in his hands.

The boy with the red-streaked hair lay at his feet, his face contorted in anguish as he clutched his abdomen. Blood ran over his fingers. He couldn't have been eighteen years old.

Miles turned away, feeling sick. A crowd had formed around the two fighters, and now everyone was talking loudly. Money changed hands. There was laughter.

When Miles looked back, the boy's two friends were helping him to a standing position. They led him away, doubled over, leaving a trail of blood on the sidewalk.

The man with the strange eyes tossed the knife into the gutter. The crowd parted respectfully for him to leave.

As he came closer, Miles saw what it was that made the man's face so unusual. He was the only Asian Miles had ever seen with green eyes. They met Miles's. Then, with a grunt of disdain, he shoved the American out of his way.

Miles stared after him long after he was gone from view. The crowd broke up and melted back into the seedy clamor of the street. Finally, the girlie-show barker prodded him with a stick and angrily shouted him away.

He walked down the street and into a place that looked reasonably quiet. The bar was full, so after a verbal struggle for a whiskey and soda – which he lost – he took a beer to an empty table. Within minutes a woman was beside him.

She wasn't the sort of woman, Miles thought, who usually cozied up to customers in a sleazy bar. She was wearing a blue suit, its skirt well below the knee, and a pillbox hat. A small handbag dangled from the crook of her elbow. She looked, he mused, almost laughing out loud, exactly like a nun out of habit.

'May I sit here?' she asked in textbook English, 'I am waiting for someone, and I would rather not sit alone here.'

When she smiled, Miles noticed how pretty she was. Her eyes were wide-set and sensitive, the eyebrows above them straight and wisped like feathers. She wore no makeup except for a small amount of pink lipstick, and her fingernails were short and unpainted.

'Sure,' Miles said. 'Are you an American?'

'No,' she said, blushing. 'But I knew you were. I heard you order at the bar.' She laughed. 'That's when I decided to sit with you.'

'Because I'm so obviously harmless?'

'Well – yes, I suppose so.' She frowned suddenly. 'I mean no insult to you, sir,' she added formally.

'None taken,' Miles said. He introduced himself. Her name, she told him, was Tomiko Sasakawa, and she was visiting from Osaka.

'Is this a favorite haunt of yours?' Miles asked. He

looked around at the rough clientele in the bar.

Tomiko blushed. 'Perhaps my friend will not come.'

'Let's go,' Miles said, rising. 'I'm sure there are nicer places to have a drink.'

'Oh, I want nothing to drink,' she said quickly. 'Please – I would like to return to my hotel.'

'Where is it?'

'The Imperial,' she said. 'On the Ginza.'

'I'll be damned,' Miles said. 'I'm staying at the Imperial myself.'

'Oh yes? Perhaps then you will join me for breakfast tomorrow. I have come many times to Tokyo. I can show you the city if you like.'

Miles smiled. 'I would like very much, Tomiko.'

At the hotel, he walked her to her room. 'You said your name was My-o?'

'Miles. Yes.'

'My-o,' she repeated, thoughtfully. 'It is a very difficult name. But interesting. My-o.'

He leaned toward her to kiss her, but she slipped away behind her door. 'Thank you, My-o,' she said. 'Good night, My-o.' The door closed in his face.

'What's new, My-o,' he muttered as he walked down the hall. Even the women here were weird. As he approached the elevator, he caught a glimpse of a face he recognized. A Japanese face with green eyes. And a hand with only four fingers. Miles shouted at him.

The man saw him and ran. Miles chased after him down the fire stairs, but at the ground floor the man's footsteps stopped, and Miles lost track of him.

Not again, he thought wearily. He thought he had left the cloak-and-dagger mystery at Nagoya's mansion, but it was everywhere he turned in this strange and senseless city.

He called Tomiko's room from the lobby. 'My-o?' a sleepy voice asked.

'Has anyone bothered you since I left?' he asked. 'A man?'

'No man,' she said. 'I am sleeping.'

'I'm sorry,' Miles said. 'Just don't open the door for anyone, all right?'

'My-o, don't be afraid,' she said softly. Then she hung up.

Tomiko appeared the next morning in a silk dress with a lace schoolgirl collar. Her black hair, now unfettered by the antique hat, was the longest Miles had ever seen. It cascaded down her back almost to her knees. Heads turned in the hotel's dining room as she walked through it on her way to Miles's table.

'Jesus, you're gorgeous,' he said, stupefied.

She lowered her eyes. 'I apologize. It was not my intention to preen.'

'Preen? You're not preening. You just can't help being beautiful.'

She waved her hand at him to stop, visibly distressed.

'Okay,' he said, 'I don't want to make you uncomfortable. But where I come from, it's a compliment. Please take it that way.'

'Very well,' she said primly, sitting down. 'You slept well?'

'I didn't sleep at all. Some guy with light eyes and four fingers . . .'

Suddenly he slammed his fist down on the table and stood up.

The man had been standing in the doorway of the hotel restaurant. Now he ducked behind the maître d' and disappeared.

'I'll be back,' Miles said, and dashed after him, crashing into a waiter on his way out.

'My-o,' Tomiko called, running after them both.

78

She caught up with Miles outside the hotel.

'He's gone,' Miles said in despair.

'My-o, I must explain –'

'Later,' he said, hustling her back into the hotel. Inside the revolving doors he put both hands on her shoulders. 'Listen, Tomiko, I don't want to scare you, but someone's following me and it would be better for you if you weren't around me.'

'But why?'

Miles sighed. 'I wish I knew. I'm sorry, but you'd better check out of this hotel as soon as you can.'

'What will you do?'

'I can't leave. I – I've got some things to take care of.'

'Important things?'

Miles stuck his hands in his pockets. 'Yeah. Important things.'

Tomiko took his hand. 'Don't worry, My-o-san, Mr Nagoya will help.'

Miles felt his heart skip. 'What did you say?'

'I was the one he sent to look after you.'

He stared at her aghast for a moment. Then he laughed. 'You? You're one of Nagoya's . . . people?'

'I am.'

'Well? What were you supposed to do with me?'

'See that you stayed out of trouble.'

'Oh, I see. And what would have happened if I'd gotten into trouble? I guess you would have slugged our way out of it, right?'

She giggled. 'I could not do such a thing,' she said. She raised her arms slightly so that she looked like an Oriental statue of the Virgin Mary. A half dozen men stepped forward, encircling the two of them. One, putting down a newspaper, was the green-eyed man with the missing finger. He inclined his head solemnly. 'But they could,' she finished.

'Him,' Miles said, pointing to the man he had chased out of the hotel. 'He was with you?'

'That is Sato. Without him, the pickpocket with the knife would have had your wallet last night, and perhaps your life as well.'

Miles felt a shudder as he remembered the fight on the street. 'He wasn't a man,' he said. 'He was just a kid. Your friend Sato opened him up like a tin of sardines.'

Tomiko looked down. 'Sato felt it was necessary,' she said quietly.

'Oh? Did you see it?'

'I . . . yes.' She did not look him in the face.

'Did you think it was necessary?'

'He was *bosozoku*,' she explained. 'One of a gang. They are young, but they carry weapons. They are dangerous to those who are weak and unskilled in fighting.'

Miles detected a gleam of amusement in Sato's green eyes at the insult, but he let it pass.

'Then I guess you thought it was all right to rip his belly open.'

Tomiko was quiet for a long moment. Finally she said, 'What I think is not important.'

'Oh, brother.' Miles stuck his hands in his pockets. 'That's a cop-out I haven't heard for a while. You mean because you're a woman?'

Now Tomiko did meet his gaze. 'Because I am Yakuza,' she said with quiet defiance. 'So is Sato. And the rest. And Nagoya above us all.'

Miles started to speak, but she touched her fingers to his lips. 'I will explain, but not here. In Japan, what I have just told you is a thing to be spoken only in whispers.'

8

Tomiko took Miles to Shibuya Park, where graceful promenades wound around hundreds of cherry trees in bloom, their petals coating the ground like snow. She sat down demurely on a wooden bench beside a pond filled with water lilies while Miles paced in front of her.

'We can talk here,' she said.

'Talk your little heart out. Tell me the moon is made of green cheese. After what I've seen in the past two days, I'll believe anything.'

'My-o, I do not understand why you are angry.'

'Angry? Me? Why should I be angry? Just because I've been treated like an imbecile? Because Nagoya sends a woman to protect me from the big, bad city? Because I'm surrounded by goons everywhere I go? Why should I be angry?'

'It is their duty to see that I am chaperoned,' Tomiko said.

'But of course. Who knows what evil the foreign round-eye will bring?'

'It is our way, My-o. But they would never harm you. The Oyabun has ordered it.'

'The what?'

'Mr Nagoya. He is the Oyabun. The master.'

'The master? Oh, for crying out loud.'

She lowered her eyes. 'Mr Nagoya has asked me to explain. He feels you have the right to know about us, but it would shame him to tell you himself.'

'Shame him? Why? Because it's so ridiculous?'

Tomiko colored angrily, but she continued to speak softly. 'He does not wish to tell you himself because the business of the Yakuza is . . . outside of the law.'

Miles blinked. 'What?'

'It is the underworld of Japan's society. The Yakuza is almost a caste in itself. No outsiders are permitted into the *ikkas* of the great Oyabuns. Its members must adhere to a strict code of ethics, our own ethics. Even the language we use among ourselves is different from ordinary Japanese. Our customs were developed over the centuries, and we keep the old ways. But the essence of the Yakuza is criminal. Every Japanese knows this.'

He sat down heavily. 'Jesus,' he said, 'the longer I stay in this country, the crazier everything gets. Now you're telling me that Mr Nagoya's the grand poobah of some secret Oriental tong.'

'Yakuza is not a tong,' Tomiko said. 'It is a way of life.'

Miles put his head in his hands. 'I don't have the slightest idea what you're talking about.'

She nodded. 'It is difficult to understand without understanding Japan itself.'

'I don't want to understand Japan,' Miles snapped. 'I only want to understand this tattoo on my arm.' He showed it to her. 'Nagoya put it there. The same design is hanging on the wall in his house. And two of his boys have the same tattoo.'

Tomiko touched it gently. 'It is the Onami, the cresting wave.'

Miles's breath hitched. 'What does it mean?'

'It is the mark of the Nagoya ikka, his house. But this house is not one of blood family. The ties in the ikka are chosen, tested.'

'Then why do I have it?'

Tomiko folded her hands in her lap. 'At the end of the

82

war, Nagoya was a man with nothing. But he became very rich, very powerful. He is respected even in the highest echelons of government. If he wished to become prime minister, he would win without opposition.'

'It wouldn't be the first time a crook got into politics,' Miles said.

'I am sorry to hear you speak with such disrespect of a man whom we regard as a father, and more than a father,' she said. The bloom of color in her cheeks deepened. 'When he heard of your birth, he was happy for the first time since long before the war.'

'How do you know?' Miles asked with more than a trace of sarcasm. 'Were you there?'

'My father was Nagoya's best friend. They served in the same ikka together. Nagoya did not want to be part of the Yakuza. For a man of wealth and position, it was shameful to sink to the level of a common criminal. But times were hard then, and it was the only way to stay alive.'

'My father explained this to me many times before he died. He was also not born to be Yakuza, but these two men did what they had to do. Then, when the Oyabun of the ikka was arrested by the Occupation authorities, Nagoya began his own house. For its symbol he chose the cresting wave.'

She traced the design on Miles's arm with her finger. 'This is a powerful house, My-o. No one would dare to harm one who bears this mark.'

'But why me?' Miles said. 'I'm an American.'

'For a man whose world collapses, anything is possible. Perhaps, in his mind, America would one day fall the way Japan had fallen. Or perhaps you might move here. I do not know his reasons for choosing you. I only know that he wishes above all things to protect you.'

'Protect me how?'

'The mark is a sign that you are of the Onami ikka. It

83

means all of the men of the ikka will fight for you like brothers. It means that wherever you are, whatever the circumstance, if you call for help, it will be answered. Others are not permitted to wear this mark until they have proven their loyalty and skill as warriors beyond question. But you have borne the sign since birth. You will always be served by the ikka, even if you make no effort to understand it.' She lowered her voice. 'It was a great honor the Oyabun accorded you,' she said.

Miles was silent for a moment. 'It's crazy,' he said finally. 'The nuttiest thing I ever heard of. You're telling me that Nagoya's a gangster.' He looked at the tattoo on his arm. 'And that for some reason I was born into his mob.'

'Your American terms do not translate well,' she said. There was an edge to her voice. 'Mr Nagoya is a proud man of ancient lineage. His family were of the nobility for countless generations. Despite his success, he was afraid to tell you of his profession. Now, after hearing the shallowness of your reaction, I see that he was wise to be afraid. He did not wish for you to humiliate him, and you would have.' Her eyes flashed.

'Wait a minute, Tomiko. I'm not judging anybody. This is taking awhile to digest, that's all.'

'What is it you do not understand?' she asked sharply.

'The same thing I've been asking all along. Who am I? How do I fit in in all this? I never even met Nagoya until a few weeks ago. Why was it such a big deal to him when I was born?'

'Do not ask me things I cannot answer, My-o.'

Miles sighed. 'I'm never going to get a straight answer, am I?'

Tomiko was silent.

He looked down at his hands. 'Why is Sato's finger missing?' he asked abstractedly.

'Long ago, in his youth, Sato offended the Oyabun.'

'What did he do?'

Tomiko smiled. 'He tried to rob someone who was a friend

of Nagoya-san's. Later, to atone for his error, Sato offered his pain by cutting off his finger at the first joint. He was forgiven, and did not bring shame upon the Oyabun again.'

'What would have happened to him if he had?'

'He would have cut another joint from his finger, and another, until his hands – and his life – were useless to him.'

'Nagoya's finger is missing, too,' Miles said.

'I do not know how he lost it. Even my father did not know that.'

Miles stared into the distance. 'It was a token for a life,' he said.

It started to rain softly. Tomiko stood up. 'I have explained all I can, My-o. I must ask only that you keep what I have told you to yourself.'

'Who would I tell?' he asked. 'Ripley?'

'The American authorities, perhaps. The Oyabun is planning to send men into America. He does not wish them to be discovered by your police.'

Miles spun around. 'What?'

'I do not know the details. Nagoya said you would understand.'

Miles felt his heart pound. Nagoya was going after the DeSantos himself.

Without Miles.

'Take me back,' he said.

'That is not possible. The Oyabun does not wish –'

'I said, take me back to him!' He shook her. Within a moment Sato and another man appeared, seeming to materialize out of nowhere. Tomiko shouted to them.

Miles let go of her, and in an instant of fury, he lashed out at the tall Asian with the green eyes. He landed the first punch square on Sato's jaw, and the Japanese reeled back in surprise.

The other man came behind him, but Miles saw the

move. Acting faster than he was thinking, he backhanded the man's throat, knocking him to the ground. Then he went after Sato again.

The Japanese was a superb fighter. He never missed. Every punch, every kick was placed perfectly, even though he drew no blood. From his boxing experience Miles knew that the man was pulling his punches. Still, the force of Sato's attack was enough to keep Miles on the ground most of the time.

He won't kill me, he thought. *He's not allowed.*

That was Miles's only advantage. He could kill Sato, and he would.

If only he could touch him.

This time there was no towel to throw into the ring. Miles took everything the Japanese had to give. His head was reeling. His knees had turned to water. Just . . . once. Just one punch like the one that had surprised the tall man at the beginning, he thought, throwing wildly. Just once.

He was not even aware at first that he had the opening. Then he felt the smash of his fist against the side of Sato's head, a perfect roundhouse right with the loud smack of victory, and Sato fell sideways onto the grass.

Exhausted, Miles hunkered over, panting, while Sato brought himself around.

The second man sat up groggily, rubbing his throat. With an effort he stood up and staggered toward Miles, but Sato put up a hand to stop him.

'Take me back to Nagoya,' Miles said.

9

This time the old man was dressed in a plain white kimono with no decoration. It was, Miles knew, a garment of mourning Nagoya was watering a bonsai tree next to a bamboo shrine which had been set up in the large room. In the center of the shrine were photographs of Matt Watterson and Susi Haverford.

'Why have you come back?' he asked without looking at Miles.

'You're going to kill the DeSantos.'

The old man held the watering can in midair for a moment, then continued pouring from it. 'That is no concern of yours.'

'You can't dismiss me that easily!' He slammed his fist against a wall. 'I was closer to Matt Watterson and my sister than anyone in my life. Now, I appreciate what you're doing. I underestimated you before, and I'm sorry. But if you're planning to get rid of the DeSantos, I want to be included.'

'That is impossible.'

'They're going to die by my hand. Do you hear me? Mine!'

'Do not shout in my presence.' The old man's voice was parched and bitter. 'What good would you be? You know nothing. You have led the soft life of a pampered pet. If you were included in this plan, you would only endanger the lives of everyone involved.' His voice softened. 'Go home, tiger cub. We cannot use you.' He set down the can and knelt in front of the shrine.

'Then I'll kill them myself,' Miles said.

The old man turned around. 'How?'

'Anyway I can.'

Nagoya frowned. 'You are an even bigger fool than I thought.' He clutched the hem of his kimono. 'They killed Shiro Ushi. They would certainly kill you.'

'My grandfather was an old man.'

Nagoya's head snapped up. 'And you are a child. You would not even see the faces of the men who murdered your sister and grandfather. Their men would kill you long before you had any chance. Idiot! Even if you should – by the most fortunate of accidents – succeed in breaking through the ranks of that organization to kill these two men, others will remain to avenge their deaths. What will happen to you then? To your father? To your mother?'

Miles thought for a long time. 'What is it you're saying?' he asked finally. 'What would you do?'

Nagoya turned to face him. 'Grandson of Shiro Ushi, a willingness to kill – even a willingness to die – is not enough. In order to dispose of those two worthless boys, one must first decimate the army which protects them. When the battle is begun, they will have no army left in the field. Only then will it be possible to fight them and win.'

Miles was stunned. 'You're talking about a war with the Mafia, for God's sake.'

'Yes.'

'How can you even think of such a thing?' Miles whispered.

The old man tucked his hands into the sleeves of his kimono. 'Death is, unfortunately, something in which I am well versed.' He turned back to the shrine and began to chant the prayers for the dead.

Miles touched his shoulder. 'I want you to take me with you,' he said quietly.

Nagoya slapped him away. 'That is out of the question. You are not one of us. Go home. Go back to your soft bed, where you belong. The matter is closed.' He gazed ahead at the photos of Matt Watterson and Susi Haverford.

'Did you ever meet my sister before?' Miles asked.

'Only at her wedding.'

'Then why do you have her picture there?'

'That does not concern you,' Nagoya said.

After a long pause Miles said slowly, 'Matt Watterson said you owed him a life. Whose life was that?'

'That does not concern you, either, tiger cub.'

Miles dropped to his knees beside the old man. 'You're wrong,' he said. He put his hands on Nagoya's shoulders and turned him until their eyes met. 'I think it concerns me most of all . . . Grandfather.'

Nagoya's eyes wavered. 'Shiro Ushi did not tell you that.'

Miles shook his head. 'No. He would never betray a promise. You did make him promise, didn't you?' He rolled up his sleeve. 'You had me branded with your mark because I'm of your blood. The ka you entrusted to Matt Watterson was my mother's.'

Nagoya looked for a long time at the crested wave tattoo, then began to tremble. 'You were never to know,' he said hoarsely. 'It was so long . . . so long ago , , ,'

'He said you would tell me the truth. I know now what he meant.'

The old man looked at him, then nodded slowly. 'I will tell you,' he said. He fingered the bamboo edge of the shrine. 'In Japan, when we say "the war," it can mean only one war. You of the West know it as World War Two, but here the war has no number. It was the event that destroyed our world. Never before in five thousand years had Japan been invaded by foreign armies. Never in five thousand years had our country been defeated in battle. We believed ourselves chosen of the gods, singled out by destiny to rule the world.

'But the war changed everything. Our cities were smashed. More than two-thirds of our buildings were destroyed. We had no automobiles, no factories. After the surrender, even our spinning wheels were confiscated so that we could not make cloth to wear. After the fire bombings, with no usable land for agriculture, there was no food. The people of my country were starving.'

He drank from his cup. 'The Americans were gracious victors. General MacArthur and his people tried, after the initial bloody purges, to bring Japan back to life, but the whole world was in chaos, and war reparations money had to first be given to the American allies, who were also hungry. For the Japanese there was nothing. Those fortunate enough to find work were paid an average of ten yen a day – enough perhaps for an apple, if such a delicacy could be found, or for a few grains of rice.

'Thousands of families killed their children because they could not bear to watch them die of starvation. Others who could not bring themselves to murder their babies abandoned them in the burned-out parks and open places of the cities, hoping that someone with a little food to spare would take them and care for them. Through the night, long after the wailing of the bombs had stopped forever, the cries of the sick and freezing children could be heard rising from the ruins.

'I too had a child,' the old man said quietly. 'Only one, after the war. The other was killed with her mother during an air raid. I tried to save them . . .'

Nagoya could not speak again for several minutes. Finally he breathed deeply and closed his eyes. 'My daughter was only three years old. I offered myself as labor to anyone who would feed us even a fish head or a glass of milk, but even that much was hard to find, and many nights all we had to eat were a few insects I dug from the ground in the parks filled with abandoned babies.'

'And every week the wail from those parks grew fainter and more feeble as the children died. More than once I held a rock over my daughter's head while she lay sleeping and thought, "This will be easier for her than the life I can offer." But every time I cast the rock away, too weak to end her life quickly.

'Those were my circumstances when I saw your grandfather,' he said. His voice was hoarse. 'We had known each other years before, when I was a rich man. Now he hardly recognized me, and I him. He was an American soldier, a prize among beggars such as myself. The Americans were generous, bringing chocolate bars and sometimes even food from their rations into Tokyo, although they were not permitted to do so. Before I even saw Shiro Ushi's face, I saw his uniform and ran with scores of others to surround him and beg him for food or a coin or even a button from his jacket that I could trade for a bowl of rice. But when he looked at me, I knew that a miracle had been sent.

'We wept in each other's arms. He had already been to my house and my business, and found only the burned plots of ground where they had once stood. He asked me if there was anything he could do to help me. And I told him, yes, there was one thing.'

A tear slowly coursed down the old man's face.

'You gave him your daughter,' Miles said.

Nagoya nodded. 'Masako.' He pulled his shoulders back. 'I begged him to raise her as an American, with no memories of her country or her family,' he said. 'I could not bear for Masako to remember those times.'

The old man clasped his hands in front of him with dignity. 'You have asked for the truth, Miles, and I have told it to you. Now you must go. Keep your life, the sweet life I wanted so much for you.'

'No!' Miles swept the air in front of him. 'Don't you see? That life is worthless now. Two thugs with a gun saw to that.' He clenched his fist, and the wave on the tattoo rippled. 'I belong with you.'

Nagoya bowed his head, as in prayer. At last he looked up. 'Keeping you with me may not help you. It may destroy you.'

'Please,' Miles said, 'you're the only chance I have.' He blushed. 'I know I'd be a liability to you now, but I can learn. I'll do anything you say. I'll prove myself worthy, I promise.'

The old man looked at him strangely. 'What did you say?'

'I – I said I'd do anything you wanted . . .'

Nagoya took a folded sheet of paper out of his kimono. 'You said you do not read Japanese.'

'I don't,' Miles said, bewildered.

The old man unfolded the paper and placed it on the floor between them. 'This is the note from Shiro Ushi.' He smoothed the wrinkles carefully. Obviously the message had been read many times. 'It says, "If he is worthy, pay your debt through the tiger cub." '

Miles sat back on his haunches, dazed. Matt Watterson had known what Miles would do before Miles himself. 'He wrote that?'

'Yes,' Nagoya said softly. 'Your grandfather – and Shiro Ushi *was* your grandfather, more than I have ever been – was a wise man.'

'Then – then you'll take me?'

Nagoya looked away.

'You owe him, Mr Nagoya.'

The old man whirled around to face him. 'If you are worthy!' he roared. The sudden shout from the quiet old man seemed to echo through the bare room. 'I need do nothing for a spoiled and demanding child. I am obligated to keep you *if you are worthy*. Only then.'

'I will be worthy,' Miles said.

'If I keep you here, you will be required to accept certain conditions.'

'I accept them.'

'You have not heard them.'

'I accept them anyway.'

Nagoya sniffed. 'You may not, for instance, contact your parents.'

'Agreed.'

'They may think you dead.'

Miles nodded.

'In the matter of these killers, I will decide what is to be done and when,' Nagoya said.

'Agreed.'

'You must understand what I am saying. Two lives for two lives will not do. They kill one, we kill one. They kill another, we kill another, and thus it will never stop. These men are from a powerful family. Our full revenge demands that the family be destroyed.'

'I understand,' Miles said, 'but how will you do it?'

The old man's eyes met his levelly. 'When you are ready, grandson of Shiro Ushi, you will know.'

There was a long silence. 'Think of this too,' Nagoya said at last. 'If you are alive when this is over, you may be no more than a fugitive. There may be no more life for you in America. Are you willing to sacrifice all that for your vengeance?'

Miles looked at the photographs of his dead sister and the man he had known as his grandfather. 'I am.'

The old man nodded faintly. 'Then you may stay while we prepare. During that time Sato will try to teach you the things you will need to know to survive. Even then it may not be enough. If you cannot learn quickly, you will be left behind. Without protest.'

'I'll do my best.'

'That goes without saying. Only your best will be

acceptable. And you must live by our rules. They are strict, and no deviation from them is permitted. If you disobey these rules, you will be cast out.'

He folded his hands together. 'In this house, your blood tie to me means nothing. I will not claim you as my kin. Here you will be a visitor only, with less status than the newest apprentice *kobun*. Do you understand?'

Miles nodded. 'Yes, Oyabun.' He bowed awkwardly to the old man.

Nagoya smiled thinly. 'You are beginning to learn already,' he said.

BOOK TWO

THE SONS OF THE WAVE

10

Hiro walked with Miles up the winding path from the big house to a small stucco building surrounded by a six-foot bamboo fence dappled with the colors of the spring sunset. 'Teahouse,' Hiro explained. 'Belong to Oyabun. Tea ceremony for you.'

He grinned and slapped Miles on the back. Miles lurched forward from the force of the gesture, almost tripping over the tall wooden *geta* shoes that were part of the traditional Japanese costume required at Nagoya's house. Hiro, in contrast, seemed completely at home in his outlandish garb, an eighteenth-century samurai warrior out for a stroll among the rolling hills and covered bridges of his fiefdom.

'Have you always dressed this way, Hiro?' Miles asked, wincing as he stubbed his white-stockinged toe on a stray rock. He remembered the streets of Tokyo, where Western clothes were the norm.

The big man guffawed. 'Not before. Nagoya like old ways.' He shrugged. 'Nagoya is Oyabun.'

'Nagoya is nuts,' Miles whispered.

'You no go back to mama, yes?'

Miles coughed. 'Yes. Er, no. I'm staying for a while.'

Hiro laughed and gave his shoulder a tap that sent arrows of pain shooting through Miles's arm. 'Good. You be kobun, like Hiro.'

'Kobun?'

'Student,' the big man said. He made his hands into two

97

fists, one on top of the other. 'Oyabun,' he said, indicating the top fist. 'Nagoya. Yes?'

Miles nodded and pointed to the lower fist. 'Kobun?'

'Hai. Hiro. Now My-o kobun also. Brothers.' He opened the bamboo gate and let Miles pass.

Inside was a garden, of sorts. Carefully tended greenery covered all four walls of the fence. On either side of the narrow wooden walkway were beds of white sand raked into intricate designs around big boulders which seemed to have sprouted out of the surreal earth. In the corner nearest the sliding doors of the teahouse was a cluster of moss-covered rocks. Jutting from them was a yellow bamboo pipe dripping water onto a single flat rock below. The surface of the enormous stone had been scooped into a bowl from centuries of dripping water, and two lazy red carp swam inside it.

A feeling of peace settled over Miles as he looked at Hiro. The big man was standing at a stone basin, rinsing his hands. He beckoned for Miles to come over.

'Wash hands and mouth here,' he said. 'Make pure, for tea ceremony.'

Miles dipped his hand into the ice-cold water. 'This is how it's been done for a thousand years, isn't it?' he mused.

Hiro nodded. 'Time change. Men no change.' He offered Miles a small cotton towel.

'Brothers,' Miles said.

'Hai.'

Other members of the ikka came into the garden, acknowledging them with a polite bow before standing in silence on the divergent paths of the walkway. Miles recognized the tattooed man from the bath. With his bizarrely illustrated body covered, he looked like a sweet-faced schoolboy.

'That Koji,' Hiro said. 'Is *sansuke* of bath. Good job here.'

Nearby, the two men who had kidnapped Miles from in front of the post office bowed to him in greeting. The smaller man, the one who had wrestled Miles to the sidewalk so effortlessly, accompanied the gesture with a broad grin.

'That is Yoshio,' Hiro whispered. 'Good fighter.'

'You're telling me.'

'Best fighter, next to Sato.'

Miles looked around. The garden was filled with men, all dressed in the antique finery of another era, another Japan. Only one face was missing.

Then Sato appeared at the entrance to the garden. He stood there for a moment, looking like a Shinto deity in a kimono of brocade and satin, the blood-red setting sun behind him. Without a word the others moved out of his way. Their bows to him were not the cordial greetings of equals which they had accorded one another, but the subdued obeisances of servants for a master. Sato walked past them briskly, nearly knocking Miles off his precarious wooden shoes. Only Hiro's swift hand on his arm saved him from sprawling into the raked sand.

'What's up his ass?' Miles asked as Sato entered the teahouse and removed his shoes.

'Sorry?'

'Never mind. Is Sato a kobun here, too, or what?'

Hiro hesitated a moment before answering. 'Sato kobun, yes,' he said tentatively, 'but higher than Hiro. Higher than all but Nagoya. One day Sato become Oyabun.'

'Kind of like the crown prince.'

'Prince, yes!' Hiro beamed.

'Great,' Miles said.

Hiro led him to the doorway, which was so low that they had to crouch to enter. Inside, the teahouse was even more spare and austere than Nagoya's room. Empty except for three tatami mats on the floor, a sunken hearth with a ceramic pot of boiling water, and a low, lacquered table with a few tea utensils on it, the single room nevertheless radiated a kind of tranquil beauty. The paper windows set against round frames which showed through in silhouette, were colored by the changing hues of the sunset. Light from the open sliding door fell on a small alcove in which a branch of blossoming plum was set inside a bamboo vase. Beside it was a calligraphy scroll.

'What does that say?' Miles whispered as the two men took positions on the side of the room opposite Sato and his circle.

'Poem,' Hiro answered. 'Oyabun write himself for tea ceremony. For you. It say, "Tomorrow come ocean." '

Miles thought about it. 'Tomorrow come . . .'

'Ocean,' Hiro finished. 'Water.'

'I see.'

'Very beautiful.'

'Ummm,' Miles said. 'Maybe it loses something in the translation.'

He heard a soft clop-clop outside and turned. It was Tomiko, dressed in a red and gold kimono, her hair dressed in the classic *shimada* style of ancient Japan, with a chignon set off by tall jade combs. She was even more beautiful than in Tokyo. Miles followed her with his eyes as she entered the teahouse, removed her shoes, and knelt silently beside him.

'Tell me I'm not dreaming,' he said.

Tomiko blushed.

Then Sato barked something from the far end of the table, where he occupied the place of honor opposite the head. Tomiko answered him softly in Japanese. All other talk ceased. After the exchange Miles could sense the tension in the air. Hiro was looking down at his hands. Yoshio and Koji and the others sat without moving, their faces masks of Zen imperturbability.

'Do you mind telling me what just went on?' Miles asked.

'Sato has said that women do not belong in the teahouse,' Tomiko said quietly, her cheeks flushed.

'That was chivalrous,' Miles said. 'I hope you told him to stuff it in a sock.'

'I informed Sato that the Oyabun has requested my presence for the purpose of translating and explaining the procedures for our American guest.' She did not meet his eyes.

'So formal? Lighten up, Tomiko.' He took her hand. She pulled it away as if he had burned it with a poker.

'What's the matter?' he began, but Hiro tapped his arm. Silently the big man shook his head.

'I – I'm sorry,' Miles waffled.

Tomiko whispered, 'It is not your fault. You do not yet know our ways.'

At the end of the table Sato raised his imperious head. An angry cascade of Japanese poured from his mouth. His dark green eyes moved from Miles to Tomiko, but lost none of their fierceness. Again he spoke.

Miles did not understand a word. He looked at Tomiko for a translation. She was staring down at the table, blinking rapidly.

'What did he say?' Miles asked.

Tomiko raised her head and breathed deeply. After a moment, in a voice that was barely audible, she said, 'Sato-san has asked me to translate exactly. He said "Tell the barbarian that here in Japan we do not touch our women lightly." And then he said that perhaps I had encouraged such advances. So Sato said.'

Miles smiled. 'Translate this exactly for me, too. Tell Sato that he is a liar with the manners of a sewer rat.' He gave Sato a mock bow. 'Translate. Exactly.'

As Tomiko spoke Sato rose to his feet. Miles started up too, but Hiro whispered 'My-o, no. Not here. Not in teahouse.'

Gently he forced Miles back into the kneeling position

the others had taken. Sato still stood, the anger in his eyes turning to mocking contempt, and he knelt back down.

After a few minutes Nagoya stepped softly through the sliding doors and closed them behind him, and the ugly moment passed.

The Oyabun bowed to the guests in his teahouse. The ceremony began. Silently Nagoya knelt before the hearth in the position of honor, farthest from the door. From the table he took one of two red lacquer bowls and sprinkled a small amount of powdered green tea into it. With slow, measured movements he ladled simmering water into the bowl with a long-handled bamboo ladle.

Miles watched, fascinated, as the old man turned a mundane occurrence into a dance of studied movement, of tension and repose. After each utensil had been used, he wiped it in a single motion with a folded silk napkin, then set it down as if each were an object to be studied for its beauty. Nagoya took an intricate whisk and swirled it in the tea until the liquid frothed. Then he set down the whisk and, bowing, handed the bowl to Sato.

Sato accepted it, bowing in return, and turned the design of the bowl toward the Oyabun before drinking it.

Not a word was spoken. As Nagoya carefully picked up the second bowl with both hands, he nodded to Tomiko.

'The Oyabun wishes for me to explain the *cha no yu*, the tea ceremony, to you,' she murmured, her head bowed. 'It is a ritual of humility, for all who partake of the *wabi cha* – the tea of poverty – are equal. The host himself prepares and serves, although he does not drink the tea.'

'He uses but two bowls,' she said, nodding toward Nagoya, who was accepting Sato's bowl. 'So he must wash each before serving the next guest. The guests, drinking from the same bowls, also express a sense of community with one another.'

One by one, each man was served his bowl of tea. The

very air in the room seemed to still, and the only sound Miles could hear was the steady drip of water from the bamboo pipe outside into the stone basin. Slowly the light behind the paper-covered windows changed from pink to blue to gray, and the figures in the room receded into shadows.

'The essence of *cha no yu* is tranquility,' Tomiko said. 'We seek to make this moment, although fleeting, an oasis in time, a communion between the present and the past, between friends and enemies alike. Even the objects in the *tokonoma*, the place of honor' – she inclined her head toward the alcove in which Nagoya's scroll hung – 'have been carefully arranged by the Oyabun. The plum blossom is a symbol of strength, for this tree maintains its beauty even during the harshest winters. And the scroll bears a haiku –'

'Tomorrow come ocean,' Miles said.

She looked at him briefly, then bowed her head again. 'On the waves of the distant sea rides tomorrow,' she translated.

Miles thought about it. 'I think I understand,' he said. 'Hiro said he thought it was written for me.'

'Perhaps,' Tomiko said. 'My-o-san, your bowl.'

Nagoya held out the tea to Miles. He accepted it, remembering to turn the design toward the old man, and drank. It was bitter, yet strangely refreshing. As he handed it back, he saw Sato staring at him. In his cold eyes was pure hatred.

Miles bowed as Nagoya took the bowl from him, then leaned toward Tomiko. 'Why does your friend look as if he's ready to drive a bamboo stake through my heart?'

She was quiet for several minutes. Finally she said, 'Perhaps he has found the same message in the scroll that you have.'

Then the Oyabun rose. The others followed. He bowed and the kobun bowed in return. Nagoya spoke in Japanese,

103

and the others smiled and murmured their assent to what he was saying. All but Sato.

'The Oyabun has expressed his wish that you be accepted not as a guest, but as one of their brothers,' Tomiko said.

'I can see that went over big with Sato,' Miles mumbled.

'Although this was not the formal ceremony of acceptance of a new pupil, or kobun – that is performed with sake in the sanctuary of a shrine and must be earned by the pupil – he hopes that the others will make you feel welcome in this house. He has charged Sato with the task of being your mentor. The term we use is *aniki*, big brother. From now on, Sato will be responsible for your training and discipline. It is to Sato that you must go with all your needs and questions.'

Miles's heart sank. 'Terrific,' he said. He bowed to Nagoya. Nagoya bowed back and then left as unobtrusively as he had come. The other men stood in silence.

'You must now acknowledge Sato,' Tomiko whispered.

With a bad taste in his mouth Miles turned to Sato and bowed. The tall Japanese raised his chin. The corners of his mouth turned down in a bitter scowl. Without returning the bow, he walked past Miles, disdaining even to touch him with his garments.

He said only one word under his breath before he left the darkened room: '*Ronin*!'

There was a murmur among the other men. Hiro wiped his face with his hand.

'What did he say?' Miles asked, looking from one stricken face to another. 'Why's everybody looking at me like that?'

'I heard nothing,' Tomiko answered. Then she too bowed and left the room.

Miles turned to Hiro. 'Am I as crazy as everyone else? He said something to me, didn't he?'

The big man nodded with embarrassment. 'Tomiko-san much lady. Cannot hear bad things.'

'Well? What did that arrogant bastard say?'

'Very insult, My-o san. He call you "ronin". It mean outlaw. Outside.' He gestured behind him. 'No useful. No belong. That is ronin.'

Miles looked at him, trying to figure out if Hiro were serious. 'Is that it?' he said at last. 'That I'm an outsider in this side-show?' He laughed. He laughed so hard that tears came to his eyes. The others stared at him, in disbelief at first, then in understanding. This naive American wasn't afraid of Sato. One looked to another, and their eyes spoke what they were too polite to say:

He will be afraid. He will learn.

One by one they bowed to Miles and left. Only two remained besides Hiro. Koji, the sansuke of the bath, approached Miles with a deep bow, a gesture of respect. He spoke at length in Japanese, maintaining the rigid posture of a soldier. When he was finished, Hiro translated.

'Koji say when he join the Onami ikka, he must give honor to Sato. But now Sato act without honor. He feel shame for his brother. Koji beg My-o-san's forgiveness for disgrace he feel in his heart.'

'Why doesn't he just tell Sato he was out of line?' Miles said. 'Why don't you all? That guy could stand to come down a notch or two.'

Hiro raised his arms, palms up, in a gesture of helplessness. 'Sato is Number One,' he said. 'Go against Sato, lose everything. Home, work, honor, all. Understand, My-o-san?'

'No one's ever gone up against him?'

Hiro shook his head emphatically. 'Cannot. Sato will be Oyabun. Even to talk with you, My-o-san, is bad mark for Koji.'

Miles looked first at Koji, then at Hiro, and realized the extent of the young men's courage in alienating themselves from Sato in the cause of a stranger, a ronin.

'Please tell Koji-san that I am touched by his friendship

and that I too will try to be a brother to him.' He bowed
deeply to Koji. Then he turned to Hiro and bowed again.
'And to you too, Hiro-san. I will not forget my first friend.'

Hiro's round face colored. '*Hai*,' he said hoarsely. He
translated for Koji, and the young man smiled. 'He invite
you to take bath before dinner,' he said.

'Oh, God, not again.'

'I already tell him yes,' Hiro said, elbowing Miles's ribs.

The other kobun who had waited for Miles stepped forward. He was the small, monkey-faced man who had first
brought Miles at gunpoint to Nagoya's house and the
strange world inside it. Instead of bowing, he thumped his
chest dramatically.

'Yoshio!' He announced his name so loudly that it
echoed in the paper-lined room. Then he extended his hand,
Western-style.

This little man, Miles knew instinctively, was afraid of no
one. He took his hand and pumped it.

'Ronin!' he shouted.

This time they all laughed.

11

The four men went into the bath chamber together. Miles, Hiro, and Yoshio scrubbed down in the shallow basin while Koji disappeared into the towel room. When he emerged, carrying two wooden buckets and a load of white towels slung over his shoulders, he had stripped naked except for a rolled cotton loincloth.

Again Miles looked with wonder at the extraordinary designs on the young man's body.

'Many tattoo, yes?' Hiro said, handing Miles a bar of soap. 'Koji is kobun here only six months. Too soon for many tattoo. Nagoya-san very mad.'

Miles checked quickly to see if Koji had all his fingers. He did. Apparently the offense of tattooing didn't warrant self-mutilation.

'Why did he do it?' Miles asked quietly.

'Oh, tattoo very good. Sign of respect. But Koji too young. Must earn respect before tattoo.' The big man leaned back and sighed. 'One day Hiro have tattoo. All over, every place.' He swept his hands in the air over his massive body.

Miles winced. 'That's got to hurt.'

'Very hurt, yes,' Hiro said, smiling. 'Yakuza no use electric needle for tattoo. Must do old way, bamboo knife, very sharp.' He poked the air gingerly with an imaginary sliver. 'Take long time, great pain. Much blood.' He grinned. 'Koji ancestor all soldier. Make proud.'

Koji poked the charcoal fire beneath the iron tub until the bed burst into flames, then invited Miles to be the first inside.

'Well, if you guys can take a bamboo tattoo, I guess I can stand a bath,' he said, lowering himself onto the wooden float. The water was scalding, and the men all laughed heartily at Miles's stifled groans. When the ordeal was over, he was glad to crouch wrapped in a towel in the steamy room while the others took their turns in the tub.

'When is it Sato's turn to bathe?' Miles asked.

'First. Before tea ceremony.'

'That figures,' Miles said. 'And Tomiko?' He tried to sound casual, but even the mention of her name excited him.

'Women always last,' Hiro said, chuckling. 'Eat last, take bath last, sleep last.'

'I don't understand it,' Miles said. 'How can you treat them that way? In America they'd revolt.'

Hiro translated for the others, and Yoshio answered. 'Yoshio say suffering make good woman.'

'But isn't Tomiko one of you?'

Hiro found the question hilarious. 'Woman not Yakuza,' he answered. 'Tomiko-san father very close to Nagoya. Not kobun like us. Big man, live in own house. Very rich.'

'Then what's she doing here?'

'Father die. Nagoya must keep Tomiko until she take husband.'

'I see.' A surge of hope raced through him. 'So she just hasn't found anyone she wants to marry yet, I guess.'

'Tomiko no pick husband,' Hiro said. The others prodded one another merrily. 'Tomiko is woman.'

'Yes?'

He tapped his forehead. 'Woman no brains. Nagoya find man to marry Tomiko.' He sighed. 'Sato.' The others agreed glumly.

'What? She's going to marry Sato?'

'He will be Oyabun.'

'But he treats her like dirt. Does she love him?'

Hiro howled. 'Who love Sato?'

Miles stomped out of the room and got dressed.

The three other men padded behind him. 'You mad, Ronin?' Hiro asked. 'Ronin . . . is okay?'

'Yeah, yeah.' He slapped his towel into a bin. 'I just don't understand your crazy customs. She ought to decide who she's going to spend the rest of her life with, at least.'

'You like Tomiko, yes?'

Miles sat down. 'Yes. I think she's beautiful and intelligent and deserves better than Sato.'

'But Sato will be Oyabun.'

'Will you stop saying that? I don't care if he's Hirohito's first cousin. She shouldn't have to marry him.'

Hiro put his hand on Miles's shoulder. 'My-o,' he said quietly, 'no good think about Tomiko-san, yes? Belong Sato. Understand?'

Miles sighed. 'Understand.'

'Good,' Hiro said, and gave Miles a squeeze that nearly broke his shoulder blades. 'Koji invite see room.'

'What room?'

'Koji room. Is very proud.'

'Of his bedroom?'

Hiro inclined his face close to Miles. 'In Japan, many house only one room. My family, eight children.' He held up eight fingers. 'One room. Koji, nine. Here, each kobun have own room. Very honor. You see, Ronin?'

'Of course,' Miles said, feeling ashamed.

In truth, Koji's room, though tiny, was as remarkable as his body. Long swords of blue steel with hilts inlaid with ivory and gold hung upon the walls, along with huge lacquer bows and a quiver of hand-carved arrows.

'This looks like a museum,' Miles said, admiring the pieces. 'May I hold one?'

Koji took the most handsome sword off the wall and

handed it to Miles. The curved blade was at least seven feet long and lethally sharp. Its hilt was of interwoven sharkskin and silk, and its silver and gold guard was intricately carved with dragons bearing small jeweled eyes.

'From his family,' Hiro said as Koji beamed. 'A hundred generations, all warriors. During war, Koji grandmother take to mountains, bury. Now belong Koji.'

The young man smiled shyly and said something to Hiro. 'He say he will teach Ronin *kendo*. Is Japanese sword fighting. He is expert with all weapons – gun, knife, even rope. In high school he help father teach new soldiers in Japan Defense Corps. But is best with ancient ways.' He smiled. 'We kobun believe Koji come from past life as samurai. Is honor to learn kendo from his hands.'

'Thank you,' he said, wondering what possible use anyone could have for knowing how to fight with a seven-foot sword. *'Arigato gozaimasu.'*

Koji grinned. 'Hey, you speak Japanese pretty good, Ronin,' Hiro said.

'I'm going to learn. Either that, or I'll have to move in with you.'

Hiro laughed. 'No room for two in Hiro's room, Ronin,' he said.

His laughter was cut short. Without a sound Sato had materialized in the doorway. Steam gushed around him like smoke surrounding some mystical demon. He spoke quietly, but the cold intensity in his voice filled the room with its power. He refused to look at Miles until he was finished, then cast him a glance of utter disdain before walking away as silently as he had arrived.

'Jesus,' Miles said to break the tense silence. 'He ought to rent himself out to haunt houses.'

Yoshio bowed politely and left. Koji went to the wall and began to remove his swords.

'What's going on?' Miles asked.

110

'Must go to dinner,' Hiro said casually.

'Why's Koji taking the swords off the wall?'

Hiro fidgeted and looked at the ground. 'Sato say Koji must hide swords.'

'Hide them? Why?'

The big man hesitated. 'He say honorable Japanese weapons no good now.'

'Why not?' Then he understood. 'Because I touched them?'

'*Hai*,' Hiro said.

'Why, that shitheel . . .'

'Is not you, Ronin. Sato hate all Americans. All.'

'But that's crazy. World War Two's been over for fifty years.'

Hiro shrugged. 'Is so. But Sato is Sato. And –'

'I know, I know. Sato will be Oyabun.'

'Is so. Hiro sorry, Ronin.'

'Oh, forget it. He's just pissed because I punched him out.'

Hiro's eyes bulged. 'You fight Sato?'

'It was a lucky punch. But I don't think he's going to forget it soon. I'm just sorry he's taking it out on you guys.'

Hiro smiled. 'Hiro not afraid to be friend.' He translated for Koji.

'*Watashi-wa kowaku arimasen*,' Koji said.

'Koji not afraid.'

'I understood him,' Miles said. He looked at the innocent-eyed young man with his brave tattoos. '*Ronin-wa kowaku arimasen*.'

He helped Koji remove one of the long swords. The young man smiled at him. 'I teach,' he said tentatively.

'I learn,' Miles said.

The low table in the large communal dining room was set with dozens of small bowls filled with unrecognizable food cut into beautiful designs. After the men took their places, two

111

empty cushions were left on the floor. Assuming the vacant spot at the head of the table was Nagoya's, Miles took the other.

The kobun beside him nearly fell off his knees. He gestured wildly to Hiro, who was holding forth at the other end of the table. When the man finally got his attention, Hiro blanched and waved his hands agitatedly.

'No, Ronin,' he said, rushing over to him. 'No can sit there. Sato place.'

Miles stood up. 'Sorry,' he said, moving to the other empty place.

'No, no!' Hiro pulled him up. 'Is for Oyabun.' He held his hand out in front of him in the universal gesture for 'stop.' 'You wait. Hiro wait also. Sato will come, make place. Yes?'

As if Hiro had called up an angry spirit, Sato swept into the room. He acknowledged no one until he took his place at the table. Then slowly he raised his cold gaze to Hiro and nodded for him to sit down.

'Sato-san . . .' Hiro began.

Sato clapped his hands twice.

Tomiko appeared in the doorway leading to the kitchen and bowed. Sato barked something at her. She hesitated for a moment. Hiro looked at Sato, then to Miles, his round cheeks blazing. Sato spoke again, this time to the room at large. When he was finished, Tomiko came softly to Miles's side.

'You must come with me, My-o,' she whispered, and led him into the kitchen.

It was a gloomy room with only one small window, a tall wooden table, a charcoal stove, and a big wooden basin filled with water, where three other women busied themselves.

Tomiko averted her eyes as she spoke. 'Sato requests that you dine apart from the kobun,' she said. 'He feels that

112

since you have not been introduced into the ikka as a true student, with the formal ceremony of acceptance, it is not appropriate for you to sit at the same table with the Oyabun.' She blinked, her embarrassment visible. 'Forgive me, My-o-san, but he has ordered me to translate exactly.'

'Don't worry about it, Tomiko.' He smiled. 'He'd spoil my appetite anyway.'

She spoke with the other women, who scurried to the cupboards and outside. 'We will serve your meals in your room, My-o-san.'

'Nothing doing. I may be *persona non grata* in the dining room, but that doesn't mean I have to stay in solitary confinement, does it?'

'I do not understand,' Tomiko said.

'Where do you eat? You and the girls?' He grinned expansively.

'Oh, no, My-o. You cannot eat with women. That would be a disgrace.'

'Not to me. I'm a ronin, remember? We do all kinds of shocking things. Tell you what. You let me have dinner with you, and I'll help with the dishes.'

'My-o!'

'I'll have you know all the men in my family have been excellent dishwashers,' he said with mock solemnity. 'Do you dare to insult the honor of my ancestors by refusing my offer?'

She looked at him helplessly for a moment. Then her porcelain-perfect face melted into a smile. 'You are a very singular individual, My-o-san.'

'Ronin. Mr Ronin to you.'

She shook her head. 'I will not call you that. But I am pleased it does not offend you. Even Sato cannot insult a man who refuses to be insulted.'

'Aha. Do I detect a note of something less than total adoration for the almighty Sato?'

113

Tomiko blushed furiously. 'I did not intend . . . I am sorry . . .'

She turned away, but Miles grabbed her shoulders, laughing. 'You can't run away that easily. The guy's a beanbag and even the Lady Tomiko knows it.'

Her eyes twinkled. 'A beanbag?'

'Right. And you don't have to marry him.'

She froze in his arms. Immediately. Miles knew that he had said something very wrong. She wriggled out of his grasp and spoke softly to the ladies.

'We dine after we have served the men, in the small room off the kitchen,' she said with the precise dignity she had used in the presence of the Oyabun. 'You may join us if you wish.'

12

The room the women used for their meals was actually more pleasant than the big dining room. A woven straw mat overlaid with a quilt had been laid on the floor, and a small, square table with ten-inch legs rested on top of it. The room was windowless, but two painted paper lanterns shed a warm light, and sprigs of lilac scented the air. Miles told them how enjoyable it was, and the women tittered.

'This room is our laundry room during the day,' Tomiko explained. 'They think you are exceedingly polite.'

Smiling, they all encouraged Miles to eat. The fare was Spartan compared with the lavish spread in the dining room. Each woman had only a small bowl of rice sprinkled with dried fish flakes, a few slices of white radish and cucumbers, and a tiny receptacle filled with soy sauce. There were a few other dishes on the table, each with two or three slivers of vegetables or fish. The ladies pushed all these toward Miles.

'Haven't you people ever heard of women's suffrage?' Miles said. 'Even the most hardened male chauvinist pig wouldn't take dibs on food. Here.' He passed the bowls back to the women, who protested politely even though it was plain to see they all cherished their meager rations.

One of them held out something brown and shiny between her chopsticks.

'Shizuko insists you try it,' Tomiko said as the woman placed the silver on his rice bowl.

'Sure.' He popped it in his mouth. It had the consistency of an eraser. 'What is it?' he mumbled, working his jaw mightily.

'Eel,' Tomiko said. 'It is a great delicacy.'

With an effort Miles swallowed it in a gulp. 'Delicious,' he said wanly.

The women immediately offered him their portions. 'No, no,' he said, waving the noxious items away. 'Actually, I'm more in the mood for . . .' He glanced down at the table. 'Radishes,' he finished. 'Nothing like a good radish, I always say.'

Before he even finished talking, the women all pushed their radish bowls toward him and smiled eagerly. He looked to Tomiko for assistance, but she was carefully covering her laughter with a napkin.

'Thanks a lot,' he told her after dinner. 'I'll have heartburn for a week. Give me those.' He yanked a pair of porcelain bowls out of her hands and dried them. The four women and Miles squatted on the floor of the kitchen beside the wooden wash basins filled with scalding water. The clean bowls and dishes were stacked on the table, reaching nearly to the ceiling.

'How many dishes do those guys need, anyway?'

'Many dozens are required for each meal,' Tomiko said. 'We Japanese eat a number of foods in small quantities.'

'Couldn't you put a lot of things on one plate?'

She shook her head. 'It is not our way.'

'How about paper plates? Now, there's an idea whose time has come . . .'

Tomiko laughed. 'The Oyabun would think we had all gone insane.'

Miles sighed. 'Then there's only one thing to do. We've got to modernize this kitchen.'

'Modernize? How?'

'Well, I don't want to sound like a radical, but running water might be a start.'

Tomiko considered. 'You are right, My-o. Our work would be much easier if we did not have to carry water from the well. But the Oyabun likes the old ways.'

'Oh, baloney. How often has he even set foot in the kitchen? I don't think one of them could care less what goes on in here as long as they don't have anything to do with it.'

'We could not have metal pipes.'

'Why not?'

'It is not the old way.'

Miles sat back on his haunches. 'Just how old do things have to be around here, anyway?'

Tomiko smiled. 'Our way of life must seem very odd to you,' she said. 'The Yakuza, like the geisha, is a kind of anachronism. The rules we live by were made for another time. Nevertheless we follow them.'

She translated for the other women, who nodded in agreement.

'For example, the Japanese spoken in this house is different from the language of Tokyo. It is older, more formal. We do not drink alcohol, except for ritual sake taken in a Shinto temple. No coffee is drunk, no soda. Indulgence in any form is forbidden. Laziness is not tolerated. That is why all the kobun here perform menial tasks.'

'I still don't see why you can't have plumbing,' Miles said.

Tomiko shrugged. 'While some of the Yakuza organizations have modernized, the Onami ikka has not. That is the wish of our Oyabun.' She went back to the dishes and spoke as she worked. 'Nagoya-sama is a complex man. He does not wish to live in the twentieth century. The modern age reminds him constantly of the war, which took more from him than he could bear. So he keeps his house as if the war never happened. As if the century in which we live had not existed.'

'But how can he make a living? From what you said –'

'This ikka is one of the largest in Japan, with nearly two hundred members. You see only the kobun here, the apprentices. They must first learn the Oyabun's ways before they are permitted to work and live independently.' She took a stack of bowls and placed them on the table. 'And his ways are the old ways. Before metal pipes.' She smiled. 'No plumbing, My-o-san.'

Two hours later, when the dinner bowls were put away, the dining room cleaned and swept and scrubbed, the kitchen floor washed, and the small room where the ladies took their meals was dismembered and transformed back into a bare, stone-floored laundry room, the exhausted women bowed to Miles and said good night.

'Thank you for your concern,' Tomiko said.

'Thank you for your company.'

She looked away. 'I hope you are soon accepted by the men of the Onami.'

'I'd rather be accepted by you.' He took her hand. She held it for a moment before letting go. 'Good night, My-o-san.' She snuffed out all the lanterns except one, which she carried to the door. 'Come,' she said, 'I will show you the way to your room. I may not enter the men's sleeping quarters, of course. That is forbidden.'

The dim light that threw an aura around her hair flickered and shook as she reached the kitchen doorway. Sato stood in front of her, his arms folded across his chest. Miles had no idea how long he had been there, watching.

The Japanese snatched the lantern out of Tomiko's hand.

'Sato,' she whispered in astonishment.

He slapped her backhanded across her face. She stumbled backward, gasping, and the lantern swung from side to side in wide arcs, illuminating first Tomiko's face, pale and frightened, then Sato's menacing green-eyed glare.

'That's enough, Genghis Khan,' Miles said, throwing himself at the Japanese.

Sato did not move a muscle until Miles was nearly on top of him. Then his leg kicked out with such swiftness that Miles saw no more than a blur as Sato's knee thudded into his groin.

Miles went down groaning, his eyes bulging, waves of nausea rising in his throat. He blinked, trying to maintain consciousness. In the flickering light he saw Sato grin with triumphant malice.

Tomiko ran to Miles, bending over him. Sato's smile vanished. He spoke sharply, then left.

Tomiko brought a cloth dipped in cold water over to Miles and wiped his face. 'Oh, My-o, you should not have tried to defend me.' Her voice was a whisper, but it possessed a high, sirenlike undertone of hysteria. 'Not against Sato. It was what he wanted. He was waiting for you to try to fight him again.'

Miles managed to sit up. 'I don't think I did a very good job of defending you,' he said. 'Are you all right?'

'It was nothing. You are the one who is hurt.'

'I suppose I've felt better,' he said, shifting position to lessen the throbbing pain between his legs. 'Have you got any ice?'

She took her head. 'No refrigerator.'

He sighed. 'Right. I forgot we're back in the Middle Ages here.' He groped for the table. 'Think you could help me back to my room?'

She took his hand. 'My-o,' she said softly.

'What now?'

'I am sorry.' She touched his face tenderly. 'You are no longer permitted to use any of the guest chambers. Sato said that the Oyabun himself no longer considers you a guest.'

His jaw tightened. 'Okay. Where am I supposed to sleep?'

'He said . . .' She bit her lip.

119

'Spit it out, Tomiko. It can't be that bad.'

'He said that since you are so fond of the kitchen, you should sleep here.'

Miles looked around him at the dark, barren room with its stone floor seeping with dampness. 'What a guy,' he said. Then he remembered the laundry room. 'What about in there?'

'In the laundry?'

'Could I make it the way it was for dinner, with the quilt on the floor and the paper lanterns?'

She smiled softly. 'Yes. Yes, we can make a good room,' she said.

Together they pulled out the mats and quilts and laid them on the floor. Then Tomiko left for a while and returned with a futon and blankets. After the bed was made, Miles lit one of the colored lanterns. It shed a rosy light over the tiny room.

'Not bad,' he said.

Tomiko giggled. 'It is a very nice place after all.'

He touched her hair. 'It is as long as you're in it.' He pulled her close to him.

'My-o, no,' she protested, but when he kissed her she did not fight him. Instead she kissed him back with an urgency that made Miles's body surge with need. He clasped her more tightly. His tongue searched for hers and found it, hot and expectant. He kissed the smooth whiteness of her neck and she moaned, her whole body quivering.

'We cannot,' she said harshly, pulling away from him. Her hands were trembling. 'We must not.'

She scurried out of the room, the lantern from the kitchen swinging in front of her.

He followed her into the hall, limping with the pain of Sato's kick, but she was gone. Everything in the house was dark. Everything was silent. It was as if she had never been with him.

Miles could not sleep for hours. He lay on his bed and watched the shadows from the burning candles play on the ceiling. 'Tomiko,' he whispered aloud. He had never felt an attraction for another woman like the violent, almost painful pull he experienced whenever she was near.

It frightened him. She was part of this world, Nagoya's world, Sato's, this place outside of time. She could never adjust to Miles's life away from here. And yet, he knew, she needed him as much as he needed her.

She was dangerous for him. Hiro had warned him that she was Sato's property. Even Tomiko herself did not deny it.

But he had to have her. And he knew that whatever the cost, he would.

13

Before dawn the next morning Miles was awake and exploring the grounds outside the kitchen. This was obviously the back of the house, with no gardens or pond or covered walkways. There was instead a ramshackle wooden porch supported by low stilts, where lengths of bamboo, firewood, and some primitive tools were stored. Beyond it lay a vile-smelling patch of black earth surrounded by flies. Walking past the area, Miles recognized the odor as human waste.

In the distance, to the west of the filthy midden, was the well. It was deep, judging from the thickness of the rope supporting the wooden buckets inside it.

He paced the distance from the well to the kitchen. The ground was inclined slightly toward the house. That ought to help, he thought as he stood on the porch. If only he could get hold of some pipe. Some pipe . .

He picked up a length of bamboo. It was almost exactly six feet long and five inches in diameter, as were the others – leftovers, probably, from the fence around Nagoya's teahouse. Rooting through the debris on the porch, he found a wooden box containing a hammer and nails and a saw. The tools were gigantic things, as old as time, Miles guessed, but the nails were not rusted and the blade of the saw was sharp.

'This just might work,' he said aloud, and carried the first bamboo pole to the well.

By six o'clock, when the women came into the kitchen to prepare breakfast, he had nearly finished. They gathered outside, ogling the rickety construction that stretched like a bamboo snake from the lip of the well down to the house, supported on gradually shorter lengths of firewood.

Miles waved to his audience and ran to them. 'Where's Tomiko?'

One of the women pointed to the kitchen. Tomiko was starting the wood fire, studiously ignoring Miles.

'Forget that,' he said. 'I want you to see something.'

'I am busy,' she said, avoiding his eyes.

'Feel guilty later,' he laughed, grabbing her hand and pulling her out the door. 'What do you think?'

She stared, horrified, at the ungainly structure. 'What is this thing, My-o?'

'It's running water!' he shouted. 'Well, nearly running water. It's a flume. Let me show you how it works.' He ran with her up the hill, Tomiko's white-stockinged feet mincing beneath her tight kimono until they arrived, panting, at the well.

At the lip of the well Miles had tilted one of the big wooden kitchen basins. 'You pour the water in,' he explained, pulling a bucket from the well and dumping it into the basin. After several more buckets the basin overflowed, and the runoff poured into the bamboo pipe.

At the other end of the flume, near the house, the women were clapping and exclaiming.

'The water goes round and round, wah-wah-wah wah,' he sang, once again taking Tomiko's hand and yanking her down the hill. 'And it comes out here.' He pointed to another basin that had been set into a depression in the ground. It was half filled with water.

Miles picked it up and set it on the porch. The women pulled the basin into the kitchen, chattering excitedly.

'It's pretty primitive, but I figure it'll save you at least ten miles of walking a day. And not a metal pipe in the whole shebang. What do you think?'

Tomiko looked up at him. The strained aloofness in her manner was gone. She was once again the soft, trusting woman he had held in his arms the night before.

'My-o, we do not know how to thank you.'

Her beauty made him ache. For a moment he considered kissing her again, in the sunlight, in front of the world, claiming her as his prize. But the moment passed, and he only shrugged.

'How do you say "It's nothing"?'

Her eyes never left his. 'It was not nothing,' she said. Then she bowed to him.

The other women bowed, too, with great solemnity. Miles stood in the middle of their small circle, grimy and sweating and feeling like a king.

'Aw, shucks,' he said, and laughed. He bowed to each of them in return. 'Well, I guess the show's over. I'll just patch up some of the leaks and reinforce – oh, hell.'

A figure in a kimono was striding over the lawn toward them.

'What is it, My-o?' Tomiko asked.

He gestured with his chin to the approaching man. 'We have company,' he said. 'Mr Party.'

'Sato,' one of the women whispered, and ran into the house.

'You'd better go, too,' Miles said to Tomiko.

She hesitated for a moment, then nodded, and went in.

Sato walked over slowly, his green eyes as deadly as a cat's. He surveyed the strange contraption Miles had built, walking its length. Then, standing beside it, his hands on his hips, he kicked one of the bamboo poles off its support. The other poles followed, crashing to the ground, rolling down the hill until they collected in a heap at Miles's feet.

125

Miles looked away. He could hear the noise as the flume fell to pieces, but he did not want to see it.

Finally it was done. Everything was quiet again, and Sato walked away, his spine rigid, his head high.

Miles sat down on the bare ground. His muscles ached. During all the hours it had taken to build the flume, he had felt invigorated and alert; now he was overcome with fatigue. He wanted only to rest.

'Was good idea, Ronin,' a voice said behind him. Hiro put his big hand on Miles's shoulder. 'All kobun know already. Watch Sato.'

'You were watching?'

'Hai. Very bad.'

'Thanks for your help,' Miles said, pushing him aside.

Hiro followed after him. 'What can do, Ronin? Sato will be Oyabun.'

Miles whirled around to face him. 'Well, maybe he shouldn't be. Did you ever think about that? If all of you would stand up to him once – just once . . . Oh, what's the use?' He stomped up the steps to the kitchen.

The women gave him a basin of water to wash in. From the window he saw Tomiko plodding up the hill to the well, carrying one of the big wooden buckets. 'What's the use?' he repeated.

Hiro handed him a clean rag to wipe his face and hands.

'What are you still doing here?' Miles snapped.

'Come with me, please,' the big man said apologetically. 'Sato have job for you.'

His job consisted of dumping the chamber pots from every room into the midden, then washing them in a wooden trough beside the foul-smelling plot. As he worked, flies buzzed around him and the stench made him retch. At noon he was given a 'sun flag' lunch, a ball of rice packed around a plum. After he was finished, he was told to spend the rest of the day cutting firewood.

He worked until sunset, when Hiro called him in for his bath. Miles was the last to bathe, and the other kobun were already preparing for dinner. Still, Koji attended him leisurely, as if there was no greater pleasure than to bathe a man who smelled like a sewer.

'You're a good man, Koji,' Miles said.

Koji cocked his head, not comprehending.

'*Arigato.*'

Koji smiled and made a dismissive gesture, then helped Miles out of the tub, and pantomimed for him to lie down on a wooden bench. He massaged Miles's back until all the soreness and disappointment of the day melted beneath Koji's strong and expert hands. Miles was asleep within minutes.

When he awoke, Koji was gone. The room was dark and the fire beneath the iron tub had gone out. Sitting up with a groan, he picked up a candle and some wooden matches that had been left for him and wended his way through the hallways toward the kitchen.

The flame from his candle was the only light in the house. The dining room was empty, as was the kitchen. A platter of food covered with a cloth had been left on the countertop. In the small room where he slept, his bed had been prepared for him.

'What time is it?' he muttered to himself as he rifled through his bag to find his wristwatch.

Four-thirty. He had slept through the entire evening.

Cupping his hand over the candle, he went back out to the kitchen and began to wolf down the food Tomiko had left for him, not bothering to examine the morsels. Eels or not, he was starving. He stared vacantly out the dark window as he shoveled the food into his mouth with his fingers.

Then he saw something outside. A deer perhaps, or . . .

He forgot about the food as his eyes adjusted to the

127

blackness outside. There was no moon to light the night, but he could see something.

Men.

He snuffed out the candle. Three of them, moving without a sound. He crept over to the door and opened it quietly. Then, stepping out on the porch, he recognized them.

'Hiro?' he called softly. 'Koji. Yoshio.'

'Shhh!' Yoshio gestured for him to join them.

'What the hell are you . . .?' Miles stopped short where the bamboo poles had been piled. They were gone now. The sound of running water broke the silence as it poured into the basin near the house.

The flume had been rebuilt.

'What you think, Ronin?' Hiro whispered.

With a thick cloth covering a jointure, Koji hammered in a final nail with a muffled thud, then looked over, smiling.

Miles walked to the well, rubbing his hands over the smooth bamboo. The flume was twice as strong as it had been.

'I can't believe it,' he said.

Yoshio stuck out his hand for Miles to shake.

'You guys stayed up all night to do this.' A frown creased his forehead. 'But you might as well know, Sato's probably going to tear it down again.'

'Then we build again, yes?' Hiro chuckled.

Miles smiled crookedly. 'Is that the way of the Onami?'

Hiro's eyes went wide. 'No, no. Is way of sneak.'

Miles laughed aloud, then hugged the three of them. 'You're all ronin now, do you know that?'

'Hai,' said Yoshio. He dipped his finger into the mud beside the water basin and drew a Japanese character onto the bamboo flume. 'Ronin,' he explained as he wrote. 'Ronin. All.'

*   *   *

From a window high above the Oyabun watched, and smiled.

The tiger cub may earn his roar, after all, he said to himself.

He knocked down a small, round doll on the windowsill. It was a cheap and gaudy thing, its red paint chipped and cracking from the years. It bobbled back and forth, back and forth, each swing rolling back the boulders of time . . .

14

Two months after his meeting with Nagoya in 1945, Matt Watterson returned to the States with his new daughter. For the Wattersons, Mickey was a dream come true. In eight years of marriage they had been unable to conceive a child, and the tiny three-year-old lent a new beginning to their lives.

For Sadimasa Nagoya, it was the end.

Watterson had given Nagoya five hundred dollars – all he had – before he left, but when Nagoya tried to exchange it for Japanese currency, he learned that Japanese were not permitted to own American money. The cash was confiscated and Nagoya thrown in an overcrowded Japanese jail.

In a way his arrest was a relief. The bowl of flavorless Navy beans he received each day was the first time in more than a year that he was able to count on steady meals. Apparently many of the other inmates felt the same way, for within a month all but the most notorious war criminals – who were given over to the Occupation forces at Sugamo prison – were released and left to fend again for themselves in the war-ravaged city.

Nagoya walked for miles through the wasteland that was Tokyo to the neighborhood where the house of his father and grandfather had stood. Not a trace of the building remained. In the rubble he found a chip of dark, cord-marked pottery. It was a piece of what had once been the urn for the ashes of his great-great grandfather, who had been a noble in the court of the emperor during the Meiji Restoration. The Jomon urn had been made more than six thousand years ago. It, and its contents, were priceless. Now they were part of the scorched and fruitless earth where nothing of the past remained and nothing would grow for the future. He tossed it away like the garbage it now was and moved on.

Only a few blocks away, some buildings were still standing, among them the old Shinto temple where his family had worshiped. Just seeing it made Nagoya's spirits soar. He remembered the New Year's celebrations of his childhood, when his parents took him to the shrine to ring its deeply pealing brass bell and offer sweet rice cakes to the thousands of deities who inhabited the place, long-dead ancestors whose spirits watched over the living to assure the continuity of the chosen people on the divine islands in the sea. Surely those spirits would help him now that he had lost everything else. Surely they would not be offended if he slept for one night in the shelter of the temple.

But the great bell was gone. The door was closed and boarded over. Nailed to the ugly, raw boards covering the carved lintel was a sign:

CLOSED BY ORDER OF THE OCCUPATION FORCES

Below it was an explanation that Shintoism, the state religion of Japan which advocated the divinity of the emperor, had been outlawed.

At the end of the war, though he was already homeless, he heard the astonished talk of people who had listened to the emperor's message on the radio announcing the surrender of their country. The emperor spoke! The emperor, whom common eyes had never seen, had appeared in public and spoken in ordinary words, like any man. The emperor's photograph had appeared in a newspaper. He had stood

132

beside General MacArthur and next to the tall American, the man-god Hirohito, direct descendant of the goddess Amaterasu Omikami, who had created the perfect islands of Japan, looked small and young and almost foolish. And human.

There was no god anymore, Nagoya realized. One had only to walk the streets of Tokyo to see that.

He slept in alleyways and on sidewalks. He worked when he was lucky. He stole what food he could. He listened to the screams of the children in the parks, and the racking coughs of the men and women who were dying of tuberculosis. He walked and watched and waited to die.

Then he found the abandoned house.

It was on the outskirts of the city, in an area which had been deprived of water for months. There was water beneath the ground, but the residents could not tap it. Their only source of drinking water was rainfall, collected in barrels set outside the ramshackle homes and guarded with every weapon available.

With the unsanitary conditions and close quarters, TB swept through the area like a plague. Wagons sent by the civil government came by daily to collect the bodies, and at night wails of mourning issuing from almost every house matched the cries of the dying.

Nagoya was looking for work. There was none among these people, whose gaunt cheeks and bug eyes betrayed the ravaging sickness. Door after door shut in his face, until he came to one house with no rain barrel in front. There was no answer to his knocking, but the door creaked open. When he pushed it open wider, a nauseating stench washed over him.

He recognized the smell. He had seen too many corpses decomposing in the corners of the city not to know it at once. He only had to find the bodies.

They were on the floor: an elderly man and woman, their

133

eyes wide and black and gummy, their skin blue. On their bedding were rags of dried mucus and blood. Dust lay in the house like a blanket. On the small shrine in the corner, hidden from the authorities behind a screen, were scattered the ashes of incense burned for their ancestors.

Nagoya moved the bodies to the street outside, along with the contaminated bedding. He opened the windows to dispel the horrible smell of putrefaction. Then he lit a stick of incense at the shrine. He no longer had a god to pray to, but the old ones, the dead whose corpses now lay rotting on the street, had in their last act defied the authorities to pray at their illegal altar.

And so Nagoya prayed, too. He prayed to the gods who had abandoned him, who had taken his wife and family, who had destroyed his city, his country, and his life. He prayed to all the thousands of souls now lost forever in the decree of a foreign government.

And he forgave them.

It was afternoon. Sunlight filtered into the small house from the paper-paneled back door which opened to a garden. He knew there would be no flowers blooming there, but it was fenced-in and at least the air would be fresh.

He stepped outside. It was an odd sort of garden, without rocks or even a small bench. The tiny plot of earth had been plowed flat, then dug into furrows. The old couple had tried to grow vegetables in a place which had not had water for two years.

Still, something had grown there. The place was filled with odd plants, dry and lanky. Nagoya touched the leaves of one of them. It looked like a weed, but all the plants were identical. Curious, he pulled it out of the ground. On its roots hung small, woody nodules. He wiped the dirt off them with his fingers, his heart pounding as he began to understand. 'It cannot be,' he said aloud. He cracked open one of the nodules and saw a small, egg-shaped thing inside.

Then he laughed out loud and danced around the garden like a man who had lost his senses, clutching the tiny ball as if it were made of gold.

It was a peanut. The old couple had planted the only food that could grow in any soil, with only underground water to sustain it, and the harvest was ready.

First he roasted them in the stove. Finding some clean rags, he parceled out the peanuts, ten to a batch, and ran as fast as he could into the heart of the city, to the teeming Shinjuku market.

It was a filthy, malodorous place stretching for miles in every direction, where merchants from all around the city gathered to sell whatever food they could get. There were thousands of makeshift stalls crowded together, many of them no more than tables with rag awnings hung to protect the perishables on them from the sun. With food so scarce in Tokyo, everyone with even a few yen flocked to Shinjuku for a scoop of dried beans or a piece of fish.

'Peanuts!' Nagoya called when he reached an open spot. 'Fresh food!'

He sold each bag for twenty yen. It was an exorbitant price, but hungry people were happy to pay it. Within ten minutes he had sold half his supply and made more money than he had seen in years.

'Peanuts,' he called to a heavyset man wearing a Western-style suit who was walking toward him. The man did not look hungry, and his expression was stony. Nagoya backed off a few steps when he came closer.

'I don't know you,' the man said.

Nagoya ignored him. The war had driven many people to the point of insanity. It was no use to argue with them. Inching away from him, he sold a bag to a woman.

The heavyset man snatched the bag out of her hand. Then he picked up Nagoya's basket and threw it down, sending the little bundles rolling at his feet.

'Stop it!' Nagoya shouted, stooping to pick up his precious wares. 'What's the matter with you?'

The man crashed his knee into Nagoya's face.

Holding his hand over his bloody nose, Nagoya tried to get up, but the man grabbed him by the collar and slammed his fist into Nagoya's mouth. He felt the coldness of the brass knuckles a split second before the pain. Two of his teeth broke off. Blood spilled down the front of his shirt.

The man reached into Nagoya's pocket and pulled out the money from the peanuts. He threw it into the street, where people fell on their hands and knees in a mad scramble to pick up the coins.

The man laughed as Nagoya watched, stricken. He had gone hungry himself to sell the peanuts. Now everything was gone. 'The next time you decide to peddle in Shinjuku, talk to Izu first,' he said. With one last kick at Nagoya's back he swaggered away.

Groaning, Nagoya tried to get up, but his legs fell out from under him. He saw his two broken teeth lying next to some blood-sprayed chestnut peelings. Everything else blurred and circled around him, and the sounds of the market faded into the high, droning whine of unconsciousness.

He came to smelling the aroma of dried cuttlefish. Even through his pain, the delicious fragrance made his mouth water. Then a face appeared in front of him, a young man with his head covered by the traditional kerchief of a fishmonger.

'Are you all right?' he asked.

Nagoya rubbed his jaw. The teeth were gone, but the bone was not broken. He nodded.

'I've made some tea for you,' the young man said, handing him a cup.

He drank, careful to avoid the broken teeth. 'Thank you,' he said. 'Thank you very much.'

'I saw what that ape Kodama did to you. My father and I

were treated to the same welcome the first time we tried to sell in the market.'

'Kodama? I thought he said his name was . . .' He searched his memory. 'Izu. That was it. Izu.'

'Izu's the boss. He controls all the stalls in Shinjuku. We pay him some "squeeze" every week. Understand?' He rubbed his fingers together. 'Then Kodama leaves us alone.'

'Yakuza,' Nagoya said. Until now he had always thought of the dreaded Yakuza gangs as a kind of myth, like the dragons of country folklore. They had never touched his life before.

'They're everywhere since the war ended. The Americans don't really believe they exist, and the Japanese police are all getting paid off by them.' He shrugged. 'I guess the cops have got to eat, too, right?' He smiled. 'My name's Sasakawa,' he said.

'Nagoya.'

The young man cocked his head. 'Nagoya? Not the auction house.'

Nagoya sipped his tea without answering.

'I never met a millionaire before.'

'That was a long time ago,' Nagoya answered softly. 'Many lifetimes ago.'

Sasakawa gave his shoulder a squeeze. 'We've all had to start over from the beginning,' he said.

Nagoya laughed bitterly. 'I think I'll leave that to you.' He rose to leave.

'Another suicide,' Sasakawa said, almost in passing. 'The *shayo-zoku* always take the easy way out.'

Nagoya felt himself getting angry. *Shayo-zoku*, or 'sunsetting class', was a new word in the postwar language of Japan. It referred to the displaced aristocrats who, despite their loss of status and money, continued to live as they had in the past, helpless and pampered, never realizing that their world had disintegrated around them. Many of these people, princesses and statesmen and wealthy old men now bereft of all their luxuries, ended their lives in the ritual of seppuku, their bodies swathed in the tattered silk garments of another time.

Nagoya had often counted his own parents fortunate to have died before the war. Perhaps they too might have died this way, with no other route of escape. And now this boy, this peasant who spent his days in a filthy market where Nagoya's mother would not even have deigned to walk, was ridiculing them.

'How dare you,' he said coldly. 'My family –'

'I wasn't talking about your family,' Sasakawa interrupted. 'I was talking about you. Big man, rich man. I lost everything in the war, too. But it's all right for people like me to try to make the best of things, isn't it, because I never had much to begin with. Not like Nagoya, who lived in a house with servants and ate dinner with the prime minister. No, your kind just crawls up and dies when things get tough.'

Nagoya was so stunned by the young man's sudden cruelty that he could think of nothing to say in return. And in the silence he realized that Sasakawa's words were true. Japan was a new country now, a frightening country where death was easy and the strong lived only through force of will.

'I have tried,' he said brokenly.

'And you have succeeded, Nagoya. You're alive.' Sasakawa grinned. 'Hey, that's something, isn't it?'

Nagoya smiled despite himself. 'I guess it's a kind of accomplishment, at that,' he said.

'You'd better believe it!' The young man picked something off the table in his stall. It was a painted red doll, a round figure without legs, heavily weighted at the bottom. 'Do you know what this is?'

'It's a *daruma*,' Nagoya said. He had seen them all his life. Every shopkeeper displayed one in his store as a sort of lucky mascot. Occasionally he had even come across rare ones at auction. The one Sasakawa held, with its garish color and crude carving, certainly did not qualify as a rarity.

'Here is why I keep it.' Sasakawa set it on the bench next to Nagoya. Then he swatted it with all the force he could muster. The doll reeled and tilted, banging from side to side against the wooden bench, but because of its bottom-heavy construction, it stood upright in the end.

Sasakawa picked it up in one hand. 'This is how we must be, my friend,' he said gently.

The first pale streaks of sunlight shone on the little doll. It was difficult for an old man to sleep, Nagoya thought, touching it. Memories were intrusive visitors. They came without being summoned and stayed too long.

When Sasakawa had died, he had left his old friend only two things: the guardianship of his youngest daughter, Tomiko, and the old daruma from their first meeting. They had been the most precious things in his life.

15

Sasakawa took him home to dinner that first night they met. 'Home' was a shack of corrugated cardboard in a Shinjuku alley, where Sasakawa's ailing father lay on a bed of straw.

'We've got some black-market wheat from the Americans,' he said, building a small fire in a hole in the dirt floor.

'Wheat?'

Sasakawa showed him the bag of brown flour. 'It's what they use for rice in the West.' He made a face. 'Not very tasty, but even the emperor can't afford rice these days.'

He mixed it with water, sprinkled the dough with cuttle-fish flakes, then steamed it over the fire.

Nagoya was ravenous, but the heavy biscuits were too painful for him to eat. The exposed roots of the two teeth Kodama had broken were throbbing. He felt a fever coming on.

'There's a dentist nearby,' Sasakawa said gently. 'That is, he used to be a dentist. His office was burned. But he can still pull those teeth. God knows, he gets enough experience around here.'

'From Kodama?'

Sasakawa laughed. 'If Kodama were all we had to worry about, things would be fine. But the Chinese are moving in, too.'

'The Chinese? What do they have to do with anything?'

'Where have you been, in a cave? The Chinese, the

Koreans, the Taiwanese – all the foreigners here – are outside Japanese law now. They're allowed to have American money, so they can deal with the American GIs. And they're protected by the Occupation government.'

'So?'

'So we've treated them like shit for the past few thousand years, not to mention what the military did to them during the war. Now that they've got the chance, they're getting even.' He lifted up the hair on his forehead. There was a deep scar there, shiny and white. 'There's not a merchant in Shinjuku who hasn't been robbed or beaten. A few dozen have been killed.'

'Why doesn't Kodama stop them?'

Sasakawa fought to chew through the hard biscuit. 'What does that fat idiot care, as long as he gets his squeeze?'

'In exchange for his money, he ought to at least protect you.'

'Sure. And arrange a marriage for me with his daughter, too.'

'I'm serious. If the Yakuza are going to take money from you, they should give something in return.'

Sasakawa shook his head. 'It's obvious you're an aristo,' he said. 'Either that, or all your brains were in those teeth Kodama knocked out.' He swallowed the last bite of his meal. 'Come on, I'll get you to the dentist. That's all I can take of this crap, anyway.'

Nagoya looked down. 'A dentist is not necessary,' he said.

'Don't be stupid. There won't be any charge. No one can afford to pay him, anyway. I'll take him some of these.' He hefted one of the leftover biscuits. 'I'll tell him they're American fish cakes. He'll love them.'

His father coughed. Nagoya recognized the sound, as well as the old man's sunken cheeks and glassy eyes. He was dying. Soon Sasakawa would be alone, too. And like Nagoya and thousands of others, he would be homeless and starving.

'What's Kodama's boss's name again?' Nagoya asked.

'Izu. Kinosuke Izu.'

'And he gets squeeze from every merchant in Shinjuku?'

'More than twenty-five thousand of us. He's got two hundred men like Kodama working for him.'

Nagoya was quiet for a moment. 'I'm going to talk to him.'

This time, even Sasakawa's father joined in the laughter. 'Good luck,' his young friend said. 'Izu's campaigning for a seat in the Diet. Maybe he'll shake your hand after one of his election speeches about cleaning up the corruption in Tokyo.' He stood up. 'Let's go.'

'Wait a minute. He's running for government office? The leader of a Yakuza gang?'

'You got it.'

'But who's going to vote for him?'

'I will, for one.'

'What?' Nagoya shouted. 'Why?'

Sasakawa grabbed his arm and pulled him out the door. 'Because I've been to the damned dentist enough times.'

That night, lying on the earthen floor, his mouth packed with cloth, Nagoya formulated his plan. It was simple. If Izu was playing politician, he wouldn't murder a voter in cold blood. Not in front of witnesses, anyway.

By asking a few questions, he found his way to Izu's headquarters, a storefront staffed with the most villainous-looking thugs he had ever seen. There was something comical about them, too, as if they had adopted their mode of dress from American gangster movies of the Thirties.

'I would like to speak with Mr Izu,' Nagoya said.

One man in a pinstripe suit, black shirt, and white tie

looked him up and down with the subtlety of a fishwife. 'You and who else?' he said. He jerked his thumb toward the door. 'Get lost.'

Nagoya breathed deeply and steeled himself. 'My name is Sadimasa Nagoya,' he said. 'Please write it down.'

'Eat shit.'

'I assure you, sir, that you will be the one performing that activity unless you comply with my request. My family is one of the oldest in Japan. Mr Izu, as well as many of the voters, will recognize it. If he wishes to meet with me, I will return here at ten o'clock tomorrow morning.'

He bowed curtly and left, walking in his rags as tall as one of his illustrious ancestors.

The next morning, Izu was present. The squat and toadlike man had the coarse features of a killer, but he wore a silk suit and cufflinks of gold. He did not bother to return Nagoya's bow. 'What do you want?' he said.

'Mr Izu, it is a dishonor to my family name that I appear before you in such a state, but like many of our countrymen, I have fallen on unpleasant days.'

'Skip it,' Izu said. 'Look, if you're here looking for a handout –'

'Thank you for your generous consideration,' Nagoya interrupted, 'but I have not come to burden you with the trivial concerns of my difficulties. Indeed, I am prepared to offer you something which may be of some slight benefit in your noble effort to bring good government to our city.'

Izu sneered. 'Like what?'

Nagoya raised his head to show the refined lines of his face. No one, he knew, was more class-conscious in a class society than a man of poor background. 'Sir, the commodity I offer is myself. Or, more precisely, my name.'

The toadlike mouth opened to laugh. But slowly a glint of intelligence shone in Izu's eyes. 'Your name?'

'That was why you agreed to see me, wasn't it? It's not

every day a person of my background is seen by the common populace.'

The thug's lips curled down. 'Who are you calling common, you asshole?' It was a question, but it sounded like a threat.

'The voters,' Nagoya answered. 'Shinjuku is a poor district. It's constituents are easily impressed by such inconsequentials as names and titles. Forgive my bluntness, Mr Izu, but you have neither. My presence would add a certain' – he paused for effect – 'legitimacy to your campaign. They would take you more seriously as a leader.'

'I've got twenty-five thousand merchants who've sworn to vote for me,' Izu barked.

Nagoya shrugged. 'One says many things out of fear. But the ballot is a secret one.'

Izu paced the room. He lit a cigarette and leaned against a desk. He smoked in silence for a while, exhaling two streams from his broad, flat nose. Then he smiled. 'A Nagoya as my front man,' he mused aloud.

His gaze returned to Nagoya. He tossed his cigarette on the ground and crushed it with his shoe. 'What's in it for you?' he said gruffly.

Nagoya hesitated. He had never really expected Izu to hear him out. 'Only one thing,' he said. 'A job.'

Izu's suspicious eyes narrowed.

'Kodama's job.'

'You're crazy. I don't even know you.'

'You know Kodama even less,' Nagoya said. 'How much does he give you out of the squeeze he collects from the Shinjuku merchants each week?'

'That's none of your business.'

'Three hundred thousand yen? Four?'

'Don't be ridiculous,' Izu said.

'Much less?'

Izu shrugged. 'What can those people afford?'

'I'll bring you half a million a week,' Nagoya said. 'Guaranteed.'

Izu stared at him for a long moment. Then he looked at his men. 'Get out of here,' he told them.

When he was alone with Nagoya, he folded his arms across his chest and scrutinized him. He no longer viewed the young man who stood before him as a shabby supplicant.

'How are you going to squeeze five hundred thousand yen out of them?'

'What does it matter? I said it was guaranteed.'

'With what?'

'With my life,' Nagoya said.

'You're doing *what*?' Sasakawa nearly dropped the heavy piece of dried squid he was holding.

'I'm collecting the squeeze. And I want you to help me.'

The young man gave him a look of incredulous disgust.

'Listen to me,' Nagoya said. 'Izu's going to take the money anyway, at least as long as Japan is the cesspool it is. The government's a shambles. The police are corrupt. Even if they weren't, they're powerless. They aren't even allowed to carry arms anymore. The Americans don't have the slightest idea what the Yakuza are doing. Under those circumstances, gangs like Izu's are going to be running the country.'

'And you want to get in on the action,' Sasakawa said, hacking into the cuttlefish with a cleaver.

'I think I can make things better. Look, you pay Kodama thirty yen in squeeze, right? But only a part of that goes to Izu. Kodama's keeping the rest.'

'So?'

'So I collect twenty-five yen. With twenty-five thousand merchants, that's six hundred, twenty-five thousand. I've promised half a million to Izu. He gets more than he's used to, the merchants pay less –'

Sasakawa laughed. 'And you're a rich man.'

'No. That is, I won't starve. Neither will you, as my partner. But we'll put most of the money back into the Shinjuku market. We'll hire people to clean it every day to slow the spread of TB. The people who earn the money by cleaning will spend it on food. At the market. The merchants will be able to get more goods to sell. The entire economy here will spiral upward. It's got to.'

Sasakawa wiped his forehead with his arm and leaned back. 'Where did you learn this stuff?'

Nagoya grinned. 'My grandfather was Finance Minister. It's in my genes.'

'The aristo to the end.' He turned back to his work. 'There's just one thing I'm curious about,' he said, almost too casually. 'Yakuza don't usually take people in off the streets. You must have offered Izu something valuable in exchange for a job like that.'

Nagoya was silent for a moment. 'I did,' he said finally. 'My name. It's the only thing I have left.' There was a long pause. 'I'm going to campaign for Izu.'

Sasakawa laid down the cleaver. 'You're going to help get that murdering swine elected?'

'He'll be elected anyway,' Nagoya said. 'No one else can afford to run against him, in more ways than one.'

The young man sighed. 'I suppose you're right. I've got to vote for the snake myself. Well, what do you want me to do?'

'Find some people to clean the market. No, not some – dozens. Hundreds. Anybody who needs a job will be welcome. Tell them we'll pay ten yen a day now, more later. I'll ask the merchants to give them a discount.'

Sasakawa laughed and slapped Nagoya on the back. 'I was wrong when I called you a *shayo zoku*,' he said. 'We're going to have some fine stories to tell our sons.'

Nagoya turned away. 'I will have no sons,' he said quietly.

Within a month, the Shinjuku market was as clean as a temple's grounds. Nagoya bought disinfectant through Sasakawa's blackmarket connections, and every stall was washed down with it. The merchants were granted 'licenses' – chits of paper guaranteeing them clean conditions, the right of exclusive trade in Shinjuku, and protection from thieves and vandals.

Now they no longer regarded the money they paid to Izu as squeeze, but as a legitimate investment. As a gesture of goodwill, Nagoya formed the Association of Shinjuku Merchants and granted them the status of auxiliary members in Izu's organization.

'What kind of joker are you?' Izu had bellowed when Nagoya told him about the twenty-five thousand new members of his ikka. 'What do I want with a bunch of dirty peddlers?'

'They make your money for you,' Nagoya said bluntly. 'As for their membership, all that does is assure you of their loyalty. You don't have to send strongarms like Kodama after them anymore. They're proud to be associated with you.'

Izu thought about it sourly. 'I hear you're paying people to clean the market. Hundreds of them, when a dozen could do the job.'

'That's right. And all those people are spending what we pay them on food, so the merchants can buy more. Surely you must know that the black market is thriving only because the legitimate merchants can't afford goods that people need. By circulating money in Shinjuku, we can drive the black-market profiteers out of existence within six months.'

This struck a chord with Izu. He had been trying since the end of the war to control the stupendously profitable black market in Tokyo, but that niche had been carved out by the *sangokujin*, the foreigners.

Chinese, Filipino, Taiwanese, and Korean nationals living in Japan had radically improved their standard of living since the surrender. As American allies they were entitled to Occupation government food, jobs, supplies, and even houses which had been confiscated from the Japanese. Once considered something less than human by the native Japanese, these same foreigners were now prospering while their former masters starved.

The sangokujin were not gracious victors. With their new-found wealth they sold necessities such as rice and firewood to the city-locked, automobile-less residents of Tokyo at astronomical prices. Quick to organize, a Chinese gang under the leadership of a notoriously bloodthirsty Cantonese family named Lee had already taken control of the profiteers and set up a burgeoning black market in the bombed-out area near the train station on the outskirts of Shinjuku.

For the Japanese populace the new arrogance of the sangokujin was salt rubbed into the wound of a lost war, but for Izu the situation was infinitely more painful. He was missing out on the opportunity to capitalize on the hottest black market in history. Without the Chinese gang bosses the lucrative sangokujin market could conceivably come under his control.

'Six months?' he asked.

'That's optimistic, but possible. We'll certainly make a dent in their business if our merchants can afford to buy rice and sell it at a realistic price.'

'The foreigners won't own our country,' Izu said, echoing a popular slogan.

'Not if we're willing to think beyond tomorrow's profits. That's why I gave out licenses. But we've got to be able to make good on our guarantees.'

'What, to sweep their grounds for them so that a stinking fishmonger can feel like a nobleman? I still think it's a stupid idea, but I'll go along with it.'

'I'm not talking about that,' Nagoya said. 'It's the other guarantees, the right of exclusivity in Shinjuku and the protection of the merchants against violence.'

He fought to control his annoyance with this stupid man who could not see beyond his own flat nose. 'As it is, the Lees and their gangs have been terrorizing the merchants just to pass the time. Now that our people have started doing enough business to hurt the sangokujin, there's no telling what the Chinese gangs will do.'

'What are you telling me, that twenty-five thousand people can't defend themselves against a few foreigners?'

'They're not fighters,' Nagoya said. 'They're afraid. That's why they need us.'

'*Kintama*, golden balls, you make things complicated. What do you want from me?'

'A force of men to patrol the market.'

'For *six months*?' Izu sputtered.

'At least.'

'What do I look like, the police department?'

'A few men, then,' Nagoya persisted. 'Led by someone like Kodama. He can at least make a show –'

'Kodama's working the gambling houses.' He smiled. 'The atmosphere suits him better than the food market.' He shook his head. 'Sorry, Nagoya. It was a mistake to promise protection from anyone besides us. Now you've got to live with it. Tell those jerks to look out for themselves.'

Nagoya felt fury rising inside him. Izu was not only a thug. He was the worst kind of fool, who could not see the threat to his own welfare simply because he could not bring himself to help another human being. A man like Izu could not have risen to power in any society other than that of postwar Japan, over a people who were desperately hungry and suicidally demoralized. He was the new breed of gangster in Japan, driven solely by greed, empowered by terror.

Even Nagoya, in the sheltered life he had led, had heard

the tales about the exploits of the famed Yakuza. Adopting the traditions of the samurai, these classless outlaws had been regarded for centuries as the defenders of the common man against the oppressive regimes of the shoguns. They were the champions of the divinely appointed emperor, the preservers of the ancient ways of Japanese life.

Their self-discipline was legendary. In the days before the war, Yakuza kobun were sent to live as beggars in order to prove their endurance and humility. Self-mutilation was the expected form of atonement for even the most minor offense. When a member of a Yakuza ikka pledged himself as a brother to another member, it was a vow that, if possible, he would die in his friend's place. He lived by the precepts of *giri*, duty, and *ninjo*, compassion, and he was honor-bound to help those who needed his help, even at the cost of his own life.

But that had changed, too, Nagoya thought, like everything else in the world he had known. Like Japan itself, the Yakuza had become a hybrid chaotic monstrosity with no rules and no heroes. It was one with the new Japan. Izu's world.

Later, as he rode in Izu's American Cadillac, dressed in a fine silk suit of Chinese manufacture, smiling and waving to the crowds of emaciated people who chanted, 'Izu! Izu!' in unison as if the thug in the big shiny car were their deliverer, Nagoya felt a shame so deep that he thought he would collapse under its weight.

At the cost of his name, the honorable name of his ancestors, he had promised these people protection from the brutality of the sangokujin. Now they would have none.

He had become a part of Izu's world.

16

Dawn was breaking.

The old man knocked the red daruma to the floor, then pulled furiously on the bell-rope near the door. Presently Tomiko ran in, wide-eyed and panting.

'Oh!' she said, nearly skidding to a halt in the doorway. '*Sumimasen*, Oyabun. Excuse me. I was afraid –'

'No, I'm not dead yet,' he snapped. 'Bring Sato to me.'

'Sato . . . Hai, Nagoya-sama.'

Her hesitation had meant she would have to have Sato awakened, he thought impatiently. The young always slept as if life would go on forever.

He knelt by his shrine and waited. He tried to clear his mind of thought, of the burden of his memories, but through the silence he could still hear the sound of gunfire . . .

Nagoya heard the first shots from the motorcade. Izu, assuming it was an attempt on his life, dived for the floor. His men pulled out their weapons and aimed them at the astonished crowd which fled, shrieking, at the sight.

Nagoya got out and listened. The volley had been fired fairly far distant from Izu's parade.

A woman screamed as she was trampled by the stampeding crowd. 'Fujiko,' she sobbed, trying to pull herself along on the ground.

Nagoya pulled her to her feet. 'Can you walk?' he asked.

'My daughter. She's at the market.'

His head snapped in the direction of the stalls. He had not believed it at first, because he had not wanted to, but now he knew it was true. The sangokujin had attacked.

'Oh, no,' he groaned. Then a second burst of gunfire rang out, along with the shrill screams of the victims. The woman in his arms pushed him away and ran.

Nagoya looked back toward Izu for assistance, but the entire motorcade had gone. Whatever was going on in the Shinjuku market, it would undoubtedly bring in the police and probably the Occupation authorities as well. By his disappearance Izu had washed his hands of the matter.

By the time Nagoya reached the market on foot, the grounds were deserted except for the dead and dying and those who had come running to care for them. The stalls had been knocked over and hacked with axes. There were nearly a dozen corpses lying in the rubble, children and old people and shoppers and merchants. A woman sobbed as she rocked back and forth on her knees with the body of a small boy in her arms. In the distance a siren wailed. And over it all were scattered the small framed licenses of the merchants, Nagoya's promise to them that they would be safe from violence.

Numbly he bent over a man with a chest wound. He took off his jacket to keep the man warm, then tore his shirt to make a dressing.

'Can you hear me?' he asked.

The man opened his eyes. He was a merchant Nagoya knew, a weaver of tatami mats whose stall was near Sasakawa's.

'Don't touch me,' he wheezed.

'The ambulance will be here soon. But you're bleeding, and –'

'I said get away!' The man raised himself up on his elbows. The effort was painful. He coughed blood. 'You and your guarantees. You're the same as all the rest. Liar!'

154

He fell back, clutching the wound on his chest. His voice was barely a rasp. 'Liar . . .'

Nagoya sat back, numb. As the ambulances arrived, he could only stare at the carnage in the market.

The Chinese gang leaders had done it to teach the Shinjuku merchants a lesson. The lesson was that men like Nagoya, with his worthless paper licenses, would not help them to stand on their feet. Their association meant nothing. They meant nothing. They were a conquered people, and the foreigners were their rulers now.

As he stood up, he saw a figure crouching against a stall. 'No, please, no,' he whispered. He ran to the stall.

Sasakawa sat on his haunches in front of it, his arms crossed over his face.

'My friend . . .'

Sasakawa's shoulders heaved, and Nagoya felt a flood of relief that he was alive.

His friend did not answer. He only continued to weep, covering his head as if the fire bombs of the war were still falling. Nagoya looked inside the stall. Sasakawa's father lay on the small wooden bench. He was still, and the pall of death was already on his face. There was a bullet wound on his neck.

'I'm sorry,' he said softly, kneeling outside next to Sasakawa.

'The damned Chinese came in shooting. Not a warning, not a word. They just shot into the crowd as if we were fish in a barrel.'

'Sasakawa –'

'No one expected it,' he went on, sobbing. 'It was so fast.' He banged his head against the stall, his face contorted in helpless rage. 'What's happened, Sadimasa?' he cried in anguish. 'What did the war do to the human part of human beings?'

Nagoya looked over the littered field of broken stalls, at

the ambulances and morgue wagons. 'We're going to fight back,' he said quietly.

'How? With what? No one except criminals and the sangokujin can get guns anymore.'

'Did you fight in the war?'

Sasakawa nodded bleakly. 'Guam.'

'Did you use machine guns? Those big monsters on tripods?'

'The *Nambu*? Sure. I was assigned to one. Why?'

Nagoya took a deep breath. 'I was stationed at Misawa as a radio operator. When the Americans attacked, we were wiped out. All our vehicles were destroyed. There were only twelve of us left out of a whole battalion of ninety-six men. We took off for the hills.'

'Yes? So?'

'Before we did, we buried the gun.'

Sasakawa's mouth dropped.

'We thought we'd be going back. As it turned out, we were all assigned elsewhere. I was wounded, so I was sent back to Tokyo . . .' For a moment he lost himself in the terrible memories of those last days of the war, the fire bombings, the collapsing buildings, the screams of his wife trapped inside a blazing inferno.

Sasakawa put this hand on Nagoya's shoulder. Nagoya licked his dry lips. 'Anyway, we never got back to Misawa. No one did, as far as I know.'

'The gun's still there,' Sasakawa whispered.

'It may not work.'

'I can get it to work.'

A Buddhist funeral was held for Sasakawa's father. Before the cremation a bowl of rice holding a single upright chopstick was placed near his head in the Buddhist tradition. The rice had cost more than a week's earnings, but without it the old man's *kami*, his spirit, would not rest.

After the ceremony Nagoya and Sasakawa set off for Misawa. They traveled by train, where the trains ran, and on foot the rest of the way up the rugged, mountainous coastline. The villages of the region resembled wood-block prints from centuries gone by: thatched houses, public hot-spring baths, wooden poles hung with dried persimmon, and ancient roads used by travelers for a thousand years which wound through the forests and over the high cliffs overlooking the sea. Here the rice paddies had begun to produce once again, with green shoots poking out of pools of water. Here, it seemed, nothing had changed since the beginning of time.

'It's as if the war never happened,' Sasakawa said.

'These places weren't affected much. Our squadron used to come to the villages for baths, and complain that we had nothing to do. We were convinced we were being wasted up on these hills.' He smiled sadly. 'In the end, we probably were.'

Misawa was located at the far northern end of the Japanese peninsula, where the coastline formed a magnificent peak over-looking dozens of small volcanic islands, many of them containing no more than one tree. The rocky ground of the cliff still bore the charred marks and deep pits where the battalion's trucks had exploded.

Nagoya looked around at the sky, the nearby islands, the sea. The village itself had not been touched by the strafing. 'We were stationed here to knock out enemy planes before they reached Tokyo,' he said bitterly. 'Idiot stategists. We were sitting ducks.' He stuck his hands in his pockets. 'The gun is at the base of the mountains. We carried it there.'

At the foothills, lichen-covered boulders rested at the feet of gigantic, time-worn fir trees.

'Any of this look familiar?'

Nagoya shook his head. 'There was a little creek nearby, with a shrine of some sort built over it. The shrine was painted green, I think.'

157

They searched for hours, overturning rocks, kicking at the dense pine underbrush, until the sun was almost down.

'It's getting hard to see,' Nagoya said. 'There's a hotel in the village –'

'Water!' Sasakawa called. He lifted his two hands, palms up. They were covered with mud.

Frantically the two men scoured the ground on their hands and knees until they found the thin trickle of a creek, then followed it. As night descended, Sasakawa took a candle lantern from his backpack.

It was nearly ten o'clock before they saw the shrine. It had rotted and fallen into the water, but the main supports, mottled with moss but still showing bright green in spots, lay crisscrossed over the running stream.

Nagoya paced his steps northward, then east. '. . . eight, nine, ten.' He raised his arm above his head as far as it would stretch and felt for a notch in the branch of a tree with his fingers. 'This is the place.' He took the lantern and held it over the ground. A bush of tinderwood-dry pine boughs stood next to the tree. 'Here,' he said.

They yanked away the pine boughs. Below them was a rectangular pile of small stones that looked like a grave. With their hands they raked off the stones until they scraped the black earth beneath.

'It won't be deep,' Nagoya said. 'We didn't have a shovel.'

The earth had settled since the burial, and the two men were drenched in sweat, their arms aching, by the time Nagoya felt the first hard section of metal.

'Easy, easy,' Sasakawa grunted as they lifted the heavy gun out of the ground. 'We can't replace any of these parts.' He examined it by lantern light.

'Will it work?' Nagoya asked.

Sasakawa cocked his head. 'Well, some of the parts are pretty rusted, and the ammunition you packed will have to be checked . . .' He turned to Nagoya and smiled. 'Don't worry. I said I'd get it to work, didn't I?'

Sasakawa labored with the gun while Nagoya helped the merchants to repair the wreckage of the Shinjuku market. On the ninth day after the massacre, the Chinese attacked again on a lesser scale, singling out merchants at random as targets for their terrorism. At night, sangokujin boys came to the empty market with cans of red paint, smearing the newly built stalls with obscenities. The police filed reports to the Occupation government, stating that the Shinjuku district was in a state of unrest. The Americans responded by declaring the area off-limits to its GIs.

The tension grew. The Japanese population began to stay away from the market. The merchants watched their produce and fresh fish, bought with their first profits, rot unsold in their stalls. Nagoya became known as *Ono*, the ax, because he had to collect the squeeze even though the merchants were impoverished. Those who genuinely had nothing were exempted, their share paid by the money which normally went to the cleaners. All the cleaners were dismissed.

Still there was a shortfall. To cover it, Nagoya had to dig into the stores of cash he had laboriously built up since going to work for Izu.

'When will the gun be ready?' Nagoya asked.

'I don't know.'

On the fourteenth day a fire spread through Shinjuku at night, razing more than half of the new stalls. Nagoya promised that they would be rebuilt. The merchants turned their backs on him.

'When will the gun be ready?'

'The bullets . . .'

Nagoya slammed the door.

On the sixteenth day Izu held another parade. He was pelted in his Cadillac with rotten food.

'Those bastards!' he shouted. 'You think I'm going to rebuild their stalls again, Nagoya? Think again!'

'They've lost everything. All the gains we made . . . Everything's gone. They're upset . . .'

'Not as upset as they're going to be,' Izu said. 'Raise the squeeze.'

Nagoya was dumbstruck. 'Raise it?' he managed finally. 'They can't pay as it is. I've had to let the cleaners go just to get you your five hundred thousand yen.'

'Seven hundred,' Izu said.

'It can't be done. They can't pay.'

Izu fixed his cold toad's eyes on Nagoya. 'Then you fault on your guarantee.'

'The price we agreed on . . .'

'The price was your life,' Izu said. 'Raise the squeeze.'

'When will the gun be ready?'

Sasakawa rubbed his bleary eyes. 'It's ready.'

They took it at dawn, rolled inside a tatami mat, to the outskirts of the sangokujin black market.

It was going to be a busy day. The Chinese merchants were assembling their ramshackle market as they did every morning, spreading their wares on blankets on the ground or on tables in the open air. Around them their children, who were exempt from Japanese compulsory education, shouted and ran around like puppies. The air was filled with the scent of strange, spicy dishes cooked in pots over open fires, so unlike the beautifully arranged but bland and unheated food of Japan.

'Where?' Sasakawa whispered.

Nagoya pointed to an elementary school. He threw a

rope with a hook on its end up to the roof, then shinnied to the top. Sasakawa fastened the rope around the gun, and Nagoya hoisted it up.

On the roof, Sasakawa assembled the monster. 'Let's just hope the ammo doesn't blow up in our faces,' he said. 'I had to refill every shell with gunpowder.'

'Where'd you get gunpowder?'

'Don't even ask,' Sasakawa said, peering into the eyepiece. 'Okay. They're in range.' He looked up. 'They've got kids.'

'Yes. So did we.'

The young man touched the gun lightly. 'One of these can down an airplane,' he said quietly. 'It'll blow them to bits.'

'They killed your father.'

Sasakawa said nothing for a long moment. 'Yes. And we killed Americans. And they killed Germans. Who killed Poles. When does it stop, Sadimasa?'

Nagoya looked down. 'It's a different world now.'

Sasakawa looked at him with terrible anguish. Then he pulled himself upright, his eyes bright with tears, and took hold of the gun. 'This I do for my father,' he said. 'For all of us.'

He opened fire.

The children screamed. Pots were overturned, toys cast aside, valuable bags of rice knocked to the ground as the sangokujin scattered.

Sasakawa fired until all the ammunition was spent, then stepped away from the gun and crossed his arms defiantly across his chest. When the smoke cleared, the market was empty. Nagoya looked through the magnifying sight on the weapon.

Not one person had been killed. Not one person had been wounded.

Sasakawa stood like a statue, his stubborn face fixed in a

scowl. Nagoya could only stand and stare at the man. Then he shook his head, and laughed, and put his arm around him. 'You're a lousy shot,' he said, and kicked the legs out from under the gun.

The old man smiled.

Sasakawa had been his conscience from that day forward. His sense of ninjo had always guided him, and it was usually a wise guide.

After the incident at the sangokujin market, the Lee family migrated to more pleasant waters in the United States, and the gang terrorism of the Shinjuku merchants stopped cold. The episode itself soon grew to the proportions of legend, and firmly reestablished the Yakuza as the champions of the people.

Ironically, Kinosuke Izu was arrested by the Occupation government shortly afterward on suspicion of underworld activities, and was unable to continue his political campaign. After his release he tried again, promising outright grants of cash to everyone who voted for him, but he was defeated.

And Sadimasa Nagoya went on to become Oyabun over the most powerful Yakuza ikka in Tokyo.

He became a man with no past. He was no longer the young aristocrat of ancient lineage. His daughter had forgotten his existence. His grandson had been reared as an American.

His grandson.

The Nagoya line, the true line, not the perversion Sadimasa Nagoya had made of his ancestors' name, was still unbroken. The handsome, educated boy from America would carry it on. Miles Haverford would live the life Nagoya would have had if the war had not happened.

But the boy had shown up with other plans. He wished to

bloody his hands in an enterprise which would cost many lives, perhaps – most likely – his own.

No, Nagoya thought angrily. The revenge of Matt Watterson and Susi Haverford was necessary, but it would not take the boy's life. Miles could not be involved.

Nagoya had kept him at the ikka from fear that Miles might try some foolish and suicidal action on his own. With a little hardship, he had thought, Miles would give up and leave the war with the DeSantos to those who knew violence and understood it.

But young Haverford had not given up easily. He was resilient, as Americans are, yet he possessed the Japanese sense of giri. And he was a natural leader.

Nagoya smiled. In his own world across the sea, the tiger cub might one day make his ancestors proud.

If he lived.

The old man lit a stick of incense on the shrine. The boy *would* live, even if it meant he would hate his natural grandfather for the rest of his days.

'Nagoya-sama?' Sato asked at the doorway. 'You asked for me?'

The old man turned away from his altar. 'I have seen how you have treated the American,' he said. 'Your tactics have been childish. I am not pleased.'

Sato fell to the floor. '*Gomenasai*, Oyabun. Forgive me. I was –'

'Let the women keep their water-carrier. It means nothing.'

'Yes, Nagoya-sama.'

'If you are to break him, do it as a man.'

The young man looked up, astonished.

'I selected you as his aniki because I knew you would hate him. *Now break him*, do you understand?' Nagoya's voice was a low threat. 'I want him gone.'

Sato rose slowly and bowed. '*Hai*, Oyabun.'

17

'*Mo scoshi, kudasai.*'

Tomiko smiled as she passed the bowl of breakfast rice to Miles. 'You are learning our language quickly,' she said.

'I have a good teacher.' Their eyes met and held. The other women looked at one another knowingly.

Tomiko turned away in embarrassment. 'We are grateful to you for repairing the foom,' she said.

Miles grinned as he did every time he heard one of the ladies fracture the pronunciation of 'flume.' 'The foom wasn't my doing. Not this time. Is there a Japanese equivalent to the story of the shoemaker and the elves?'

Just then Hiro walked into the kitchen, his huge body filling the narrow doorway. 'Ronin-san?'

'Well, speak of the elf,' Miles said. 'I was just about to explain to the ladies how you and the others rebuilt their –'

'Hai, hai,' Hiro said nervously. 'Ronin, you must come. Sato wait for you in *dojo*.'

'Dojo?' Miles asked.

'Dojo. Is – is . . .' Hiro looked to Tomiko for assistance.

'The dojo is the room where the martial arts are practiced,' she explained. 'It is a gymnasium but smaller, and the floors are matted. Ours is for the use of the kobun.' She glanced at Miles hopefully.

'Maybe Sato teach fight, yes?' Hiro said. 'Open-hand fight, Sato very strong. Good teacher.'

'Why would he teach me anything?' Miles asked. 'He hates me.'

'Sato is aniki to Ronin. Big brother. Is duty.' He muscled Miles off the chair with a scowl. 'You come.' The ladies tittered.

The dojo was a bare room with white lime-washed walls. Its only decorations were the woven mats on the floor and a scroll hanging near the door. Sato stood on the opposite side from the doorway, barefooted and dressed in a *gi*. When Miles entered, the Japanese strode over to him purposefully.

Miles attempted a bow. When he straightened up, Sato slapped him backhanded across his face. The force of the blow sent Miles sprawling into a corner of the room, where he landed painfully on his shoulder. He sat up slowly. One side of his face felt numb. His nose was bleeding. When he could finally focus, all he saw were Sato's cold emerald eyes mocking him.

'It's time you learned how to fight,' the Japanese said.

Miles banged the side of his head with his hand. He couldn't have heard correctly. The tall Japanese had spoken in perfect, unaccented, American English.

'What did you say?' Miles asked thickly.

'Get up,' Sato said with a sneer. Again he had spoken in English. 'Stinking coward.'

Miles wiped the blood from his nose onto his sleeve and tried to stand. But before he was on his knees, Sato kicked him in the stomach, a violent, gut-wrenching blow. Then he picked the American up by his clothing and smashed him against the wall.

'You're allowed to fight back,' Sato said, his lips curving into a malevolent smile.

Heaving, Miles held his stomach as he tried to inch up the wall. All the images in the room, the corners of the ceilings, the doorway, the scroll, the green-eyed Oriental, blurred together into one whirling, nauseating spiral. Vaguely he recognized the taste of blood in his mouth.

Sato came at him again. Miles tried to hold his hands in front of him. They shook.

The Japanese kicked his legs out from under him and Miles fell, unprotesting, to the floor.

'Get up. Get up, I said!' He dragged the American to the middle of the floor and kicked him again. Miles did not even have the strength to curl his body into a ball. He lay like a limp rag. The only sensation he felt was that of blood pooling beneath his cheek.

Sato spat on him. 'I'll send your nursemaid for you.' He walked out.

Hiro carried Miles into the kitchen. The women gasped when they saw his swollen, bloody face.

'How did this happen?' Tomiko demanded in Japanese as she prepared some cold towels and hurriedly took some unguents from a basket.

Hiro laid the unconscious American on the floor. 'It was Sato,' he said wretchedly. 'And we thought he was going to teach the Ronin.'

'I will not stand for this,' Tomiko said.

While the women dressed Miles's wound, she stood up. Her eyes were wild. 'The Oyabun must know.'

She knocked deferentially on Nagoya's door before entering. The old man knelt on the floor amid piles of papers, a pair of bifocals perched on the end of his nose.

'Nagoya-san, there is a matter which must be brought to your attention,' she said formally. 'A few minutes ago the kobun called Ronin was badly beaten. It was Sato.'

He hesitated for a moment, his pen poised in midair, but when he spoke, his voice was calm. 'The American is not a kobun,' Nagoya said. 'And it is not your place to meddle in the affairs of men.'

167

'But it was an inexcusable –'

'Did you not hear me? It is not your concern. To be the daughter of my *kyodai* does not excuse your bad manners.'

'This is more than a question of courtesy,' she said hotly. 'Sato tricked the American. He believed he would be taught to fight. Instead he was beaten almost to death. Sato cannot be permitted to continue this way. You must –'

'How dare you tell me what I must and must not do!' he shouted. 'Sato is my chosen successor, and your husband-to-be. Whatever his judgment is in the operation of this *ikka*, I will support him.'

'Then you will be alone,' she said with equal ferocity. 'Sato is not fit to become Oyabun. The others know that. His hatred clouds his vision. One day it will destroy his honor.' She swept her arm out in front of her as if she held a sword. 'I will not have him for my husband.'

She had spoken the unthinkable. For a moment the beautiful woman and the old man faced each other in the thick silence. Then Nagoya rose.

He took the glasses off his face and folded his arms across his chest. He spoke in barely a whisper, his voice hard as steel. 'Had any other woman spoken so presumptuously I would not tolerate her presence in my house,' he said. 'Your marriage to Sato was arranged by your dead father. The alliance cannot be refused. Now go.' He turned his back to her. 'Get out of my sight.'

Tomiko touched Miles's eyelids, and they fluttered open.

'Did he break the flume?' Miles rasped.

She smiled. A tear dropped from her cheek onto his face. 'No, My-o-san. It stands.'

'That's more than I can say for myself.' He propped himself up on one elbow, grimacing with the pain.

'No, please. You must rest –'

'Let him stand,' Hiro said in Japanese. He took the cold

168

towel off Miles's forehead. 'He is still a man. Grant him a man's pride.'

Together they helped him to his feet. Miles was still dizzy. His legs buckled, but Hiro stood stolidly, supporting him. 'Good news, Ronin,' he said cheerfully. 'No bone break.'

'This must be my lucky day,' Miles groaned. He blinked. 'The strangest part was, he spoke English.'

Hiro frowned, puzzled. 'Sato? Is mistake, Ronin. Sato no speak English.' He laughed. 'Sato hate English, almost much as hate American.'

Miles looked at Tomiko. She lowered her face. 'But he did speak English,' he insisted, grabbing her shoulders. 'Perfect, flawless English.'

Hiro pried Miles's hands off the woman, then shook a finger in front of his face. 'No touch Tomiko-san,' he whispered. 'Big rule, yes?'

'Oh, for God's sake. He did speak English, Tomiko, and you know it. Why all the mystery about it?'

'Maybe you sit down, Ronin,' Hiro said.

'I don't want to sit down.' He untangled himself from the big man's arms. The effort sent a terrible pain down his hurt shoulder. 'Oh, God,' he moaned.

Hiro held him up. His fleshy face was somber. 'Maybe is time to go,' he said. 'Sato no break bone because Sato know how hurt' – he pressed the knuckles of his hands together – 'without break. Understand? Sato know hurt.' He backed away from Miles and bowed. 'Hiro must go now,' he said. 'You go too, Ronin. Cannot win against Sato. He will be Oyabun.'

When he was gone, Miles moved his shoulder painfully in its socket. He checked the swelling of his eyes and nose. He examined the bruises on his body.

'Hiro is right,' Tomiko said softly. 'You must leave the ikka. Sato will not stop. His hatred will not let him.'

'What in the hell does he have against me?' Miles shouted.

Tomiko quietly sent the other women away. When they were alone in the kitchen, she prepared a tea table for them. 'Please sit,' she said, 'and I will tell you about Sato.'

She seated herself across from him – her small teacup held in her hands. 'He speaks English so well because his mother was an American,' she said. 'Hiro does not know this. No one knows except Nagoya and myself. It is something about Sato which he keeps hidden.'

Miles sat back. 'Go on.'

'As far as I know, his mother was a prostitute in America, brought here from Los Angeles with many others to fill the brothels all over Asia. Since the war there has been great demand for white women.'

She looked away from him. 'It is a shameful thing. The American women came thinking they would become movie stars, or wealthy courtesans. Sometimes they did not give their consent at all. They were treated like animals.

'This was the work of the Yakuza, though not Nagoya's ikka. Neither Nagoya nor my father could tolerate such practices, and there was much bloodshed between the Yakuza houses.

'Still, it went on. The women were only useful to these men so long as they were young and beautiful. Later they were simply turned out. It was so with Sato's mother. After he was born, she remained in Tokyo, in Shinjuku, working as the lowest form of streetwalker. She drank heavily and took drugs. Sato cared for her until he was ten years old, when she died of a morphine overdose.

'After that he was on his own. He never attended school. He became a *bosozoku*, one of the young criminals who work the streets. My father found him there. Sato had tried to rob him. Of course, he was unsuccessful.'

'So your dad took him under his wing?' Miles asked. 'Why?'

'Because of Sato's green eyes,' she answered. 'Let me

explain.' She turned the cup around in her hands. 'This is difficult for me to say to you, but you must understand. You see, Japan is not the melting pot that America is. We are a homogeneous people, with the same background, the same ancestry, the same distant gene pool. We welcome foreigners as visitors, but . . . Forgive me, My-o –'

'But you don't want us to marry your women.'

'It is so,' she said. 'Here, those of mixed race are shunned, even by their own families. They are considered as low as the *burakumin*, the untouchables who work in the slaughterhouses. They can never be accepted as Japanese. They have no future here. Do you see?'

Miles nodded.

'This is Sato,' she said.

'My father was an unusual man, particularly for a leader of the Yakuza. He despised bigotry. He saw the suffering it had caused so many children born of American soldiers after the war. And he saw in Sato a boy of great courage and strength. He asked Nagoya, his *kyodai*, to accept Sato as a kobun in his house.'

'What's a kyodai?'

'It is a brother. An equal brother, the highest pledge one Yakuza man can make to another. There is the pledge of aniki, elder brother, and *shatei*, younger brother, made between two friends of unequal rank. But to be kyodai with another is a bond that cannot be broken. For us it is stronger than a blood tie. A man will give his life without hesitation to protect his kyodai. It is understood with his pledge.

'This was the case between the Oyabun and my father. Nagoya could not refuse to accept Sato.

'In time he began to see that my father had been right. Sato proved himself to be a man of high intelligence and complete loyalty. Upon acceptance into the ikka, Sato's first act was to cut off his finger in atonement for trying to rob my father.'

Miles sighed. 'Sounds like you're pretty close to him.'

'I have known Sato since I was a child,' she said. 'Once, when the marriage was arranged, I thought he was the most beautiful man in the world.'

'In spite of his being a half-breed?' Miles asked acidly.

Her eyes flashed. 'My father placed no value on that hypocrisy, and neither do I.' Her fingers closed tightly around the little teacup. 'It was something else that made my heart grow cold toward Sato. His hatred . . . It seemed as if in trying to prove himself completely Japanese, he had to loathe the part of himself that was American.'

'But his green eyes,' Miles said. 'Doesn't anyone think –'

'It would be too farfetched for anyone to believe that a man of mixed race could be accepted into the ranks of the Yakuza, let alone be chosen as successor to the Oyabun of the Onami ikka. Because no one would believe the truth, Sato's eyes have always been regarded as a freak of nature, as part of his extraordinary character.

'But there is nothing extraordinary about him,' Tomiko said bitterly, 'except his emptiness.' She stared out the small window across the room. 'He is like a rock in the ocean, with no grass growing upon it, no life.'

She looked up at Miles. 'When he looks at you, My-o, he sees himself. That is why he wishes to destroy you.'

Miles took a deep breath. He remembered his sister's constant battles with their mother, and Susi's firm belief that she had been born in disfavor because she looked Japanese.

The subject had always made Miles uneasy because, deep inside, he had somehow known she'd been right. Susi, not Miles, had had to face all the bullies on the school playground, had had to listen to the taunts of children. Susi, not Miles, had watched the surgical changes that had transformed their mother's soft Oriental face into a chiseled European one, knowing that her own features were the same as those Mickey Haverford had chosen to discard.

172

Susi had been the outsider, the ronin, all her life.

Now it was Miles's turn.

'It seems funny, being ostracized because I'm half Caucasian,' he said. 'I guess I never thought it worked that way.'

She took his hand. 'Ignorance is not confined to one race,' she said. 'That is why it is so powerful. Go now. As long as you are here, you will be humiliated, excluded, punished without cause. Perhaps one day Sato will kill you. He is capable of it. And the Oyabun will not intervene.' Her fingers pressed into his palms. 'Go now, while you still can. There is no other way.'

He looked down at their hands. They were in the same position as his sister's and her husband's when they died.

'I'm not leaving,' he said quietly. 'Not until I've got what I came for.'

'What is that?' she asked, stricken.

'Nagoya owes a debt,' he said. 'Whatever happens to me, I'm going to see that he pays it.' He stood up and limped toward the door.

'Where are you going, My-o?'

He smiled crookedly. 'I've got work to do,' he said. 'That was my end of the bargain.'

Tomiko ran to him and embraced him with a fierce tenderness. Gently she held his face in both her small hands and kissed him. Her eyes were filled with tears. 'Ronin,' she whispered.

Even now he will not go, Nagoya thought as he watched Miles carrying the buckets of excrement to the midden.

His eyes stung. 'Oh, Sasakawa, kyodai,' he whispered. 'Is my *ninjo* strong enough for this?'

173

18

Miles did not see Sato the following day or the next. On the third day Tomiko and Hiro woke him before dawn with their laughter.

'*Okinasai,*' Tomiko said with a giggle. 'Time to wake up, My-o.'

'Huh?' Miles squinted at them. Tomiko was dressed in a blouse and skirt, her long hair pulled into a ponytail. Hiro wore a polo shirt, a pair of chinos, and loafers. 'What kind of getup is that?'

Hiro laughed. 'Special clothes, Ronin. Special day.'

'What's so special about it?'

'No work.' The big man moved aside to let Miles up.

'For you, maybe,' Miles said, rising from his mat on the floor. 'But unless everyone in the house came down with constipation, there's work for me.'

Then he saw them, a pile of gleaming chamber pots stacked into a pyramid.

'All done, Ronin,' Hiro said with pride.

'What – what did you do that for?'

'Cleaning stinkpot Hiro's job before Ronin come. Also Hiro's job in *heya*, school for sumo.' He shrugged. 'Stinkpot is stinkpot, yes? Hiro no mind.'

'He did it so that you could go to the festival,' Tomiko said excitedly. 'The others are already gone.'

'What festival?'

'Mibu,' Hiro said. 'Village where Yoshio born. Yoshio

want you see.' He looked up in frustration to Tomiko. 'You talk, Tomiko-san, yes?'

She beamed. 'Every spring the village of Mibu holds the Ohanataue, the festival of the rice god. There are parades and dances and competitions in the old Japanese martial arts. Since Yoshio is from Mibu, he goes back every year to take part in the archery program. He's won four years in a row.' She tugged at his arm. 'Come on, My-o. We can bicycle to the train station, but then it's a two-hour ride.'

'Wait . . . wait a minute. What about Nagoya?'

'Oyabun gone,' Hiro said. 'Sato gone.'

'They both left for Yokohama yesterday evening.' Tomiko's eyes danced.

'Sato very busy,' Hiro said weightily. 'Too busy even to pay attention Ronin. You feel bad?'

'It breaks my heart,' Miles said. He looked back at the glistening chamber pots. 'Well, what are we waiting for?'

Miles felt strange to be in his modern clothes again, riding the bullet train down the length of Honshu Island with a carload of people dressed in business suits or blue jeans, but he felt even more strange stepping off the station platform into what could have been the sixteenth century.

On Mibu's narrow main road, lined with low wooden buildings that looked as if they had been built during Japan's Middle Ages lumbered a parade of oxen, elaborately decked with bright silken banners and ornate carved saddles of silver and gold, loaded with flowers. Behind them minced a long line of celebrants in ancient dress. They were carrying umbrellas made of enormous flowers that extended well below their knees. Between the legs of the umbrellas, the dancers' costumes could be glimpsed, but not their faces.

'What's on their heads?' Miles asked.

'Flower dancers cover their faces with boxes so that none

but the rice god, Sambai-sama, will know them,' Tomiko said. The boxes were painted red on three sides, with the fourth side a slatted bamboo curtain.

'Are they men or women?'

'Men,' Tomiko said. 'But the costumes are ambiguous. They celebrate the victory of the local warlord over a rival in 1578, when he dressed his soldiers as flower dancers and led them into his enemy's castle. The rival soldiers were expecting women, but saw, after it was too late, a legion of samurai and their swords instead.'

Following the flower dancers came the musicians, rows of flute players trilling on lacquered bamboo pipes, and drummers with their instruments bound in nets and tied around their waists, carrying sticks that ended in long, tufted horsehair. They wore checkered kimonos dyed with local indigo and new straw hats tied to their heads with ceremonially knotted cotton scarves. Their shrill music, tuneless and arrhythmic to Miles's ear, filled the valley of Mibu with sounds as ancient as the mountains surrounding it.

Next came the planters. 'Is women now,' Hiro explained. 'Of course.'

'Why "of course"?' Miles asked as the dozens of women, identically dressed in their blue rural kimonos and straw headdresses, passed.

'Only women plant rice seedlings,' Hiro said haughtily. 'Man supervise.' He pointed to a solitary figure dancing behind the women. Elaborately costumed in sumptuous fabric, sporting a long gray beard and a shiny, boxlike lacquer hat over a fierce mask, he carried a handful of long pampas grass as he leaped and spun, followed by shouting children who clopped along on wooden *geta*.

'That is Sambai-sama, the rice god,' Tomiko said. 'You see, his legs are bound in black cloth so that he may enter the rice paddies without soiling his fine clothes.' They all bowed ceremoniously to the god as he passed. 'Sambai-sama is also the god of the mountains here. At sunset he will return to the hills for the rest of the year.'

At the end of the parade were the participants in the athletic events. Swordsmen, karate contestants, and even a few huge sumo wrestlers wrapped in bright robes marched down the narrow dirt road. Hiro's carriage straightened at the sight of the goliaths, and his normally ebullient face grew ineffably sad.

'You studied to be one of them, didn't you?' Miles asked.

'Hai.' The big man answered hoarsely. 'Three years. Is not enough. To be professional sumo, one must study many years. Must be favored of gods,' he added quietly, blinking.

The archers were last, in bizarre costumes of red and white silk covered with dark cloaks. On their feet were shiny, high black wooden clogs; on their heads were small lacquer pillboxes with stiff bristles standing at the back, like ponytails forced to stand upright. The hats were tied around each archer's head by four strings. Each man held a long, narrow bow, and on their backs they carried quivers of wood or carved leather, filled with colorful arrows.

'Is Yoshio!' Hiro shouted. The three of them cheered as their friend marched past, his little monkey face stony and proud.

'He win, you see,' the wrestler confided cheerfully. 'Nobody is beat Yoshio with bow and arrow.'

The crowd followed the parade to the rice paddies, neat rectangular tracts of wet mud. Near them the women planters built a pyre of rice straw and lit it, chanting prayers to Sambai-sama.

'They are summoning the god's presence,' Tomiko said.

'I thought he was in the parade.'

'That was just the dance master dressed up like Sambai-sama. The real spirit of the god has to be lured from the mountains to ensure a good harvest.'

The keening song of the women grew louder as the fire billowed into bright flame. Then the dance master, dressed as the god, broke out of their ranks in a wild gyration that led him around the crowd and into the wet paddies.

'What flower blooms in the field?' he shouted in Japanese. 'Rice flowers. Money flowers. Blossoms of virtue. Flowers of prosperity!'

The drums beat. The pipers trilled their ancient melodies. Decorously the women waded into the paddies after him, baskets filled with tender green rice seedlings at their sides. They planted in perfect unison, bending low as the drummers hurled their horsehair-ended sticks into the air and the dance master chanted the commands of the rice god.

Afterward, when the planting was done and the participants slogged, muddy and exhausted, out of the paddies, Miles, Hiro, and Tomiko followed the crowd to the sports fields.

'The archers are this way,' Tomiko said. 'Hurry. They've already begun.'

A row of archers stood before stationary targets. Their bows, between six and seven feet long, were asymmetrical, with more than two thirds of the bows' lengths above their left ears.

'Where's Yoshio?' Miles asked.

Hiro pointed beyond the archers. More than a hundred meters away stood a second row of men on horseback. The animals were covered with bamboo and gilt armor, and stamped on the soft ground.

Yoshio was astride a black stallion. He looked like a wizened child playing cowboys and Indians. Even from so far away, Miles could see that Yoshio's bow was longer than those of the other archers.

'Is he going to shoot from there?' Miles asked.

'Hai. Yoshio bow, ten men.'

'What?'

Tomiko explained. 'The strength of a bow is character-ized by the number of men it takes to string it with the silk cord they use. Most are two-or three-man bows. Yoshio uses a ten-man bow.'

After the first archers had finished, the horsemen paced their animals. Then the first broke away from the others, bringing his horse to a gallop and circling behind them before making his run.

Gripping the horse with his legs, the archer stood up in the small saddle and let fly all the arrows in his quiver. Every one of them made the target, and the crowd cheered its approval.

The second man dropped one arrow as he pulled it from his quiver. When he was finished, he bowed profusely to the onlookers in apology.

Then it was Yoshio's turn, and the laughter and shouting of the spectators ceased. The field was deadly quiet as the little man maneuvered the stallion to the starting point. The other archers moved away to give the champion room, and Yoshio urged his horse back another fifty meters.

'His bow is so powerful, he does not wish to destroy the target,' Tomiko said. 'Also, to be fair to the others, he gives himself the disadvantage of greater distance.'

With a cry Yoshio kicked the stallion into a gallop. The animal thundered over the field as the little man stood up in the saddle, his posture as rigid as if he had been forged of steel. Slowly he reached back in his quiver for the first arrow.

After that was only sound, the galloping hooves of the stallion, the whistling of the arrows in flight, and the faint sucking noises as they struck the target, each within seconds of the last, every single arrow in the flight lodged within the red bull's-eye.

Only when Yoshio turned the horse away did the cheers and stomping begin, and then they went on for so long that the small monkey-faced man was forced to ride among the crowd, accepting gifts of flowers and food, before the spectators allowed him to leave.

'Yoshio good, yes?' Hiro asked as they walked toward the other areas.

'I never saw anything like it in my life,' Miles said. 'How did he learn that?'

'Old archer from Mibu teach when Yoshio small. He make Yoshio shoot one thousand arrow every day. Learn shoot fast,' he said, grinning.

'Why did he join Nagoya?' Miles asked.

Hiro shrugged. 'No job for archer these days, Ronin. Yoshio can be . . . like us,' he whispered, careful not to use the term 'Yakuza' in a crowd, 'or he can be farmer. But brother inherit farm, kick Yoshio out. No choice.'

As they approached the site for the sumo matches, the crowd once again hushed.

'The sumo exhibition is always held near the shrine,' Tomiko said softly.

They passed beneath an H-shaped *torii* gate and walked toward the small wooden building housing the village shrine. In front of the shrine was a raised platform inscribed with a circle.

'That is the *dohyo*,' Tomiko said, 'where the wrestlers fight. It is near the shrine because sumo is favored by all deities. It is said that a sumo match decided which gods were to rule the islands of Japan. But the sport has always been performed especially for rice planting.'

Hiro went silently to the shrine and clapped his hands three times before it.

'It is difficult for him to watch the wrestlers,' she whispered. 'He had dreams of becoming a *Yokozuna*, the highest ranked among the sumo. But his family is very poor. Even though Hiro did not have to pay to attend the sumo *heya*, the school, he could not continue because it was

181

necessary for him to help support his parents.'

Hiro did not join them again, but sat apart, his hands folded in his lap, as the huge wrestlers, clad only in silk *mawashi* belts, entered. Standing around the dohyo, they began the slow ritual preceding the bout, clapping their hands to attract the attention of the gods, stamping their feet to drive away demons. They bowed, touched the ground and threw salt into the air to purify themselves.

'Each gesture has a meaning that is centuries old,' Tomiko explained. 'The sport is so ancient that no one knows when it began. It is mentioned in the oldest known histories of Japan.'

The two men in the ring grappled with one another for no more than thirty seconds. Then, with a thud, one knocked the other to the floor, and the crowd cheered deliriously.

'That was it?' Miles asked.

'The bouts themselves are very short, but there are many of them. In a real tournament the matches go on for fifteen days.'

'Fifteen days!' Miles groaned inwardly. 'How long is this going to take?'

'No more than a few hours,' Tomiko said.

Miles nudged her as the next pair of wrestlers entered the ring. 'What do you say we leave and come back for Hiro later?' he whispered.

She smiled at him. 'Let's go.'

As they stole out, they waved to Koji, who was making his way toward Hiro.

'Good. Hiro'll have good company,' Miles said. 'They can talk about how things used to be in the good old millennia.'

'Oh, look!' Tomiko pointed to a small tent on the other side of the shrine, where children dressed in exotic costumes and masks peeked out of the flap. '*Karuga*,' she said. 'Children's dances. We must see them, My-o.' They stood

182

among the gathering crowd as one small boy, his mask pulled on top of his head, cried pitifully. A woman scurried from the audience, kissed him, replaced his mask over his face, and shooed him inside the tent.

Presently some flutes began to play, and the same little boy leaped out from the tent slashing a wooden sword.

'That is the warlord,' Tomiko explained.

Several tiny samurai scampered out, growling and stomping. From behind the tent another warlord and his army emerged and the fighting began, complete with beating drums and loud encouragement from the audience.

The fracas stopped suddenly when a bespectacled middle-aged woman stood up and clapped her hands, at which point all the soldiers faced each other and bowed.

'That is the end of the battle,' Tomiko whispered.

Miles laughed. 'Someone ought to send that lady to the UN.'

The first group of samurai ran behind the tent, shrieking and giggling, while their warlord swaggered manfully in a circle. Then, accompanied by the boos and hisses of the spectators, some warriors from the second group sneaked up on the unsuspecting noble and stabbed him with their swords.

The warlord went into a frenzy of dying, twirling wildly and bobbing his head before crashing to the ground, his feet kicking in the air. A lone flute played a plaintive melody to signify his passing, but halfway through the song the warlord sat up with an anguished expression and proclaimed something in Japanese. The audience laughed uproariously as the bespectacled woman came up and took him firmly by the hand.

'What was that about?' Miles asked.

'The slain lord has wet his pants,' Tomiko said as the child was led away to the cheers of the crowd.

Act two was more difficult for Miles to understand. The

dead warlord's soldiers, now dressed in rags and carrying tiny bamboo flutes, with baskets over their heads, staggered blindly in front of the tent as sad music played. In the spirit of the dance, the audience even refrained from laughing when two of the performers bumped into each other and tumbled to the ground.

'Why do they have baskets on their heads?' Miles asked.

Tomiko squeezed his hand. 'This is the legend of the forty-seven ronin,' she said. 'A great favorite.'

As the children continued their dance, she explained quietly. 'During feudal times, ronin, or "wave-man," was the name given to samurai warriors without masters, because these unfortunates were doomed to wander the earth without direction or purpose, like drops of water upon a wave of the ocean,' she said.

'In the legend, a noble lord was killed through the trickery of a rival. Upon his death most of the lord's samurai joined the ranks of other great houses. Some even went to serve the man who had murdered him. But forty-seven of the warriors remained behind, masterless, since they wished to fight for none but their dead leader.

'Without a liege lord to serve, these ronin were reduced to begging for their livelihood. They traveled about from village to village, covering their faces like monks with bamboo baskets as a sign of their humility, playing musical instruments for the amusement of the villagers. So complete was their change that no one would have thought them to have once been the most fierce and courageous of warriors, and even their own families were ashamed of them.

'But they accepted the mockery and humiliation of the people, because this was part of their plan. Knowing that the murderous lord's guards would never permit a band of armed samurai near their master, the ronin pretended to be fools and actors, musicians and clowns, until at last they got the opportunity to perform for the hated nobleman.

When he was within their circle, the forty-seven ronin unsheathed their swords and killed the evil lord and all his men.'

The audience cheered. 'You see?'

The children had removed the baskets from their heads to reveal flushed and sweating faces that were grinning wickedly as they yanked their toy swords from inside their rags. The ensuing battle between the ronin and the evil samurai went on until one warrior threw down his weapon and pounced upon another. They tussled and rolled into the audience until two angry fathers separated them, whereupon the rest of the troupe bowed serenely to wild applause.

'Wave men,' Miles mused. 'Maybe that's what I am.'

Tomiko smiled. 'At least you have seen that the term "ronin" was not always a derogatory one,' she said. 'The legend has influenced many great deeds. Perhaps even the flower dancers celebrated in the rice-planting parade. I know it is the meaning for the cresting wave symbol of Nagoya-san's house. The Oyabun and my father called themselves the Sons of the Wave.'

They walked toward a stand of cherry trees whose petals had already fallen. 'They were both ronin back then, with no one to follow, and nothing more to lose.'

'So they went back in time five hundred years and stayed there,' Miles said.

'The old world made more sense to them,' she answered softly.

A fragrant breeze sang through the branches of the trees and tugged at the loose hair around Tomiko's face.

'What about you? Why do you stay?'

She looked to the distant mountains. 'I left once,' she said. 'I went to the university, where I learned English.' She smiled. 'I even worked for a time, as an editor of textbooks. But that was not where I belonged.' She turned back to

Miles. 'It is hard to explain to a man of your world . . . of your time,' she said, 'but in my way I am as much a part of the old world as Nagoya is. My life is with the old ways. I can change no more than he can.'

Her beauty made Miles ache. He touched her lips with the tips of his fingers, then held her close to him, tenderly, jealously. 'I love you, Tomiko,' he said.

She buried her face in his chest. 'Do not say it,' she whispered. 'It cannot be.'

19

Nagoya could see from the awkwardness of Toshiro Yamaoka's bow that he was not a man accustomed to lowering his head before anyone. For that matter, the man was probably unused to courtesy of any sort. Still, Yamaoka made the effort, carefully bowing more deeply than the aged Oyabun from Tokyo.

'Greetings, Nagoya-san.' He directed Nagoya to a chair. It was not, as befitted custom, in the place of honor farthest from the door; that spot was occupied by Yamaoka's own desk, and he sat behind it grandly.

'It is a great honor to our house that you have deigned to visit Yokohama to help us in our misfortune with your valuable advice.'

'It is an honor to have been invited,' Nagoya said, knowing full well that Yamaoka had protested the intrusion with everything short of violence when the All-Japan Consortium of Yakuza organizations insisted that he enlist Nagoya's aid.

Yamaoka had a problem unique in the annals of organized crime: he was being sued by the populace. And it was not one suit he had to worry about; one hundred thirty-two different injunctions were pending against him and his merry band, from infractions of noise-pollution laws to carrying submachine guns in public.

'I don't understand it,' Yamaoka said dispiritedly. 'Twenty years I've been here. Almost forty since Kodama

187

first moved in. Forty years of peace. Now suddenly everybody in town's turned into a vigilante. Shopkeepers take pictures of us coming and going. We're followed like pickpockets in a department store. The business has come to a standstill.' He shook his head. 'The outside of this building is covered with rotten eggs. They throw them at us. It's embarrassing.'

Nagoya sat back, ostensibly in thought. Actually he was concentrating all his effort in not laughing out loud. From the corner of his eye he saw Sato standing beside Yamaoka's bodyguard. Sato, he knew, could not share in the exquisite pleasure of this interview because he was too young to remember.

Yamaoka had inherited the stewardship of the Yokohama ikka from Sessue Kodama, the man who had first introduced Nagoya into the world of the Yakuza with a set of brass knuckles. After Nagoya's brilliant dispersal of the sangokujin gangs, it was clear that the Shinjuku merchants would stay with Nagoya.

Kodama moved to Yokohama, with its long tradition of Yakuza control, and set up one of the most ruthless gangs in the country. Squeezing local merchants was only one of Kodama's enterprises. Through the busy Yokohama port he smuggled in Chinese opium by the ton during the chaotic postwar decade, setting up a drug empire rich enough to make his ikka a powerful force.

He also became involved in prostitution, carrying the oldest profession to new heights. It was Kodama who introduced white slavery to the Orient on a massive scale, kidnapping Caucasian women from Europe and America and transporting them to brothels throughout the East. This business venture – and Sadimasa Nagoya – eventually caused Kodama's death.

Nagoya had warned the Consortium that he would not stand for the Yokohama Oyabun's practices. The spreading drug problem alone would cripple Japan, he argued, but the slavery of women – foreign women at that – would cause worldwide repercussions. He called for severe restraints on Kodama's operation.

The Consortium paid Nagoya lip service, but since all of the Yakuza ikkas in Japan except for Nagoya's dealt in the drug trade, they were heavily dependent on Kodama's opium imports. So they averted their eyes from the issue of white slavery.

Nagoya did not. In the early sixties, the Onami ikka waged a war on Kodama that bloodied the streets of Yokohama for three months. Kodama himself was gunned down in a gambling den, along with six of his lieutenants. When the bloodshed reached its peak, Nagoya threatened to use his influence in the Diet to purge Yokohama of its corrupt officials and reorganize its dockworker's union so that the drug traffic into Yokohama port would cease.

The Consortium quickly called an end to the war.

Kodama's successor, Toshiro Yamaoka, was ordered either to make rapid amends with Nagoya in Tokyo, or to murder him if he dared. Yamaoka apologized. The business of white slavery returned once again to the province of independent traffickers. But the general tenor of the Yokohama ikka never changed. It was an organization of thugs led by a man who looked even more like a thug than his predecessor.

Yamaoka had thick, greasy black hair, bushy Russian eyebrows, and a ragged mustache that curled down past the corners of his mouth. The tip of his nose was turned up, very much like a pig's, exposing nostrils in which long black hairs were visible, as they were on the backs of Yamaoka's hands.

He was clad in a light gray plaid suit with red and blue stripes running through the fabric. The suit jacket was open and his vest buttons strained to cover his stomach which cascaded down in levels like a string of rice paddies inset down the side of a hill. The man wore heavy gold cuff links with diamonds inset in the form of a star, the symbol of his ikka.

Like Kodama before him, Yamaoka wore his profession on his sleeve. The muscle and swagger of his organization had been enough to terrorize the citizens of Yokohama into submission for four decades, but times were changing. Japan now had laws that worked. The days when a Yakuza boss could order the beating of an ordinary citizen without reprisal from the authorities were over.

Moreover, the people's traditional trust in the rightness of the Yakuza had eroded to nothing since the war. These men were not the ronin of centuries past, defending the common man from the shoguns; they had instead become the gangster caricatures they imitated. Now, instead of inspiring awe, they drew only jeers.

The ultimate slap in the face was the lawsuits. Nearly every businessman in the neighborhood of Yamaoka's new 'office' building protested its presence in a way that was so radical that it might work: they were going to sue the Yakuza out of existence.

'Perhaps the problem is the building,' Nagoya said.

'The building? It's brand-new. We haven't been here for six months.'

'It is black,' Nagoya said softly. 'And the first-floor windows are covered with bars, like a prison.'

'It was made to serve as a fortress in the event of a war.' Yamaoka looked at the old man defiantly. During Nagoya's attack in the sixties, more than thirty of Yokohama's top Yakuza men were killed.

'In a war, bars will not keep an enemy away.' He watched Yamaoka fidget.

'I don't see what the building's got to do with it.'

'In the minds of the residents here, it is the Yakuza

building,' Nagoya said. 'It is a symbol of something they do not wish to have in their midst.'

Yamaoka snorted. 'Ingrates. Without us they wouldn't have anything. Where do they think the parks came from?'

'Politicians cost money,' Nagoya said.

Yamaoka laughed resignedly in understanding. 'Yeah. I guess they don't have to love us. But they've gone too far with this lawsuit business.'

Nagoya clasped his hands together. 'They do have to love you.'

Yamaoka sat back in his chair and lit a cigarette. 'I have to get the people who are suing me to love me,' he said, exhaling a cloud of smoke. 'Terrific. That's great advice, Nagoya.' He exchanged a glance with his bodyguard, whose face reddened with contained mirth.

'I am quite serious,' Nagoya said. 'The citizens are working against you because they do not feel you are one of them. Perhaps they even feel that you are not on their side.'

'Golden balls! What I do doesn't have anything to do with them. I only keep my offices here.'

'Exactly,' the old man said patiently. 'You are an outsider. Therefore you should move.'

'What?'

'Publicly and noisily. Sell the building. To one of your own subsidiaries, of course. Paint the building white. Remove the bars from the windows. Invite the neighbors in to see the interior. Open a child-care center on the first floor. Make a room or two available for community groups.'

Yamaoka stared at him like an ox. Nagoya looked to the other two men. Yamaoka's bodyguard had the same uncomprehending, vaguely distrustful look on his face. To Nagoya's dismay, so did Sato.

'What harm would it do?' he went on. 'After a month you can quietly move your operation back in here. The

191

building will again be your headquarters, but it will not be advertised as such. And the people, now with a stake in the building, will not be so quick to attack you.'

Yamaoka finished his cigarette in silence. After he stubbed it out he said, 'Seems like a lot of trouble to go through for a few cranky neighbors.'

'Those few neighbors have warranted the attention of the Consortium,' Nagoya reminded him.

'Yeah. Well, it's easy for you to be the country gentleman, sitting out there in never-never land. Yokohama's not going to change just because I turn the building into a babysitting center.'

Nagoya shrugged. 'I have given you my considered opinion.'

'What do you think?' Yamaoka swiveled suddenly toward Sato. The insult to Nagoya was plain. By consulting his subordinate, Yamaoka was obviously discarding Nagoya's advice.

Sato looked up glassily. 'I – I trust in the wisdom of the Oyabun,' he said.

'Oh, bullshit. I want to know what you really think. Go on. We're friends here, right, Nagoya?'

Nagoya smiled tightly. 'By all means, Sato. I would like to know what you really think.'

They waited, expectant. Sato took a deep breath. 'Well . . . If you want to know the truth, it seems simple. Make an example of one or two of the more troublesome neighbors. When their bodies are found floating down at the docks, the rest of the complainers will quiet down. The suits will be withdrawn.'

Yamaoka narrowed his eyes appreciatively. 'What about the police?'

Sato paused for a moment. 'Police can be bought,' he said. 'Especially since it would bring an end to all this trouble. I don't think the local officials like the publicity this

192

thing is generating any more than you do. Of course, the deaths would have to look accidental enough to keep the government's hands clean.'

Yamaoka nodded. 'I had the same idea myself,' he said, turning back to Nagoya. 'You've got a smart boy there.'

Nagoya said nothing, but Sato did not miss the flash of anger in the old man's eyes.

Yamaoka thanked him for his time, again bowing low before him. But he shook Sato's hand. 'Come by my home for dinner sometime. Anytime you're free. I'll send a helicopter for you, all right?' He slapped the young man's arm 'We have a lot to talk about.'

Sato bowed to him, confused.

'Why did he say that to me?' he asked as he drove the limousine away from the ugly black building.

Nagoya looked out the window. 'You will be Oyabun after me. He thinks he can deal with you.'

'Nagoya-sama –'

'Not now,' the old man snapped.

Sato glanced at him in the rearview mirror. Nagoya's eyes were still angry.

They spent the night in the Princess Hotel in Yokohama. Although they were less than three hours away from Tokyo, Nagoya had ordered Sato to make the reservations.

'But what about the kobun?' Sato had protested. 'The festival in Mibu is this week. With both of us gone, they'll run off like children.'

'Nonsense,' Nagoya had said. 'We won't tell them we're staying away.'

After Sato had gone, the old man called for Tomiko. 'Make sure the Ronin sees the festival,' he had whispered.

He sat at dinner with Sato now, eating silently.

'Oyabun, forgive me,' the young man said quietly in the ancient formal dialect of the Yakuza. 'I apologize most

193

heartily for causing you embarrassment today.'

Nagoya answered in modern Japanese, refusing Sato the intimacy of speaking in the old tongue. 'I was not embarrassed,' he said tersely. 'I was disappointed.'

Sato looked down at his food.

'Your solution was that of a killer. It appealed to Yamaoka because that is what he is.' The old man set down his chopsticks. 'I know what you are thinking, Sato. That this old man beside you is no better than Yamaoka.'

'No, Oyabun –'

Nagoya gestured for silence. 'It is true. I have lived most of my life as a criminal. I like to think I have not stooped to the level of moral repugnancy that some have, but really, there is only one difference between Yamaoka and myself: I am not stupid. I know what is coming.'

Sato blinked. 'What's that?'

'A new country,' Nagoya said. 'Yet another Japan. The first ended with the expulsion of the shoguns toward the end of the last century, when our country joined the industrial nations of the world. The second Japan was destroyed by the war. The third Japan, the Japan of defeat and deprivation, was my country. There was a place for the Yakuza there, for the Kodamas and the Izus and the Nagoyas to own their share of a decaying world. But that era, like the others, has come to an end.'

He picked up his chopsticks again and held them up. 'Do you know that schoolchildren now have to be taught in the classroom how to use these?' His eyes twinkled. 'The new Japan uses high tables and silver utensils. The young marry whom they wish. And for the first time in our history, the laws reflect the wishes of the people.' He stared at the wooden chopsticks for a long time. 'It will be a good thing, this new Japan,' he said quietly.

'I don't understand,' Sato said. 'What about us? What will happen to the Onami ikka?'

'It will die,' Nagoya said simply. 'You will lead it to its death.'

Sato expelled a gust of breath, as if someone had punched him in the stomach. 'I?'

'You will be Oyabun,' the old man said. 'I knew by your response to Yamaoka that you, like him, would cling to the old Japan with its diseased ways and die with it, as he surely will. And with it you will take our two hundred men and their families and employees.' He ate quietly. 'That was why I was disappointed.'

Sato gripped the edge of the table with white-knuckled fingers. 'What – what would you do?'

'If I were in your place?' He shrugged. 'I would buy businesses. Banks. Construction companies. Hotels. I would expand all our legitimate enterprises while I phased out the illegal ones.'

'The merchants?'

'I would merge with some, loan others money, discard a few . . .' He smiled. 'Sato, what I am proposing will take a lifetime. I cannot lay out a blueprint over dinner.'

'But how am I to do these things? How do I begin?'

Nagoya drank tea from a porcelain cup. 'Begin by arranging to buy the black building.'

'I beg your pardon?'

'Yamaoka will lose it. He will follow your advice – it was a reflection of his own thoughts – and he will be driven out of business. The press will destroy him. The legal entanglements will go on for years. Perhaps he will go to prison. He certainly deserves it. At any rate, the building will come up for sale. Prepare to buy it as soon as it does.' He sat back. 'As for the rest of it, the Oyabun must make his own decisions. When I relinquish my place as head of the ikka, its future will no longer concern me.'

Sato swallowed. 'Yes, Nagoya-sama.'

That night Nagoya lay awake in bed for a long time. He

had not spoken the truth at dinner. The future of the Onami concerned him a great deal. And he was leaving it in the hands of a man whose first instinct was not to think, but to kill.

'But Sato will be Oyabun,' he whispered.

BOOK THREE

RONIN

20

The next morning at Nagoya's home, a special breakfast was held in honor of Yoshio's victory. To Miles's surprise, he had learned enough Japanese to follow the conversation and even occasionally speak. His accomplishment did not go unnoticed by the kobun. They made a point of including him in their jokes and songs, and soon he became caught up in their festive spirit.

Without Nagoya and Sato present, it was a convivial, loud affair, with music and laughter. Even the women joined in the singing, except for Tomiko. She stayed apart from the rest, and through the noisy celebration Miles caught an occasional glimpse of her watching him, her eyes filled with the same desperate longing he felt in his heart.

It cannot be, she had said. She belonged to another man and another world. It could not be.

'Ronin,' Hiro said, pulling on his arm. Miles looked up, startled. 'You come, okay?' He dragged the American outside, to the back of the house. The others followed them, patting Miles on the back. 'Still holiday,' Hiro said, laughing. 'Koji want to teach you sword fight.'

'Oh, no,' Miles said. 'Really . . .'

Koji bustled toward them carrying a large lacquered box. It was finely wrought, decorated in the manner of some chopsticks Miles had seen, with layer upon layer of different colors. The design on the box had been painstakingly carved through many levels of lacquer, melding the brilliant

199

hues into the configuration of a dragon. Miles recognized the dragon as one of the tattoos on Koji's body.

The young man opened the box proudly. Inside gleamed the two long swords that had hung on the wall in his room.

The other kobun murmured in approval. Every one of them had had occasion to use the flume Miles had designed. They had watched every day as the American went about his tasks, the most unpleasant and menial chores in the house, despite the fact that he was a man of wealth and learning. They knew that he slept in the damp kitchen at night, that he was fed next to nothing, and that he was denied even the company of men in the evenings. For a Japanese, the forced isolation which Miles endured would be a humiliation beyond bearing, yet the American accepted it, and all the other hardships Sato had imposed on him, without complaint. Even after the notorious beating Sato had inflicted on him, Miles had stayed on to learn their language and customs, showing respect to both the Oyabun and his house.

No, the American called Ronin was not an object of ridicule, no matter how hard Sato tried to make him one.

The men had all heard about Sato's ordering Koji to hide his weapons in shame after having let the outsider touch them. By offering them now to Miles, Koji was publicly discrediting Sato. It was, Miles realized, their way of including him into their inner circle. He stood up slowly and bowed to Koji. 'Thank you for your generous offer to teach this unworthy pupil,' he said in awkward Japanese. 'I accept, but I will not defile the ancient swords of your family with my clumsy hands. If you will teach me with sticks, I would be honored to learn from you, Koji-san.'

Koji's eyes moistened. 'No,' he said stubbornly. He lifted the weapon from the silk lining of its case with utmost delicacy, balancing it in his left hand, revealing the blade inch by inch as he pulled it from its scabbard. When it was free, he held it aloft for Miles to take.

It was, Miles knew, a gesture of extreme trust and intimacy. Koji was a samurai. He would allow no one, not even Sato, to tell him to hide his swords.

With a bow Miles accepted.

Koji showed Miles how to grip the heavy weapon with both hands. The resinous hilt was wrapped in lacquered bamboo, and felt like thin satin ribbons under his hands. Koji spoke slowly, so that Miles could understand him. 'First, before you wield the sword, you must learn to yell,' he said.

'Yell?' Miles looked at Hiro, to be sure he understood correctly.

The big man nodded solemnly. 'Yell,' he repeated.

'I'd yell soon enough if you came at me with that thing,' Miles said. The others laughed appreciatively at the American's first joke in their language.

Koji shook his head. 'I don't mean yelling out of fear,' he explained. 'The noise is for your enemy.' He demonstrated by letting out a sudden wailing shriek. 'Do you see?' he asked pleasantly when it was over. 'It should frighten them.'

'It worked for me,' Miles said.

'Good. You try it.'

The two men screamed until they were hoarse, while the onlookers applauded each bloodcurdling chorus. After a half hour Koji began to teach in earnest. Feet spread, knees bent, he guided Miles's arms in a horizontal swing, all the while speaking softly in Japanese.

'Do not think of the sword as a weapon, but as part of yourself. Use it not for victory over your enemy, but for the perfection of your own being.' He looked up at Miles impishly. 'Hai?'

'Hai,' Miles grunted. Under his breath he added in English, 'And I'll also try not to chop off my legs with this damned thing.'

Hiro chuckled. 'You do good, Ronin. No sweat.'

The young man spoke again, but this time Miles could not understand him. *'Wakarimasen,'* he said, still trying to hold the sword in the strange position Koji had shown him. *'Sumimasen, wakarimasen.'*

Hiro stepped forward to translate, eager to show off his knowledge of English in front of the others. 'Koji say in modern kendo, must make seven blows, one push. Push?' He looked to Tomiko.

'Thrust,' she corrected. 'In kendo, there are seven points of the body . . .' Her voice fell away. 'Oh, no,' she whispered.

The men followed her eyes. Sato was standing near the house, watching them. Even from that distance the naked fury in his face was visible.

Koji took a step backward, leaving Miles with the sword. Sato was wearing a Western suit and tie, and as he walked swiftly over to them, he discarded the jacket. The lean muscles beneath the tame clothing rippled like a panther's. *'Dete uke,'* he commanded. 'Leave us.'

Most of the kobun obeyed, retreating silently into the house. But Koji remained, and so did Hiro. In the background stood Tomiko, the silk of her kimono trembling with her fear.

Sato stopped in front of Miles, but he was looking at Koji. 'You are not worthy to own the swords of your ancestors,' he said. For a terrible moment Miles was afraid the tall Japanese was going to grab the sword out of his hand and break it. But instead Sato took the second sword from the case, examining it carefully. 'This is a beautiful blade.' He ran his finger along the steel.

Koji flushed. It was an unbearable insult for a man to take another's sword without permission. In ancient times such an offense had been punishable by death. But this was Sato, and Sato was going to be Oyabun. Koji said nothing.

Sato circled Miles like a cat. 'So you think you're a swordsman,' he said softly in English. He held the point of the sword to Miles's throat.

Miles stepped back. Sato came after him again, smiling, jabbing. He slit open a seam of Miles's kimono. He drew blood. With each attack Miles retreated, holding the useless, heavy sword in front of him as Sato used his weapon as deftly as a samurai warrior.

Miles could smell the midden nearby. The ground was growing soggy. Sato was pushing him faster, thrusting only enough to open small wounds, his green eyes glinting in the sun. Miles slipped on a rock and fell backward, instinctively rolling into a ball. He was not fast enough. With a swing like the arc of a sickle, Sato cut a long line across the width of the American's chest.

The pain of it was exquisite. With each breath the wound opened wider. He made himself breathe shallowly to ease it, but Sato was standing over him, sword poised.

'What do you want from me?' Miles asked finally.

The corners of Sato's mouth turned down bitterly. 'I want you to die, round-eye.'

'Will that make you less of a half-breed?' Miles spat, scrambling to his feet. 'Will that change the fact that you're as much a ronin as I?'

Sato swung the sword in an arc over his head, his green eyes blazing. As it came down, Miles raised his own sword.

'No!' Tomiko screamed. 'Don't fight him! He will have a reason to kill you!'

But it was too late then. Miles clumsily swung the heavy weapon across his body. Sato dodged it easily, grinning, then came at the American with a downward sweep. The swords struck each other, gleaming in the sunlight. Sato parried it with a swift, circular motion so that the long sword whistled by Miles's ear, nicking it where it joined his head. The blade was so sharp that he did not feel the cut at first, and the sensation of blood running down his neck surprised him.

'You had your chance to go home, little boy,' Sato growled. 'Now even Nagoya can't help you.'

'You're insane,' Miles said.

'Am I? You're armed. I'd call this self-defense.' He spun the sword expertly with both hands, so it looked like a flashing silver torch for the split second before it crashed down.

Miles managed to get out of the way, splashing into the foul mud of the midden, then took a wild swipe at Sato. He could not control the blade; it sliced through the air like a living thing. But it stopped when it struck flesh. Sato's flesh.

Everything froze in that moment: Tomiko's hand in front of her mouth in shocked amazement, the movement of the fighters, the breath of the onlookers. The very air seemed to still as the two bright slashes on Sato's legs opened up. His Western trousers seeped blood.

The cuts were not deep, Miles knew. But they were Sato's wounds. The Ronin had drawn the blood of the crown prince.

The midden was slick and watery. Miles tried to keep his feet, but slipped and fell down again, dropping the ungainly sword into the mire. While he skittered and slipped deeper into the muck, searching vainly for the lost sword, Sato stood at the small stone ledge and prepared to strike.

Just as Sato's sword was about to sing into the American's belly, a wild cry rang out. Hiro clapped his hand over Sato's, and the sword flew out of it. With a mighty shove the big man picked Sato up over his head and threw him into the stinking midden.

As Sato sat up, shaking with astonishment and anger, Koji pulled Miles out of the vat of human excrement.

Sato no longer even noticed the American. Hiro had

dared to attack him, and Hiro would pay for his mistake.

The wrestler stood on the stone ledge, his arms folded over his chest, his mild eyes glassy with fear. But the irrevocable step had been taken. Nothing could stop him now.

'You dare . . .' Sato began. The rest of his words were drowned as Hiro leaped off the ledge to fly belly-first into the midden on top of Sato. He caught the tall Japanese around the neck with the crook of his elbow and held until Sato's mud-spattered face turned dark red and his eyes bulged. Then, without a word, Hiro flung him from him.

Sato seemed to unroll from Hiro's grasp like a carpet, flying spread-eagled through the air to land with a smack on the deepest part of the midden. Hiro sloshed after him. When he caught up with Sato, he grabbed him by the back of his collar and forced the man's head under the muck.

Sato kicked out awkwardly with his legs. Hiro spread his knees and squatted on them until they disappeared. His arms flailed as they sank deeper, deeper. Soon all that could be seen of Sato were his two hands jutting out convulsively from the slime.

'O taihenda,' Koji whispered. *Holy shit*! He ran in after Hiro. Miles joined him, wading through the thick mud to reach the wrestler before he killed Sato.

He pushed forward with all his strength, his legs straining against the ooze, his wounds screaming with every step through the fetid swamp. Flies buzzed incessantly around him, lighting on the fresh cuts on his body and sucking his blood.

Koji reached Hiro a full half minute before Miles, and was pulling at the big man's arms as if he were trying to climb a greased pole. Hiro stood stolidly, the muscles of his back taut, his huge arms like tree trunks growing out of the mud, his face utterly expressionless as Koji tried vainly to pull him away.

A few thick bubbles escaped from the mud between

Hiro's arms. *Sato's last breath*, Miles thought.

Rearing back, he did the only thing he could think of: he clenched his right hand into a fist, hurled it forward, and delivered the hardest blow he could muster onto Hiro's cheek.

The big man flinched, tossing his head to one side. Blood flowed from his nose and mouth. But he did not move. It was as if Hiro were in some sort of trance, a trance of death, and that nothing short of killing him would take him out of it. Perhaps, Miles thought fleetingly, not even then . . .

Tomiko screamed. The scream, like the scene itself, seemed endless, frozen in time. One last bubble rose to the surface of the mire and, with infinite slowness, burst open.

Then Nagoya's voice cut through, clear and dry and carrying with it absolute authority.

'I command you to stop,' he said in the most archaic form of Japanese.

Hiro cocked his head toward the voice. Slowly his glassy stare focused, and the sharply defined muscles in his arms relaxed. He looked about him as if he had no idea where he was.

Miles and Koji bent to pick up Sato and drag his inert body to the ledge, where they slid him over the stone wall. Slimy rivulets trailed from Sato's shoes.

While Koji loosened the man's necktie, Miles wiped Sato's face with his hands, scooping the muck out of his mouth. Then he bent over to blow air into his mouth. Three short puffs, then a compression of the chest . . .

Brown slime poured from between Sato's open lips. He coughed, his body jerking spasmodically. He opened his eyes. Miles's face was the first sight he saw.

For a moment the two men stared into each other's souls. They were both ronin in their way, both outcasts. One had hidden himself in his American ways, the other in his Japanese pride, but both had lived lies for so long that the glimpse of the truth they each saw in the other seemed alien to them, incomprehensible.

Tomiko's sobs punctuated the morning air. In the midden Hiro stood, his arms hanging low like an ape's, his body smeared with black mud. His lips were slack. His head hung sideways, as if he were still listening to the faraway voice of the Oyabun's command. The young sumo who had worked for so long to make a place for himself knew that he had just thrown away any future he may have had.

Koji waded back to him silently, picking up his ruined swords, and put his arm around the big man.

'You are past all shame,' Nagoya said, his thin body trembling with rage. 'Come to the teahouse at sunset. Do not let me see your faces, any of you, before then.' He turned away and walked inside.

21

As the red sun went down, the participants in the Folly of the Swords, as the incident was already referred to among the kobun of the ikka, gathered at the teahouse. Miles sought out Hiro, but he had closed the door to his room and refused to answer.

In the garden Tomiko and Koji stood silently, their heads bowed. On orders from the Oyabun, none of the men had been permitted to use the bath. Miles had last seen Koji at the cold stream in the hills beyond the house. He had apologized for causing the trouble that had resulted in the ruin of the old swords. The young man had answered politely, but Miles could feel his shame and despair at having ruined his family's most prized treasures.

'I wish there were something I could do,' Miles said in halting Japanese.

Koji wrapped himself in the clean kimono he had brought, then picked up the tied bundle that contained his other garments. They would be burned. 'There is nothing to be done,' he said.

Now in the garden, he walked over to Miles and put his hand on the American's arm. 'This will pass, Ronin,' he said gently. 'Have you seen Hiro?'

'He won't answer his door. You don't think he wouldn't come, do you?'

Koji looked back toward the main house sadly. 'He will come. It will be the last time.'

A tear trailed down Tomiko's cheek. She and Koji would be punished, Miles knew; reprimanded, restricted, given extra duties. Miles himself would doubtless be sent home. It was the promise he had made Nagoya. Any infraction of the rules . . . All of his work here, his patience, had been for nothing.

But Hiro, among them all, would suffer the worst fate. Hiro had tried to kill Sato, the crown prince, the man who would become Oyabun. Hiro would be lucky to live through the week.

Wordlessly Koji and Tomiko entered the teahouse and took places at the foot of the table. Miles waited outside for Hiro. The bandages Tomiko had wrapped over his wounds were binding him. Nearly his entire chest had been cut open by one wound or another. But they were all shallow. Odd, he thought. Sato could easily have killed him with any of them, yet he had chosen to keep the wounds superficial.

Why?

When he heard footsteps he looked up, but it was not Hiro. Sato came into the garden, limping slightly from Miles's one blow. He walked slowly, without his usual arrogant bluster. He looked straight ahead, but just as he passed Miles, he stopped abruptly.

For a moment he said nothing. Then, still staring ahead as if he had not seen the hated American, he spoke. 'Why did you save my life?' he asked sharply.

Miles took his time to answer. He looked the tall man over from head to foot. Sato, the great warrior. He could do anything except understand the principles of simple human decency. Miles let out a sigh. 'You really don't know, do you?' he said.

Sato colored and walked in quickly without a backward glance. In his pride, he could not even grant the American the sight of his eyes. Miles smiled and shook his head. Poor bastard, he thought.

Inside the teahouse the shadows were already deep. Miles looked at his two friends at the far end of the table, and at Sato, seated next to the Oyabun's place at the head. Then, with a start, he saw Hiro.

He was kneeling, pressed against the wall near the *tokonoma*, where an empty scroll hung against the wall. Below it stood the small wooden table holding the same bamboo vase Miles had seen before. The vase too was empty. Hiro huddled beside it, his hands on his knees, his eyes closed.

He must have been here all along, Miles thought. *How deep the man's humiliation must be.*

No one disturbed him. No one spoke. When the Oyabun entered, they were all kneeling, their backs straight, the room silent. Nagoya ignored the huddled figure of Hiro as he directed his furious gaze on the others.

'What shame you have brought upon this house!' he whispered hoarsely.

Miles felt a palpable chill as the old man spoke.

'You!' he said to Koji. 'You have allowed the ancient weapons of your samurai ancestors to be desecrated in a fool's game. For this you will rise two hours before dawn for a hundred days. You will spend the time prostrate before the swords, which you will repair, in prayer to the spirits of your fathers. I hope they forgive you.'

Koji bowed, his face flushed with relief. It was a small penance, one he would have imposed upon himself.

'The woman has overstepped her bounds,' Nagoya said without looking at Tomiko. 'Her speech and actions are brazen, and a disgrace to her dead father. She should not have been witness to this debacle, and would not have been, had she remained in the house where she belonged. Therefore, the woman Tomiko Sasakawa will henceforth confine herself indoors, and is prohibited from serving or having any other interaction with the men of this ikka.' He waved the back of his hand at her as a signal of dismissal. She stood up shakily, bowed, and left.

Now the old man's gaze rested on Miles. 'Ronin,' he said quietly in English. 'That is what you are called, is it not?'

Miles nodded.

'Do you know what "ronin" means?'

'It means outsider,' he said. 'Someone who doesn't fit.'

'And yet you remain. Why is that, Ronin?'

Miles swallowed. 'I have promised to avenge my family's loss,' he answered in Japanese. 'I have come to learn your ways so that I will not fail. I have waited for your teaching.'

The old man looked down. 'And you have waited well,' he said. 'I know it has not been easy for you. You have shown *gambari*, the endurance of a man of will.' He took a deep breath. 'However . . . it is my desire that you leave.'

Miles felt a clutching at his heart. He knew it was coming, but the pain of Nagoya's pronouncement still hit him like a blow.

The old man went on quietly: 'When I saw you with the others, I believed I had found my chance to be rid of you.' He fumbled with his fingers. 'But Sato tells me that you had no involvement in the affair, that you were present only to learn the way of the swords. And that you tried to stop the attack on him.'

With a sharp intake of air Miles snapped his head toward Sato. The Japanese sat expressionless, betraying nothing.

He lied! Miles thought. *For me*. He had fought Sato. He had drawn his blood. And yet the man had said nothing about it to the Oyabun.

'And so you will be permitted to stay. For a while.' Nagoya narrowed his eyes. 'We will see how much gambari the Ronin possesses.'

Miles felt his breath rush out, quivering. 'Arigato,' he managed. 'I will try to prove myself worthy.'

But the old man did not hear him. He had already turned

212

toward the miserable creature huddled against the wall. 'I will not speak your name,' Nagoya said with disgust. 'No-name, show your face, that your brother whom you have betrayed may see your shame.'

Hiro stood up. His face was white. His broad back was hunched over like a beggar's. Slowly he shuffled toward the table and knelt there, his big shoulders trembling.

'You have tried to take the life of one you have pledged to serve, one who will be Oyabun. For this there is no punishment great enough. In ancient times you would have been killed, hacked into thirty pieces by the sword, and your remains left to be eaten by carrion birds.'

'Yes, my lord,' Hiro answered.

'What will be your punishment?'

'As you will, Oyabun.'

Miles listened, fascinated, as the ritual went on, the memorized, archaic words droning like a catechism.

'Do you fear death?'

'I do not, for it is my fate.'

'And the spirits of the Old Ones . . .'

'. . . will flay me and keep me from the succor of my ancestors in the world to come.'

In time the recitation was over. Nagoya straightened up, the masklike set of his features utterly devoid of emotion, like an ancient deity passing down his judgment from a mountain peak. 'Your name will be forgotten,' he said. 'Go from this place.'

A sob escaped from the big man. 'I accept,' he said.

From the folds of his white kimono, Hiro took a white cloth and a knife.

Miles started in fright, thinking that his friend was about to kill the old man, but Koji held his arm tightly.

As Hiro wrapped the cloth around his hand, Miles felt Koji's fingers gripping his arm with the force of ten men. He wanted desperately to ask what was happening, but he sensed that the moment was meant to be spent in silence. Still, every nerve in his body was strung taut as Hiro took another white cloth and wrapped it around his finger.

The big man's eyes were calm now. As he raised the short knife above his hand, he looked at the blank wall in absolute concentration. Then, in a slow, rocking motion he brought the knife down and through the white cloth until it spread with blood.

'Oh, my God,' Miles whispered.

Hiro's face had only contorted for a moment, when the pain flashed in his eyes like steel. But now it was again composed, his body still. He pushed one of the cloths toward Nagoya. It contained, Miles knew, the severed finger.

'I beg your forgiveness,' Hiro said quietly.

Tears were streaming down Koji's face. Miles was shocked beyond emotion. Waves of nausea ran through his body, yet he could not take his eyes off the bloody scrap of white cloth lying on the table.

Nagoya turned formally to Sato. 'The man with no name has offered an atonement for his transgression against you. Do you accept it?'

Hiro was bending low, his head almost touching the floor. Sato took the cloth and held it in both his hands.

'I accept, Oyabun.'

Hiro sobbed openly now.

'Your brother seeks no further revenge,' Nagoya said softly. 'Go from this place and find a new life.'

Hiro lumbered up. Clutching his blood-soaked hand, he bowed first to Nagoya, then Sato, then Koji and Miles. Then he backed away to the door and disappeared into the night.

The room was quiet. They all sat in the deep shadows like unseen spirits, unable to move, not daring to disturb the dreadful finality of Hiro's departure.

Koji let go of Miles's arm.

'Jesus Christ,' the American said at last. He stood up, feeling weak. 'You're not still insisting that he go, are you?'

Nagoya's face was impassive. 'It was the judgment that he accepted.'

'He cut off part of his *body*, for God's sake!' Miles shouted. 'Can't you stop him?'

'I cannot,' Nagoya said quietly. 'It is not our way.'

Miles hesitated for a moment, looking wildly from Nagoya to the door, then ran out.

Hiro's room was already empty. The white kimono he had worn was folded neatly on the floor. Miles caught up with him near the iron gates leading to the road. Hiro was on foot, carrying his belongings in a knotted square of cloth.

'Hiro! Hiro!' he shouted, running toward him.

Hiro was dressed in the chinos and polo shirt he had worn to the festival. His left hand was still wrapped tightly in the white cloth. Miles caught up with him, tried to speak but couldn't. Instead he slapped the big man on the shoulder with the heel of his hand, then embraced him. In the pitch darkness the two men held on to each other as if they were drowning. Now it was Miles's turn to weep.

'Why did you do it?' he asked, still clinging to Hiro's massive arms. 'You could have gone back to wrestle. You could have –'

'That was not my destiny, Ronin,' he answered in Japanese. 'This was.' He held Miles at arm's length. 'Be strong, my friend. Perhaps our paths will cross again.'

'Where – where are you going?'

'My family owns a fish market in Shinjuku. I will work for them.'

Miles nodded. 'I will see you again,' he said hoarsely. 'I promise you that.'

They bowed to each other. Then Hiro walked into the darkness.

*   *   *

215

In the teahouse, Nagoya dismissed everyone but Sato. The old man's face was haggard. 'It was your right to exact this revenge on your brother,' he said quietly. 'Are you satisfied?'

'I am,' Sato said.

'Then remember this moment of triumph. When you lay dying alone in your own spilled blood, the memory of a good man who might have served you all his life will be all that you have.'

He stood up and left.

22

Miles stayed outside for hours, wandering through the woods, listening to the lonely drone of the night insects. In the distance was the house, growing smaller as the lights inside it were extinguished one by one until, when the moon was high and small overhead, only one lamp remained lit.

It came from Sato's room. Sato, his enemy.

Miles sat down by the cold stream. Waves of anger rushed over him as he relived Hiro's awful ordeal. The big, kindhearted man who had befriended Miles had given up his future just because for one terrible moment that friendship had overridden his fear of Sato.

And yet Sato had lied for Miles.

Why? *Why?*

He must have known that Miles would have left if the Oyabun had ordered it. That was the agreement. Endure anything, accept everything. His dismissal would have made things easier for Sato. There would be no Ronin to sway the others, no round-eye to stir the ancient soup of this strange house where time had been turned backward.

Why did he lie?

Miles had to find out. He hurried back to the house, slipped into the men's sleeping quarters, and threw open Sato's door.

The Japanese looked up from his place on the floor. He was sitting in full lotus position, his hands palm-up on his knees, a thick bandage wrapped near his ankle. His missing little finger was starkly noticeable now. Hiro's hands would be the same after they healed. Mutilated by his own hand in a bizarre custom that had no sense behind it, only the strange concept of honor that these men clung to.

There was anger in Sato's intense gaze, but something else as well. If it weren't for the man's towering arrogance, Miles would have called it loneliness.

'Why did you lie for me?' Miles asked.

Sato stood up. 'I owed you a debt,' he said softly, turning away. 'Now that debt is paid.'

Miles remained silently in the doorway. There was a great tension in the room, as if the two men wanted to speak to each other across the ocean of differences that stood between them.

'You never intended to kill me,' Miles said softly.

Sato whirled to face him. 'I don't need to kill you,' he spat. 'And I don't need to have you banished. You will give up of your own will, because inside you are soft, like your life. You will never stay to the end, little boy. And when you leave, I will laugh at your cowardice.'

Miles felt himself shaking. 'Then you'll wait a long time,' he said, and left.

With a crack one of the wooden floorboards splintered as Sato slammed his fist into it.

Nothing was the way it should be. A kobun had attacked him. His betrothed woman was openly flaunting her affection for another man. Even the Oyabun had turned against him. All since the Ronin came.

Nagoya had charged Sato with getting rid of him, yet at every turn the old man seemed to embrace him while pushing Sato farther and farther away. Sato had done everything he could. He had ability. He had courage. And yet the old man despised him. He had even begrudged him the sumo's apology – after the man had tried to kill him!

In Yokohama the Oyabun had made it clear that he was

not happy with his chosen successor. After training Sato for more than ten years in the ways of the Yakuza, the old man now wanted to transform the entire ikka into a legitimate business empire. Who was supposed to run it? Sato, with barely an eighth-grade education?

Or a rich lawyer from America?

Would the Ronin take this too away from him?

No!

He would break Miles Haverford.

It was just a matter of time. The round-eye was stubborn, and he had a way of ingratiating himself to those around him, but for him, this was still an adventure, a vacation in a quaint new place. He could stand a beating or two . . . It was part of the adventure.

Something had to make him leave! Something that would take his hope away, his ninjo.

Sato could no longer concentrate. Whatever focus he had managed to attain through meditation had been shattered by Miles's rude visit.

Sato could have had him sent away for that alone. But then the Ronin would be leaving only because he had been ordered to leave. That was not what Sato wanted. The American had to realize in his heart that he had no place among the Sons of the Wave. He had to break and die inside. Then and only then would Sato win against him.

He dressed in his Western clothes. There was only one person who could help him when he got like this. He would never sleep otherwise. One person who listened, who knew without asking. Sato quietly slipped out the door and drove through the gates.

His car was common enough, a black Toyota, but Sato still parked it blocks away from his destination. It was always good insurance not to leave one's car exposed. More than one member of the Yakuza had gone to join his ancestors prematurely because they had not taken precautions against bombs.

Sato locked the car, then walked through one of the roughest sections of Shinjuku, taking shortcuts through a maze of narrow alleys. Sato knew the district like the back of his hand. He had been raised here, if that term could be applied to his upbringing.

In these dark alleyways he received his first beating from the neighborhood kids at the age of three; smoked his first cigarette at six; had his first girl at twelve; committed his first robbery at fourteen; joined his first gang at fifteen; killed his first man at seventeen. Here was his life spread before him amid the garbage and stink of Tokyo's underside.

He walked easily through the maze of dirty, unmarked streets until he came suddenly to a curve where the narrow pavement suddenly blossomed into a pretty, flower-lined lane. There were three buildings on the street. On one end was a small grocery. A noodle restaurant was on the other, with a teahouse in between.

The teahouse was sparkling clean, with the characters for 'Half Moon' written in red above the door.

Sato rang the bell, and bowed when a smiling old woman opened it to him. From within he could hear the strains of samisen music and the slightly drunken laughter of the guests.

'It is so late, Sato-san,' the woman chided. 'But you are always welcome.'

'Thank you, Mrs Yamamoto,' he answered, removing his shoes inside the door. She had managed the Half Moon ever since it opened more than twenty years ago. Sato had heard rumours that she had once been Nagoya's mistress, and that the Oyabun had built this place as security for her old age.

Sato had never seen Nagoya with a woman, or ever heard

any discussion of one. Still, the rumor was possibly true. It was the only teahouse Nagoya ever visited.

He walked into the inner room, looking for a face. A particular face, a beautiful face. When he didn't see it, his heart sank with disappointment. He sat down heavily on a cushion. 'No food,' he said to the old woman who seated him.

Then a door slid open and he saw her.

Her name was Midori.

Midori, with her flawless, white-painted face and slim, perfect body dressed in an elaborately decorated violet kimono. She hesitated on the wide single step for just a moment, a tray of sake balanced in one hand. But that moment was enough to make Sato's loins ache with need for her.

The brief look that passed between them did not escape the notice of Mrs Yamamoto. She discreetly said a few words to one of the other geisha, who took the tray from Midori and directed her to Sato's table.

'Thank you for gracing this humble teahouse with your presence,' she said softly, her eyes lowered.

'The honor is mine,' he replied.

They had opened all their exchanges with the same words for almost two years, since Midori first came to the Half Moon as a *maiko*, an apprentice geisha. She was nearly twenty now, at the peak of her beauty. Sato knew she had passed up many offers to work in more prestigious teahouses to remain in the Half Moon, which Nagoya owned, in order to stay close to Sato.

She had given him her virginity. It had been, Sato knew, a gift from the Oyabun himself, presented so discreetly that, had Sato dared to thank the old man for his gesture, he would have been roundly reprimanded for even giving voice to such a thought.

Nevertheless, it had been Nagoya's doing. He and

Sasakawa had brought the young man to the Half Moon after Sato had settled some trouble among the merchants in Shinjuku. The new *maiko* had just arrived, shy yet poised with the long training of her profession. She had played for them on the twelve-stringed koto and danced to show off her skills to the powerful Oyabun and the ailing man who was his great friend; but it was the handsome young one with the green demon eyes who had taken her heart from the very first moment.

Sato had felt it, too. He still did, every time he looked at Midori's beautiful face or heard the soft sound of her voice. He had never loved a woman before. He distrusted them as much as he distrusted men. Yet from the first, something about Midori told him that she was special.

He came to the teahouse infrequently at first, telling himself that he was far too busy for such dalliances. Sato had never used his leisure time for anything other than study or perfecting his fighting skills. He had never had a friend. But something drew him back to the teahouse, and there, for the first time in his life, he found some measure of peace in the comforting atmosphere of ancient music and ritualized pleasure.

Of course, he could not afford to take the beautiful young maiko to bed with him. As a kobun, even one of advanced standing, he received almost no money. Even if he could, he thought ruefully, such a magnificent woman would never accept him, a man of no social standing, with little formal education, whose light eyes aroused the worst kind of suspicion. He could keep men from voicing those suspicions with his fists, but there was nothing to be done with a woman. She would simply say no, smile sweetly, and leave him to his humiliation. No, he would never ask.

Then Sasakawa died, finally succumbing to the cancer that had eaten away his lungs for more than a decade. Nagoya retreated more and more into the large room with the shrine, where he continually lit incense and chanted prayers for his kyodai, delegating the bulk of his business affairs to his lieutenants, and leaving Sato to function as his go-between. In accordance with her father's wishes, Tomiko moved into Nagoya's ikka, adding another annoyance.

Sato did not wish to be reminded that he was betrothed. He had nothing against Tomiko. She was, if anything, even more beautiful than Midori. But she was different. Tomiko, despite her lineage, was not quite Japanese.

She was an educated woman. Too educated perhaps. She had travelled. She had worked in offices with men. She had a sense of the world that did not wear well on a woman. Not Sato's woman.

Although Tomiko pretended to follow the traditional ways, they did not seem to be ingrained in her the way they were in Midori, who seemed to radiate the serenity of Japan with every movement, every syllable. Midori's femininity was so much a part of her that she carried it without thought; Tomiko seemed always to struggle with hers. On more than one occasion he had heard her actually talking back to men, using logical argument, even allowing her voice to become strident.

No, the world had spoiled Tomiko, now and forever. The thought of being married to such a woman made Sato shudder. However hard she might try, she could never be the wife he wanted.

Even through the fog of grief over the death of his friend, Nagoya seemed to understand. 'The daughter of Sasakawa-san is yet too spirited for marriage,' he announced formally to Sato. 'Therefore, it is my decision that Tomiko remain in my house as my daughter for two years.'

Sato almost gasped with relief. Two years! It was an eternity!

'At that time, you will be prepared to begin taking over my duties as Oyabun of the Onami ikka.'

'What?' Sato said aloud. The smell of incense from the old man's shrine suddenly made him feel dizzy. 'But – but I can't . . .' He tried to collect himself. 'There are many others who are older and know more about the Oyabun's businesses,' he said.

'Yes. About one aspect or another. None of my senior associates know every part of my work, and none will ever know. They are rich men, content with their lot. They cooperate with one another. If I were to make one of them my successor, the others would rebel. The friendship between them would turn to treachery and deceit. Many would leave my employ to strike out on their own. There would be bloodshed. The police would become involved, the government. No, my son.'

He shook his head. 'The Oyabun must have more than experience. He must be a leader. He must be the glue that binds everything together. Most important, he must groom the kobun of the ikka to carry the Onami into the future.'

Sato looked down. He had never given any thought to the other kobun. To him they were children, nonentities who remained in the background while he shone.

'They are your brothers,' Nagoya said. 'You must care for them like brothers. They are the strength of the house. Without them the Oyabun is no more than a man alone.'

'I will try,' Sato said.

And he had. For two years he had devoted himself to the kobun, to their discipline and growth. But they had been two years of drudgery for Sato. He was a lone knight, the best fighter in Nagoya's entire organization, not a mother hen to boys barely out of school.

He felt the years rolling forward without him. Somewhere along the line, he had missed the path of his destiny. But now his destiny was to be Oyabun, to marry Tomiko, and he would follow that path whether it was his wish or not.

Along with Nagoya's announcement that he intended to make Sato his successor, Nagoya gave the young man ten thousand yen, a legacy from Sasakawa. 'Spend this on a pleasure,' the old man had said. 'There will be few enough in your life.'

Sato had spent it – all of it – for one evening with the beautiful maiko at the teahouse. It had been the grandest of gestures, left discreetly in a knotted silk handkerchief near the shrine in the room where she had brought him, along with a poem.

He had not had the nerve to ask her, but on the night he arrived at the teahouse with his ten thousand yen, she seemed to be waiting for him. Midori was dressed in the most elaborate kimono he had ever seen her wear, of bright red with gold embroidery and a flight of white herons across the skirt. She did not enter the tea room until summoned by Mrs Yamamoto. When she did, she went straight to Sato, knelt beside him with a shy smile, and began the ritual greeting.

'You look beautiful tonight,' he said, feeling himself tremble. 'More beautiful than ever.'

'It will be a special night,' she answered softly.

After dinner and sake she led him quietly to the back of the teahouse, to a perfectly appointed room fragrant with fresh matting. It was September fifteenth, the night of Otsuki mi, or moon-viewing. The traditional moon dumplings, white rice-dough spheres called *odango*, were stacked in a pyramid in front of the large paper-covered round window, surrounded by fronds of pampas grass. It made an enormous, beautiful shadow on the floor. Midori took a white futon and coverlet from a sliding cupboard and laid it carefully within the shadow.

She excused herself for a moment and left the room. While she was gone, Sato felt a twinge of apprehension. He had listened for years to the sounds of his mother having sex in an adjoining room with strangers. Even now he could remember the squeaking springs of the rusty, Western-style bed, the nocturnal grunts of men whose faces he would never see, the soft closing of the front door in the middle of the night. He remembered the smells of her room in the mornings, the dank, sweat-soaked sheets, the odor of semen and his mother's sex, and the rank fumes of cheap whiskey and stale cigarette smoke.

She was never awake when he left for school, during the early days when he still bothered to attend. He would see her on the bed, her straw-like blonde hair black at the roots, a dirty sheet wound around her plump, too-soft body, her mouth open slightly to snore. And on the dresser would be a few bills, five or ten dollars' worth.

Was this any different?

Then Midori came in, her shiny face stripped of the heavy geisha makeup, her black hair straight and flowing. She was wearing a thin silk robe tied loosely at the waist, and walked toward him almost hesitantly. She looked so young, like a schoolgirl, so clean.

'Are you pleased, Sato-san?' she asked timidly, with a small smile.

She knelt beside him and he touched her hair. It smelled of violets. This was not his mother. This was Japan.

'I am pleased,' he answered softly.

Slowly she undressed by the moonlight, revealing little by little her perfect skin and slender limbs.

'I give you my gift tonight,' she said. 'Accept it with joy.' She held out her arms to him, and Sato moved to fill them.

Her body quivered as he touched it, her creamy smooth shoulders, the small buds of her breasts, and as he held her she felt so fragile and delicate that he thought she might break. Tenderly, languidly, he made love to her, kissing the dot of blood on her lip when she bit it to keep from crying out at the pain of his first, slow thrust, holding her close to him through every minute, lying with her afterward in the silence of that room where the moon shadows played.

Afterward she found the money near the shrine.

'No, Sato-san,' Midori had said. 'This was my gift.'

'And that is mine.' He held her two hands and kissed them. 'You are a geisha. I am your patron. It is the right way.'

She bowed her head. 'Then I will have no other man.'

He knew it was not a light vow. When a geisha made such a promise, it was forever.

'No, Midori. I cannot accept. I am betrothed.' He put down her hands. 'I have been for many years. I don't love her, but –'

'I understand, Sato-san. It changes nothing.'

He had made love to her a hundred times since that night, and she had never mentioned his impending marriage again.

Now he lay beside her again, smelling the sweet fragrance of her hair as she slept in his arms. *Oh, Midori, how could I ever leave you?*

She might have been – might yet become – one of the great Tokyo geishas. But she had given up all possibility for advancement by choosing to remain Sato's lover. In a few years, by the time she was thirty at least, her career would be over. Without the prospect of marriage Midori would have no future. How could he do this to her? If it weren't for Tomiko . . .

Tomiko!

He sat up with such a start that Midori awakened. 'What's wrong?' she whispered.

He stroked her arm. 'Nothing,' he said. 'Go back to sleep.'

She kissed his chest. Her eyelashes fluttered once against his breast before she fell asleep again.

Tomiko was the answer. He could feel his heart thudding.

Tomiko loved the Ronin, anyone could see that. If she were to compromise herself with him, Sato could legitimately nullify the marriage plans, freeing himself of the unwanted woman.

Without her the Ronin would lose his ninjo.

And without that he would break like a dead tree.

23

Hiro's departure signaled a change in Miles's life at the Onami ikka. On Sato's orders he was moved into Hiro's old room, and no longer had to sleep on the kitchen floor. He was left undisturbed to his work. There were no more beatings, no more surprise visits in the night. The other kobun began to speak freely to him even in Sato's presence. Miles was permitted to join the others at dinner.

But he missed Tomiko with a longing that was nearly an obsession. He lay awake at night remembering her scent, her laughter, the softness of her hands, and during the day his thoughts were filled with her.

He made a point of staying in the public rooms when he was inside the house, hoping to catch a glimpse of her in the kitchen or in the halls, but she never left her room.

Shizuko served Tomiko her meals, as well as those of the men. Her duty to report the running of the house to the Oyabun was taken over by Sato. To all appearances, Tomiko had ceased to exist.

Her sudden seclusion baffled Miles. Nagoya had commanded her only to remain in the house. There was no reason for her to make a prisoner of herself.

Unless something was wrong. The thought shot through him like a bullet. Was she sick? Was that why she never left the women's quarters?

He cornered Shizuko in the kitchen. 'What's wrong with Tomiko?' he demanded.

The woman lowered her eyes.

'What is it? Tell me.'

Shizuko looked around, flustered. 'She is well,' she said quietly.

'Then why doesn't anyone ever see her? She was restricted to the house, not to her room.'

'The punishment was changed.' She blinked. Her eyes were suddenly shiny with moisture. 'Please do not ask more.'

'Changed?' Miles shouted. 'What do you mean, changed?'

Shizuko hunched her shoulders, as if warding off a physical blow.

'When did Nagoya change the punishment?'

'It was not the Oyabun,' Shizuko whispered, her voice catching. 'It was Sato. He has ordered Tomiko-san to stay in her room until after you have gone.'

Miles stepped back from her, unable to find anything more to say.

'I must go now,' Shizuko said quietly.

That night at dinner, Miles ate nothing.

'Why so glum, Ronin?' Sato asked pleasantly. The conversation at the table stopped. It was the first time Sato had ever addressed him publicly.

Miles looked over to him with eyes filled with pure hatred. Sato smiled. Miles got up from the table and went to his room.

He sat on the floor, staring at the wall. He would never see the woman he loved again. It had been decreed by Sato, and Sato would be Oyabun. Miles let out a feeble puff of air. He thought that if this all weren't so sick, it would be funny.

He picked up one of the books Tomiko had lent him and leafed through it. The illustrations were reproductions of woodblock prints by Hokosai and Hiroshige, with their beautiful mountains and oceans and bridges and faceless, interchangeable people.

Who would ever understand the Japanese? he thought bitterly. They would spend a thousand years contemplating the shape of a mountain without sparing a moment of concern over a living person.

The anger Miles felt toward Sato was spilling over onto everything, to Nagoya, to Japan itself, even to Tomiko. What woman would allow anyone to keep her a prisoner in her home? And for what? For *seeing* something? For being no more than a witness to the fight between Sato and Hiro?

All women, regardless of rank, were slaves here. The tragic part of it was, they didn't have to be. Why didn't Tomiko object? All she had to do was to walk out. Pack a bag and head for civilization. Tell those macho idiots to take their self-serving customs and shove them. Why didn't she *do* something?

But he knew the answer. As difficult as it was, Tomiko accepted her place, as they all did. As Hiro had cut off his finger, knowing he would still be cast out of the ikka. As Koji fulfilled his hundred-day penance for using his sword, his own property. As Miles himself had accepted an unjust beating from his aniki, his so-called brother. They were all slaves, he knew, but not to Sato, not even to the Oyabun. Their master was the time they lived in, and they had chosen that themselves.

Tomiko would stay in her room until Sato saw fit to release her. And later she would marry him. It was the way of the Onami.

Inside one of the books were the poems Tomiko had tried to teach Miles, the eighth-century *renga* which linked one short verse with another. In the margins were Tomiko's penciled transcriptions of the Japanese characters into English.

At the time Miles had been more interested in being with Tomiko than in learning the rigid verse structures. She would teach him Japanese after he had finished his work for the day and before the women had to begin preparations for dinner. Often they would go outside to walk alongside the raked sand gardens beside the stream while Tomiko recited *tanka*, the fourteen-syllable poems which were the basis of the long *renga*.

'These were almost always love poems,' she explained with the eagerness of one who loves learning. 'They were the fashion at court. When a man presented his short *tanka* to his favored one, she was expected to reply in a seventeen-syllable poem which both acknowledged what he had written and developed the subject in another direction. For example –'

'For example, you're the most beautiful woman I've ever known,' Miles said.

'That is not a poem of fourteen syllables,' she said primly.

He counted on his fingers. 'How's this: You are the most beautiful woman I have ever known,' he said. 'That's fourteen. And still the truth.'

'Then I would be obliged to answer in seventeen syllables,' she said quietly.

'I'm waiting.'

She stopped walking. 'What you call beauty is illusion; in the heart alone is there truth.' She blushed. 'Seventeen syllables. I am pleased that you understand the concept.'

And she had fled from him like the scent of spring in winter.

He closed the book.

There was a way to reach her. Hesitantly he picked up a brush and the dark, fragrant *sumie* ink Tomiko had bought to teach him the rudiments of Japanese calligraphy. He would not attempt to write in Japanese. English would be difficult enough. But the way was Japanese. She would accept it. Perhaps.

> My heart is filled with you
> Yet it cries with hunger for more.

Fourteen syllables.

. He blew the ink dry, then folded the paper carefully. The next morning he made an excuse to come into the kitchen while Shizuko was there, and pressed it into her hand. 'Give this to Tomiko,' he said. 'Please.'

'No, Ronin-san,' she said, turning away from him. 'I cannot. I must not.'

'Shizuko, I beg you. It's the only way I can think of to reach her.'

Reluctantly she agreed.

At dinner that evening, as she was clearing the dishes away from his place, a small scrap of paper fell from her kimono sleeve into Miles's lap. He eased it under the obi around his waist, then sat through the remainder of the meal feverish and silent, breathing shallowly.

In the privacy of his room he unfolded the paper. On it was written, in Tomiko's smooth hand, another poem.

> Time satisfies all hunger,
> Quells all hope.
> In time, we too will forget.

She had answered! He picked up his brush again. This time, painstakingly, he wrote the characters in Japanese.

> Time is a paper dragon.
> Fire it with love:
> It crumbles,

233

'No, Ronin-san, absolutely not!' Shizuko hissed. 'I cannot do this. If I am caught, I will be sent away forever.'

Miles looked down at the piece of paper clutched in his hand. He was already responsible for one person's exile. 'I'm sorry,' he said. 'I just wanted so much . . .' He crumpled it into a ball.

Shizuko clasped his hand with her own. 'She loves you, Ronin,' she said softly. 'I will do it once more. But this is the last time.' She took the ball of paper from him. 'Go now.'

He kissed her cheek and rushed out the back door. Shizuko shook her head, smiling. She prepared Tomiko's tray, refolded Miles's poem carefully and placed it on the corner.

'Hello, Shizuko,' Sato said silkily.

She gasped.

He was standing at the entrance to the kitchen, his arms folded across his chest. 'What's this?' He picked up the square of paper.

'It's just . . . Sato-san . . .' the woman stammered. Then she fell silent, her head bowed as he read it.

'I see our American Ronin has become a poet. Did you tell him his *kanji* looks like it was written by a four-year-old?'

'No, Sato-san,' she whispered.

He refolded the paper. 'No matter. Westerners attempting civilized behavior are like dogs who walk on their hind feet. It is so remarkable that they do it at all, one doesn't criticize their imperfections.' He placed the poem back on the tray.

Shizuko looked at him in disbelief, but he only smiled and walked away.

'He was listening!'

Tomiko sat on the floor, her long hair streaming behind her onto the reed mat as she heard Shizuko's story.

'He was there the whole time I was talking with the Ronin.

234

But he was not angry. He did not even keep the note.'

'He is planning something,' Tomiko said quietly.

'Maybe not. He has changed, Tomiko. He has given the Ronin a room to sleep in. Sato has permitted him to take his meals with the others. Perhaps he wishes to make amends.'

Tomiko did not look up from the folded note in her hands.

When she was alone, she read the poem once, then set fire to it. 'Our time is over, my love,' she whispered as the paper curled into gray ash.

Sato dismissed Shizuko an hour later. Her clothes and personal possessions had been packed for her and were waiting in a car outside. 'There is no need for good-byes,' Sato said coldly as he escorted the weeping woman through the long corridors. 'You should have said them when you decided to disobey my instructions.'

Before she entered the car, she turned to him. 'The Oyabun himself brought me here,' she pleaded.

'Then perhaps he will take you back someday.' He helped her inside, then closed the door with a click.

It was working, he thought triumphantly. By tonight everything would be complete. He had waited patiently for the Ronin to set the wheels in motion with a mistake, and it had come to pass. Just as Sato knew it would. The American could not resist his impulses.

Now they would destroy him.

'Where is Shizuko?' Miles asked the woman who served him his dinner. She avoided his eyes. The woman had already seen Shizuko's empty room.

'She's gone to visit her family,' Sato said, then quickly changed the subject.

Miles's heart sank. There would be no response from Tomiko that evening, no contact at all until Shizuko's return. 'Excuse me,' he said, rising.

'I'm afraid not,' said Sato. 'I have a special duty for you tonight. If you don't mind.'

The conversation at the table stopped dead. All the men could sense that something was going to happen. Sato sat back like a big cat, satisfied with a good kill.

When the meal was over, he excused himself. 'Please wait for me,' he told Miles as he left the room.

The other kobun also left quickly, except for Yoshio and Koji. They said nothing, but instinctively moved closer to Miles.

Yoshio was the first to speak. 'Something stinks,' he said, his ugly little face scowling. It was enough to make the other two laugh.

'Maybe he's changed his mind about you,' Koji offered. 'It's about time his conscience spoke up.'

Yoshio shook his head. 'That one hasn't got a conscience. Only a nose, a vulture's nose. He smells blood.'

'Will you take it easy?' Miles said. 'He just said he wanted me to do something. For all I know, he found a chamber pot I missed.'

'If he did, you can be sure he's taking a big shit in it now to get his money's worth out of you,' Yoshio said.

The minutes ticked by. 'We saw Hiro yesterday,' Koji said, almost too loudly. He knew Hiro's name was not to be mentioned in the house, but he also knew that the man's punishment had been unwarranted.

After Hiro left, the kobun had gathered secretly to take up a collection for their friend. His hand would need medical attention which his family could not afford. With this and a hundred other small gestures, the kobun of the Onami ikka showed their defiance of Sato.

Unfortunately, Miles knew, their defiance would eventually affect the ikka itself. The kobun were drawing away from it as they drew away from Sato. When it came time to take their places in the organization, these men would lack the unity to keep Nagoya's empire intact.

'How is he?' Miles asked.

'He wouldn't talk to us. The vulture has drunk his blood. He is ashamed. Perhaps if you went to him, Ronin . . .'

'I can't. I'm not supposed to leave the house.'

'How do you speak with your family, then? We have no telephones here.'

'I've never spoken with them since I came. They don't know I'm in Japan.'

'You have broken from them?' asked Koji.

'No. But the less they know, the safer they are. In America there are some men . . . They killed my sister and grandfather.'

The words were difficult to say, but he was glad he'd said them. Sharing the terrible thing which had happened made it less lonely a burden. 'The law won't touch them. If they're going to be punished, I have to do it. But I can't do it alone. That's why I came here. The less my parents know about everything, the better.'

Yoshio breathed deeply, raising his chin. 'I will help you with your revenge, Ronin,' he said.

'I too,' said Koji.

Miles looked from one, then to the other. He was tempted to accept. 'No,' he said finally. 'I can't let you do it. But thanks for the offer. I won't forget it.'

An hour passed.

Two.

'There's no point in waiting around any longer, Ronin,' Yoshio said. 'It's almost midnight. This was just another cheap trick. Sato's not coming.'

'Why would he do that?' Koji asked.

'Who knows? He's the damn king around here, now that the Oyabun won't get involved in our affairs. He can do anything.'

'Go on to bed,' Miles said. 'I'll stay awhile longer.'

He had nothing better to do anyway, he thought. He would never sleep tonight, not knowing what Tomiko had written to him.

He caught himself remembering their poems to one another, poems he had memorized, and felt vaguely embarrassed. Miles Haverford, attorney-at-law, Yale man, semi-pro drunkard, certified cocksman, was agonizing over a poem. From a lady he would never make love to, no less.

But he loved her. The words broke into his mind like bricks through a window.

It was crazy, he thought, as crazy as everything else here. Her whole existence was entirely alien to him. Tomiko might as well have come from another planet, for all they had in common.

But he loved her. And he would find a way to her.

When the last candle in the last lantern had nearly guttered, Sato ambled into the room. 'Forgive me for making you wait so long,' he said. 'Something came up.'

'What do you want, Sato?'

'Ah, yes. You Americans do like to come to the point. It's Tomiko.'

'What about her?' Miles asked anxiously.

Sato laughed. 'Nothing grave. It's just that she hasn't eaten. When Shizuko left, I forgot to assign someone else to take Tomiko's meal to her. Would you care to do it? I'm still in the middle of some things.'

Miles blinked. He could hardly believe what he was hearing. 'I . . . sure,' he said. 'Where is it?'

'The women have probably left something in the kitchen for her.'

Miles nodded and started to move away. 'That's it?'

'That's all,' Sato said expansively, spreading out his hands. 'Again, my apologies for returning so late.'

He took a deep breath as Miles rushed from the room. *You fool*, he thought, smiling.

*   *   *

Miles knocked softly at Tomiko's door. The light inside was still on. 'Come in,' she called softly.

Miles entered with the tray. 'Surprised?'

She only stared at him.

'Tomiko, what's wrong?'

'You are not permitted in the women's quarters,' she said harshly. 'Leave at once.'

'Wait a minute,' he said, laughing. 'I didn't come here to ravish you, for God's sake. I just brought you your dinner. Sato knows about it.'

'Sato?' Her voice was a whisper.

'He's the one who sent me here. It's all right, I tell you.'

'What's happened to Shizuko?'

'She went to visit her family,' he said, puzzled. 'Didn't she tell you?'

Tomiko's face drained of color. She stood up in a rush and pushed him toward the entrance. 'Go, My-o. Go now. Hurry.' She slid open the door.

It was too late. Sato and the Oyabun were striding toward them down the corridor. Tomiko sank back on her knees, her eyes closed in anguish.

'What the hell's going on?' Miles said.

Outside the open door Sato raised himself to his full, awesome height. 'I refuse marriage to this woman,' he said.

'What are you talking about?' Miles asked. Throughout the hallway, doors slid open discreetly. 'I only brought her dinner. On Sato's orders. Ask him.'

'It was Sato who saw you coming here,' the Oyabun said in a fierce whisper.

Miles could not believe what he had heard. Sato stood behind the old man. His features were still, but he could not disguise the triumph in the gleam of his green eyes.

'You lying bastard!' Miles screamed, leaping at him.

Sato was ready. He swatted him like a fly down the length of the corridor.

'Leave my house,' Nagoya said, so quietly he was almost inaudible. The old man's whole body was trembling with rage.

Miles stood up slowly, wiping the blood from his mouth. 'No,' he said. 'Not this time. That lying scum set me up.'

'Get out,' Nagoya said.

'I will. Gladly. But you're going to hear me out first. For once someone's going to tell you the truth. This – this vermin, this person you've designated to succeed you as Oyabun –'

'Stop,' Tomiko pleaded.

The eyes of all the men turned to her. There was not a sound in the house now, although everyone in it was awake.

'Say nothing, My-o. I beg you.' Before the Oyabun, she bowed the Grand Obeisance of a thousand years past, the elaborate *kowtow* once reserved only for emperors. 'I beg for your mercy, Oyabun,' she said, touching her head to the floor. 'I beg your forgiveness.'

'What?' Miles said in astonishment.

She seemed not to have heard him. 'I have offended you, as well as the spirit of my father, for in my heart I have loved one who was forbidden to me. The shame is mine, master. Punish me, but show mercy to one who is innocent, and only followed the path I marked for him.'

'What the hell are you saying?' Miles said in English.

Nagoya paid him no notice. He stared at the woman for a long moment, his face a mask of bitterness. 'Be prepared to leave in the morning,' the old man said at last. 'The betrothal is nullified.'

'She's not telling the truth, can't you see that?' Miles burst out.

'Be silent!' the Oyabun commanded. 'You will have your chance to speak tomorrow. But you will not stay in my house tonight.' He turned abruptly and walked away.

'What's wrong with you people?' Miles shouted. 'Isn't anything even supposed to make sense?' Softly he felt women's hands pulling him back and heard the soft murmur of their voices. He turned to Tomiko for an explanation, but she remained kneeling on the floor, her features serene, her dark eyes soft and asking for forgiveness.

24

Numb, Miles watched as one of the women closed Tomiko's door. She did not move from her position, not an eyelash. But her gaze never left Miles's face until she was gone from view, a still shadow behind the paper wall that separated them.

'I am sorry,' the woman said.

Miles stumbled away. He was beyond bafflement now, beyond anger. Tomiko had chosen to lie to protect Sato rather than tell the truth to save herself. Leaving the house, he walked aimlessly into the woods and sat down near the stream.

It's over, he thought despairingly. He was going to lose everything he had come to Japan for. His time here had been for nothing.

Oh, Nagoya had said he would see him, and Miles was going to have his say, but it would mean nothing. Obviously, honesty carried no weight at the Onami ikka.

What had possessed him to believe he could ever fit in with these people, to whom morality meant no more than speaking the right words? Nagoya had no interest in the truth, and Sato had no concept of it. For all their apparent concern about honor, they possessed the ethics of cave men.

And Tomiko . . . he closed his eyes in anguish. Even Tomiko had betrayed him. In the end, after all that had passed between them, she had cast her lot with the Onami against him.

He lay down under the starry sky and listened to the soft sounds of the brook nearby. He had no choice now. He would have to face the DeSantos alone.

One good thing had come of his stay in Japan: enough time had elapsed that the DeSantos would not be expecting him now. If he planned carefully, he might be able to take at least one of them by surprise. Then afterward . . .

Who was he kidding? he thought. There would be no afterward.

A soft rustling through the fallen leaves of the woods brought him to his feet, listening. They were not the sounds made by an animal, but human footsteps.

'My-o,' a voice called gently.

Through the darkness he saw Tomiko walking toward him. 'What are you doing here?' he asked sharply.

'My-o, I must speak with you.'

'Why?'

She stopped. 'Do not hate me,' she said softly. 'We have so little time now.'

Her words cut into his heart, but he said only, 'That was your choice.'

She came up to him and bowed her head. 'What I did was necessary.'

'For what? To protect that scum who beats you?'

The nape of her neck was silver-white in the moonlight. 'For the Oyabun,' she said softly. 'He is an old man. If we had made him accept the truth about Sato, he would have been forced to send his successor away.'

'That really breaks my heart.'

She looked up at him. Her eyes were shining with tears, but the sharp intelligence in them snapped through. 'You do not understand, My-o. Sato is a dangerous man. He would form his own ikka. At this stage it would be difficult for Nagoya to choose a new successor. The kobun are already divided in their loyalties.'

'Divided by what?'

'You,' she said. 'It was not your purpose, but your presence has driven a wedge between Sato and the men he will guide for the next generation. He is the only leader they know. Without him, Nagoya's world – my father's world – will die when he does.'

She touched his hand. 'Against this, My-o san, the question of whether or not we have made love weighs little.'

Miles was silent for a long time. Finally he asked, 'What's going to happen to you?'

'Tomorrow I will be sent to live at a shrine in the country.'

'For how long?'

She did not look at him. 'Until the Oyabun calls me back.'

'If he does.'

'If he does,' she repeated.

He shook his head. 'You're willing to be locked away in a convent for life just to keep from rocking the boat here? Tomiko, that's insane.'

'That is because you are not of the Onami.'

'Don't give me that,' Miles said angrily, brushing off her hand. 'This place isn't the Vatican, you know. And Nagoya sure as hell isn't the pope.'

'No,' she answered acidly. 'He is not. He is Yakuza. He takes money from the merchants of the city, and in return he gives them protection from the bosozoku and the other Yakuza gangs, with their drugs and their guns. If one of the merchants dies in debt, Nagoya provides for the man's family. When the big conglomerates threaten to push the small merchants out of business, Nagoya intercedes with his influence to stop them.' Her voice quavered with passion. 'That is how the Yakuza was three centuries ago, and that is how Nagoya keeps his house. In the old way. My father's way.'

'Is it Sato's way?' Miles asked sarcastically.

Her jaw set. 'The Onami must remain whole.'

In the silence that followed, Miles could smell her scent mixed with the warm night air. He longed to put his arms around her, not to comfort her, who was strong enough to sacrifice her future without a thought, but to take some of her strength for himself.

She broke the silence. 'And there is something more,' she said quietly.

Miles sighed. 'What else?'

'What we were accused of . . . what the Oyabun thought about us . . . It was true in my heart.'

Then Miles did hold her, and he felt drunk with her touch. 'I wish I didn't love you,' he said. He kissed her gently. And this time when she responded, he felt a heat rush from her, unbridled by conscience.

'I am no longer Sato's woman,' she whispered. 'Make love to me.'

'Here?'

'There is no other place. There is no other time.' Slowly she untied the heavy gilt sash of her kimono and let it fall to the grassy bank, already blooming with lilies of the valley and periwinkle. He slipped the brocaded kimono over her shoulders to reveal the thin, bright red undergarment beneath. It was even more beautiful than the kimono itself, designed with swirling carp hand-painted in gold that shimmered in the moonlight as though alive.

She helped him untie the silken cord that closed it. Then gently he put his hands beneath the garment, on her shoulders, and it fell away like air. Her breasts were beautiful, larger than he would have expected, their nipples already puckered with anticipation. He stooped to kiss one, and when his tongue slid over the taut, erect flesh, she put her arms around his neck and cried out in pleasure.

Slowly, like a dance, she undressed him as he explored

her, their clothing coming off like insubstantial things scattered around them, until their naked bodies glistened on the dark earth. Then he lowered her slowly to the ground and entered her.

Her body pressed into his, needing him as much as he needed her, her tongue searching hungrily for his, her strong fingers stroking his back, until she sobbed with the pleasure of him.

Miles kissed her forehead, beaded with sweat. 'I won't let you go,' he said. 'We'll leave together. We'll go back to New York. Or somewhere else. I don't care, not if you're there. We'll start a new life . . .'

She put her finger to his lips. 'No, My-o,' she whispered. 'It cannot be.'

The hope in his eyes faded, then turned to anger. 'Why not? Because I'm not a "real" Japanese? Because I don't belong to the Onami?'

'You do belong,' she said. 'But you have another world too. And it is the other that will claim you from me.'

He began to protest, but she touched his cheek. 'It is so, My-o san. For this time, this moment, your worlds came together in one. But one day you will have to make a choice, and I do not believe you will choose the old way, the way of the Onami.'

'What about you? You can choose, too.'

A tear rolled down her face. 'I have chosen,' she said.

He held her close to him, wanting to hurt her for her stubbornness, for her honesty, wanting her to love him more. 'I guess you have,' he said finally.

She kissed him. 'What will happen tomorrow is never certain. Tomorrow may never come. But I am here tonight, my love. You are here. We do not need to look beyond.' She kissed him again, and he felt himself being swept into the aura of her strength, her gambari.

Yes. Tonight was all there was.

When they finished making love, it was almost dawn. She sat up, gathering her clothes together.

Miles clasped his hand around her wrist. 'Don't go,' he said.

A bird sang overhead. Tomiko raised his hand to her lips and kissed it. 'Tomorrow has come after all,' she said quietly.

He held onto her until she pulled away.

'Leave the Oyabun in peace,' she said as she turned to go. Then, without looking back, she left him.

Within an hour she came out of the house with an escort of four men. A car was waiting for her at the front gates. She walked proudly, her head held high, her features composed. There was not a trace of regret or shame or self-pity about her as she walked away from everything that had ever been of importance to her.

And Miles realized that at last Sato had won.

25

'Sato has asked me to tell you that your appointment with the Oyabun has been postponed until tomorrow.'

Miles sighed, looking down at his dirty kimono.

The young man reached behind him and handed Miles his suitcase. 'These things were taken from your room, Ronin,' he said, avoiding Miles's eyes. 'I am sorry.'

He was a gentle boy whom Miles had gotten to know recently. 'It's not your fault,' he said, and walked toward the iron gates.

He checked his pockets after he changed out of the kimono in the woods. He had seventy-one dollars American, five thousand yen, and four credit cards. And unless he could hitch a ride, he was still going to have to walk the eight miles into Tokyo.

He dreaded the phone call he had to make. He had left his parents' home saying he was going to bum around for a while. Now, months later, they would surely believe he was dead. It would be better not to contact them at all, he knew. For what he had to do, they were better off not knowing of his existence. But he owed them a good-bye. He had to give them that much. He only hoped that when the DeSantos killed him, they would get rid of his body so that his parents would not have to grieve twice.

Had Nagoya ever intended to help him? he wondered absently as he walked along the dusty highway. He pushed the thought away. It didn't matter now.

By the time he reached Shinjuku, it was after noon. It took another two hours to work his way through the maze of unmarked streets to the fish market Hiro's family owned. It was in the middle of a cluster of small markets surrounded by larger buildings, many of them either under construction or demolition.

This was Nagoya's doing, he knew. The merchants were kept alive by the old man's influence. Miles finally reached it as the workers in the small stalls were preparing for the final onslaught of the day, when the din of the construction machinery would stop and the white-collar workers from the big buildings would pour out into the market.

Hiro was stacking paper-wrapped slices of tuna onto an outdoor table. Beneath the rubber gloves he wore, his left forefinger was encased in bandages. When he saw Miles, he pretended to be busy, turning away, but Miles grabbed hold of his arm. 'I came to say good-bye,' he said in Japanese.

The big man's eyes were compassionate. 'Sato had his way, then.'

'You were my last champion,' Miles said, smiling.

Hiro stripped off the rubber gloves. 'Come on. I'll buy you a drink.' He nodded to a narrow, shingle-fronted place across the busy street, then said something to an old woman, who eyed Miles suspiciously before taking over Hiro's job with a sour look.

The bar where Hiro took him was noisy and brightly lit. Without bothering to take their orders, the bartender served them two beers, followed immediately by two more. The place was packed with men in aprons and muddy boots who dashed in, drank, and left just as quickly. Many of them paused for a moment to slap Hiro on the back and exchange a few words. The air inside was redolent with the smells of the city, of sweat and meat and fish and machinery and uprooted pavement.

Miles settled easily into the place. Japanese was almost

250

second nature to him now, and he found that without the language barrier between them, Hiro's personality took on a whole other aspect. Instead of the silly, pidgin-speaking buffoon who ended every sentence with 'yes?' Hiro was a pleasant, funny man with a keen intelligence.

'So what did Sato finally come up with to get rid of you?' he asked, downing a beer in one swallow.

Miles explained the circumstances, leaving out his final meeting with Tomiko.

Hiro shook his head sagely. 'I told you not to go near his woman.'

'Yeah.'

'Then again, who am I to give advice about keeping your head, right?' He called for another beer. 'Well, one good thing's come out of it, at least.'

'What's that?'

'She doesn't have to marry him anymore. I'd rather be a nun than have to crawl into that snake's bed at night, wouldn't you?' He laughed, but Miles didn't answer.

'Am I walking on swampy ground?' Hiro asked.

Miles looked at him for a moment, then smiled. 'No,' he said. 'No, friend. None of it matters now.'

'Ah. You have become Japanese.'

Miles sniffed. 'Maybe.'

Hiro took a long draught of his beer. 'Has the ikka changed?' he asked awkwardly.

'The kobun miss you.'

Hiro shrugged dismissively. 'Some of them came here once, but I didn't have time for them.' He took another drink.

As the two men talked, the noise of the construction machinery outside ceased abruptly, and for a moment everyone in the bar seemed to be shouting at one another. The bartender put a radio on top of the bar and played some music. The lights in the place remained glaringly bright,

251

although the windows darkened and the open doorway took on the dark blue hue of evening.

Miles looked at his watch. 'Jesus, it's nine o'clock,' he said. 'I've got to call my folks.'

Hiro laughed. 'So you're finally taking my advice and going home to your mama?'

'Where's the phone?'

'Not here. The nearest pay phone is three blocks away, at the Striped Cat. I'll walk you there.'

'I can find it.'

'You don't know this neighborhood. And if I may say so, you're shitfaced. So I'm going with you, and afterward, you're staying at my house. Period.'

'Pain in my ass,' Miles said.

Sato walked along the same streets, barely noticing the familiar sights and sounds. Everything had worked like a charm. Tomiko was out of his way, the engagement broken, the American was leaving in disgrace, and Midori was waiting for him. Nothing could be better.

It had been a shame to make Tomiko the scapegoat. He had not wanted to hurt her. Her father had been like his own. But he'd had no choice. Maybe now Tomiko would forge a new life for herself, the one she should have followed in the first place. She was of legal age; she had no obligation to remain either at the ikka under Nagoya's dominance, or locked up in the shrine. She had plenty of money of her own, left by her father and entrusted into Nagoya's safekeeping. Any lawyer could get it for her, if she even needed one. More likely, it would take only a word to Nagoya for her to be free of any obligations to the Onami. She could travel the world, marry whomever she pleased. Even an American, if she had become as corrupt as that. She would be a fool not to go.

As for the Ronin, he would go back to his soft life in

America with no real harm done. He would have stories about the 'real' Japan to tell his rich friends for the rest of his life. The thought almost made him laugh. The American would go on forever believing that his experience at Nagoya's house was typical of the way most Japanese lived. He was too stupid even to realize what an anomaly it was, how strange the life-style at the ikka was. How strange Nagoya himself was, a Don Quixote of the underworld who believed that the Yakuza were still bound by the *bushido* code of honor.

The old man should never have opened his door to the outsider, Sato thought bitterly. Yet he had taken him into the secret world of the Onami, of the Yakuza. For what? So that the boy would enjoy a vacation? So that he would tell his friends, who would tell others, until the ikka was destroyed? No, Sato thought, he did not regret what he had done to the Ronin. He only wished it had been done sooner.

He was so deeply engrossed in his thoughts that he did not notice the gang of bosozoku who looked up at him as he passed. One of them, a youth with red streaks dyed into his hair, narrowed his eyes. His hand touched his abdomen, where the stitches from a knife wound had left a long red scar like a caterpillar. He tossed his cigarette aside and motioned to the others with him. Then he began to follow the man with the missing finger who had opened his belly on the street.

Holding his finger in his ear to hear above the din of rock music inside the Striped Cat, Miles listened to the electronic buzz of a telephone ringing in New York City. Then there was a click, and his father's voice.

'Hello, Dad,' he said, sounding hoarse and timid.

His father hesitated for a moment. 'Enjoying yourself in Japan, son?' he asked tightly.

Japan? How did he know?

'I suppose we should thank you for the postcards. At least we knew you were still alive.' His words came out slightly slurred.

'Dad, I –'

'Don't bother. We're used to your vanishing acts. I should have known you'd disappear as soon as things got tough. You need money, I suppose.'

'No,' Miles said. 'I'm fine.'

He could hear the clink of ice cubes near the phone. 'Find a rich woman to play with?'

Miles felt suddenly sick. 'Yeah,' he said. 'Yeah, that's it.' He forced a laugh. 'Is Mother all right?'

'She's home.'

There was a long silence, with no words to fill it.

'Okay, then,' Miles said lamely. 'I think I'll come home soon.'

'What's the hurry?' his father said sarcastically. 'Nothing's changed.' Then he added, almost to himself, 'Nothing ever changes.'

'Dad?' Miles tapped the phone. 'Dad?'

But his father had hung up.

'Are you all right?' Hiro asked.

Miles hung up the receiver slowly. He wasn't sure how long he had been standing there, staring blankly at it. 'Let's get out of here,' he said.

Outside in the night air of the busy street, his head began to clear.

'Did you get some bad news from your folks?' Hiro ventured.

'Nagoya's been sending them postcards. From me. They knew I was in Japan.'

Hiro laughed heartily. 'Just like him.'

'But he wouldn't allow me to write to them.'

'That's because you might have told too much.' He pantomimed a puppeteer, waving his big fingers delicately. 'He keeps all the strings. That's what makes him the Oyabun.'

After a few blocks, he held out his arm across Miles's chest. 'Slow down,' he said, nodding toward a group of bosozoku across the street. 'I don't like the looks of those punks. They've got more weapons than brains.'

Miles shrugged. 'They're not paying any attention to us.'

'Famous last words. I bet the guy they're following said the same thing five minutes ago.'

The slim, tall man ambling a half block ahead of the gang obviously had no idea he was being followed. He walked purposefully and swiftly, his head down, his hands in his pockets. Miles straightened up, feeling an alarm go off inside. 'It's Sato,' he said.

Hiro squinted. 'Are you sure?'

Sato turned a corner into one of the winding alleyways off the busy street. At a signal from their leader, the bosozoku split into two groups. The first followed Sato into the alley. The second ran the way they had come, back-tracking into another alley, and then running into its darkness at full speed.

'They're going to cut him off,' Hiro said.

'He needs help.' Miles started to cross the street, but Hiro held him back. 'There are twelve of them, Ronin,' he said. 'And it's Sato.'

Miles shook him off him. 'Yeah. And he's going to get killed.' He raced through the traffic to the other side.

Sato knew there was someone behind him within twenty feet of turning into the alley, but by then it was already too late. He spun around, his hands ready. The silhouette of a young man stood starkly outlined in the entrance to the alley. The shadow raised its arms slowly, silently. With a click the silver gleam of a switchblade shone in the darkness, and other shadows swarmed out of the walls, moving toward him.

He backed up. Even Sato knew he could not defeat an entire gang with no weapons but his hands. If he ran, he might get away. If there were a way out . . .

The six bosozoku who had splintered from the original group ran in, breathless and laughing, the sound of their footfalls incredibly loud as they stopped behind Sato.

The tall man spun around again and back, as they all crowded closer toward him.

'Here, chickie, chickie,' the leader said, moving close enough so that Sato could see his face. The youth with the red-winged hair beckoned teasingly with the switchblade.

'Remember me, four-fingers?'

'No,' Sato answered coldly.

'Bet you will after tonight.' There was a rumble of low laughter in the alley.

Sato took a deep breath, trying to calm the despair that was welling up inside him like a tide. How could he have been so stupid? After a lifetime of training on these very streets, he should have known to keep his wits about him. Now, no matter what damage he might inflict on these swine, they would probably kill him.

He crouched down, readying himself. Sweat trickled down his forehead. Killed by a bunch of boys in a dark alley. It was a death without honor. The shame of it would stay with him for eternity.

The leader slashed the blade at him. He jumped back, into the waiting arms of the group behind him. Someone tried clumsily to pin his arms behind him. Sato threw him overhead, hoping to hit the leader with the other's body, but the red-haired youth dodged out of the way, slithering close to Sato. With a kick behind him, Sato put out another assailant and bent low to avoid the switchblade. Then he set out an expertly aimed kick to the red-haired youth's hand, and the blade went flying. Sato went after it, but stopped suddenly when another knife appeared at his throat.

And another. And another.

He felt a sharp kick in the backs of his legs, and they buckled to the packed earth of the street as he felt the rain of blows falling around him. They were not good blows, he knew. Not one of them could kill a child; yet together they would kill him. Like the stag brought down by yapping dogs who could do no more than snap at his feet, he knew that once he was down, he would stay down. He swung widely, delivering a powerful blow into the chest of a boy who flew backward into the wall, but the others did not stop.

A blade slashed at his ear and caught it. Shaking his head, blood spraying over the young faces that surrounded him, he swerved and flailed, trying to escape, but there were too many of them and their grip on him was too strong. Finally he lay still.

'He's mine,' the leader said, panting. He stooped to pick up the switchblade and swaggered toward the fallen man.

'Fight me without your friends holding my arms down,' Sato said.

'But I don't want to fight you,' the boy said with a smile. 'I want to kill you.'

He moved in close to Sato, teasing the blade near the tall man's eyes. When Sato turned his head away, the boy laughed. 'Afraid, Yakuza man?' he cooed. 'Sure you are. Why, underneath those nice clothes, you're just a stinking coward, aren't you? A coward.' He spat in Sato's face.

A coward . . .

Those words, Sato knew, were his ka coming back to him. They were so like the words he had spoken to the American when he innocently came to ask why Sato had not handed him up to the Oyabun. The Ronin had never had a chance against him, just as he himself had no chance now against these yapping dogs.

Was this, then, the judgment of his ka, that he should die

without honor in a filthy alley just like the alleys where he had spent his childhood, like the alleys he had tried for so long to escape?

'Kill me, then,' he spoke at last. 'Get it over with.'

Then he heard a scream like that of some tortured spirit reverberating through the alley. As if they were a single organism, the gang members looked up toward it, their faces pale and blank. In a split second Sato was up and swinging, not caring if the goddess Amaterasu Omikami herself had made that bloodcurdling noise, only grateful that it came in time to give him a fighting chance again.

He ranged his body over his terrain, finding his center, taking one assailant at a time, ignoring the incidental blows, going after the weapons. There seemed to be fewer of them than he remembered. Out of the corner of his eye he saw a face straining under the effort of the fight. The Ronin's face.

Sato's astonishment broke his concentration utterly. In a flash he saw the red-haired leader hurtling toward him in the air, the switchblade singing in front of him. Sato tried to roll out of the way, but knew he would never make it.

That was when the second bizarre occurrence happened.

Suddenly the young thug veered violently off course, screaming, hitting the ground with a thud. Two enormous arms had pushed him away in mid-flight. At the end of one of the tree-sized arms was a thick bandage. At the other end was Hiro's face, wearing the same expression it had when the big man had tried to drown Sato in the midden.

With the addition of two grown men in the alley, most of the bosozoku fled. The only ones left behind were the boy Sato had flattened against the wall, who was crawling slowly toward the lights of the big street, and the gang leader. The carefully spiked mercurochrome-colored wings at his temples were drooping and disarrayed. He looked like a foolish child as he scrambled around frantically in the dirt.

'Looking for this?' Miles said, brandishing the switchblade. He held it up by the tip and cocked it over his shoulder. The boy's eyes widened with fear. He turned his back and ran out of the alley for all he was worth, his spindly legs pumping like pistons. Miles threw the blade into the dirt, where it quivered. 'You all right?' he asked Sato over his shoulder.

Sato only stood there, staring at the quivering blade. He could not find the words to speak. It was wrong, all wrong. Why had they come, these men whom he had betrayed?

Miles turned to Hiro. 'Thanks for coming along,' he said.

'I came for you,' the big man answered. 'Not him.' He jerked his head contemptuously in Sato's direction. 'Let's go.'

The two of them walked away into the glossy blackness of the alley. Sato heard their voices receding with the soft click-click of their footfalls.

'Where did you learn to scream like that?' Hiro asked.

'From Koji, remember? I was a bust at sword fighting, but I learned all the preliminaries.'

The two of them laughed.

Ashamed, his breath still coming in gasps, Sato crouched against the brick wall.

After all I have done to break him, he thought, *still the men of the Onami would follow him to the end of the world.*

26

The Oyabun knelt in the middle of the large room containing the shrine, his eyes like flint. Sato was beside him. Miles had planned his speech carefully, with a list of Sato's lies and injustices, with a plea for Tomiko and a final word about Hiro, who just last night had saved the worthless life of Nagoya's successor, despite his ill treatment. It was to be a speech about justice and morality and honor, about the insanity of living in the feudal age in the latter part of the twentieth century. But when he knelt on the tatami mat and breathed the incense from the shrine, he could almost see Tomiko's face before him. It was a face as timeless as this place, with the wisdom of the centuries on it.

Leave the Oyabun in peace.

She had wanted to keep the ikka as it was, even if it meant her own imprisonment. Her honor – not the outward honor she had forfeited by accepting the undeserved shame of a faithless woman, but the honor of her own ka deep inside herself – had demanded it. For Tomiko, her choice had been the only one. It was the way of the Onami.

And Miles understood. Finally, in this spare room, looking on the old king and the young warrior, he knew that protecting their world from destruction was more important than the rightness or wrongness of a few petty acts. This was Japan.

Miles bowed to them both.

'You have requested this audience,' Nagoya said coldly.

261

Sato turned his face away.

The American's back was straight, his features calm. 'I am deeply sorry, Oyabun, for having offended you, and will no longer press for the favor I once asked of you.'

Sato wheeled around to stare at him. Nagoya blinked in surprise. 'Is that all you wished to say?'

'It is all, Oyabun.'

The old man's eyes softened. 'Then you will go?'

'I will.'

A cry escaped from Sato. 'Do not dismiss him, Oyabun,' he said in a hoarse whisper. 'He has done nothing wrong.' He stood up, his hands covering his face.

Nagoya seemed to freeze where he sat. 'What are you saying?' the old man demanded.

'The charges I made against him were false. It was my envy . . . my fear. . .' The tall Japanese threw himself prostrate on the floor in front of Miles. 'Forgive me, I beg you,' he said.

'Sato –'

'I have wronged you in a thousand ways, Ronin, though you have shown me nothing but honor in return. In my stupidity I interpreted that honor as weakness. But the weakness was in myself.'

Collecting himself in a kneeling position, his shoulders bent humbly, he took a knife from his sash and laid his unmarked right hand on the tatami mat.

'This I do for my ka, which is filled with shame.'

As Nagoya gasped, Sato raised the knife high in the air above his head.

A strong hand gripped his wrist. 'No,' Miles said.

Sato bowed his head in misery. His hand holding the knife hung limply above him. 'You saved my life – twice – and in return . . .'

'In return, you will save mine many times over by teaching me what you know. I don't need your blood, Sato. I need your help.'

262

The Japanese looked up. 'How could you trust me?' he said in shame.

Miles helped him to his feet. 'Because you are my *aniki*.'

Miles turned to Nagoya, and the old man saw that his grandson, before whom the strongest and wildest of his warriors had knelt, was no longer the frightened, pleading boy who had come to him from across the sea. The cub had grown into a tiger. And his name was Ronin.

The Oyabun nodded slowly, feeling his heart break. 'My debt will be paid,' he said.

From the moment Miles held back the knife in Sato's hand, the Japanese warrior and the American he had named Ronin truly became *aniki* and *shatei*, elder and younger brother.

'What can I teach you?' Sato had asked that night.

'How to stay alive,' Miles had answered.

'Against what?'

'Guns.'

Sato laughed. 'For how long?'

He had not expected an answer, but Miles gave him one. 'Long enough to kill two men.'

Sato considered. 'Only two?'

They spent the first three weeks of their new association almost exclusively in the dojo.

'Show me how you fight,' Sato said during their first session.

Miles assumed the classic boxing stance, feet apart, hands up, head down, and jabbed into the air.

Sato cupped his own hands lightly around Miles's. In a flash he threw his knee into Miles's groin, spun around, and thumped him on the back with his two clenched fists, sending the American to the floor. 'That will not keep you alive,' Sato said.

*　　*　　*

Breathing was the beginning.

'There are four kinds,' Sato told him. 'Through the shoulders, chest, belly, and toes. When one sees a loved one breathing with his shoulders, it is time to call the priest, because he is dying. The chest breathers can puff themselves up like blowfish, but they make themselves dizzy with their foolishness. Athletes and artists breathe with their bellies, toward the seat of their ka.' He demonstrated, closing his eyes.

'But to fight when the alternative is death, you must learn to breathe as far as your toes, and beyond.'

He helped Miles, pressing on his stomach muscles as the American breathed. 'Breathe as if the wind were rushing through every pore of your body. Belong with it. Become a part of the air.'

Miles followed his instructions, breathing hypnotically. 'Now control it, and your breath will be your strength,' Sato said. 'Do you remember your scream in the alley?'

Miles laughed. 'It was the only thing I could think of at the moment.'

'It scared the wits out of the bosozoku, but it served more than that. By screaming you focused your strength and your mind.'

So Miles screamed. He breathed. He learned the principles of tension and contraction. He was taught the basic karate forms of the hand. After that Sato tailored his training to Miles's own abilities.

'Perhaps one day we will make a karateist out of you,' he said. 'When you have ten years to spare. For now, you must learn how to defend yourself with the skills you have.'

Sato showed him how to stand, not like a boxer who presents as little of his body as possible to his opponent, but full front, in perfect balance so that he can move in any direction with speed. He developed his abdominal muscles,

264

and learned to base his movements on them. He spent hours exercising his fingers, hours practicing jumping, hours in the dark learning to identify the location of moving objects by sound alone.

He was exempted from all his chores at the ikka so that he might work without interruption. At the beginning of the fourth week he moved into Sato's room with him, and the two of them spent every waking and sleeping moment together, having no contact with anyone else. They rose at five in the morning and worked until eleven o'clock at night, yet Miles felt no fatigue. He fell asleep instantly, and rose without a trace of grogginess.

In the sixth week Sato began to wake him at three-thirty. 'The day will be longer now,' he said as he led Miles outside in the darkness to a place beneath a red maple tree. And he began to train Miles's mind.

They were to spend an hour in silence, their bodies devoid of movement, their minds devoid of thought. Sato gave Miles a nonsense phrase to repeat again and again in order to help his concentration. Miles obeyed, speaking the words, but behind them were always other thoughts. Memories, plans, fears . . . and behind them all, something else, something that never left him.

He had last seen Tomiko in a place not far from where they were now. He had made love to her there and said good-bye to her forever. Tomiko was always with him, the beauty of her face, the terrible longing he felt.

'What's the matter?' Sato asked.

'Who said anything was the matter?'

'You don't have to say it. Your face shows it.'

Miles picked up a leaf and twirled it between his fingers. 'It's Tomiko,' he said. 'I'm sorry. You asked.'

Sato looked at the ground. 'I have already asked the Oyabun to bring her back. I have offered to make a public apology to her.'

'And he refused?'

'No, he agreed. But not until the mission in America is finished.'

Miles cast the leaf away. 'Why not?' he said angrily. 'She's imprisoned in some temple somewhere –'

'She is free to leave it whenever she likes. She has family to keep her, and money. She chooses to remain at the shrine.'

'What?'

'And she knows everything.'

'She knows I'm here?'

Sato nodded. 'She will follow the Oyabun's will.'

Miles stood up abruptly. 'I'm going to talk to him.'

'Ronin!' The Japanese stood up. In an instant the man who had become his friend disappeared, replaced once again by the samurai warrior. 'Who will go with you when you face the men with the guns?' he demanded.

'Whoever the Oyabun chooses,' Miles answered.

'Then they will be his best men. Are their lives not worth your whole mind and heart?'

'Their *lives* . . .' Miles began angrily.

'Yes! To be distracted by a woman now will weaken you. Perhaps later it will kill you. The Oyabun knows this. Tomiko knows. I know. Only you are too arrogant – too foolish – to understand. If you do not care about your own life, then at least consider the lives of the men who will rely on you. If you cannot, then go home.' He walked away.

'Sato!'

Miles stood beside the maple tree for a long time. At last he knelt on the ground. 'I *am* home, aniki,' he said softly.

27

By the tenth week Miles and Sato had grown so used to each other that they communicated almost entirely without words. Miles could sense, rather than hear, the rhythms of Sato's breathing, his moods, his feelings. Now when they meditated, Miles could feel himself giving up his consciousness and melting into the same state of passive awareness as Sato.

The relationship could not be described as friendship. There was no real camaraderie between them, no laughter, yet Miles knew that Sato was closer to him than any other human being – even Tomiko or his sister or Matt Watterson – had ever been. Sato was a part of his very being.

It's as if there were two of me, Miles thought, watching Sato's face as he slept.

The green eyes opened.

'How did you know I was thinking about you?' Miles asked softly.

'I just knew.'

A long moment passed. Silence was no longer an awkward state for Miles; he accepted it, just as he now accepted his odd intimacy with another man. 'Why did you hate me so much?' he asked in time.

Sato answered simply, 'Because I wanted to have your innocence.'

'My what?' Miles laughed. 'If that's something like my virtue, you've missed the boat.'

'Your innocence,' Sato repeated. 'Your parents. Your childhood. Your college fraternity drinking parties. All those stupid things that protected you from the scum in the gutters.'

Miles smiled bitterly. 'They didn't protect me much in the end.'

'No.' Sato flopped onto his back again. 'I should have known we all have to pay in one way or another.'

'I am ready, Oyabun,' Miles said, kneeling before the old man.

Nagoya stiffened. He looked to Sato.

'It is so.'

The old man was quiet for a long time. 'I do not wish to send you into danger,' he said finally. 'But you have proven yourself a man. I have no choice.'

'Thank you, Oyabun.' Miles bowed. 'Whom will you choose to assist me?'

'You will choose,' the old man said.

Miles inhaled sharply. It was an honor he had not dared hope for.

'It is your mission. You are ready to lead it now.'

The air almost crackled with his excitement. 'I choose Sato,' he said.

Nagoya nodded.

'And three others. Koji, Yoshio, and Hiro.'

The old man hesitated for a moment, then nodded again. 'They are good choices,' he said.

Koji and Yoshio accepted gladly.

In the afternoon Miles and Sato walked into the city. Where the walk had seemed so long before, it was now an easy stroll, barely raising a sweat despite the heat of August. Miles's slim frame had filled out considerably, but there was more to the change in his appearance than his body. He no longer looked like a handsome college boy. He was a man, a warrior, with the discipline of a thousand years behind him.

They wore the traditional garments of the ikka, and when they stopped at the fish market, people turned to stare at them. But no one laughed. These were not men to laugh at.

'Hiro,' Miles said softly. His voice carried across the wild din of the place. The big man looked up. He smiled when he saw Miles, but the smile vanished when he saw Sato.

'What do you want?' he asked, looking from one to the other.

Sato bowed from the waist. 'I apologize publicly for the wrong I have done you, my brother.' The people milling around the market turned to stare at the strangely dressed man speaking an archaic language none of them could understand. 'Ask what you wish of me. If it is in my power to give, I will give it. Punish me as you will, and I will accept. Forgive me.' Then he prostrated himself on the ground, among the fish scales and slime, waiting for Hiro's verdict.

Hiro could only stand and stare, astonished. He looked at Miles, but the American's face was impassive.

The Ronin, he thought. He looked so different now. The fresh exuberance, the easy laughter of the man was gone. Now there was something else – power – about him. But he was still the Ronin, and Hiro knew what the Ronin would do in the same situation.

'Sato . . .' the big man said brokenly. Then he bent down and put his massive arms around the man. 'You are forgiven, my brother,' he said in the same ancient tongue, and pulled him to his feet.

Miles's face broke into a grin.

'It is you, after all,' Hiro said, putting his arms around Miles. 'I guess nothing can get you to leave this place.'

'I'm leaving soon,' Miles said. 'Sato, Yoshio, and Koji are coming with me.'

Hiro's face fell.

'And one other, if he is willing.' He took Hiro's big hand in his own. The mutilated finger had healed. 'It will be difficult and dangerous, and there is no shame in refusing. You will still have a place at the Onami ikka whether or not you join me.'

'I will go, whatever you want me for,' Hiro said.

'Thank you, my friend,' Miles said. 'Now all the Ronin will be together.' He put his arm around Sato. 'All of us.'

The five men gathered before the Oyabun in the candlelit stillness of the Shinto shrine. The Oyabun took the sake cups from the priest and passed them to each of the kobun. Miles was the last to receive his. When they were finished drinking, the old man spoke.

'I have no wish to send you on this mission,' he said. 'You are the seeds of tomorrow. Without you the house of the Crested Wave cannot continue.' He turned to the American. 'For this reason I charge you, the initiator of this mission, with their lives. If one dies, it is your responsibility, and you will answer to me and to the spirits of your ancestors for it. Do you understand?'

Miles bowed to him. 'I will bring them back, Oyabun, or I will not return.'

Nagoya nodded. 'Welcome, then, to the way of the Onami. May you live your life, however long, with honor.'

He drank, as did the others, in silence.

Long after the sun had set, Sadimasa Nagoya remained in the darkened shrine. Tears filled the gullies of his weathered face.

Gambari. Giri. Ninjo. The Ronin had proven himself in all these. He had a right to his revenge, and Nagoya would not stop him.

In the darkness of the room, the old man shambled over to the *tokonoma*, the sacred place. In it was a scroll containing a poem he himself had written:

> O waves thundering
> Against distant rocks!
> Return gently to your shore.

With his gnarled hands he touched the delicate blossoms beneath the scroll.

'The gods be with you, Ronin,' he whispered.

Miles was in charge of everything from that point on. He arranged the passage of the four Japanese and himself to New York. Using another name, he rented a place for the men to stay.

He met with the Oyabun, prepared to outline his plan for the foray into New York. But the old man asked only, 'Have you thought through everything?'

'Everything I can.'

'Have you calculated the risks?'

'The risks are high, but I believe I can bring my brothers home.'

'How many of the others will die?'

Miles's face set hard. 'All of them,' he said.

'Then there is nothing more I have to tell you.' Nagoya bowed his head.

'Oyabun –'

'This mission must be yours alone. It will be the measure of your learning, and of my trust.'

Miles stood straight before him. If he failed, he knew, he and his men would die. 'Thank you for this honor,' he said, bowing.

And he knew he must not fail.

*　　*　　*

271

'How many guns do you want to ship?' Sato asked while the five kobun were going over their plans.

'None,' Miles said.

A silence fell over the room.

'We will have Koji's ceremonial swords, Yoshio's bow, Hiro's body, and Sato's hands. They're all the weapons we'll need.'

The men looked from one to the other. Yoshio grinned. 'Sounds good to me,' he said.

Koji pressed the palms of his hands together. 'To fight with the swords of my ancestors,' he whispered.

Hiro burst out laughing and slugged Sato on the arm. For a moment he recoiled, realizing whom he had struck, but Sato only smiled. 'Whatever the Ronin says.'

Later, in the room they shared, Sato brought up Miles's decision again. 'Is it wise to take no guns?' he asked. 'After all, your Americans will have them. And no matter how fast a fist is, it cannot beat a bullet.'

The American was calm. 'No, it can't,' he said. 'But a man with the discipline to use his fists well thinks better than a man who knows only how to pull the trigger of a gun.'

He walked over to the small window and looked out at the moonlight-bathed hills. 'Since I've been here, I've learned something about honor,' he said. 'It doesn't have anything to do with sense or intelligence or the right way to do things. It's bigger than any of that.'

He turned back to Sato. 'Back in America, I'm a lawyer. That is, I trained to become one. But the law doesn't have any connection with justice or good. It's just a way to keep order. Here, in this house, we're all criminals. What we're planning to do amounts to a mass murder. There is no law. But there's honor. There's right and wrong.' He clenched his hand into a fist. 'That's what's going to keep us alive.'

Sato nodded slowly. 'I think I understand,' he said. 'Yoshio's bow –'

'It's part of his soul. It's the same for Koji's swords, and Hiro's strength, and your hands. Our ka will be our weapons.'

Sato smiled. 'You are a different man from the one who arrived in this house half a year ago.'

'I was never Japanese before.'

The drive was a long one, over mountains and across rivers. Miles had left with Sato before dawn and had driven without stopping to eat; it was nearly ten o'clock at night now.

'Where in the hell are you taking me?' Miles asked crankily.

Sato smiled. 'You'll see when we arrive.'

'That's what I was told the day I was kidnapped from in front of the post office. Look, if it's going to be much longer –'

'We're here.' Sato pulled the car into a clearing on the grass. There were no lights anywhere, but in the moonlight Miles could make out a large *torii* arch nearby.

'What is this place?'

'It is the shrine of Kumano-michi,' Sato said softly as they passed under the gate and began climbing up a seemingly endless stone stairway.

There was an eerie silence as they ascended, with only a low drone in the background that grew louder.

'What's that noise?'

'A waterfall. We'll see it before long.'

At the eighth level of the stairway they could see part of the magnificent falls off to the left. It was far below them, in a canyon beside the mountain where the shrine had been built. As they climbed higher, they moved closer to the waterfall, and the sound became deafening.

'You'll get used to it,' Sato assured him. 'This shrine has been here for a thousand years. It's run by nuns. In the old days, women who'd been mistreated by their husbands came here for refuge.'

'But, why –' Miles stopped in his tracks. 'She's here, isn't she?' he asked softly.

'Yes, Ronin. This is the place.' He stood on the step below Miles. 'The car will be here for you. I will take the train back.'

Miles stood in the soft mist of the waterfall, feeling its cool moistness on his flushed face. 'Why, Sato? Why have you done this for me?'

'You have the right to say good-bye to the woman you love,' he said.

Miles bowed to him. 'Thank you, aniki.'

Sato shook his head. 'I am no longer your elder brother, Ronin. We are kyodai now.' He turned and walked lightly down the long stairway until he vanished from sight.

Miles walked upward, his breath coming quickly, his heart pounding. How would he find her? How long would he have to wait to see her?

He opened the hammered brass door to the shrine and entered. It was cool and dark inside, the air fragrant with incense. One corner was lit by a dim wax candle inside a brass offering dish, revealing the miniscule dimensions of the small antechamber where visitors received the ritual cup of sake before entering the larger chamber of the shrine. In the other corner were three stone steps beneath a curtain of white cloth leading to the priests' quarters.

Miles waited in silence. It was late. He was surprised the door had even opened to him. Tomiko would surely not be here. She would be asleep in one of the outbuildings. Even the priests of the temple were not in the shrine at this hour.

Strips of folded paper, prayers left to be burned by the priests, were hanging on long strings across one wall. Looking at them waving in the slight breeze, he lost his nerve. He would not ask for her. Whatever they had had together was perhaps better left a memory. She had, after all, chosen to remain here, even though she knew Miles had stayed at the

274

ikka. If Tomiko had wanted to see him, she would have.

On a narrow shelf above the folded prayers were squares of colored paper and a bamboo cylinder filled with slim brushes and cakes of dry ink.

He would leave her a message.

He chose a paper of light green. Holding the brush carefully, he dipped it into a small bowl of water, mixed the ink, and wrote:

> I walk as a stranger
> Seeking your face,
> Stopping only when the gods still my breath.
> Yet even then I will yearn for you.

It wasn't seventeen syllables, but it was the truth.

He read it over, then crumpled the paper into a ball, and placed it in the flaming prayer dish. Some things were perhaps better left unsaid. He turned to go.

'Don't leave,' Tomiko whispered, stepping from behind the curtain. She was dressed in the white robe of the order. Her hair was pulled back into a braid. Miles had never seen anything so beautiful in his life.

Tears stood in her eyes. 'I thought I would have the strength to obey the Oyabun, but I do not.'

Miles walked up the three steps to stand before her. 'Tomiko,' he said softly, and they embraced for what they both knew would be the last time.

'I've come to say good-bye,' he said, feeling her tremble in his arms.

She looked up, her shiny eyes smiling. 'Not good-bye, My-o. In my heart, there will be no parting between us.'

He kissed her then, in the cool darkness of the holy place, as the flame in the prayer dish consumed his words and sent them toward the gods.

BOOK FOUR

OYABUN

28

The look on Joey DeSanto's face when he entered the Peyton Place was the kind usually reserved for dead puppies and terminal illnesses. His older brother laughed aloud at him.

'Hey, lighten up,' Nick called out as Joey approached him down the empty bar. 'There's nothing in the world that bad.'

Frankie Lupone, sitting next to Nick at the bar, echoed the sentiment. 'Yeah, ain't nothing that bad.'

'Unless it's being as ugly as Fat Frank,' Nick said.

'Yeah, unless . . .' Frankie stopped in mid-sentence. He knew when he was being made fun of.

Joey slid on to the bar stool next to Nick and slapped a legal-sized white envelope down on the bar.

'A lot you know,' he said sourly. 'Look at that.'

'Well, what have we here?' Nick said as he picked up the envelope and held it up to the light, pretending to examine its fibers. 'Looks like an envelope to me. What do you think, Frankie?'

'Looks like an envelope, Nick,' Fat Frank said.

Nick turned the envelope over. 'And that looks like a return address on it, doesn't it?' He showed it to Frank, who nodded.

'Read me who it's from, Frank,' Nick said.

A worried expression crossed Frank's face as he squinted at the letters in the upper left-hand corner of the envelope.

He shook his head. 'Come on, Nick,' he said plaintively. 'You know I don't read so good.'

'He don't read so good,' Nick said mockingly to Joey. 'He don't read so good.' He wheeled on Frank and slapped the top of his balding head. 'You don't do nothing so good, you're so dumb. Getatta here. Go outside and scare away customers or something. I gotta talk to my brother.'

As Frank was walking away, Nick said without lowering his voice, 'He's so stupid he makes me puke. They all are, all these losers the old man keeps around.'

'Nicky, I've got my own problems,' Joey said despondently.

A man came out of the kitchen, saw Joey at the bar, and automatically made him a sloe gin fizz, Joey's drink of preference these days. As soon as he had set it on the bar, Nick swiped the glass away so that it spilled all over the bartender's yellow suit.

'What are you giving him a drink for? He's underage,' Nick growled as the bartender tried to towel off the red stain from his jacket. 'Christ, even the manager here don't have any brains.' He took the towel from the man and cracked it across his face. 'Get lost, Salvo. Go hide in the kitchen or something.'

The man behind the bar walked away obediently. 'Clean up the broken glass first, stupid. Jeez.' He jerked his head toward the back tables. 'Come on, Joey, let's talk.'

The brothers slid into a banquette in the far corner of the room. Joey slapped the envelope on the table. 'There it is,' he said disgustedly.

Nick put a hand over his and squeezed it affectionately. 'So you been accepted in college, Big Brain, right?'

'Yeah,' Joey said glumly. 'Morehead State College.'

'Where the hell is that?' Nick asked.

'Tennessee. What the hell am I supposed to do in Tennessee?'

Nick shrugged. 'They got girls there, don't they? Hey, I'd go to a place with a name like More Head.' He laughed at his own joke.

'Come on, Nicky,' Joey said. 'I don't want to go to school. I want to stay here and be like you.'

'Dumb and uneducated, right? Is that what you're saying?'

'You? Dumb? Nick, you're the smartest guy I ever met. You know what I mean. You're in the business up to your nougats and me . . . I'm left out in the cold, like I wasn't even part of this family.'

Nick spread his arms, revealing the embroidered lining of his lightweight cream-colored suit. 'Hey, what can I do, okay? Pop don't want you in the rackets. Me, he got no hope for.' He laughed again. 'He wants you to get an education. Who knows? Maybe he's right. Maybe it's the best thing for you to do.'

Joey shook his head. 'The best thing for me to do is to be with you, Nick. Didn't we have fun this summer?' He sat forward eagerly. 'Remember the night we clipped Mannie for five thousand dollars playin Hole 'em with the marked cards, and then we spent it all on those bimbo showgirls down in Atlantic City? I thought my pecker was going to fall off. And the big hit we made at Belmont with that jockey who owed Pop money?' Joey looked at his older brother earnestly. 'This has been the best summer of my life.'

'Yeah? Well, it's not all booze and broads and winning at poker either, you know? The family business is business sometimes. You didn't like it when we bopped those two people up at Central Park. You threw up all the way home. That's part of the family business, too.'

Joey looked down, his jovial mood broken. 'They were just getting married,' he said softly, afraid to reopen an old wound. 'And it wasn't real business.'

'No? Well, part of business is not letting our family get pushed around. You let people push you around once, it gets to be a habit. Then everybody pushes you around because you got no respect.' He lit a cigarette and blew out the smoke angrily. 'Nobody would've gotten hurt up there if they had just shown us a little respect.'

'But I didn't *say* anything, Nick. I didn't enjoy it much, but I didn't say anything,' Joey said.

Nick affectionately mussed his brother's hair. 'No, you didn't. You're a good guy, Joey, and when you get out of college, you'll be even better.'

'Ahhhh,' Joey growled and pulled away in mock anger. 'What makes me nuts is that I know I flunked the entry exam for this school. I answered everything wrong. I told them that Mario Cuomo discovered America. That Bobby Kennedy was president and got shot by Martin Luther King. I don't know how they let me in.'

'You have to ask?' Nick said. 'You got in 'cause Pop wanted you in and somebody owed him a favor.'

'He controls some college in Tennessee?' Joey said.

'No,' Nick said slowly. 'But he controls somebody who controls somebody whose fag brother-in-law or something is a dino at some fag college, and he puts on a little squeeze at this end and at that end. They never heard of him, probably, but oh, yes, young Joseph DeSanto will make a wonderful addition to our student body. That's the way it works.'

'Dino? What's a dino?'

'You know, it's college talk. Like the Dino Students or the Dino Admissions? Like that,' Nick explained patiently.

'Oh,' Joey said. 'Anyway, it's not fair. I shouldn't be let in if I flunked the test. Maybe there's somebody out there who couldn't get in because I did.'

Nick shook his head. 'Shit, you start thinking like that, you might as well join the fuckin' Peace Corps. What the hell's the matter with you?' He swatted his brother across his head.

'Nicky . . .'

'Aw, cheer up.' He came forward in his seat and looked around the big empty dining room before reaching into his pocket and bringing out a little brass vial. He upturned a glass ashtray and with practised hands spread a thin line of white powder on the back of it, then handed Joey a dollar bill.

'Here, take a blow. The best Colombian coke. We hit one of the Estebans' stashes last night.'

'The Estebans?' Joey said in an agitated whisper. 'Holy shit. Does Pop know about it?'

The Estebans were a growing Colombian mob which was making deep inroads into the cocaine traffic in New York City. Nick regarded their success as a personal insult.

'Pop knows what I want him to know,' Nick said airily. 'Go ahead, it's good stuff.'

'Maybe not today,' Joey said. 'I'm too depressed.'

'Your funeral.' Nick rolled the dollar bill and used it to sniff the fine white powder into his nose. 'Aaaah, nothing better than that,' he said as he leaned back again in the banquette. 'You know, Joey, maybe college isn't such a bad idea.'

'I'd like to know how you figure that,' Joey said.

'Go down there and learn something. You know, maybe learn to be an accountant or something.'

'Yeah, so I go down there and I hang out with a bunch of hayseeds and I read books about a lot of dead English fruits in leotards and then what? And then what do I do? Come back here and work in an office at the World Trade Center and if I get lucky, make enough money to buy a Yugo?'

'That's not my idea,' Nick said. 'You know, Pop's not going to live forever. Times are changing. And when he's gone, Joey, I'm going to need somebody to handle business, to invest our money, to make sure we ain't getting ripped off. That would be your job, Joey.'

The sparkle returned to Joey's eyes. 'You mean it, Nicky?'

'Of course I mean it. Did I ever lie to you?'

Joey wanted to say, 'Only a million times,' but he knew that with blow in his nose, his brother had no sense of humor. 'No,' he said. 'Never.'

'Damned right. And I never will,' Nick said. 'When I take over, you come back here and we'll run this thing together.' He stopped, thought a moment, and smiled. 'I'll kill them and you'll write the checks for their funerals, okay?'

'Okay,' Joey said.

'I can't trust nobody around here to do nothing.' Nick scowled at the ashtray. Already the cocaine was starting to make him edgy. Joey knew the signs. 'Pop's old pepper-sucking goombahs are no good and Fat Frank's got no brains and that juicehead Salvo who runs this place and tries to get you all liquored up is thicker than shit.'

Joey swallowed, then smiled confidently. 'I guess you do need me, then,' he said. 'Thanks a lot, Nicky.'

'Yeah, a partnership. Sound good?'

'Nicky, you're the best brother anybody ever had. I just hope I don't rot in that school before you call me.'

'You won't,' Nick said. 'I'm pretty sure of that.' He paused for a moment as he felt a warm glow suffuse his body. 'Hey, you know what?' he said, leaning closer over the table. He whispered, even though no one else was in the room with them. 'I got an idea for you. Chance to get a little extra cash to take with you to Sticksville.'

'A job, Nicky?'

'Cigarettes. You take a truck down to North Carolina, you pick them up cheap down there, and sell them on the street here at a discount. Nothing big, but there's two, three

284

grand in it for you. I'll front you the cash for the smokes and you can pay me back after you sell them. Interested?'

'Sure,' Joey said. 'What about the truck? Does it go down empty?'

Nick chuckled appreciatively. 'You belong in college, kid. You got some brains after all. No. The truck doesn't go down empty 'cause that'd be bad business. You take down some TVs, some radios, a few car parts. There'll be a guy waiting for them down there. He'll unload them and pay you. But that money comes right back here. To me and nobody else but me. Understand?' He pressed the ends of his two index fingers hard into the dark red tablecloth.

'No sweat, Nicky. I understand,' Joey said. 'What Pop doesn't know . . .'

'Doesn't hurt us,' Nick finished.

'So Nicky finally found some pigeon to make that run down South for him?'

It was 11 P.M. The last diners had just left the Peyton Place. Guy Salvo, the manager, was alone with Fat Frank Lupone and a tall, good-looking guy who was sitting alone at the end of the bar near the door, too far away to hear.

'Shaddup,' Fat Frank said. 'Get me an anisette.'

'Sure. What's eating you?'

'Don't be knocking Nicky. He wants something done, he does it, huh?'

'Who's knocking Nicky?' Salvo said as he poured the anisette into a short fluted glass. 'I just asked if he found somebody to make the run.'

'And I said it ain't none of your business,' Fat Frank said, 'so whyn't you just forget it?'

'Okay, okay,' Salvo said. 'Keep an eye on the bar, huh? I want to see how the kitchen's doing.'

He brushed his hands down the front of the sloe gin-splattered yellow suit and walked through the sliding doors that led into the restaurant's brightly lit kitchen.

A young Oriental was washing down the front doors of the walk-in refrigerator. Angrily Salvo kicked the toe of his soft black loafer against a plastic garbage pail. 'What the fuck you think you're doing?' he shouted.

He stomped across the floor as the Oriental turned to face him with a bewildered look. Salvo snatched the sponge from his hand and tossed it across the kitchen.

'You got nothing to do, you don't wash the frigging walls, you shit-for-brains slope. Get out there and sweep the carpet.'

He pantomimed the activity, moving his hands back and forth as if wielding an invisible broom. 'Sweepee, sweepee, got it?'

'Hokay, Mista Boss,' the Oriental answered, his head and shoulders bobbing up and down in a series of bows. He grabbed a broom and went out through the swinging doors.

Behind him, Salvo looked around at the immaculate kitchen and shook his head. *Mista Boss*. What was the world coming to that he was forced to hire people who couldn't speak goddamn English?

But he had to admit, it did have certain compensations. His budget for the unskilled kitchen help was two hundred dollars a week per man. When he hired the junior wiseguys he was generally forced to hire, Salvo had to pay them the whole two hundred. But once in a while when he could employ some foreigner, he only paid a hundred and fifty a week and the other fifty dollars went into his own pocket.

This Chink had been a lucky find. The regular nighttime cleanup boy had gotten himself beaten up on the street – nobody knew why or by whom – and fifteen minutes later, the Chink had shown up at the kitchen door saying, 'Jobbee, Mista Boss, got jobbee?'

So Salvo had made him wait while he called the two names on his must-hire list and found out that both young men were in jail. So the Chink got lucky and got a job and Salvo got another fifty dollars a week that he could stick in his pocket. Add that to what he could clip out of the bar till at night, and he was able to take two or three hundred dollars a week from the Peyton Place without anyone suspecting.

That was the key – that no one suspected. Because if anybody, especially that arrogant bastard Nicky DeSanto, thought that he was tapping the till, Guy Salvo knew he'd be dispatched with no more ceremony than road kill.

So maybe hiring gooks wasn't such a bad thing after all. They were happy for the jobs, they didn't complain, and they didn't talk well enough to rat on him to anybody.

And Christ knew, they were better than shines. Jesus, he thought, cheat a black out of a nickel, and you got seventy-five of his relatives dancing and waving their fists outside your door. Not to mention a year of TV cameras up your asshole.

He looked into the highly polished reflective door of the stainless steel refrigerator and moaned at the reflection of his ruined suit. He opened the refrigerator, took a bottle of scotch from the back of a shelf, and raised it to his lips. There was barely enough left inside to wet his lips. He cursed under his breath, then stashed the bottle at the bottom of a garbage pail.

In the bar, the kitchen boy was sweeping the dining area and Fat Frank was still sucking away at his anisette, but the young guy at the other end of the bar had gone.

Salvo went over to take away the man's empty glass and saw there was no money on the bar.

'Hey, Frank. This guy pay his bill?'

'Yeah. He dropped ten bucks there. I put it in the register.'

Salvo nodded and turned away to wipe the bar. Lying bastard, he thought. The young guy had been coming in every night. He always paid his bill and left an extra ten spot for Salvo. Fat Frank had copped Salvo's tip.

It was a lowlife business when you had to work with petty thieves, Salvo thought peevishly. He put the empty glass in the washing tray and said, 'I could use a drink.'

Fat Frank shook his head with a particularly nasty smile. 'Well, you ain't getting one,' he said. 'You know what Nicky says. You don't do no drinking on the job.'

'Place is closed,' Salvo said.

'It don't matter. Nicky's rules is Nicky's rules. Hey, you want a drink, go someplace and get one. I'll close up for you.'

Salvo thought for a moment. If he left, Fat Frank was sure to line his pockets with the register receipts. On the other hand, Salvo himself was going to steal them anyway. 'What the hell, why not?' he said as he came out from behind the bar. 'Just remember to let Charlie Chan out, will you?' and nodded toward the Oriental, who was still sweeping the carpet in the dining room.

'Sure. Go on. I'll take care of everything,' Fat Frankie said with a self-satisfied smirk.

Like bartenders everywhere, Guy Salvo had a favorite nearby bar where he liked to sneak for a drink whenever he got the chance. Zorelli's was three blocks away, right on the fringe where the tidy streets of Little Italy started to give way to the filth of the Bowery. The bar was big and usually not too crowded, and Salvo was known just enough to command respect, but not so much that people pestered him when he wanted to do some serious drinking.

The bartender saw him, waved, and without being told, poured a double shot of Chivas over ice and put it in front of Salvo.

'Start me a tab,' Salvo said.

'This one's on that guy down there,' the bartender said. He pointed to the end of the bar, where the young man who had been at the Peyton Place earlier was sitting.

He was tall and thin, with a face as pretty as a girl's, but Salvo knew by the man's bearing that he was no fag hustler. His clothes were impeccable and he had money written all over him. And there was something hard about his eyes.

When the man saluted him with his glass, Salvo waved for him to join him.

'How's it going? Michael, isn't it?'

'That's right,' the young man said. 'Michael Hall. Call me Mike.'

'You sort of took off in a hurry.'

'Yeah, well, I got tired of Fatso sitting at the end of the bar, scowling at me. I suppose you hired him as a bouncer.'

'Hire him? Hire him? I'd sooner hire Dracula,' Salvo said. 'But I'm stuck with him. The bucket of shit's Nicky DeSanto's little pal. Goddamn moron acts like he owns the place.' He sighed. 'You know, I'm forty-two years old. I'm smart, damn smart. And all I do is I get pushed around by a bunch of animals with no brains who think they're all hot shit. You know what that fat turd does?'

'What's that?' the young man asked.

'Whenever my back is turned, he nips tips from me. Mike, I swear to God.' He crossed his heart and held his hand up for celestial witness. 'You turn around for a minute, and the son of a bitch is swiping money off the bar. You want proof? I'll give you proof.' He waved to the bartender for a refill on his drink. 'You leave me a tip tonight?'

'Sure,' the young man said.

'Right. See? Fat Frank said you didn't. You just paid your bill and left. See? He swiped my tip. Not that it matters to me, you understand.' He shook his head. 'I just don't understand thievery.'

'Whatever happened to honor among friends?' the young man said with a smile.

'Honor? That's a laugh,' Salvo said. 'Fat Frank steals

my tips, the old man would steal anything that isn't nailed down, Nicky steals from the old man . . .' He tapped his companion's arm. 'Hey, listen to this. That Nicky's even sending his kid brother off on a cigarette run for him. The kid's nineteen years old. He gets nailed, he could go away for five years. Nicky don't care. Sheesh. Honor, huh?'

He finished his drink. 'I tell you, the only honest man in that whole place is me. And I'm not just bragging, you just ask anybody and they'll tell you. Hey, that's a nice suit. What do you do anyway, Mike?'

'I'm a businessman,' the young man responded and hunched forward so that no one could overhear them. 'I'm looking around, thinking maybe of buying a restaurant. Is the Peyton Place for sale, do you know?'

Salvo looked at him a long time before answering. What the hell. Mike was his friend. He shook his head. 'You know it's a . . . well, you know, a place for wiseguys.'

'Wiseguys?' the young man said.

'Yeah, you know. Wiseguys. All right. The mob. It's a mob place.'

'I didn't know that,' the man said.

'Well, you wouldn't, 'cause I run a tight ship and I don't let them get away with any of their crazy crap in there,' Salvo said. 'But that's why I don't think it's for sale, you know? They'd never let go of it. It's like a restaurant and an office and a hangout for all those jerks. But, boy, I'll tell you, it could be a real crackerjack restaurant if they just let me run it.'

'I can tell just by watching you that you really know this business,' the young man said. 'If I find a place . . . well, don't be surprised if I make you an offer.'

'Don't be surprised if I take it,' Salvo said. He took a large swallow from his fresh drink. 'And I could invest too. I've put together a few bucks working there. I could put up some money, maybe get in on the profits some.'

'That's possible,' the young man said. 'But I wouldn't need your money. Your expertise would be enough of a contribution.'

'You serious?'

'Why not?'

Salvo grinned. 'Another drink for my friend!' he shouted to the bartender. Then he leaned on his elbow. 'Expertise,' he repeated, savoring the word. 'I've got that, all right. Mike, I tell you, when you're ready to make a deal, you let me know. I'll check the place out. I know every way that a bartender and a manager and the help can cheat. You look at a place, then send me in and I'll tell you what it really should be taking in. Nobody's going to pull the wool over my eyes.'

The young man chuckled. 'You're a fox, Guy. Is it all right if I call you Guy?'

'Sure. Guy and Mike. Not a bad name for a place, you know. Guy and Mike's.'

'Terrific. But I want the Peyton Place. I like the looks of it. Think you could introduce me to the boss?'

'Nicky? I don't know, Mike.' He shook his head nervously. 'I mean, sure, sure I can do it. But the time has to be right, you know? Let me find the right time.'

The young man stood up. 'All right. But try to make it soon. I'm not going to be in town much longer.'

He threw a fifty-dollar bill on the bar. 'Have a nightcap on me,' he said.

Salvo waited until the young man went through the door before picking up the money and sticking it in his pocket.

On the street outside the bar, the young man inhaled deeply to get some fresh air into his lungs, then walked off to his car. Who said that being the best drinker in his Yale law school class didn't count for anything?

Guy and Mike's. He thought about it again and laughed aloud, startling a wino who was sleeping on a stoop. The man grimaced at him and said, 'Hey, fucko. A little quiet down there. I'm trying to get some sleep.'

Miles Haverford laughed again as he walked off down the street.

He got back to the tenement on Avenue D in Manhattan's rundown Alphabet City at three and waited in the car until he saw Sato coming down the sidewalk. Without greeting each other, they walked upstairs to the third-floor apartment. Inside, Koji, Hiro, and Yoshio awoke and sat up, alert, when the two men entered.

Miles and Sato stripped, showered, and clothed themselves in the cotton kimonos waiting for them before they joined the others. Koji had made tea.

'Joey DeSanto's going to North Carolina in a truck,' Miles said. 'To pick up illegal cigarettes. I don't know when.'

'Next Saturday,' Sato said.

'How do you know?' Miles asked.

'Chinkee no speakee English, learn many thing in kitchen, chop chop, Mista Boss.' There was an edge to his voice, but Miles ignored it. He would speak to Sato later.

He turned to the others. 'You will begin it, Yoshio,' he said in Japanese. 'The first death will be by your hand.'

The little man bowed low to him. 'I will not fail you, Ronin-san.'

29

Joey whooped as the tractor trailer rolled out of Charlotte and headed north on Route 77. 'We did it, Hooks, we did it! Not a hitch. Nicky's going to be happy as a clam.'

Dominic 'Hooks' Aiello, the driver, only grunted and shifted his weight to ease the pressure off his hæmorrhoids. He was a veteran in the DeSanto army. For him, the cigarette runs were kids stuff. To prove it, they had put a kid in charge of it.

Now the kid was looking at a map that he had folded in his lap. 'Why're we taking 77, Hooks? Why don't we just get onto 95 and take it right up to New York?'

Hooks sighed. Kids in charge of an operation wasn't a real smart way to do things. Not like the old days. Still, Joey and Nicky were the old man's boys and it wouldn't pay to lip off to the kid, no matter how dumb he was.

When Aiello answered, he spoke slowly with a thick, raspy voice that seemed more suited to growling than speech. That voice and an ugly red scar that ran across the full front of his size 18 neck were the only reminders of the night the Morelli boys had slit his throat and left him for dead. He always wore turtlenecks now, no matter what the weather was, to cover the scar, but there was no way to hide the damaged vocal cords.

'Let me ask you, Joey. You think Nicky's the first guy who ever thought about coming down here and buying up cigarettes cheap?'

'No,' Joey said cautiously.

'Right. Everybody does it. So many people in New York do it now that niggers even caught on and they do it. And niggers got no brains. So what they do is they buy up some cigarettes, and they stick 'em in the trunk of their broken-down old Cadillacs. They can't wait to get back to New York, so they jump on 95 and they don't get ten miles before the state troopers arrest them.'

'Patrolled heavy, huh?' Joey said.

Hooks nodded. 'The road's filled with state troopers and if they got any time left over after arresting all the niggers, they look for trucks that look like they might be carrying cigarettes in them and then they stop you and you get nailed and off we go for a vacation in the slammer, okay?'

'Yeah,' Joey said, enthusiastic about even that aspect of the operation.

'So what we do is we take 77 up to 81 in Virginia and then we go into New York and we stay out of the troopers' way and we let them go on arresting niggers.'

'No arguments from me, Hooks. I was just wondering,' Joey said.

'Yeah. I know,' Hooks said. He shifted his weight again. It was going to be a long trip. Only a little while on the road and already his hæmorrhoids were throbbing like a Puerto Rican dance band. That came from no sleep. He would talk to Tony DeSanto and tell him that his asshole wouldn't let him make any more cigarette runs, except that Nicky had told him that this one had to be kept quiet from his father.

'It's a surprise,' Nicky had said, which meant that the kid was running something that he didn't want the old man to know about. Well, he'd tell Nicky, then. No more. Not until he got refitted with a plastic ass.

Running cigarettes from North Carolina was retard work, anyway. Anybody could do it. Back in the old days, when he was hijacking cargo off the docks and doing it all

294

with the cops and Feds on three sides of him and the Morellis on the fourth, that was a job he could sink his teeth into. Not like this pussy stuff.

But what the hell. That was a long time ago. At sixty-two, Hooks had not had a bullet put into him in almost twenty years. He had a house on Long Island with a pool, a wife who still had a fair set of tits on her even if she did have a mouth that could melt bone marrow, three grand-kids, and a Lincoln Continental that was paid for. He wasn't complaining.

Hell, he was a different generation and he knew it. Most of the kids today didn't even know that he got his name from his habit, during the gang wars around World War II, of using his longshoreman's hook to rip out the guts of enemies and leave them dying in a locked warehouse for the rats to eat.

Those were the good old days.

But the Morelli boys were all dead now and the gang who had replaced them, those crazy Esteban spicks from Colombia, were people he'd just as soon leave alone, thank you. Because they were nuts.

It used to be, you'd pop a Morelli and another Morelli would pop you back. Or your uncle, if he was in the business. But fuck with the Estebans, boy, and they'd tear the arms off your children. Rape your daughter and leave a Coke bottle inside her. Set your mother on fire in the old folks' home. They had done all that and more.

Crime wasn't what it used to be. He'd drive cigarettes for Buster Brown here from now until doomsday before he'd get mixed up with the big stuff anymore.

Joey peered into the passenger side mirror as Hooks rolled past Dobson, NC, a dozen or so miles from the Virginia state line. 'Is that a tail?' he asked nervously. 'They've been following us for a while. Think it's the Feds?'

'Jesus Christ,' Hooks sighed. The temperature was in the nineties, the cab of the semi wasn't air-conditioned, and his hæmorrhoids were itching like a bastard. If Joey weren't the boss's son, he'd have hung him out the window by his balls.

'It's not the Feds,' Hooks said flatly. 'Feds would have pulled us over by now. They been behind us for ten, twelve miles.'

'Maybe they're waiting for us to cross the state line,' Joey said. Hooks slowed down and the car behind them drew closer. 'Look again, Joey,' Hooks said, deadpan.

Sticking his head out the window, Joey was inclined to think Hooks was right. For two reasons. One was that the car behind them was a Jeep, a yellow convertible. It didn't look like anything he ever expected to see the FBI in. The second reason was that the two men inside it were Chinese.

'Uh, I think I see what you mean,' Joey said, and both of them laughed. Joey looked back again, then pulled his head inside and said, 'Jeez, that driver's the fattest Chink I ever saw.'

'Eats his puffed rice, I guess,' Hooks said, and they laughed again. Neither of them paid attention to the fact that the Jeep clung doggedly behind them for the next hour.

'Gotta tap a kidney,' Hooks grunted as he pulled into a big Exxon rest stop on Interstate 81. 'Used to be I could go three states without a pit stop, but that goes with age.'

'I could stand a Coke myself,' Joey said. 'Get you something?'

'Nahhh,' Hooks said. He used the toilet, put a suppository up his rectum, filled the truck with gas, and pulled over to the parking area to wait for Joey.

Hooks squirmed on the seat, his posterior feeling as if a million fire ants were having a picnic inside. He gave the

296

semi's horn an angry blast. 'Get the fuck out here,' he screamed in the direction of the restaurant, knowing full well that Joey could not hear him, but doing it anyway just to vent his anger.

Then he saw something that, perhaps because of the heat or his irritation or the state of his hæmorrhoids, caused him a moment of concern. It was the yellow Jeep convertible with the two Chinks in it, pulling out of a spot in the waiting area.

Funny, he thought. They had not been at one of the gas pumps, and he hadn't seen either of them near the men's room. Maybe they had gone into the restaurant, but if they went in after Joey, why the hell were they out already?

He reached under the driver's seat and unhitched the clips that held a small shotgun, a sawed-off Lupo that could spray hard enough to kill three men in one blast. He held it in his hand as the Jeep moved around the parking lot. The two Chinks – God, the driver was a fat bastard – pulled into a parking spot, then backed out, and drove around the lot again. He put both hands on the Lupo as they passed the truck, but neither of them looked at him as they went by.

Hooks let down the gun, feeling a little embarrassed. The Chinks were a couple of tourists weaving around the lot, probably lost. Everyone knew they were the worst drivers in the world. But were they bad enough to raise the short hairs on a man who'd spent forty years with the mob?

I must be going buggy, he thought. *Hell, who wouldn't, with that blabbermouth kid sitting next to you, all the time wondering if the Feds are chasing us.* He didn't need this kind of aggravation on a day this hot. What he needed was to be home beside his pool, with a can of beer in his hand and an icepack on his piles.

He glanced at the truck's three mirrors again, but the Jeep was not to be seen. Nothing. Just a pair of dumb Chink tourists who were right now probably speeding west, on the wrong side of the road, into the face of eastbound traffic.

He replaced the shotgun. When he straightened up, he heard the truck door open. Joey slid into the seat with two cans of Coke and two chocolate bars.

'Where the hell you been?' Hooks growled.

'Sorry. I saw this video game I never played before. The House of Sinanju. It's a blast, Hooks.' He laughed.

Hooks was not amused.

'I guess I just kind of got involved with it,' Joey said apologetically.

Hooks cursed under his breath and started the motor. He moved the truck out on to Interstate 81, heading northeast toward the Maryland border.

After a while the suppository started to work and Hooks felt a little less grouchy. There was no sign of the yellow Jeep anywhere. The North Carolina troopers were far behind him. Even the kid wasn't talking so much. The day might not turn out so badly after all.

The scenery was pretty here. To the right lay the vast woods of the Shenandoah National Park. With luck they'd be back at the New Jersey warehouse before dark.

'Hey, Hooks, mind if I conk out for half an hour? I've been so up about this job, I haven't gotten any sleep for a couple of days.'

Hooks shrugged. 'Suit yourself. Use the bunk if you want.' He gestured with his thumb toward a deep shelf behind the seat.

'Is that what that's for?' Joey asked. 'Hey, there's even a blanket in there.'

Hooks rolled his eyes and sopped the perspiration off his forehead with his sleeve. 'Good thing,' he said. 'Wouldn't want you to freeze to death.'

Joey laughed good-naturedly and climbed into the cab bunk like a kid at summer camp. Within five minutes he was sleeping the kind of worry-free, comatose slumber attainable only by teenage boys.

Least he'll be out of my hair for a while, Hooks thought. *And quiet, for a change.*

The semi swerved momentarily as he looked up at an overpass in the distance and saw a car parked on it. A yellow Jeep convertible.

Slowly he took the Lupo from under the seat. As the speeding truck drew within a few hundred yards of the overpass he saw one of the Chinese men, the skinny one, stand up in the Jeep.

What the fuck . . . The crazy slope was as naked as a jaybird, Hooks observed, except for a towel or something around his dick, and he was holding up a bow at least twice as big as he was. Then he reached back behind him for an arrow.

That was when Hooks threw the Lupo into his right hand and stomped on the brake. But before he could fire, the windshield of the truck shattered and Hooks heard the soft *thwack!* of the arrow hitting his chest.

He looked down, gasping, at the quivering wooden shaft as his blood sprayed into his throat from the bellows of his lungs. Like its driver, the semi wheezed and shrieked as it skidded toward the embankment just below the overpass.

The naked Oriental lowered his gigantic weapon. Then he bowed to the dying man.

Hooks Aiello's last thought was that things sure had changed since the days of the Morelli boys. With his final breath his finger reflexively tightened on the trigger of the Lupo and it fired through the roof of the cab, inches from Joey DeSanto's face.

'Huh?' Joey mumbled fuzzily, sitting up. Then he saw, in rapid succession, the hole in the roof, a red beard of blood cascading down Hooks's chin onto his neck, the smoking barrel of the Lupo clutched in his hand, and the arrow still vibrating in the man's chest.

'Hooks! Oh Jesus God!' he screamed, vaulting over the cab bunk onto Aiello's inert body. The weight of Joey's fall broke the arrow and forced a fresh stream of blood out of the wound, but Joey was no longer paying any attention to the dead driver. He was looking out the windshield, and what he saw was a wall of concrete growing larger by the millisecond.

Sobbing and screaming at full throat, Joey straddled Hooks's paunchy carcass and pumped his foot on top of the dead man's covering the brake. At the same time he managed to downshift, stripping most of the gears, while muscling the wheel back toward the road.

'Stop, you fucker! Stop, oh, please stop, you *fucker*!'

The chant went on for several minutes until the big truck came to a standstill on the shoulder of the highway.

Joey's hands gripped the steering wheel as if he were trying to fold it in half. His knuckles were bone-white. Tears streamed uncontrollably down his face. There was a spreading dark stain on the lap of his jeans. His back was scraped. The broken arrow that protruded from Hooks's body had torn Joey's shirt and drawn blood.

Joey was not aware of any of these things. Feeling as if his body had been created from Jell-O, he crawled on all fours to the passenger seat, opened the door, and tumbled onto the pavement.

Cars and trucks whizzed by as if nothing were amiss.

He was killed by an arrow, *for God's sake*, Joey thought, and his hands started shaking again. He forced himself to breathe deeply a few times. This wasn't the place to fall apart. He had to get out of there fast, before the cops came and asked him to explain Hooks Aiello's puzzling condition.

He had to get to Nicky and his father. The family would know what to do.

Joey scanned the horizon once more for any sign of a roadside archer, but there was nothing. Nothing but cars and trucks and a dead man with half an arrow in his chest.

30

'Didn't you see nothing? Robin Hood steps out on Interstate 81, shoots a four-foot arrow into the guy sitting next to you, and you don't see *nothing*?'

'I told you, I was sleeping.' Joey wiped the tears off his face with the back of his hand, then fended off his brother's slap. 'Quit it, Nicky.'

'Quit it, Nicky,' he mimicked, slapping Joey again.

'Enough, enough,' Tony DeSanto said, waving them both down. He was pacing in front of the red leather desk in his study, his brow creased. 'It could have been you,' he said. 'It was supposed to be you.'

'Hey, relax, will you, Pop?' Nick poured himself a glass of scotch from the bar and leaned against it. 'The hit couldn't have been meant for Joey. He don't have no enemies.'

'*I* have enemies!' his father shouted. '*You* have enemies.' He strode over to the chair where his younger son was sitting and pulled him up. 'Go on, Joey. You've been through enough. Go watch TV.'

Joey shambled away. He wore no shirt, and the spot where the broken arrow had scraped him was bandaged.

'But don't leave the house,' his father added.

'I won't, Pop.'

Nick put away his drink. 'The leak had to come from the guy who lent me the truck,' he said after Joey had closed the door behind him.

DeSanto looked at his older son with fury in his eyes. Nick had directly disobeyed him by sending Joey along on the cigarette run. But this was no time for a family argument. There were other things to sort out first.

Joey had done the right thing. After he left the truck with Hooks Aiello's body in it, he walked for more than a mile down the highway, then thumbed a ride to the first roadside restaurant and called home to tell his father the bizarre details of Hooks's murder.

Since then the DeSanto organization had been working at top speed. The first thing Tony DeSanto did was to call Aiello's unsuspecting widow with the bad news. He expressed his deepest regrets at the death and said it was always untimely when a man of great honor died. He mentioned to the widow how proud he had been to know Dominic Aiello and then told her that when the police came, she was to tell them that Hooks had been retired for many years, but that recently he had been doing some part-time driving for a truck company in New Jersey. No, she did not know the name of the company.

Meanwhile, Nick called the owner of the company from whom he had borrowed the truck to tell him that he should act surprised when the cops arrived and told him that one of his trucks had been stolen.

'You didn't even know it happened until they told you,' Nicky said. 'You got it?' He listened to the answer and said, 'All right. Make sure that's the way it goes down. I'll make it up to you later.'

Then Tony DeSanto called a friend of the family in Virginia to send a car to pick up Joey at the highway restaurant and drive him home. Later he would arrange for some maintenance worker at the Virginia state police pound to wipe down the truck to make sure that none of Joey's fingerprints survived.

Security around the DeSanto home was tightened, and

around the city family members were put on alert to keep an eye on the Esteban gang.

From the first moment DeSanto had felt instinctively that the Colombian cocaine dealers were behind the killing. How many nights had they sat up, drugged on their own poison, dreaming up the most brutal way to kill Tony DeSanto's beloved younger son? There was no doubt in the Don's mind that Joey had been the actual target and Hooks Aiello just had the misfortune to get in the way of an errant arrow.

'Savages,' he said aloud in his den lined with unread but expensively bound books. 'Who but savages would use a bow and arrow?'

He closed his eyes for a moment and an expression of ineffable sadness cloaked his face as he thought of the brutal savagery of a bow-and-arrow attack that killed a man whose nickname had been won by disemboweling his enemies with a longshoreman's hook.

'But why?' DeSanto sat down heavily on a leather sofa. 'Why would the Estebans try to kill Joey now, knowing what we would do – what we must do – to them in return?'

He looked at his son. Nick's gaze was shifting around the room, looking for escape. 'You know,' DeSanto said.

Nick shrugged uneasily.

His father roared. 'Tell me!'

'Take it easy, okay?' He fiddled with his empty glass on the bar. 'We had a little run-in with them the other night,' he admitted, tapping a little tattoo with his glass.

'A run-in over what? Drugs?'

'Well . . . yeah.' He smiled boyishly. 'We hit one of their houses and copped their stash. No big deal. A few grand worth of coke, that's all.'

'So for a few grand worth of coke, you enrage the Estebans and send them off on a killing mission against your brother, whom you made vulnerable by sending off on a nickel-and-dime petty theft?'

'There you go again, blaming me for everything!'

'I told you not to involve Joey!'

'Joey's a big boy –'

'He is my son!'

'God damn it, so am I!'

Both men stopped shouting.

DeSanto rested his face in his hands. 'Nicky, Nicky,' he said softly.

Nick was indeed his son, he thought, in more ways than one. Nick belonged in crime; by his nature, he had no other option. But Joey was made of finer stuff. Joey could make something of himself, if he could stop hero-worshiping his older brother. Joey had a future.

'How much did you spend on the cigarettes?' he asked wearily.

'Twenty thousand.'

'It comes out of your own pocket,' DeSanto said. 'The Feds now have your cigarettes, and your money is lost. Don't look to me to bail you out. I did not authorize that job, and I will not pay for it.'

Nick sat silently, his seething anger betrayed only by the throbbing vein in his temple. 'Whatever you say, Pop,' he said finally, and stood up to leave.

'Where are you going?'

'The restaurant. Nobody's secured the place yet.'

'Be careful. No one lives forever.'

Nick DeSanto stood in the doorway and appraised his father coolly. 'Now you're catching on,' he said quietly.

By the time Nicky reached the Peyton Place, the dinner crowd had vanished, not an uncommon occurrence in some restaurants in Little Italy where late-night hanging-on was discouraged. Fat Frank and another man were standing guard outside the door when Nick pulled in front of the place.

'Who else you got around here?' he asked Fat Frank.

'A guy at each end of the block in a car. And Jerry's around out back.'

'All right, Fatso. Don't go to sleep. Keep your eyes open.'

'Right, Nicky.'

Ernie 'The Driller' Tullio was sitting at the far end of the bar drinking a Dr Pepper. Physically, Tullio was the biggest man in the DeSanto organization, dwarfing even Fat Frankie Lupone. The Driller was six foot six inches tall, weighed almost four hundred pounds, and had a head as smoothly bald as a billiard ball. Perched on top of his behemoth body, it looked like the cherry on top of a hot fudge sundae.

Tullio had been in the Marines – a rarity among the members of the DeSanto circle – until he had been discharged under other-than-honorable conditions four months into his second tour in Vietnam. The suspicion was that Tullio had murdered two of his officers along with a half-dozen civilians during the liberation of a Vietnamese village. The deaths of the villagers had not posed much of a problem, but it had been difficult for the armed services to explain to the families of the dead Marine officers that their loved ones had been killed in action by strangulation.

Both men had been found in their bunks with large and unmistakable fingermarks around their necks. But there were no witnesses – at least none who were willing to testify against Tullio – and since even the Marines couldn't convict someone on a suspicion, Tullio was allowed to resign from the Corps and no charges were ever filed.

To anyone who wondered how he came by his nickname, The Driller, he explained that it came from his days on the pro wrestling circuit. But the fact was that it reflected Tullio's unique specialty as a strong-arm enforcer with the DeSantos. In the trunk of his car he kept a fully charged portable electric drill with a flared carbide bit which he used on the kneecaps of people who had made the mistake of borrowing money from the DeSantos and not paying it back on time.

Only when Nick had slid onto the bar stool next to him did he notice anyone else in the bar besides himself and the massive Tullio. At the far end sat the same young guy who had been there a lot in the last few weeks. He was sitting in the corner near the door, talking to the manager.

'Hey, Salvo,' Nick shouted. 'Come here.'

The manager came down the bar and stood at attention before Nicky.

'Lean over. I don't want to yell.' When DeSalvo bent forward, Nicky asked, 'Who's that guy down there?'

'Name's Mike Hall. A friend of mine. He comes in a lot,' Salvo said. 'He's an okay guy.'

'Well, I don't want him around here tonight. Tell him to fuck off.'

Salvo shrugged. 'Okay. Let's just let him finish his drink.'

Nicky snarled, 'If I wanted him to finish his drink, I'd say let him finish his drink.' He stood up. 'I'll throw him out myself.' He stalked off angrily along the bar.

Miles saw him coming. It would be easy, he thought, to do it right now, to wait until DeSanto got within reach and then to crush his windpipe and get out the door before the gorilla at the end of the bar could even move.

But that was not the plan. The Oyabun had told him that one death would not be enough. He would wait. Wait, even though the thought of delaying his vengeance on his family's killers sickened him. Wait, and destroy them all.

Angrily he grabbed the brass railing that ringed the top of the bar and forced himself to center his breathing. Calm. Calm. Calm, he told himself. Be calm with this butcher of children. He will be dead a long time.

'Your name Hall?'

'That's right,' Miles said. 'Are you Nick DeSanto?'

'I didn't come down to chitchat,' Nicky said. 'I just want you out of here. We're having sort of a business meeting.'

Behind him, Sato, wearing a menial's whites and carrying a broom, came slowly through the swinging door that led to the kitchen.

'Sorry, I didn't know that,' Miles said. 'I'll finish my drink and be on my way.'

'Can't you take a hint? Why don't you just go and forget about the drink?'

'Because I already paid for it,' Miles said. 'So I'll finish it.'

'And suppose I ask my friend there' – he nodded in Tullio's direction – 'to come down here and ask you to go now, what would you say?'

'I'd say you're going to a lot of trouble to get me to leave my drink so you can pour it back in the bottle and sell it again.'

The two men's eyes locked for a few long seconds, and then Nicky laughed and said, 'You're okay, Hall.' He held out his hand and Miles shook it. 'You from around here?'

'Nope.' Miles offered no other explanation about his origins. 'I'm in New York looking for a restaurant to buy. I like this one.'

Nick laughed. 'I don't think it's for sale.'

'Most things are for sale, Mr DeSanto,' Miles said levelly.

Nick shrugged. 'How much you want to pay?'

'How much is the place worth?'

'Say a million bucks,' Nick said, smiling.

Miles smiled back. 'I can get a million.'

'Yeah? What do you do?'

'This and that.'

'I asked you a question,' Nick said.

'And I didn't answer it.'

Nick cocked his head at the stranger. 'You got a set of balls on you, you know that?'

'Not enough to hang around here after my glass is empty,' Miles said, rising. He saw Sato moving more quickly out of the bar area to sweep the main dining room. 'I'll be back later.'

'You do that,' Nick said. 'We'll talk about that million bucks.'

As Miles left, he nodded once to Sato. The tall Japanese nodded back.

'Those Estebans are totally out of control,' Nick said to Tullio. 'We rip off a little bit of their blow and they start playing cowboys and Indians on Aiello's belly.'

The Driller opened his mouth and wrinkled his lips in what passed for a smile. 'We was easy on them when we knocked off the drug joint. Maybe it's time to teach some of those spicks a lesson.'

'That'll have to wait,' Nicky said. 'The old man is pissed and he wants me to come up with the twenty G's for the cigarettes that the Feds got. Fuck that. Hey! Watch that broom, asshole.'

He snarled at Sato, who was sweeping close to their table in the far corner of the dining room. Sato smiled and nodded nervously, bowing over and over. 'Hokay, sorry, Mista Boss. Hokay. All right? Hokay. Mista Boss.'

'Where the hell do we get these coolies?' Nick picked up an ashtray and threw it at the kitchen boy. Without dropping his broom, the Oriental caught the flying glass disc in one hand, grinning.

'Christ,' Nick said. 'Anyway, I need to come up with some money fast. We got to do that truck deal. Right away.'

'I'll get hold of my nephew today,' the Driller said. 'We should be able to do it tomorrow night.' He looked down at

310

his hands as if surprised they belonged to him and began to crack his hairy knuckles.

'All right. I'm going to go with you.'

'I ain't going to steal anything, Nicky,' Tullio said with hurt in his voice.

'That ain't it,' Nicky said. 'I just want to see if anything out of the ordinary happens. If those goddam Estebans are hanging around. Just consider me backup.'

'Okay,' Tullio said.

Neither of them paid any attention to the coolie sweeper slowly working his way around the rest of the dining room. He might just as well have been invisible.

'What's the matter with Yoshio?' Miles asked as he looked across the living room of the apartment. The small Japanese bow-man sat in a black kimono, his hands folded in his waist, staring silently at a large golden candle that burned steadily only a foot before his eyes.

'He has taken a life,' Sato explained. 'He is saying prayers for the dead.'

Miles watched him for a moment. 'Then pray well,' he said softly, 'because there will be more.'

He looked back at the faces of the other three men around him. Mammoth Hiro was filled with bubbling life but ready, he knew, to sacrifice it for him in a moment. Koji, with his sweet child's face and the forbidden tattoos of an old soldier, would carve the Ronin's enemies to pieces with his samurai sword on command. He looked at Sato, his kyodai.

There was no bond stronger than the one which held Miles to Sato. Their months spent together, never leaving each other's side, had given both men a deep knowledge of the other's every shift in mood or thought. And now, Miles knew, Sato was suffering.

He was a man of pride, a great warrior, the Oyabun's

311

chosen successor, yet his role in the plan was to play an ignorant, grinning coolie, catering to thugs unworthy to wash his feet. If Miles had still hated him, he could not have devised a more cruel punishment for the man.

'Come, Sato,' he said gently, and led him to the shabby coffee table. 'So that we do not forget who we are.'

He took out the teacups and utensils, and in the early morning darkness of the city, performed the tea ceremony for his kyodai.

The Japanese accepted his bowl, turning it three times in his hands.

'What do you wish to say, my brother?' Miles asked gently.

Sato set the bowl down. 'I do not understand why you wait,' he said. 'We have all the opportunities now, because no one suspects us. Why do we not simply dispose of the two young men who brought tragedy to your house?'

The other men looked up. It was a question they too had asked themselves.

'Waiting is not an easy task. But endurance and humility, gambari, are attributes not easily won.'

'Your gambari is stronger than mine,' Sato said stonily.

Miles smiled. 'That is because I am fortunate enough to have an enemy with power over me.'

Sato bowed his head, but Miles handed him the bowl of tea again. 'This is the time for truth, not shame,' he said. 'Do you know the legend of the forty-seven ronin?'

Sato looked amused. 'Of course. Everyone knows that.'

'Not everyone,' Miles said mildly. 'I never heard it until a few months ago, and then it was in a play acted by children. But I understood the message.'

With his gaze he signaled for the others to gather around the small tea table. Even Yoshio halted in his prayers to listen to the Ronin.

'When the samurai disguised themselves as fools, they suffered the scorn of the same people who had once hailed them as heroes,' he said. 'Surely they must have wanted to take out their swords a thousand times and show their true skills to the mocking onlookers. But each time their pride threatened to burst from them they forced it away and waited.'

His voice lowered. 'They waited until they were inside the castle of the lord they had sworn to slay. And there they killed him and all his followers.'

Miles prepared another cup of tea and passed it to Koji. 'That is our plan,' he said.

Hiro blinked. 'To kill all of them? Are we enough to fight a war with so many?'

'Perhaps not,' Miles answered. 'But we are enough to start a war.' He passed the third cup to Yoshio. 'Today was the beginning. Yoshio began to topple the enemy castle when he killed one soldier in it. Now the DeSanto family believes that a rival clan, the Estebans, were responsible for that killing. They will punish the Estebans unjustly, and the Estebans will repay the injustice in blood. And so it will go on until both sides are decimated.'

'But the men who killed your sister and grandfather,' Sato said. 'Surely you will not leave your revenge to outsiders.'

'Oh, no,' Miles said. 'That satisfaction will be mine.'

He gave the last bowl to Hiro. 'Tomorrow is your day, my friend,' he said. 'Let us see if you can knock a few more stones out of the castle.'

The big man beamed. 'I am ready, Ronin.'

Sato looked down at the table.

'Gambari,' Miles said. 'Give me your endurance.'

Sato's jaw clenched. 'It is a difficult thing for me to give.'

'Perhaps, then, it is why you were chosen for this task.'

Sato was about to speak, but he restrained himself. He was a soldier. He would follow the orders of his superior. 'Yes, Ronin,' he said, and bowed.

31

'Sorry, Boss,' the voice said over the intercom from the compound's front gate. 'There's a cop here to see you.'

'Does he have a warrant?' Tony DeSanto asked.

'No, but he said you'd see him. His name's Halloran.'

DeSanto sighed. 'All right. Have somebody bring him up to the house.'

Halloran. Again.

Lieutenant Vincent Connor Halloran had been a thorn in DeSanto's side for twenty years. He had started out patrolling a beat in Little Italy, and when he had been promoted up the ladder, he was still one of the department's main men whenever any investigation had overtones of organized crime.

Not that he had ever been able to seriously damage the organization's operations. DeSanto's mob was too far-flung, too well connected for one cop – no matter how honest he was – to make a difference. But Halloran had been like a mosquito, always flitting about, always buzzing in their ears, always stinging, never deadly but always annoying.

It was Halloran who had been assigned in the spring to check out Nick and Joey's possible involvement in the Inn on the Park murders. He had been furious about the two DeSanto sons' airtight alibis, which included a sworn statement by a state court judge who said he had been with them all night at the Peyton Place.

Halloran was acquainted with the judge, a pompous, corrupt old man who had been acquitting mobsters for decades. He doubted that the man had ever set foot in the Peyton Place. Still, Halloran did not rage publicly about it. It would take more than an NYPD detective to rout the halls of justice. Instead he went about his business. Win some, lose some. This round went to DeSanto, but the fight wasn't over yet.

When Halloran came into the spacious, expensively decorated living room, DeSanto resisted the urge to offer him a bribe. The detective was wearing the same suit he'd been wearing the last time DeSanto saw him, at an arraignment hearing two years before. It was, in fact, the only suit DeSanto had ever seen him wear. Never much in the way of sartorial splendor to begin with, it was shiny in the seat and baggy in the knees and looked as if it had been willed to him by his father. There were sweat stains around the leather band of his snap-brim fedora, and his shoes were so worn that the outline of his toes showed through them.

Such a man was obviously not susceptible to bribery.

Besides, DeSanto had tried before and gotten a punch in the jaw for his efforts. Naturally, he couldn't press an assault charge under the circumstances; Halloran had won that round.

The cop could have been a rich man if he had accepted the offer to turn. Others had. But Halloran was different. Tony DeSanto had the feeling that somewhere deep down in the soul of this raggedy middle-aged man with the hangdog face and the stooped shoulders of the born plodder was a crazy idealist who genuinely hated the DeSantos and everyone like them.

And the feeling was mutual. If DeSanto could have removed Halloran from the planet without a lot of legal problems, he would. But a cop who had been hounding him for twenty years . . . it was too big a risk.

So they played their game of cat-and-mouse. Win some, lose some. But on the big scores DeSanto invariably won.

He smiled charmingly and gestured for Halloran to sit down as a manservant brought in coffee on a silver tray. To his surprise the detective accepted a cup.

'See this morning's paper?' Halloran asked without preliminaries.

'No. I dislike news. Sugar?'

Halloran shook his head. 'There's a story about a war brewing between your people and the Estebans.'

DeSanto chuckled. 'Where do the reporters dream up these things?'

'They didn't dream this one up. I leaked it.'

DeSanto clinked his cup into its saucer in annoyance. 'You must be insane,' he said. 'I could sue you for that.'

'But you won't, because it's true. I know you've got your guys out in full force ever since Hooks Aiello got plotzed by a bow and arrow.'

DeSanto clucked sympathetically. 'I was told of that. A shame. I had thought that Dominic was enjoying his retirement. What a tragic end.'

'Sure beats being fried in the electric chair.'

'Such bitterness, Lieutenant. It is bad for the spirit.'

'Unlike murder,' Halloran said.

DeSanto ignored him. 'To me, Dominic Aiello was always just a longshoreman. A pleasant man as I recall, even though we were not close. You think he was killed by these Esteban people?'

'It's obviously what *you* think,' Halloran said. 'That explains the tight security around all your places. But there was a report that there was a young man in the truck with Hooks and he escaped on foot. Some witnesses gave a description that sounds very much like your son Joey.'

DeSanto shook his head. 'That would not have been

317

possible. Joey is getting ready to go to college. He was here all day yesterday, packing his clothes.'

'I suppose you have the usual witnesses,' Halloran said.

'I wouldn't call it that.' DeSanto smiled charmingly. 'But yes, there were many people who saw Joey throughout the day. Tell me something.' He leaned forward, avidly changing the subject. 'If these people – the Estebans, whoever they are – committed this vicious crime, then why do you not go after *them*?'

'What makes you think I'm not?'

'Because you are not likely to find them here,' DeSanto said dryly. 'More coffee?'

'No. One is a hello. Two is a bribe,' Halloran said. 'I just don't understand why you're taking chances with Joey's life. If the Estebans want him, they'll get him.'

'Do you have children, Vincent?'

'No.'

'A mixed blessing,' DeSanto said. 'A little piece of you will live on. But they have their own minds. So we do what we can. Is that not so?'

'I think you should tell your kids to stay out of reach,' Halloran said. 'Not that I give a damn about them because I don't. I just don't want any gang war where innocent people are going to be hurt.'

'Like poor Dominic,' DeSanto said.

Halloran laughed bitterly. 'Hooks was about as innocent as Hitler. You ask me, I think he got what he deserved. But I think it ought to end there.'

DeSanto looked into his coffee cup. 'If only it could.'

'What?'

'I meant only that times have changed. In the old days, even the lowest thug would not kill a man with a bow and arrow.'

'Yeah,' Halloran said. 'Not when a meat hook was available.'

318

'You are impossible. This is harassment.'

'Oh, save your legal bullshit for all the judges you have in your pocket. When your people go on a rampage, none of them care who gets hurt. The cemeteries are packed with innocent people who got in your way. You know and I know that your sons killed those newlyweds in Central Park. And then killed the grandfather and dumped him in a Jersey landfill. You're a class act, DeSanto, you truly are.' He set his cup down so hard that it broke, spilling black coffee onto the white plush rug. 'I'm sorry about the china-ware,' he added angrily.

DeSanto laughed. 'You always play by the rules, don't you, Vincent?' He stood up and said in a stage whisper: 'That's why you're a loser.'

'Maybe. And maybe that's how I'm going to nail you. You *and* your kids.'

After Halloran left, DeSanto stared for a long time at the dark stain on the rug.

Ernie 'The Driller' Tullio picked Nick up a block from the Peyton Place in an old blue Ford a few minutes after 9 P.M. Tullio was wearing leather gloves and handed a second pair to Nicky.

'Is the car safe?' Nicky asked.

'Yeah. I stole it myself. And the plates too.'

'Good,' Nicky said. 'Let's hit it.'

While Tullio drove, Nicky took a large automatic out of his inside jacket pocket and checked it to make sure there was a shell in the chamber.

'What's that for, Nicky? You expecting trouble?'

'I don't know. I just want everything to go down the way it should.'

The traffic slowed them up and they were fifteen minutes late getting to the rendezvous in Brooklyn. It was a deserted side street in an industrial part of the old Red Hook section.

Tullio spotted the truck parked off the road in a parking lot.

They pulled into the lot, turned off their lights, and parked alongside the truck. The driver stuck his head out the truck's window and gave Tullio a nervous little wave. He was a short, husky man with thinning hair and a wide mouth whose lower lip hung open like a broken screen door.

'How you doing, Uncle Ernie?' he asked, his eyes flitting toward Nick DeSanto.

'Hey, Rocco,' the Driller grunted.

Rocco got out and walked, bobbing, toward Nick DeSanto. He did not know who his uncle's companion was, but understood instinctively that that was just as well. 'How you doing?' he repeated to Nick, bobbing more actively.

Nick nodded. His eyes were busy scanning the parking lot and the dark road for headlights or signs of movement. 'You got a full load?' he asked.

'Whole truck,' Rocco said. 'New color TVs. Maybe forty, fifty thousand smackers' worth. Zeniths and Panasonics.'

'I didn't ask for no fucking inventory,' Nick snapped. 'Let's get this show on the road, okay?'

'Okay, sure.' The depth of Rocco's bobs at this point threatened to upend him. 'And then you're gonna take care of me, right?'

Nick looked him over coolly. 'Sure.'

'Okay.' Rocco bobbed in gratitude. 'How we doing this?'

'I'm gonna have to hit you,' Tullio said matter-of-factly.

'Hit me? What for?'

'Hey, this is a hijacking, stupid,' Nick said. 'You didn't just give us the truck. We held you up at gunpoint. Two big niggers. Can you remember that?'

'Yeah,' Rocco said hesitantly.

'Yeah. So the two coons stopped you with a gun and forced you into this parking lot and then one of them hit you. Then when you wake up, you get in the car they left behind, and you go call the cops. And you don't hurry about it, you understand?'

'Yeah, yeah,' Rocco said nervously, bobbing in the direction of his uncle. 'You're not going to hit me hard, are you?'

'Naah,' Tullio said. 'You're family.'

He punched Rocco in the face. His nephew dropped to his knees in the parking lot. The Driller looked down at him for a moment, then bent over, and punched him again. Rocco fell to his side, moaned once, and then passed out.

Tullio checked him out again, then punched him in the stomach. Still not satisfied, he punched him again in the face, breaking his nose, then on the side of the head. He had his fist raised to punch Rocco again when Nick grabbed his hamlike hand.

'Hey, easy on that,' Nick said. 'You don't want to kill him. He's your family, remember?'

'Yeah, but I always hated the little fuck,' Tullio said.

With Tullio at the wheel, they left the area and headed toward the Verrazano Bridge that connected Brooklyn with Staten Island. Their destination was a garage once used by a man who had built custom cars as a sideline business. It now stood abandoned, but it was tall enough to accommodate a truck. All through the drive, Nick DeSanto had been watching the rearview mirrors, but there was nothing to see. He reached into his pocket and snapped on the automatic's safety. The trip had been a waste of his time.

Tullio backed the truck into the garage, then pulled down the garage's doors.

'Long as I'm here, open it up,' Nick said. 'I might as well get a look at it. Then you unload it and take care of getting rid of the truck, okay?'

'That's what you're paying me for, Boss,' Tullio said, taking off his gloves.

The Driller was strong. New television sets still in their packing cases were heavy and unwieldy. It took two men and sometimes a forklift to get them onto a truck. Only a muscular monster like Tullio could unload them by himself.

Tullio swung open the back doors of the truck and glanced inside. There was the sudden crack of flesh against flesh, and Tullio recoiled backward, holding his chin.

Nick drew the automatic, but he never had a chance to use it. A body, the widest human being he had ever seen, seemed to fly from the back of the truck. Barefoot and clad only in what looked like a diaper, the man soared in a perfect horizontal line with his arms stretched over his head like some cartoonist's vision of Baby Huey leaping tall buildings in a single bound.

When he landed, his back was to Nick, but the giant seemed to know someone was behind him. With reflexes faster than Nick DeSanto's trigger finger, he swung in a colossal arc and swatted Nick with the back of his hand.

It was like getting hit with a piece of two-by-four. Nick felt the lights around him dimming, and then he dropped face-first onto the floor, the gun skidding away from his outstretched hand.

'You big motherfucker, I kill you!' Tullio shouted, massaging his jaw. With a scream he charged across the floor of the garage, his arms raised over his head.

Hiro stood stolidly, facing him. When Tullio reached him, he crashed his big arms down, his forearms cracking against the sides of Hiro's head.

The Japanese did not flinch. In the next moment it was Hiro's arms that were moving, cracking against Tullio's ears. The Driller stumbled backward, and Hiro slammed the vast bulk of his body on top of him. With an *oof*, Tullio managed to get his arms around the Oriental, but he could feel the pressure building on his ribs. For the first time in his life he felt the taste of fear on his tongue.

Releasing his own bearhug around Hiro's chest, he used his free hands to grope behind his belt for a switchblade he kept clipped to the back of his trousers.

The sound of the knife clicking open sent a flood of relief washing through Tullio. Feeling triumphant, he ducked low and slid out from under the Chinaman's death hold. He started to bring the knife in his right hand out in front of him, but Hiro saw it, jumped forward, grabbed the arm, and bit Tullio's wrist so hard that an artery popped and began to spurt blood.

With a roar Tullio dropped the knife. Hiro picked it up and snapped the blade off in his big fingers.

'Now you got me mad,' the Driller growled. He jumped forward again, punching, but while the punches landed, the big Oriental could not be moved. The man seemed to be made of limestone.

Then Tullio remembered something from his Marine Corps days. He moved in close enough to lash out his foot and kick the big Chink in the balls. Just before the kick landed on target, Hiro took a deep breath. Then he smiled sweetly. The kick had had no effect.

Tullio backed up and looked at him. 'Don't you got no balls?' he shouted, panting from his exertions.

'Pull balls in,' Hiro answered politely. 'You try.' Then he launched his own attack on Tullio's groin. In that split second before his foot made contact with the thin-membraned organs between Tullio's legs, the Driller tried with all his might to suck up and pull his testicles in, but . . . Holy ShiiiIIIIIT . . . it didn't work.

Tullio crumbled to the floor. Moaning, he crawled toward Nick DeSanto's unconscious form and the automatic nearby. His body was over Nick's and his hand was reaching for the gun when Hiro hurled himself into the air like a gigantic beachball and flew across the garage at him, landing with a bone-crushing thunk.

Nick groaned beneath the weight of the two behemoths, then lapsed back into unconsciousness.

But Tullio had the gun. He spun onto his back to plug the big bastard.

Only with this last action did the Chinaman seemed to lose his pleasant demeanor. The look in Hiro's eyes suddenly suffused Ernie Tullio with a realization that accepting this job tonight had been one of the major mistakes of his life.

Hiro grabbed Tullio's hand with the gun in it and squeezed until the bones cracked. But before Tullio could scream about that, there was a worse pain as the Oriental landed with his knee on Tullio's shoulder.

With a wild shriek from its owner, the shoulder separated with a crunch of cartilage. Impelled by his reflexes alone, Tullio's thumb released the safety of the automatic and he squeezed the trigger. The bullet ricocheted off the walls of the garage, its report echoing like a roar.

The pain in Tullio's hand was terrible. The pain in his shoulder was worse. And then Hiro fell forward, elbow first, into Tullio's nose, and the Driller understood what real pain was.

The nose flattened in an instant, sheeting blood over Tullio's shirt. With eyes pigged in panic, he saw the three-hundred-pound Oriental rear up over him and then throw himself forward, landing square on Tullio's midsection.

And then there was only silence in the garage. Blood trickled from Tullio's mouth and ears, and his unfocused eyes stared sightlessly up at the ceiling. His crushed nose was just another slight mound in a tundra of bleeding flesh.

Hiro rose to his feet.

Nick DeSanto groaned. He tried to open his eyes but

couldn't, then squeezed them tightly shut and forced them open. At first he thought he was seeing double, then realized that he was looking at only one man, the fattest man in the world, wearing a loincloth, with the cheeks of his butt hanging out like two prize watermelons at a county fair.

Then he saw, on the middle of the cement floor, Tullio's obviously dead body.

'What the fuck . . .' he muttered as the fat man ran silently and with amazing speed from the garage.

Nick watched him go. Then he forced himself up off the floor, wincing as he held onto his bruised ribs. He walked unsteadily across the floor to where Tullio lay.

'Jesus H. Christ,' he whispered as with his toe he prodded the mass of bruised tissue that had once been Ernie 'The Driller' Tullio.

Then he limped out, clutching his side.

32

When they were summoned to an early afternoon meeting at the Peyton Place restaurant, they expected a lot of food, wine, and one of Tony DeSanto's rambling monologues on the honor of the extended criminal family.

But this time there was no wine. There was no food. There was only the tight-lipped and obviously irate don of the DeSanto family sitting at the head of the table with his son Nicky alongside him.

The restaurant was closed and several tables had been put together in the dining room so that the six men there could be comfortable. DeSanto got down immediately to business.

'We are at war,' he said. 'We have been attacked, and we must respond in kind.'

The men at the table glanced around at each other surreptitiously, looking to see if someone there knew just what the hell DeSanto was talking about.

They were all powerful men, the heads of the satellite mob families which orbited around the central DeSanto organization. There was Pronzini from Brooklyn and Avalone from the East Village. DeAndrea had come up from Staten Island and Madonna had come down from Harlem. Those four were sitting at the sides of the table. DeSanto and Nicky were on one end. At the other end was an elderly, white-haired man. Nobody looked to see if he understood what the day's problem was; they all knew that the old man was senile.

DeSanto spoke again. 'This time the Estebans have gone too far. They want to kill each other, that's fine. There are too many spicks in New York anyway.'

The lieutenants nodded their heads in sober agreement.

'But now they kill us,' he said gravely. 'And for that they will pay.'

'The rose will be plucked,' said the white-haired man at the other end of the table, and the others nodded, although none of them had the slightest idea what he meant.

The white-haired man was Giovanni Andalucci. He had beautiful false teeth which always seemed locked in a mirthful grin, and the spotted skin of a man about to die from cirrhosis of the liver. He was called the mob boss for the Bronx, but in reality all he had left of the operation was the very considerable drug action in the war-zone South Bronx, which he monitored from his Victorian mansion in Little Silver, New Jersey. The rest of the action in the Bronx was handled by the DeSantos themselves, who also maintained control over Manhattan, the richest province in the city's crime empire.

Andalucci was a first-generation Sicilian and one of the few links between the men at this table and the old forms of Mafia behavior and etiquette. In his home, guests were treated to homemade port wine and scratchy tenor recordings of Beniamino Gigli. While across the river and uptown, his men were turning eight-year-old black kids on to heroin – first shot free, boys, step right up – he was usually at his lavish home reminiscing about the days of real honor and lamenting the fact that today's young men did not have the character of those he had grown up with.

The truth, and each man around the table knew it, was that he was an ineffectual old fart who was only kept around because he had been Tony DeSanto's predecessor as *capo di capi* in New York and had peaceably passed the reins of leadership to DeSanto.

328

The men at the table thought he was kept on as a symbolic gesture and an expression of DeSanto's goodwill. None of them knew that Andalucci's peaceful retirement had been prompted by one of DeSanto's lieutenants getting in to see him and sticking a gun barrel in his mouth. The lieutenant vanished soon afterward, of course, and both Andalucci and DeSanto had let the story spread that the passage of power was just the civilized nod of a civilized old man to an equally civilized but more vigorous younger man. And the reason that DeSanto continued to include Andalucci in his inner circle had nothing to do with tradition or respect. As he had explained it to Nick, the old windbag still kept a lot of valuable connections to himself. At seventy-eight, Giovanni Andalucci knew how to stay alive.

The old man looked around the table at the other men there. He repeated: 'The rose will be plucked. And the rose will blacken with rot.'

He smiled. Nick DeSanto rolled his eyes.

There was silence for a moment and then Madonna, the boss of Harlem, spoke. As he talked, he kept looking down toward the table, as if he feared making eye contact with Tony DeSanto.

'The Estebans have not been threatening the Harlem area,' he said. 'They have their businesses and we have ours. They leave our numbers alone. Should we start bigger trouble than there already is?'

He looked across the table at the other lieutenants, who agreed but stopped themselves in mid-nod when Tony DeSanto roared, 'And what is bigger trouble than that they try to kill our children?'

He glared around the table and no one answered. But the look in all their eyes said: the Estebans have made no attack on *our* children, only on yours, and your kids probably brought it on themselves. But no one would say that. It fell to Nick DeSanto to respond.

'Pop, I think we've got to be double sure it *was* the Estebans.'

'What do you mean?' Andalucci croaked. 'You said the man was naked.'

'Yeah.' Nicky drummed his fingertips on the table. 'He was naked. That don't mean he was an Esteban. I didn't see his face.'

'You know anybody else would send a naked fat man running around a warehouse killing people?' Tony DeSanto snapped testily at his son.

'*Loco in cabasa*.' Andalucci tapped his forehead. 'It could only be the spicks. Plus the arrow. Crazy. Very crazy.' He stopped and sipped some ninety-proof vodka from a silver flask he kept in his inside jacket pocket. The flask was empty. He held it upside down. Nothing came out. He looked around the room helplessly.

'Mr Andalucci, Pop, I'm only saying it might not be so. It doesn't make a lot of sense. I was right there, you know? I was knocked out. If the Estebans wanted to kill me, it would have been the easiest thing in the world.'

'This fat man jumped on you, hurt your ribs, maybe he thought he did kill you,' his father said stubbornly.

At the other end of the table Andalucci was waving his arm over his head, trying to signal a young Oriental busboy who had just come out of the restaurant kitchen.

'The guy could have broke my neck, just like that.' Nicky snapped his fingers. 'He could have done to me what he done to the Driller. But he didn't. And look at Joey. Maybe the arrow wasn't meant for him. Maybe it was for Hooks.'

The busboy had taken the silver flask from Andalucci and was taking it to the bar to refill it.

'Kill Hooks Aiello?' DeSanto shouted. 'Why? Why would anybody want to kill him, an old fool with a diseased ass? Why would somebody want to kill Tullio? Who cares about such garbage?'

'When the aphids feed on the dead rose, the garden must be pruned,' Andalucci said sagely.

'Oh, Jeez.' Nick buried his face in his hands.

'Respect,' Tony DeSanto admonished in a whisper.

Nick reluctantly straightened up, locking his hands together on the table in front of him. But the damage had already been done. The door had been opened a crack by one of DeSanto's own sons, and the other mob men, who were happy to live and let live with the Estebans, began to talk slowly, one after the other.

DeAndrea from Staten Island said, 'Perhaps, Don DeSanto, before we go to war, it would be best if you were to speak to the Estebans. Find out if this is their work. They will not be able to deceive one of your wisdom. And if it is so, then we will go to the mattresses as in the old days.'

The other men at the table nodded, and as Tony DeSanto looked from one face to another, his own expression one of cold contempt, he saw that he had already lost the argument. Best to put a good face on it.

'I do not know why the Estebans would choose to start a war with us in so strange a manner,' DeSanto said. 'But I agree. Your proposal is sound.'

The Oriental busboy put the filled flask again in front of Andalucci. The old man grabbed it and slurped from it happily.

'I propose to meet with Rodrigo Esteban personally,' DeSanto said. 'We will talk of the responsibility for these attacks. We will talk about reparations.'

'What reparations?' Nick said. 'The fat guy didn't touch the video equipment. He even left the truck.'

Giovanni Andalucci squinted ominously at Nick over the neck of his silver flask. 'Who is this young man?' he wheezed.

Tony DeSanto sighed. 'He is my son, Don Andalucci,' he said patiently.

'Oh.' Andalucci sipped again from the flask.

'I will report back to you at another meeting as soon as I have information from the Estebans,' DeSanto said.

The men around the table nodded. Andalucci burped.

The busboy vanished into the restaurant kitchen.

'DeSanto is going to meet with Rodrigo Esteban.'

As he used the curbside telephone three blocks from the Peyton Place, Sato looked behind him to make sure he was not spotted.

Back in the apartment, Miles said, 'Good. I've been checking old newspapers, and I found out that the Estebans are big drug dealers.'

'If the two men reach a compromise, there will be no war,' Sato said.

'Then we'll force one.' Miles hesitated for a moment. 'You will be the instrument, Sato.'

He could almost feel Sato's relief over the phone. 'I am ready, Ronin.'

'It will not be pleasant.'

'I will do as you say,' Sato answered without hesitation.

33

Under a hand-carved wooden crucifix mounted on the wall and before an out-of-focus picture of his wife and four children on the end table, Rodrigo Esteban was being serviced in his waterbed by two fifteen-year-old girls who found the soft, pudgy Colombian physically repulsive but would and did do anything for a few grams of his cocaine.

One of the girls, a slim blonde with full, firm breasts, looked up at him as the bedside telephone rang. Esteban shoved her back down roughly with his hand.

'You want blow, you do blow,' he growled and waited a moment until he was convinced the girl had seriously resumed her duties before he lifted the receiver.

'*Hola. Si.* How many times I got to tell you not to call when I got my two knob-a-job cuties here?' He looked down and watched the girls, their heads side by side as they worked him over in tandem.

'Wait,' he snapped into the phone. 'What?' He sat up, pulling away from the two girls. 'You sure it was Tony DeSanto?' He listened, then said, 'What that bastard want with me?'

He listened again and said, 'What papers? I don't read no papers, I don't know nothing about no war.'

Finally he sighed. 'Okay. I meet with him. But not at his house. You pick a restaurant or someplace. Now I get dressed and meet you downstairs. Get a couple of tough guys to go with us.'

He hung up the telephone and, ignoring the girls who were kneeling on the bed waiting for instructions, got up and padded heavy-footed across the room to a built-in closet that covered an entire fifteen-foot wall. Half of it was filled with linen suits in light pastel shades, the other half with dark silk shirts. A double over-head rack that ran the length of the closet contained more than seventy-five pairs of shoes.

As he stood before the closet trying to decide what to wear, the blonde girl spoke to his back.

'Mr Esteban?'

'Whatchoo want?'

'Will we still get our . . . you know, our coke?'

Esteban pulled a coral-colored suit from the rack and hung it on a hook on the wall alongside the closet door, then riffled through the shirts before settling on a red one.

'I didn't get off,' he said crankily.

'Please, Mr Esteban. We'll make it up to you.'

Esteban considered. It took time to button a shirt, after all. 'Okay,' he said. 'I tell you what. Come over here and do me while I get dressed. You do it right, I take care of you.'

The two girls clambered from the bed and knelt in front of Esteban, and worked on him as he carefully, lovingly put on his clothing.

As he slid his feet into his soft patent leather oxblood loafers, Esteban looked down at the tops of their heads and said, 'You the future of America. Eating *chorizo* for drugs.' He laughed harshly. 'The future of America. You. And me.'

Esteban thought about the summons from DeSanto as he was driven uptown in the back of a four-year-old Lincoln Continental. He sat alone in the back seat; his two body-guards were crammed in the front seat along with the driver.

It was true, he did not like the DeSantos, and he coveted

the money they made by owning the best crime territory in the world, Manhattan. He thought the way they ran their business was out-dated and inefficient. That was true. And if he were to be perfectly honest, it would not have grieved his heart terribly if Anthony Buonasera DeSanto and both his sons were to be covered with dogshit and stuffed into the nether cavity of a syphilitic whore.

But fight a war with them? *Madre mia*, no. And he would like to know just who gave them that stupid idea.

The DeSantos had enough men and muscle to wipe out a small country if they wanted to. They had been in the United States for over sixty years, the Estebans for barely five. Even with a direct pipeline to the purest cocaine in the world, the Esteban operation barely netted enough after payoffs, payrolls, theft, lawyers' fees, and the not inconsiderable funeral expenses, for Rodrigo Esteban to live like a moderately wealthy man. Moderately – nothing like the life-style of Tony DeSanto.

And Esteban faced much greater danger. The men who were his lieutenants, including nine of his brothers, lived barely above subsistence level and were frequently killed by rival Colombians, ordinary muggers, and sometimes by their own customers.

There was a lot to learn in America. The hardest thing, it seemed, was how to stay alive when the only people you could trust were brainless relatives with huge amounts of cocaine stuffed inside their mattresses. And you couldn't trust them too far, either. Of his nine brothers, he knew that four of them actively coveted his position and would be willing to put a knife in his belly at any time.

He was sure Tony DeSanto had no such problems. The Italians were light-years ahead of the Estebans.

His three bodyguards preceded him into the restaurant on York Avenue near 75th Street. Esteban saw Tony DeSanto sitting alone at a table in a far corner of the room, then noticed three men at the bar, obviously DeSanto's bodyguards, staring at him with hatred in their eyes.

In Spanish Esteban said to his men, 'Sit at the bar. Watch those three turds. If they make a move, kill everybody. Except, naturally, me, you *stupidos*.'

DeSanto rose to meet him as he approached the table alone. The Mafia don was wearing a dark blue pin-striped suit with a white shirt and dark tie, and Esteban suddenly felt garish and out of place in his pastel linens and silks, like a peasant in his best rags going to the palace to see the king.

The men shook hands. DeSanto offered Esteban an already poured glass of wine.

'Thank you, senor.' He took the glass in his sweaty hand and added, 'Bless your holy name.' He downed the glass in one gulp before the thought even occurred to him that the wine might be poisoned.

'I want to thank you for meeting me, Mr Esteban,' DeSanto said. 'I hope this meeting will benefit both our families.'

Esteban nodded nervously, waiting for the burning to begin in the pit of his stomach. 'Sure thing,' he said.

'I will get right to the point. In the past few days two of my men have been killed. I think these men were killed in unsuccessful attempts to kill my two sons. I have asked myself over and over again: who would try to harm my boys, my family? I have no solution to this problem. And then the newspapers talk about a war between your people and mine, and I think, Is there such a war? Must there be? And I think too that maybe it is time to call my old friend, Rodrigo, and ask him what he thinks of all this.'

DeSanto watched the Latino's eyes carefully. He prided himself on being able to read a lie. If this overstuffed sausage was lying to him, he would be dead before he ever put his fat ass back into his automobile.

But DeSanto knew instantly that Esteban was clearly telling the truth as he sputtered, 'No war, no war. We kill nobody, Senor DeSanto.' He shook his head for emphasis.

'One of my men was killed with a bow and arrow in Virginia. Another was crushed to death by a big man inside a garage,' DeSanto said calmly.

Sweat began to bead on Esteban's forehead. 'No, no,' he said again. He raised his hands and essayed a sickly smile. 'Bow and arrow? My men would shoot themselves in the foot. We kill nobody, sir, and we harbor no ill will to you and your sons.'

'It was my understanding that there might be bad blood between your group and one of my sons. Some kind of trouble over a little bit of white powder,' DeSanto said.

Esteban said, 'May I have more wine, please, sir?'

As DeSanto poured, Esteban said, 'There was a little difficulty over some of our product in one of our houses. But it was not a serious thing. It was the kind of thing young people do. It was an annoyance. It was not a thing that we go to war about.'

Again he drained the wineglass in one long gulp, and this time DeSanto filled it again without being asked.

'I believe you, Rodrigo. That is why I sought out this meeting, so that we could talk to each other and stop difficulties before people who wish us ill might push us both into corners.' He paused for a moment. 'Have you heard of anyone who might harbor a grudge against me or my family?'

Esteban shook his head again. 'I have heard no such thing. Under your wise leadership, senor, peace reigns in this city. But I will tell my men to keep their eyes and ears open. I promise you, if we hear so much as a word spoken against you in anger, I will report it to you.'

He was not lying. DeSanto knew that as surely as he knew that night followed day. He nodded, then said, 'I thank you

337

for your good wishes, friend Rodrigo, and I appreciate your offer of help.'

He stood, indicating that the meeting was over. Esteban was so happy to have survived that he did not even consider that he was being dismissed like a child. He rose too, shaking DeSanto's hand vigorously, then left the table.

As he left the restaurant, surrounded by his bodyguards, he whispered a prayer to the Virgin for delivering him from a war in which he surely would be crushed like a bug.

Peace, he said in his prayer, was his mission, his one overriding goal. Peace would give his family room to grow; peace would enable them to fill their treasuries to hire new men; peace would allow him to sleep at night without fear of his life. And then, when he had reaped all the benefits of peaceful growth, Rodrigo Esteban would rip the heart out of that arrogant donkey turd, DeSanto, and his two cowboy sons and every living member of his family. Amen.

The farther his car moved away from the restaurant, the better he felt. He was absolutely expansive by the time the car turned onto his street in the West Fifties, regaling his men with his account of how he had told DeSanto that the Estebans had started no war, but if one started, they would rip the hearts out of the DeSanto family and the old man had been so frightened that he had sued for peace.

'He done everything but kiss my ass in that restaurant,' Esteban said. 'Them dagos got no *cojones*, no stomach for a fight.' By the time the car parked, he had almost convinced himself that this was truly the way the meeting had gone.

He felt good. Maybe he would invite those two junkie girls back to do him again. It was a night for celebration.

As they always did, his two guards walked with him into the old brick building where his apartment took up the second and third floors. He whistled as he walked up the steps to his apartment door, but the whistle turned dry in his

338

mouth as a young man stepped out of the shadows of the hallway.

'Mr Esteban?'

Esteban snapped his head around but his two *stupido* body-guards were not behind him, not on the stairs. Where had they gone? Who was this guy?

'I'm Miles Haverford. I work for Mr DeSanto. Something came up right after you left the meeting, and he would like to talk to you again.'

'We just talk a lot,' Esteban said.

'This is something new. It just came up, sir. Mr DeSanto knew you'd be interested in it. Please. It's very important.'

And because the man had said 'please', Esteban knew there was no danger involved and even if he would rather be climbing into bed with a couple of teenagers, that would wait. He could be gracious, too. He would favor DeSanto with yet another meeting.

He nodded and Miles said, 'It's not far. We can take my car.'

Miles parked his car on West Street not far from Greenwich Village.

'Hey, where is this place?' Esteban said.

'It's one of our businesses. A meat-packing plant,' Miles answered. 'Mr DeSanto has an office inside.' He came around the car and opened the door for Esteban. 'It's sort of a place where the police can't bother him. You know how that is.'

'Ah. I understand.' Esteban clambered from the car.

Miles pushed open a side door to the plant. The overhead lights were all on. There were big porcelain tables lining one whole wall, with flecks of red flesh dried on them.

They walked past the tables into a chilled meat-storage room, where huge sides of beef hung on hooks. Esteban exhaled noisily. He loved to see his breath in the cold. Until moving to New York, he had never once experienced that. Then the cold bit through his linen suit and he shuddered. If it were anybody else leading him through this place late at night, he thought, he might be nervous, but this kid obviously was no Mafia guy. He looked more like a college kid.

'The office is right up there,' Miles said, pointing ahead of them as they left the meat room.

There was a glass cubicle before them, but it was dark.

'Hey, there ain't nobody –'

Esteban got no chance to finish the sentence because he saw a flicker of movement off to his right. He wheeled around, away from Miles.

Sato came out of the shadows. He was dressed in a white karate gi, and there was a white sash around his forehead. His feet were bare.

Behind him, Miles said, 'Number three. We will have our war.'

'What the fuck is going on?' Esteban shouted. He spun around toward Miles, but the young man was gone.

It was a trap. He had set enough of them himself to know one when he saw it. With surprising speed for someone who seemed so soft, Esteban hit the concrete floor and rolled. As he did, he pulled a small pistol from the holster under his armpit. He came up into a crouching position, the gun aimed at the apparition in white who had come from the shadows, but before he could fire the gun, or even level it, it was kicked from his hand. It clattered faraway into the darkness of the warehouse.

Miles had walked away because he did not want to see it, but he could hear it even in the far corner of the warehouse. There was only one scream and then there were dull thuds, followed by sharp cracks, and then the deep, heavy sound again of soft flesh being struck over and over again, without discernible rhythm. It was the same sound Miles had heard once in his life before at an art festival, when he had watched a young potter slapping her hands against a lump of wet clay, forming it into a bowl.

Finally Sato's voice rang out. 'It is finished, Ronin.'

Miles walked back slowly, reluctantly. When he saw Esteban's body, he thought that he would be hard-pressed to think of something worse than dying at Sato's hands.

What remained of Rodrigo Esteban was something like a Ziplock bag filled with liquid. The bag was leaking from the ears, nose, and mouth. His abdomen was curiously misshapen, and his arms and legs were splayed out at strange, acute angles to each other. His joints appeared to have been pulverized. When Miles leaned forward to touch the man's chest, his hands sank into the flesh as if it were a wet sponge.

For a moment Miles was forced to suppress a feeling of revulsion. This man, for all his sins, was not his enemy; he was only a tool, a part of the plan. But the plan had to be followed. The lives of his men depended on that.

He looked up and saw Sato's green eyes staring at him with unspoken questions. There was an expression in them Miles had never seen before – an ineffable mixture of sadness and disgust at the butcher he had become, and Miles was overcome with sympathy for his friend.

'I know this is distasteful to you, Sato,' Miles said softly. 'You are a warrior, not a murderer. This death – and the others – are part of my ka, not yours.'

The pain did not leave Sato's eyes, and Miles hesitated a moment, then took a handkerchief from his pocket, and dipped it into the blood that was puddling below Esteban's feet. He swiftly began to paint in blood on the concrete floor. First a circle. Then inside it, some curved lines. When he was done, he stood up, looked down at the crude drawing and nodded his satisfaction. Sato was glancing at him quizzically.

'Is that wise, Ronin-san?' he asked.

'The DeSantos will know they had nothing to do with Esteban's death. Perhaps it is time to give them something else to worry about.'

Miles looked levelly at Sato, trying to hide his feelings, but the young Japanese was able to read the message in Miles's eyes. Miles had painted the blood symbol to relieve Sato of the sole burden of Esteban's terrible death. Now the responsibility for it lay with all of them.

Sato stepped forward and touched Miles's shoulder. 'You are my brother,' he said. 'My kyodai. Your ka and mine are the same.' He looked back at the dead man. 'I have no regrets.'

34

Antwan Martin Luther Jackson pushed open the steel doors of A-One Meats at six the next morning.

That was his first tipoff. The doors were supposed to be locked. When he had been hired as janitor two weeks before, he had been told that he had the only key, so if any sides of beef were found missing or if any of the office equipment was taken from the glass room, he, Antwan Martin Luther Jackson, would personally pay for the theft with his tongue: it would be ripped out of his head like the pull-tab on a can of beer.

That admonition, plus the fact that the man who hired him wore a shoulder holster with a .45 the size of a Pershing missile inside it, might have discouraged Jackson from taking the job if it weren't for the fact that the pay at A-One Meats was a lot better than it was at McDonald's and if he didn't settle into a *real* job before the week was out, he was going to have to go back home to Ebbetts Hill, Alabama.

His mother had strapped eighty-seven dollars – enough for busfare plus lunch and dinner at the Post House restaurants on the bus route – onto his chest with tape and had made Antwan promise not to take it off, not ever, not to wash, nor to fool around with loose women, not ever, until he had another eighty-seven dollars in a bank somewhere because she didn't want her boy stuck in New York City with no way home.

Jackson had promised her he would keep the money

taped to him and he had, despite the fact that he was living in a bug-infested room near Times Square and getting pimples from a steady diet of Big Macs, large fries, and strawberry shakes.

It really wasn't the New York he had expected to find.

But A-One Meats was a step up, at least. When he accepted the key to the steel doors from the man with the .45, Jackson had an image of himself in a nice place sometime in the not-too-distant future, maybe a little house with a nice girl in it to get him his supper and warm his bed. A nice girl, not like that damned Emma Mae Watts, who looked so sweet even though she was screwing three different guys besides him, including Tyrone Walker, who went around telling everybody about it.

Oh, Emma Mae put on a good show about it all right, crying and carrying on, saying she wasn't really a whore or nothing, she just wanted to get out of Ebbetts Hill so bad and the guys she did it with gave her some money and one thing done led to another. But she never took no money from Jackson, did she, never even asked for it, even though a couple of dollars from him might get her out of Ebbetts Hill faster and she would have taken Jackson with her, on account of she loved him so much and that was the proof of it, that she didn't ask him for none of his money, but maybe someday he might give her some out of the kindness of his heart.

But Jackson instead had shown her just what he thought of her damned whoring by getting out of town himself before he felt obliged to kill Tyrone Walker, who was not a bad person, really, and was also the best pool player in Ebbetts Hill. So he had come to New York and he would show Emma Mae Watts just who belonged in Ebbetts Hill and who didn't. He was going to make a big score and live like a king in silk suits with diamond rings on his fingers and he would send her pictures to prove it and she could whore her ass off for all he cared.

Except the door to the meat packing plant was open.

'Sheeeeit,' Jackson said under his breath. But inside the lights were on and none of the cutting tables had been knocked over, so he felt better at once. Probably some of the bosses had come in early to do some of their strange business.

'The bosses' meant any of a number of mean-looking men who strolled into the plant. As far as Jackson knew, they had nothing to do with meat packing. They would walk through the cold room, where the sides of beef were stored, pulling their suit jackets close around them, scared to death that they might accidentally brush against one of the bloody carcasses.

Jackson always wanted to laugh when they did that, but of course he kept his laughter to himself because every one of those bosses carried a gun and every one of them looked as if he was just dying to use it on a skinny black kid with a broom in his hands.

It didn't take any genius to realize that A-One Meats was a front for whatever the real business of the bosses was. That had become clear when Jackson had received his second work instruction. The first one had been not to steal anything or else. The second had been that if he ever came in and found something 'not right' – that was the phrase the man with the .45 had used, 'not right' – that Jackson was never, under any circumstances, to call the police.

'What do you mean, "not right"?' Jackson had asked.

The man with the .45 had slapped him upside the head for that, so Jackson assumed it meant in case the place got broken into. The man had given him another number to call instead of the police.

'But it's got to be an emergency, got it?' the man with the .45 said. 'If it's not an emergency . . .' He poked two massive fingers smelling strongly of pepperoni into Jackson's mouth and grabbed his tongue.

Jackson nodded that he understood perfectly.

So he had taped the emergency telephone number to his chest just below his eighty-seven dollars of traveling money, and had gone to work. Who knew? Maybe a job in a place like this might lead to the big score he wanted, just to wave it in front of Emma Mae Watts's nose.

'Anybody here?' he called out tentatively. The bosses wouldn't like him talking to them, but he had to at least locate them. The place seemed too quiet. When the bosses came around, they were always talking and yelling at each other.

Maybe they were all in the office, Jackson thought. Maybe they were so quiet because one of them was on the phone. He walked through the cold room to find out if they were there.

But just when he saw that the lights in the glass office were out, he noticed the body on the meat hook and screamed.

The body didn't belong to any of the bosses he had seen, but it was a man. Or at least he thought it was a man. It had on a man's clothes, even though there did not appear to be any shoulders inside them. The figure was, in fact, a huge pyramid of flesh. The face was completely white. The arms looked like Popeye's – skinny at the top but the bulging forearms and fingers so swollen that they had ruptured at the fingertips and two pools of blood had coagulated on the floor below the enormous dangling burst sausages of fingers.

It was the same with the thing's legs. The calves were so big that the white linen trousers were stretched tight from the knees down. Blood still leaked from one patent leather shoe.

But the strangest thing was not the body at all. On the floor nearby, someone had drawn a picture with the blood. After his initial bout of screaming, Antwan Martin Luther

Jackson had examined the drawing with some curiosity.

Sheeeit, he thought. After something like this, you'd expect a message or something, at least a 'fuck you.' He had read somewhere once that some Hollywood movie star was found murdered with a picture of a dick and balls carved into his stomach with a razor blade.

But this?

The blood drawing was a circle and inside it was something like the curlicue on the top of a Dairy Queen. If that didn't beat all, Jackson thought. Somebody turns a guy to hamburger, hangs him on a meat rack, and then draws ice cream cones on the floor with his blood.

Fuck New York, he thought. Fuck the big score. Fuck getting even with Emma Mae Watts. He was going back to Ebbetts Hill, where if folks were going to kill you, at least they had the decency to use a gun.

He left his key to the front door on the desk inside the glass-walled office, then walked outside to a pay phone, ripped all the tape off his chest, and dialed the emergency number he had been given in case something was 'not right'. Something was not right, all right.

'What?' the voice at the other end answered angrily.

'There be a dude hanging on a meat hook at the A-One,' Antwan Martin Luther Jackson said. 'And you can take this job and shove it up your white ass.'

He hung up and walked straight to the Greyhound Bus Terminal.

35

Enrique Esteban stripped off his cotton print shirt and tossed it into a wastepaper basket next to the dresser in his brother Rodrigo's gold-walled bedroom. He took a silver silk shirt from the wall-length closet, put it on, smoothed the soft fabric with his hands, and turned to his eight brothers, who were sitting around the edge of the king-sized water bed.

They were passing around a reefer the size of a Bill Cosby cigar. Through the closed door of the bedroom could be heard the screaming wails of what seemed like a whole schoolyard of children and the shouts of their mothers to hold the noise down.

Enrique opened the door a crack and shouted, 'Shut up with the noise or we bust your heads, okay? We doing business in here.' He slammed the door shut and turned to face his eight brothers. Then, because he had seen a businessman once in a movie do the same thing, he began to walk back and forth around the bed as he lectured the other men.

'Rodrigo's dead,' he said. 'We gotta face that.'

He looked at their faces, but their only interest seemed to be in the joint they were passing around. The heavy marijuana smoke hung in the bedroom like bug spray in a swamp.

Finally Antonio, the next eldest, squinted through the haze and spoke. 'How you so sure Rodrigo is dead?'

349

'Because those two dopes that was with him got their heads bashed in,' Enrique shouted with an explosion of hand gestures.

'Some bodyguards, huh?' one of the other brothers croaked between tokes, setting up a chain reaction of wild giggling among the men.

'Maybe they was mugged,' someone else offered.

'They wasn't mugged,' Enrique explained patiently. 'They had money on them when they came to. Only Rodrigo was missing.'

'What time is it?' the youngest brother asked.

'One o'clock.'

'Rodrigo missed his blow job. He got to be dead.'

The brothers laughed so hard that the bed squealed.

'Yeah. Funny,' Enrique said, obviously not amused. 'Your brother's laying dead in a rathole someplace, and you're laughing.'

Antonio bounded off the bed like a rocket, his mouth suddenly twisted in anger. 'Yeah, I'm laughing, Enrique,' he said, furiously poking a finger at his elder brother's face. 'You know something? I hope you right. I'm glad that no-good shit's dead. You talk about ratholes. Want to see a rathole? Come to my apartment, that's a rathole. Maria and the kids, they got to fight off the rats with a broom, while Rodrigo lives here like God Almighty. Look at this.'

He flung open the doors to Rodrigo's closet.

'*Dio mio*,' the youngest said. 'Such shoes.'

One by one the brothers slid off the bed and drifted toward the closet with its riches.

'Fifteen suits. The *porco* got fifteen suits.'

'Not counting the one he was wearing when they offed him.'

'I ain't got one suit.'

'These shirts are silk. He got five pink silk shirts.'

'I don't like pink.'

350

'What color you like, Paulo? He got every color.'

'Got anything in a 15 neck?'

'Lemme look.'

'Hey, Enrique! Rodrigo don't need these no more, right?'

Enrique closed the closet door grandly. 'Later,' he said. 'Now we talk business.'

The brothers muttered in dismay. Paulo tried to stuff a pair of shoes into the seat of his jeans.

'With Rodrigo gone, we got to have a new boss, a new head of the family,' Enrique said. 'That's me.'

'Sez who?'

'Yeah,' Antonio yelled. 'How come you get to be boss?'

'Because I am the oldest,' Enrique shouted over him.

The room palled into silence.

'The last boss was a shit,' Antonio grumbled. 'He keep everything for himself.

'Things will be different now. With me it'll be share and share alike.'

Eight pairs of eyes swiveled toward the closet.

'This place will be our new headquarters. For the war.'

'What war?'

'You think them DeSanto wops are going to stop with Rodrigo?'

There was silence.

'Well, do you?'

Someone coughed.

'What make you think the DeSantos offed Rodrigo?' Antonio asked, relighting the joint.

'*Madre Dio*, who else? Yesterday he go to meet with Tony DeSanto, then he disappear. What you think, he join the Moonies? Of course they kill him. We cut into their business, so they steal our stash. Now they want more. They want to see the Estebans dead. All of us.'

Enrique paused for a moment to let his words sink in.

'You want to live in this crummy town?' he shouted. 'Then you got to fight. You got to fight or die. That's all there is.'

Paulo cleared his throat. 'How . . . uh, how we going to fight the DeSantos?' he asked timidly. 'They got about a million guys.'

'With *cujones*,' Enrique said, grabbing his crotch. 'We don't wait for them to come wipe us out with our families in our homes. We attack first. We surprise them. How many guns we got?'

'Sixteen handguns, two Tommies,' Antonio said.

'How much ammunition?'

'Not much, but I can get what we need.'

Enrique smiled. 'Good, Antonio. You are with me, then?'

The brothers roared their support.

'War!'

'We going to kill them wop pigs!'

'We teach them some respect!'

Enrique flung wide the closet doors. 'Share, my brothers!' he shouted magnanimously.

As they sprinted toward the closet, stripping off their clothes, he warned them: 'Don't tell nobody about we going to hit the DeSantos, understand?'

'You got it,' Antonio said, modeling a black silk shirt in the full-length mirror.

'We don't tell nobody,' another brother affirmed.

'*Silencio*.' Paulo put his finger to his lips and winked. The others nodded.

Enrique smiled. Now he wanted to get them out of his new apartment. He had a lot of things to do. The first thing was to send his wife and their three children back to Colombia. Then he wanted to find out who those two girls were who came up to take care of Rodrigo every afternoon.

Then he had to figure out when and where to attack the

DeSantos. It would have to be soon. The element of surprise would be crucial.

Even though it was Saturday, Halloran was at his desk in police headquarters. Ten minutes after the meeting of the Esteban brothers broke up, he got word through the grapevine that Rodrigo Esteban was dead and the brothers were planning to take their revenge on the DeSantos.

'Goddamit,' he snarled as he slammed the receiver down.

'What's the matter with you?' another plainclothesman called across the squad room.

Halloran shook his head. 'Something's going on out there and I can't figure it out. All I know is the DeSantos and the Estebans are going to turn this city into a war zone.'

The other plainclothesman shrugged. 'It's like the joke, Vince. If you throw a wop and a spick out a window, who hits the ground first?'

'Huh?'

'Who cares?' The other detective laughed. 'Get it?'

Halloran rose to his feet. 'I care, dammit. If I could put all those sons of bitches in Yankee Stadium and have them shoot it out, I wouldn't care, either. But they're going to do it on the streets of Manhattan.' He thrust his hands in his pockets. 'How many people are going to get in their way and die for it?'

'Yeah,' the other detective said. 'It's a shame. And no matter who's to blame, you know the NYPD's going to take the heat for it.'

Halloran screwed his sweat-stained fedora on his head and walked toward the door. 'I'm going to see what I can find out,' he growled.

Despite the fact that it was a pleasant late summer Saturday and the streets were filled with pedestrians – there was a closed sign on the front door of the Peyton Place. Halloran spotted the guards sitting in parked cars on both ends of the block. When he walked toward the front door of the restaurant, Fat Frank waddled in front of him menacingly.

'Can't you read? Joint's closed,' he said.

'Yeah, I can read. How about you?' He flashed his badge. 'Read this, Frankie.'

'You got no business here.'

'I hope not. Where's DeSanto?'

'I don't know. He ain't here.' He made a move to push Halloran aside, but the detective stepped back.

'Careful, greaseball,' Halloran said. 'Touch a finger to me and you're going to spend the next ten years making little ones out of big ones.'

'Hey, you got me real scared,' Frank said, but he dropped his hands to his sides. 'Look, I told you Mr DeSanto ain't here. And I bet you ain't got a warrant, anyhow.'

Before the situation could grow into an impasse, a dark brown, chauffeur-driven Lincoln Continental pulled up in front of the restaurant. Tony and Nick DeSanto got out of the backseat. Nick bristled at the sight of the policeman, but DeSanto greeted him as cordially as if their last meeting had never taken place.

'Hello, Lieutenant. What brings you here?'

'We've got to talk, DeSanto,' Halloran said.

DeSanto gestured toward the open door of the car. 'In here, perhaps.'

'Good enough.' Halloran and DeSanto both slid into the rear seat. Nick came in, too, sitting astride the jump seat facing them. Halloran shot him a silent look of disgust, then spoke to the father. 'I got an informant tells me Rodrigo Esteban is dead,' he said. 'Is that true?'

'What's the matter, you don't trust your snitch?' Nick said with a smirk.

'I'm asking you, DeSanto.'

Tony DeSanto spread his hands. 'Why would I know?'

'Maybe you killed him.'

'Watch it, Lieutenant.' He clenched his jaw. 'Unless you're prepared to arrest me –'

'Simmer down,' Halloran said tiredly. 'I'm not going to arrest you. I don't even think you killed him, if you want to know the truth. All I'm trying to do is to make some sense out of this.'

DeSanto settled back into his seat fractionally, but his eyes were still wary.

'When did you meet Esteban last?'

He knew the answer already and wanted to see what DeSanto would say. The don surprised him by telling him the truth.

'Last night. We talked about the bad blood that seemed to be brewing. I told him we bore him no ill will. He said the same. He knew nothing about any attacks on our family. We shook hands and he left.'

Halloran pushed back the brim of his hat. 'The word's out that the Esteban boys are going all-out for an attack on you.'

Nick blew out a dismissive puff of air. 'Let 'em try.'

'You'd like that, wouldn't you, Nicky?' Halloran snapped.

'Please.' DeSanto put up his hands in a gesture to halt. 'Please. There are troubles enough.' He turned to the detective. 'We are not responsible for the death of Rodrigo Esteban,' he said. His voice was soft, but there were pinched lines on his forehead, and his eyes were agitated. 'As for talk of an attack on us by the Estebans, I suggest – as I did the last time we talked – that you discuss that with them. We do not want a war. I hope that is clear.'

'And I hope that's the truth,' Halloran said. 'Because if anything starts, you're all going to jail, fancy lawyers or not.' He started to get out of the car. 'I just hope we can get you before you kill a lot of civilians.' He looked at Nick. 'If we can't, I'll make sure you get a life sentence.'

He slammed the door behind him.

'Somebody is setting us up,' DeSanto said quietly.

Fat Frank was still in front of the Peyton Place when Halloran got out into the street. He noticed a young dark-haired man walking up to the restaurant, but before Frank could bar his way, Nicky DeSanto stepped up alongside him. Halloran heard him say, 'Sorry, Mike. Place is closed this afternoon. Catch you tonight.'

The young man nodded and started to walk away. He glanced to his left and his eyes met Halloran's for a moment. Then the young man looked away and walked briskly down the block.

The face looked familiar, Halloran thought. He had seen that young man somewhere before.

But his name hadn't been Mike.

Who was he?

36

'This is a photograph of what was found in the A-One meat packing plant,' Tony DeSanto said.

He passed an eight-by-ten black-and-white photo to Matteo DeAndrea, the Staten Island lieutenant, who was sitting next to him at the table in the dining room of the Peyton Place. DeAndrea looked at the photograph and winced, then quickly passed it across the table to the Harlem boss, Madonna, who looked at it, then covered his mouth, jumped from the table, and ran toward the men's room. He brushed past Fat Frank, who was standing guard at the dining room archway.

Slowly the picture worked its way back and forth down the table. Pronzini and Avalone glanced at it, trying to be stoic about it, but their pursed lips showed their gut reaction.

Finally the picture reached Giovanni Andalucci at the far end of the table. The old man first took a sip of vodka from his silver flask, capped the container, and put it back into his jacket pocket.

Then he looked down at the photo.

'Aaaaah.' He smiled broadly. 'Justa like the old days.' He held the photo closer so he could examine its features more carefully. When he put it down, it was obviously with reluctance.

'Every bone in the body was broken,' DeSanto said. 'Every main blood vessel had popped. We had a doctor look at it an hour or so ago. He said that if Esteban were a piece of beef, he'd be unfit for human consumption because of the amount of internal damage.'

Pronzini whistled softly, impressed. Madonna returned to the table and sat down quietly.

'But the important thing isn't the body,' DeSanto said. He reached into the leather briefcase. 'There was something on the floor. A drawing. Here's a blowup.'

He handed the photo to Madonna, who barely glanced at it before passing it across the table to DeAndrea.

'Is this blood?' DeAndrea asked.

'Yeah,' Madonna said.

DeAndrea studied the photo for a moment and passed it on in silence.

Pronzini took it eagerly, squinting at it, turning it upside down. 'Looks like a Dairy Queen,' he said solemnly.

DeSanto closed his eyes. He pointed to Pronzini to give the picture to Andalucci.

The old man took the photograph with shaking, palsied hands as DeSanto said formally, 'Don Andalucci, in your years you have seen many things. Look at this carefully. Tell me if you see something of significance in this drawing made of blood.'

Andalucci studied the photograph at his leisure, absent-mindedly taking another swig from the silver flask as he did. 'Perhaps . . .' he said slowly. 'Perhaps . . .'

Everyone waited. 'Perhaps what, Don Andalucci?' DeSanto asked, trying hard to conceal his impatience.

'I saw something like this once,' Andalucci said. 'In Chinatown, a long time ago. We had some dealings with the tongs. They used symbols like this.'

Nick DeSanto and his father changed glances. 'Go on,' DeSanto said.

Andalucci shook his head and laid the photograph back on the table. 'But that was many years ago.' He took another drink.

Nicky spun in his chair. 'Fatso,' he called to Frank Lupone. 'Is that guy working in the kitchen?'

'The gook?' Frank called.

'Yeah.'

'Get him out here,' Nicky ordered.

Sato had kept the door to the kitchen open a crack, and by squatting with his ear close to the door he had been able to hear much of the conversation at the table. When he heard Frank's footsteps approaching, he ran softly back and stood at the sink, washing vegetables. He pretended not to hear the fat man as he entered, then came up, and punched Sato hard in the upper arm.

Sato spun around, pretending to see the man for the first time. He forced himself to put on the silly smile he always wore around these animals. Especially this fat one, who managed to sneak into the kitchen at least once every night and punch Sato up a little.

'Yessir, Mista Boss,' Sato said.

'Come on outside, you yellow-skinned turd,' Frank said. He grabbed Sato's upper arm and yanked him to the door. 'And don't act like no stupid slope, either. Nicky wants to talk to you.'

Still in the grip of Fat Frank, Sato shuffled to the table and stood, eyes downcast, in front of DeSanto father and son. Nick handed him the photograph.

'Do you know what this is?' Nick asked.

Sato bit back the impulse to tell him it was a Dairy Queen. Instead, he looked up and said, 'Yessir, Mista Boss.'

'Well?' Nick demanded. 'What is it?'

'Yessir, Mista Boss.'

'What the fuck is the picture?' Nick screamed.

'Yessir, Mista Boss,' Sato said.

'He don't speak English,' Nick said with a gesture of disgust, but Tony DeSanto stopped him.

'Wait a minute,' he said. He took the photograph from

Sato and pointed to the drawing it pictured. 'Is this Chinese?' he said slowly. 'Chinese?'

'Chinee, Chinee,' Sato agreed happily. 'Chinee, Chinee.'

'Thank you,' DeSanto said.

'Yessir, Mista Boss.'

'Get him out of here,' Nick said.

Frank dragged Sato back toward the kitchen. As he pushed him through the door, he booted him in the rear end. 'You're one stupid bastard, even for a gook.'

Sato forced himself to turn around and grin. 'Yessir, Mista Boss.'

At the table, Nicky said, 'We can't trust anything that asshole says. He don't talk English good enough.'

But his father was not listening. He looked down the table at Andalucci. 'These Chinese,' he said. 'Who can I contact?'

The old man thought for a moment. 'There is one I knew once. He would be an old man by now, but the Chinese live long. His name is Lee. A common name. But I could find him. I could take you there.'

DeSanto bit his lip. Nick was watching him, and caught his eye. The unspoken words between them were clear. Could this old fossil be trusted to talk sense? Even if Andalucci *was* lucid, DeSanto thought, how long would he stay that way? Finally he shrugged slightly, as if to say, 'What other choice do we have?'

He looked around the table. 'Someone is trying to frame us,' he said. 'Whoever killed Esteban wants to see us at war with the Colombians. Before we are forced into such a war, we must discover who these others are and why they have singled us out for attack.'

Avalone, the leader from the East Village, cleared his throat, and all eyes turned toward him. He was a tall, cadaverous man who had earned the respect of his peers. Avalone did not speak often, but when he did, the other *capi* listened.

'Don DeSanto,' he began in his sonorous voice, 'you are the *capo di capi*, and a man of respect. I do not wish to speak against you. But this has gone too far.'

The other men at the table all seemed to exhale at the same time. Avalone was speaking for all of them.

'Two days ago, you urged us to war with the Estebans because you believed they had attacked your sons without provocation. I said nothing then, but it was common knowledge that your son Niccolo had stolen drugs from the Estebans.'

Nick rose, glaring, his hands clenched into fists, but his father restrained him.

'Forgive me, Don DeSanto, if this is the first you have heard of it.'

DeSanto looked down, hoping that his anger appeared to be shock. He had known about Nicky's escapade, but he had not known the others were aware of it.

Avalone went on, 'Had I been Rodrigo Esteban, I would also have sought revenge on the thief.'

Several of the heads around the table nodded.

'Who you calling a thief?' Nick shouted.

'Leave the room, Nicky,' his father said quietly.

'I'm not going any –'

DeSanto nodded to Fat Frank, who lumbered over and grabbed Nick in a double hammerlock.

'I'm sorry, Nicky,' Frank said dolorously. 'Your pop's still the boss.' Then he dragged Nick, who continued to curse and kick savagely, through the heavy outside door.

The *capi* watched his progress through the room with distaste. When he was gone, they turned back in silence to listen to Avalone, ignoring the look of shame and horror on Tony DeSanto's face.

'Now you bring us a new development – that Esteban himself is dead, and that the Chinese have killed him.' He spread his arms wide. 'Tony, Tony,' he said sadly. 'How can we believe this? In my lifetime, I have had no trouble with the Chinese.' The other men at the table shook their heads vigorously. 'They keep to themselves. They do not instigate wars.'

DeSanto looked up coldly. 'So what are you telling me?'

Avalone looked to the closed door where Nick had exited. 'Do I have to say it, Don DeSanto?'

'My son did not kill Rodrigo Esteban!' DeSanto rasped. 'He was at home last night. I have witnesses . . .'

He looked from one face at the table to the other, but each man turned away from him in embarrassment. Only the alcohol-fuzzed gaze of Giovanni Andalucci met his own. Only one vote that DeSanto could count on in an emergency, he realized, and that from an old relic who was not in command of his senses most of the time.

'Are you finished?' DeSanto asked quietly.

'Almost,' Avalone said. 'I did not wish to sting you with my words, but now that I have spoken, I will say what I must. I will not fight a war for your sons, Don DeSanto. Not with the Estebans, not with the Chinese.'

'Same here,' Madonna said.

'No way,' said Pronzini. 'I'm with Avalone.'

DeAndrea knocked on the tabletop. 'Count me out.'

Tony DeSanto stood up slowly and with dignity. 'Come, Don Andalucci,' he said. 'We will go to Chinatown together.'

Without even acknowledging the other men, he turned and walked away from the table.

Andalucci insisted that they take his limousine to China-town. DeSanto readily agreed, since Andalucci's chauffeur and confidante, a particularly ugly thug nicknamed Joe the Goat because of his proclivity for juvenile rape, had been on DeSanto's payroll since he had taken over control of Andalucci's crime empire. With Joe the Goat reporting every new wrinkle in the remnants of Andalucci's organization, DeSanto had been able to trust the old man.

Now, it seemed, he was the only one DeSanto could trust.

As they passed an alley near Mott Street, Andalucci told the driver to stop. Joe the Goat pulled over at a fire hydrant.

'You wait here,' Andalucci said.

He and DeSanto got out of the car and walked into the alley. In a rundown building they climbed a flight of steps to an office bearing the name of an Oriental importing company.

'Are you sure this is the right place?' DeSanto asked as a cockroach crawled out from beneath the door. Andalucci's sanity was, he knew, a sometimes thing. He only hoped the old man wasn't unwittingly leading them both into a den of Chinese muggers.

'Don't be deceived by appearances,' Andalucci said as he turned the doorknob. 'Mr Lee is the biggest morphine dealer in Chinatown. But the Chinks don't like to wear their gold on their sleeves.'

'You never mentioned him to me before,' DeSanto said, making a mental note to have Joe the Goat executed.

Andalucci shrugged. 'That's what makes good neighbors, eh?'

The office was no more than a cheap desk in an otherwise bare and dirty room, but the desk was piled with papers and a young Chinese man wearing a suit and tie sat at it, writing busily and working an abacus. He glanced up in annoyance as the two men walked in.

'Mr Lee, please,' Andalucci said.

'Not here,' the Chinese quipped automatically, going back to his work.

'Tell him it's Andalucci, an old friend.' He chuckled, showing his gleaming false teeth. 'Tell him I got him his first piece of white meat.'

The young man looked at him uncertainly, then ducked behind a ratty red curtain. DeSanto heard voices speaking in the singsong cadences of Chinese, and then the young man appeared again. 'You can go through here,' he said, opening the curtain for them.

At the end of a short, filthy hallway was a door. It was open and a man stood in front of it. He was old – as old as the earth, it seemed, bald and stooped and sour-mouthed. Next to him, DeSanto thought, Andalucci looked like a youngster. Yet the man's eyes were clear and mocking, seeming to take the measure of both men with a single piercing, predatory glance.

'Been a long time, Mr Lee,' Andalucci said, extending his hand.

The Chinese man bowed, unsmiling. He kept his own hands hidden inside the sleeves of his Mandarin gown as he stepped aside to let the visitors enter.

DeSanto's mouth gaped open when he walked into the room. It was palatial, with lushly brocaded chaise longues of Chinese style resting on a gleaming teakwood floor. One table was inlaid with mother-of-pearl intricately designed to resemble a dragon with a wild, heavy-maned horse between its teeth. Scrolls and antique fans hung from the walls, as well as a mirror in an elaborate golden frame.

Surreptitiously DeSanto scratched the mirror frame, then looked at his fingernail. There was gold dust on it.

'It is quite real,' Mr Lee croaked, settling himself on one of the settees.

DeSanto coughed in embarrassment and sat down beside Andalucci.

'What do you want of me?' The old man's voice sounded like a death rattle.

Andalucci grinned, rather vacantly, DeSanto thought, and pulled out his silver flask for a drink.

Don't get senile on me now, he thought fervently.

But Andalucci seemed to have his wits about him. 'It is a pleasure to see you again, Mr Lee. I have been telling my friend Antonio DeSanto about our good times together.'

The old Chinese waved the conversation away with a scowl. 'We had no good times,' he said slowly and with obvious physical difficulty. 'Only business dealings in which I was permitted to operate in my own territory by paying you an extortionate percentage of my profits.'

Andalucci's skull-like grin wavered only momentarily. 'Ah, but perhaps you forget that when you arrived in this country, a poor immigrant, none of the other Chinese would lend you money. You came to me seeking capital.'

'And I paid you back tenfold before I was able to break your hold on me.'

'When our contract was dissolved, you promised your undying allegiance to me,' Andalucci said sullenly.

Mr Lee laughed. It made him cough. Flecks of mucus landed on his long, stringy mustache. 'Come to the point, old man,' he said. 'I have little time left.'

DeSanto took the initiative. He opened his leather briefcase and took out the photograph of the symbol found near Esteban's body on the floor of A-One Meats.

'I'd like you to take a look at this,' he said. He was careful to betray no emotion as he handed it over, watching the old man's face for any sign of recognition.

Mr Lee looked at the picture for a long moment. Then he dropped it and squeezed his eyes shut. 'Take that away,' he whispered.

'What is it?' DeSanto demanded, leaping up from his seat. 'Whose tong uses this symbol? Tell me!'

He was ready to beat it out of the old man, but Andalucci stopped him with a frown and a shake of his head.

Mr Lee remained motionless with his eyes closed for so long that DeSanto had seriously begun to wonder if he were still alive, but at last he stirred.

'Which tong made this mark?' DeSanto asked.

'It is not a tong,' Mr Lee said. 'It is not Chinese.'

'What? Don't tell me you didn't recognize it.'

'Oh, I did. I did.' Mr Lee smiled. 'Tell me, have you received a threat from these people?'

DeSanto looked away.

'That mark was drawn in blood beside the body of a murdered man,' Andalucci said.

The Chinese hawk eyes narrowed. 'Then write your will,' he said. 'Your life is over.' The old man eerily began to laugh in dry, cracked peals.

DeSanto bristled. 'Who are they?'

'Yakuza,' Mr Lee hissed, drawing out the word with relish. 'And the Onami at that. The most dangerous of all.'

'Yaku . . .' DeSanto began, uncomprehending.

'Tell us about it, Mr Lee,' Andalucci said. 'Please.'

Lee sat forward, his eyes growing bright with remembrance. 'At the end of World War Two,' he said, 'when the Americans occupied Japan, I was working the black market in Tokyo. We had access to food, and the Japanese would pay any price for it.' The corners of his mouth turned down bitterly. 'Oh, they came to us then, the arrogant Jap dogs who had thought they could destroy China and make slaves of us all. They came starving and begging, willing to trade family heirlooms for a bowl of rice. We showed them who the slaves were then.'

The old man shifted uncomfortably on his divan. 'But the Yakuza drove us out with machine guns. Where they got them, I will never know. But the Yakuza is capable of anything. They have been organized criminals since the days of the shoguns.'

'A mob?' DeSanto asked, bewildered. 'There's a Cosa Nostra in Japan?'

'Most of them are no better than you,' Mr Lee said laconically. 'They deal in drugs and female flesh. They are loan sharks and racketeers, gamblers, union fixers. But there was one who was different. An aristocrat who used the Yakuza to create a sort of government among the poor. He was not interested in making money out of the chaos of his country, as were the others. Instead he used his power against us.' The old man took a deep, rasping breath. 'His name was Nagoya, and his house was called the Onami, the Crested Wave.'

He took a brush and a piece of rice paper from a drawer inside the low table. He dipped the brush into a well of ink, then formed a figure on the rice paper. The symbol was identical with the one in DeSanto's photograph. 'These Yakuza are known as the Sons of the Wave.'

All three men sat in silence.

Finally DeSanto picked up the drawing. 'What do they want with me?' he asked in a small voice. 'We have done nothing to them.'

Mr Lee shrugged. 'I know nothing about it.' He took back the design he had painted and folded it in half so that he would not have to look at it. 'But whatever it is the Onami want, they will have it.'

Scowling with pain, he stood up. 'That is all I can give you,' he said. 'My bed and my opium pipe await me. They are the only comforts I have left.'

'Mr Lee, please,' DeSanto said with an edge of desperation in his voice. 'These men – these Sons of the Wave – if they attack us, would your tongs help us fight them? I will pay.'

'As a favor between old friends,' Andalucci said, smiling.

Mr Lee looked at him steadily, unsmiling. 'That would not be a favor, Don Andalucci. That would be suicide. I do not owe you that much.'

Neither man spoke as Joe the Goat steered the Cadillac limo through the narrow streets of Chinatown. DeSanto could not make any sense out of what was happening. Two of his men murdered. Esteban – his natural enemy – murdered also. And by a Japanese tong or whatever it was. The Yakuza. That was it. The Crested Wave. It all sounded like a lot of crazy talk. And yet the look in Mr Lee's eyes when he saw the photograph was unmistakable. It was fear.

Suddenly the car veered crazily.

'*Marone*,' Andalucci said, thumping on the partition between the rear passenger seats and the driver with his flask. Joe the Goat held up his hand in apology.

Some bicyclists ahead were swarming by on the two narrow lanes beside the Cadillac limo in the tight alley. The driver had slammed on his brakes to avoid hitting them. Joe the Goat opened his window. 'Move your gook asses before I run over you!' he yelled.

The cyclists passed on both sides of the Cadillac. Just as the last cyclist went by, the car suddenly surged forward with a jerk, accelerating through the alley and knocking over a stack of boxes outside a produce store.

'Slow down, Joe,' Andalucci ordered, thumping on the partition again. 'Crazy *stronzo*.' He tipped the flask to his lips.

But this time Joe the Goat did not respond. His head was slumped forward. His hat had slipped off and covered his face. And still the car shot ahead, veering slightly to the left now, heading directly into the corner of a brick building.

'Get down,' DeSanto yelled and threw Andalucci onto the floor. He fell down on top of the old man and covered his head with his crossed arms.

The impact was colossal. The front half of the limo folded up like a concertina, although the two men in the back were safely cushioned between the two rows of padded seats. When the car finally settled into a cloud of steam from the burst radiator, DeSanto pulled himself up off the old man.

'You all right?' he asked.

'I need a drink.'

'Never mind that. We got to get out of this heap before the engine blows.'

His door opened with a squeal of metal. DeSanto clambered out and extended a hand to the old man.

Then he saw it.

Joe the Goat's eye had a ten-inch knife growing from it.

'Jesus Christ,' DeSanto whispered, yanking Andalucci from the car.

'My flask . . . it dropped –'

'I said, let's get the fuck out of here,' DeSanto roared, then abandoned the old man and ran for his life.

Fifty feet down the alley, he realized that if the auto's engine had not blown already, it probably wasn't going to. He looked back. Andalucci was making his way forward, stopping for a quick drink from the silver flask.

'Fuck 'im,' DeSanto muttered and turned around again. He almost collided with a kid on a bicycle.

'Watch where you're going, jerk,' he shouted after the cyclist, who now looked as if he were going to collide with Andalucci. Damn Chinks, he thought. They were like flies, always up your –

'Oh, Jesus.'

It happened so quickly that at first his mind tried to deny that it was happening at all. What his mind was denying was that the boy on the bicycle was holding a sword at least eight feet long and swinging it in a long arc aimed directly at Giovanni Andalucci's neck.

By the time Tony DeSanto's mind had stopped denying this and his lips were forming the words 'Oh, Jesus,' the sword had already severed Andalucci's head, which was now looping through the air like a softball thrown by a child. It hit the cobbled pavement with a muffled, fleshy crack and then rolled toward DeSanto's feet, where it stopped. The wavy white hair atop the severed head fluttered softly in the faint breeze.

DeSanto drew his gun and fired, but the cyclist had already dashed behind the wrecked limousine. DeSanto chased after him for a few steps, but he knew it was no use.

His legs felt weak, as if suddenly the bones had been removed from them. He fell to his knees in the alley, indifferent to the hole he had just torn in the trousers of his thousand-dollar suit. He knelt in the alley and screamed.

37

Tony DeSanto groaned awake.

His vision was blurry, but he could make out bars. White bars and dingy green walls . . . He bolted up to a sitting position, causing the bedsprings to creak.

'Relax,' Halloran said. The detective was sitting in a chair beside the bed. 'You're in a hospital.'

'What – what . . .'

'You're not hurt, okay? You just snapped. The China-town cops couldn't get you to talk sense. After they checked out your ID, they called me.' He looked at his watch. 'That was about four hours ago.'

'Andalucci,' DeSanto said, licking his cracked lips.

Halloran handed him a glass of water. 'He didn't make it,' he said tactfully.

Suddenly DeSanto's eyes filled with tears and he began to sob uncontrollably.

'If I didn't know you better, I'd think you were crying over the old man.' Halloran tossed over a box of tissues. 'But it's just a reaction from the sedative. The nurse said to watch for the waterworks.'

He sat back and waited while DeSanto wept, gagging and honking loudly into the tissues. After a few minutes the jag subsided somewhat and the don took another drink of water.

'Feeling better?' Halloran asked. ' 'Cause we've got a lot to talk about.'

'I want my attorney,' DeSanto said, hiccupping.

The detective resisted the impulse to punch him. 'You're not under arrest,' he said. 'I'm here to talk to you as a witness.'

Slowly DeSanto's face screwed up again, threatening to explode into another burst of hysterics.

'Can it,' Halloran ordered.

DeSanto buried his face in his hands. 'They used a sword,' he whispered. 'They cut off his fucking head.'

The detective took out a notebook. 'Who did?'

DeSanto's shoulders stopped heaving. He sat immobile for a long time, his hands covering his face. Then slowly he dropped them and turned to face Halloran. His eyes were dry and blank.

'The Yakuza,' he said.

'What?'

DeSanto scrambled out of bed, looking for his clothes.

'Sit down,' Halloran said, pushing him back on the mattress. 'You can talk to me here or at the station. And if it's at the station, I'm calling in the FBI. Now, what's it going to be?'

DeSanto sighed. 'They're Japanese,' he said quietly. 'It's a gang of Japs that want to start the war between my people and the Estebans.'

'How do you know?'

DeSanto looked at him. The fuzz had cleared from his head. There was no way he was going to tell the police about finding Esteban's body in the A-One meat-packing plant.

Halloran recognized the look. 'All right, I'll let it pass for now. You sure it's Japs? Not Chinese? Japs don't live in Chinatown.'

'Yes, yes, I know. I'm sure.'

'What'd you call them?'

'Yakuza. They're a syndicate.'

'Here?'

DeSanto shook his head. 'In Japan.'

'What do they want with you?'

DeSanto laughed bitterly. 'That's the sixty-four-thousand-dollar question.'

'You know these guys?'

'No.'

'Did Andalucci?'

'No.'

'How about your kids? Nick –' He pushed his hat to the back of his head. 'Jesus Christ, the wedding.'

'What?' DeSanto asked. 'What are you talking about?'

Halloran stood up. 'Your pants are in the closet,' he said, and rushed from the room.

The living room of Rodrigo Esteban's former apartment had been transformed into a military bunker. Dozens of dirty bare mattresses were stacked against the walls. In the center of the room was a pile of weapons – stolen handguns, mostly, short-range Berettas, some Brownings, a few Smith & Wessons, a massive Colt .45, several zip guns, dozens of knives and switchblades, an old AR-18 submachine gun, a prize Uzi in perfect condition, and a handful of grenades. Apart from them were boxes of ammunition, organized and labeled.

'*Bueno*, Antonio,' Enrique Esteban said, walking slowly around the cache. 'You have done even better than I thought.'

Antonio puffed up his narrow chest proudly. 'Many more men are willing to fight, now that the DeSantos are so weakened.'

Word of the New York Mafia leaders' refusal to go to war with the DeSantos against the Estebans had spread like wildfire. 'Luck is with us today,' Enrique said. 'After the attack we will have many more men. Then the Estebans will be a force that all the dagos in New York will not be able to stop, eh, Paulo?' He slapped his youngest brother on the back.

Paulo grinned. 'You done good by us, Enrique.'

The other brothers agreed loudly. They were all dressed in Rodrigo's finery, their pointed-toed shoes polished to a high gleam.

'Look at yourselves,' Enrique said, spreading his arms toward his men. 'Did I not tell you this would be a new era? Did I not say I would lead you to new heights?'

'A new era!' one of the brothers shouted. 'The Estebans will be kings!'

'This is only the beginning,' Enrique said. 'Tonight we make an empire.'

'An empire!'

'Take your weapons!'

The brothers scrambled for the guns on the floor, stuffing their pockets, but they backed off when their leader approached. Enrique picked up the Uzi and four grenades, and handed them ceremoniously to Antonio. 'For you, my brother,' he said. 'My captain.'

Antonio accepted them with a smile. 'No one will be safe from us now,' he vowed.

The brothers agreed. Loaded down with weapons, belts of ammunition strapped across their chests, the Esteban men raised their guns in salute.

The Peyton Place was doing a brisk dinner business, despite the fact that all the customers were put through a search at the front door.

'Get a load of this,' Guy Salvo said, pulling out a box from beneath the bar. It was nearly filled with guns. 'All of 'em taken off the customers.'

'I guess it says something about your clientele,' Miles said.

He had been sitting at the bar for the past two hours. From the beginning he had felt the tension in the air, as if the restaurant were floating peacefully in the eye of a hurricane.

'It's on account of Andalucci,' Salvo said.

'Who's that?'

Salvo wiped down the bar. 'Some old geezer. Got killed today when he was with Tony DeSanto, the big boss.' He leaned over. 'Got his head chopped off,' he whispered.

Miles grimaced. 'Who did it?'

The manager shrugged. 'DeSanto ain't been in. He was so shook about the whole thing, they took him to a hospital in Chinatown. Nick and Fat Frank had to go get him, take him home. They just left a few minutes before you came in.'

Miles felt a wave of annoyance. He had hoped to make his first move on Nick DeSanto that night. 'Are they coming back?' he asked.

'Dunno. His brother Joey's supposed to come around, though. Not that you'd want to talk business with him. He's just a kid.' He laughed. 'I give him a drink once in a while. He likes pussy drinks, you know? Pink with lots of fruit. Cracks me up. Anyway he might know if Nicky's on his way or not.'

Miles hesitated for a moment. He didn't want to say too much. Despite Salvo's friendliness toward him, Miles had no doubt that if the restaurant manager suspected that 'Mike Hall' exhibited too much of an interest in the DeSantos, he would blow the whistle on him.

On the other hand, though, time was running out. Once and for all, Miles had to know the truth.

'I heard Joey DeSanto wasn't that much of a kid,' he said.

'Huh?'

'You're the one who told me about this place . . . its connections,' Miles said.

'Oh, that. Yeah.' Salvo looked around to make sure no one was eavesdropping on the conversation. 'Well, you couldn't frisk this many rods out of Lutece,' he said, looking balefully at the confiscated guns.

'So I did some checking on the DeSantos.'

'Hey, like the lawyers say, "Indictments, but no convictions." ' He chuckled. 'You couldn't pin a rap on Tony DeSanto in a hundred years.'

'I wasn't talking about him,' Miles said. 'What I found out was about Nick and Joey.'

'What was that?' Salvo's voice lost some of its amiability.

Miles decided to push. 'It was something about a shoot-out at a wedding a few months ago. The papers thought Joey might have been mixed up in it.' He held his breath. None of the city newspapers had carried any such story.

'Yeah, well . . .' Salvo said, washing some glasses.

'You knew about it?'

'Sure I knew. Nicky made everybody swear to the cops that him and Joey spent the whole day here.'

'But they didn't,' Miles said.

'Naah. But Joey wasn't in on it. He was there with Nicky, but Joey didn't kill nobody. Hell, he come in here vomiting and bawling so bad, Nicky had to slug him to keep him quiet.' Salvo shook his head. 'Poor kid. He don't deserve to have Nicky for a brother. Crazy bastard gets all coked up and then loses his cool. You know why he shot that bride and groom at the wedding? Huh?'

Miles shook his head.

'Because the manager wouldn't let Nicky in. That was it. Just 'cause the place was closed.' He lit a cigarette and exhaled the smoke noisily. 'What an asshole. It cost the old man a ton to cover it up, too, believe me.'

'He paid you to testify about Nicky and Joey being here?'

'Not us. We were small stuff. We talk, Nicky just puts a bullet between our eyes. The investigation was closed, but this nosy detective – I think his name's Hallahan or something – he kept coming back. So Tony had to buy a judge to swear he was here, too.' Salvo laughed. 'So now the judge has the biggest boat in the Fifty-ninth Street Marina.'

'So much for the law,' Miles said, feeling his stomach knot.

'That's how the world works, huh, Mike?'

A waitress came over with a drink order. Miles sat quietly while Salvo filled it. When he returned, Miles offered to buy him a drink.

'Don't mind if I do,' Salvo said, pouring a double scotch for himself. 'Fat Frank's not around to pull my chain about it.' He downed it at a gulp. 'Damn, that's good.'

'You'd think the families would put pressure on after something like that,' Miles said.

'What? Oh, the wedding. You still on about that?' He poured himself another drink. 'Yeah, well, they tried.'

Miles felt his heart beating faster.

'Some old guy came to the place. Somebody's grandfather. He had a gun. He was going to shoot Nicky.'

'What happened?'

'Fat Frank and some of the boys took him out back and smacked him around. Beat him pretty bad. He died.'

Miles saw that his hands were gripping the raised wooden edge of the bar so hard that his knuckles had turned white. 'Oh,' he managed to say. His voice sounded faraway to him, as if it were coming from someone on the other side of the room.

At last he knew the truth.

Nick DeSanto had murdered his sister and her husband on their wedding day.

Tony DeSanto had bribed a judge to make sure the crime went unpunished.

Frankie Lupone had beaten his grandfather to death in an alley.

And he thought, *God, do not let me forget the truth.*

Miles checked his watch. 'It's almost nine,' he said. 'I don't think Nicky's coming tonight.'

'Hey, like I said, Joey'll be here soon.'

'Never mind,' Miles said, throwing some bills onto the bar. He had no more stomach for Salvo's small talk.

It was a sultry, breezeless summer night, and as Miles walked out of the air-conditioned restaurant, he felt his clothing stick to his body. Traffic on the street was light. There were only two pairs of headlights moving slowly toward him. At the curb, Nick DeSanto's blue Corvette was parked, its engine still cooling. It must have pulled up only seconds before.

Miles waited for Nick to get out, but the driver was someone else, a young, clean-looking boy whose resemblance to Nick was unmistakable. He smiled at Miles as he strode past him.

Then he saw the two slow-moving cars pull up in tandem in front of the Peyton Place. The cars were old, virtual wrecks, quite unlike the Lincolns and Cadillacs that filled the parking lot, and they were full. Miles counted nine heads.

The man who had replaced Fat Frank to stand guard in front of the restaurant went up to them at once. 'Place is closed,' he said.

One of the men inside raised a gun and fired it into the man's face. It exploded like a melon, spraying blood and bits of flesh over the building.

Joey DeSanto screamed as the body slumped onto the sidewalk, shooting out blood in thick, rhythmic spurts. In the next instant the door on the passenger side of the car opened. A man with a machine gun hoisted himself out and stepped aside, while the others poured out the doors, laden with weapons. The young man looked from one face to another, his head moving in quick jerks, his hands spread out in front of him.

'Joey!' Miles shouted, then dived and tackled him to the ground as a barrage of bullets exploded all around them.

The lights remained on while the plate-glass windows in

front of the restaurant fell down in sheets, so that the carnage going on inside appeared to be happening on some sort of stage. People were running everywhere, their backs arching as the bullets hit them. Many were slumped over their tables; others were on the floor, using whatever they could find as protection against the Estebans' guns. The glasses over the bar burst and rained down like fireworks. Between bursts of machine-gun fire the screams of those still living shrilled in the hot, still night.

Miles muscled Joey into his arms, then rolled to the side of the building. 'Stay down,' he said, shoving the young man's head to the ground.

Then came the grenade explosion that set the entire building rocking. Miles covered Joey, hunching over him as pieces of brick and cement block fell out of the sky.

When it cleared, they heard the sound of car doors slamming and then a heavily accented voice crying out, 'Don' fok with us no more, you stinkin' guineas!'

There was a squeal of tires as the cars peeled away and screeched around the corner.

After several seconds Miles stood up. 'You okay?' he asked.

Joey nodded, but his eyes were the size of saucers and his teeth were chattering. 'I – I'm cold,' he said.

Miles took off his jacket and draped it over the young man. As he did, Joey saw the tattoo on his forearm.

'I'll be back,' Miles said.

He went around to the front of the restaurant. The guard's body was still there, riddled with bullets. Inside, the lights had finally gone out. Miles stepped through the gaping holes where the windows had once been and looked around.

There had been more than twenty people in the Peyton Place when the Estebans arrived. They were all dead. Hard-faced men, dowdy wives, showgirls, young punks in expensive suits, people from the neighborhood, couples celebrating anniversaries, old folks – all dead. Near the bar lay Guy Salvo, his arm draped over the box of firearms. The top of his head had been sawn off by a line of bullets.

All dead except for Nick DeSanto.

And Tony DeSanto.

And Fat Frank Lupone.

The gods had saved them for Miles.

He went back to the side of the building. Joey was on his feet, dusting off Miles's jacket. 'Thanks,' he said, handing it back to him. 'That doesn't seem like enough. Just saying thanks, I mean –'

'Forget it,' Miles said coldly.

'What's your name?'

'It's not important,' Miles said. 'You'll see me again soon enough.'

38

MOB WAR!!
22 DEAD IN GANGLAND ATTACK
Gunfire Riddles Little Italy Restaurant;
DeSanto Survives Assault on Family Lair
Cops Suspect Colombian Drug Rivals;
Raid Follows Andalucci Execution

The Sunday *Post* played the story on page one with the kind of red type generally associated with the outbreak of another world war.

Nick DeSanto read only the headlines, then slammed the newspaper across Joey's head. 'You jerk, you could have been killed!' he shouted. 'Didn't Pop tell you to stay home?'

Joey put an elbow up to protect himself. 'Leave me alone, Nicky. I've already been through all this with Pop.'

'Where were you when we needed you, huh? The old man was hysterical about you being gone. Shit, I couldn't blame him, what with Andalucci getting his head sliced off, and then hearing about this.' He slapped the newspaper with his fingers.

Joey clutched his hair with both hands. 'Nicky, what's going on?' he squeaked. His eyes were rimmed in red. 'All these weird things are happening, but nobody ever tells me why. First Hooks. Then the Driller. Now Andalucci, and the massacre last night. It – it's all so crazy, but nobody ever says anything to me except "Get lost, Joey." ' He wiped his nose on a handkerchief. 'Look, if I'm old enough to get killed, I think I ought to at least know why.'

'Numbnuts,' Nick shouted. 'Don't you think we'd tell you if we knew?'

'No, I don't,' Joey shouted back. 'As far as this family's concerned, I'm like some little pet that you kick out of the room the minute you've got something important to do.'

Nick threw down his napkin and was about to reach across the table to collar his brother when the door to Tony DeSanto's study opened.

DeSanto's *consigliore*, a tall, graying man who looked like a Park Avenue attorney, nodded briefly to the two sons before leaving. DeSanto stood in the doorway, holding a pile of papers. His face was ashen. When he came over to the table, Joey stood up and pulled his chair out for him.

DeSanto was wearing a maroon satin smoking jacket. He hadn't left the house since coming home from the hospital the day before. In twenty-four hours he seemed to have aged ten years.

He pushed aside a plate of food and sat for a long time, not looking at either of his sons, but only staring blankly at the papers in front of him. The don had not spoken much since Nick and Fat Frank had driven him home from the hospital. Then DeSanto had only mentioned the murder of Giovanni Andalucci. He had said nothing about his conversations with Mr Lee or Lieutenant Halloran. Once at home he had cloistered himself inside his study.

Jesus Christ, the wedding.

What wedding?

He had wracked his brains trying to make sense of Halloran's remark. They had been talking about the Japanese. The Yakuza.

Did you know these guys?

No.

382

Did Andalucci? Did Nick?

Nick.

Jesus Christ, the wedding.

There had only been one wedding in which Nicky had been involved.

DeSanto called his *consigliore*. 'Find out everything you can about the wedding at the Inn on the Park,' he said. He did not have to say anything more. The lawyer remembered perfectly well that the nuptials had included a double murder. He had arranged for the bribe to the judge himself.

Then he had gotten word about the shooting at the Peyton Place, and the rest of the night had been spent in a nightmare. DeSanto called each of the other New York *capi*. Perhaps now that war had really come, he thought, the others would stand by him.

Not one of his once faithful lieutenants would speak with him.

And Joey was missing.

By the time Fat Frank found the boy, DeSanto was beyond despair. He had screamed at Joey and beat him and then finally gone to bed, hoping to die in his sleep.

Then this morning, the *consigliore* had come with his briefcase filled with papers, and Tony DeSanto finally understood why he was doomed.

'I have found the source of my troubles,' he said. His voice sounded cracked and feeble.

Nick laughed. 'Yeah, I guess so.' He buttered a roll and took a bite from it. 'About fifty people saw the Estebans blow away the Peyton Place and everybody inside it.'

DeSanto's eyes narrowed and his jaw clenched. 'The Estebans started their war,' he said bitterly, 'but they were put up to it.'

Nick looked at him, then threw his roll down on his plate. 'So what are you staring at me for? I didn't kill Rodrigo Esteban.'

383

'No. You did much worse,' DeSanto said. 'Much worse.'

Nick rolled his eyes. 'Right, Pop. Everything's my fault, as usual. What's the matter, didn't you find the Chink you were looking for?'

'Yes, I found him,' DeSanto said quietly. 'He knew the mark. It was Japanese.'

'Oh, Christ,' Nick said. 'Now it's the Japs. Who's next, Polacks?'

'Japanese!' DeSanto roared, throwing his pile of papers at Nick. They flew everywhere. Nick shielded his face with his arm, looking at his father as if the old man had lost his mind.

'The bride you killed at her wedding was Japanese! The guests at the wedding were Japanese!' He picked up a handful of papers in his fist and shook them at Nick.

'So? A bunch of gooks. So what?' Nick said defiantly.

'They weren't just gooks. They were killers. Killers that make you look like a schoolboy.'

'Nicky,' Joey said. He had been silent until now, afraid that he would once again be sent away from the company of men, but he had to speak. 'Remember those guys? How they got your gun and threw you into the 'vette?'

'There were six of them,' Nick said with a shrug.

'Yeah, but they moved like they weren't human or something.' He turned to his father. 'They were so fast, you almost couldn't see them.'

'Were they Japanese?' DeSanto asked.

'I guess so. Some kind of gooks, right, Nicky?'

'Shaddup, what do you know?'

'*I* know,' DeSanto said. 'It's the only possible explanation. These Japs have come after us in revenge for your killing. They are the ones who murdered Hooks Aiello and the Driller. They are the ones who killed Esteban. They are the ones who executed Andalucci and his driver. All to cause a war which we cannot win, because the dons think

384

you are to blame and will not fight for us.' He sat down. 'To get even with you, they have set out to destroy everything we have.'

'But they haven't touched us,' Joey said. 'Not the three of us. They had plenty of chances, too.'

'Yeah.' Nick swept the papers in front of him away. A photograph fluttered across the table. 'If they want me so bad, why haven't they come for me?'

DeSanto ran a hand through his thinning hair. 'They will. They will come for all of us.'

Joey picked up the black-and-white photograph in front of him. It was the picture of the design that had been drawn in blood on the floor of A-One Meats under the battered body of Rodrigo Esteban.

'What's this?' he asked, turning it around in his hands.

Tony snapped the photo away. 'Go to your room. Pack a bag.'

'Why?'

'You can't stay here, not until these Japs are dealt with. And right now we don't even know who they are.'

'Does that picture have something to do with them?'

His father sighed. 'Yes, son. It is the mark of their clan. Now go –'

'I saw the same design yesterday.'

Both heads swiveled to face him.

'On someone's arm. It was a tattoo.' He took the photograph from his father. 'I'm sure it was the same. A wave inside a circle.'

'Who was it?' DeSanto asked in a whisper.

'The guy who saved me in the shooting. He gave me his coat . . .'

'Did this man say anything to you?'

'Not much. He didn't hang around. I asked him what his name was, but he said it wasn't important.'

'What'd he look like?' Nick asked.

Joey shrugged. 'Tall, maybe six feet. Dark hair. Good-looking guy. I thought he was maybe Spanish or something. But he was wearing nice clothes, you know, not like a spick.'

'Did he have an accent?'

'No. He sounded like a college guy.'

'And he was standing right outside the Peyton Place?'

'Yeah. He came out just a couple of seconds after I pulled up in the car.'

'He was inside?'

'Yeah. Yeah, I guess so.'

Nick nodded and looked at his father. 'I think I know who he's talking about,' he said. 'There's a guy been hanging out the last week or so. Said he wanted to buy the place. He offered a million bucks, but I didn't think it sounded square.'

'Does he talk to anybody there?'

'Yeah,' he said excitedly. 'Salvo.' Then he looked at his father's disgusted face and remembered that Salvo was dead. 'Guess that connection don't do us a lot of good. Hey, wait a minute, I know his name.' He searched his memory. 'It's Hall. Mike Hall.'

DeSanto looked frantically through the papers strewn over the breakfast table. He picked one up and read through it carefully. 'There were no Halls in the families of either the bride or groom,' he said. 'Belmont, Haverford, Watterson . . . No Halls, and no Japanese names, either.'

He almost tossed the sheet away, but something on the paper caught his eye. 'The bride's maiden name was Susannah Haverford. She had a brother named Miles.'

'M.H.,' Joey said. 'Same initials.'

'With a name like that, he can't be a Jap,' Nick said.

'The bride was,' Joey said softly. 'You remember, Nicky.'

The three of them were silent for a long time. Finally

DeSanto said, 'Miles Haverford. He's the one we've got to find if any of us are going to get out of this alive.'

'The man with the tattoo . . .' Joey looked into his father's eyes. 'The last thing he said to me was that I'd see him again.'

DeSanto stood up from the table. 'Get your things packed.'

'Pop, I can't leave you and Nicky –'

'Now!'

Joey left the room.

DeSanto walked slowly after him, but at the door he turned to face Nick. 'You have caused this,' he said through gritted teeth. 'You have caused this, and you will deal with it.'

Nick lit a cigarette and smiled. 'It'll be my pleasure.'

39

A man is born and dies,
weightless and insignificant as dust.
Yet I would have climbed a thousand mountains
to see your face once again.

'*Sayonara*, Tomiko,' Miles whispered, then folded the piece of rice paper into an envelope.

The only light in the room came from a paper lantern on the low table. Miles knelt before it, dressed in a black kimono, and poured five bowls of sake from a porcelain jar. As he passed each bowl the men who received them bowed, their faces illuminated by the candle in the lantern.

There was Koji the swordsman, young and pliant, the keeper of a samurai legacy centuries old; Hiro, the happy giant who had little idea of his immense strength; small, monkey-faced Yoshio, the archer who could put an arrow through a man's eye without compunction, but then had to pray for the dead man's spirit; and Sato. Sato, the half-breed, the man torn between worlds, the warrior driven by hate and revenge. Sato, Miles's true brother.

These were the men whose lives the Oyabun of the Onami had entrusted to Miles Haverford, an American who did not possess any of their skills, an outsider who had had no right to their secret knowledge. They were Sadimasa Nagoya's payment for a debt of honor incurred more than forty years ago. The old man had owed a life; he had given Miles four. And all he had demanded in return was that these lives not be wasted in a foreign land.

I will bring them back, Miles had vowed, *or I will not return*.

He would not forget his promise.

'You have come on a long journey with me,' Miles said softly in Japanese. 'Now the end of that journey is in sight. The DeSanto organization is crippled beyond help, unable now to protect the family at its rotten core. Thank you, my brothers, for your trust and your courage, for your honor. I will try to be worthy of these great gifts.'

They drank. 'The best is yet to come,' Yoshio said. The others laughed. All but Miles.

'Have you been watching the house?' he asked.

'Hai, Ronin.' He handed Miles a sheet of paper with a finely detailed drawing of the DeSanto family home drawn on it. With his finger he traced an imaginary ring around one of the second-story windows. 'The younger son's bedroom is here,' he said. 'The house is surrounded by two trip wires connected to an electronic alarm.' He pointed out two thin lines. 'Here, at a hundred meters from the building, and here, at thirty-five meters.'

'The best route of entry is through the woods in back of the house,' Koji added. 'Only two windows face in that direction. One is in the laundry room, and the other is a spare bedroom. Neither is likely to be in use.'

'A pair of guard dogs are brought in at night,' Yoshio continued. 'Also, three men armed with heavy weapons patrol the house. I can take out the dogs with arrows, then Koji and Hiro and I can deal with the men while Sato climbs up to the window.'

'I have a hook and a silk rope with me,' Sato offered, 'and some weapons that will kill more silently than guns or fists.'

390

Miles nodded. 'Thank you, gentlemen. I know about the hook. With your permission, Sato, I will take it.'

Sato bowed and stood up from the table, then went into the adjoining bedroom where all five men slept.

'May I ask a question, Ronin?' Hiro asked deferentially while they waited for Sato to return.

'Of course,' Miles said.

'Why the younger son? Did you not say that he was innocent of the crime against your family?'

Miles looked at his hands. 'All of the deaths we caused were levers to open the gates shielding Nick DeSanto and his father,' he said. 'This boy is the last lever.'

Sato came back holding a lightweight, three-pronged hook on a black cord. 'When do we move?' he asked.

Miles took it from him. 'I am going alone.'

'What?' Hiro, Koji, and Yoshio all rose at once.

'Your work here is finished.' Miles reached in his kimono sleeve and pulled out four envelopes. 'These are your airline tickets,' he said, placing them on the table.

'You can't break into that house alone,' Sato sputtered. 'You're not trained. The risk –'

'The risk is too great to subject you to it,' Miles said, his voice rising in anger. 'I promised the Oyabun only one thing: that his men would return to him alive. I intend to keep that promise.'

He walked over to the one dingy window in the room and looked out. 'I did not go to Nagoya looking for assassins. I only needed a way to make the DeSantos vulnerable. You have done that. Now, when Nick DeSanto dies, no one will strike a blow in return. His life has become unimportant.' Miles turned back to them. 'Except to me.'

'You must reconsider,' Sato said, crossing his arms over his chest. 'Without us, you will die.'

'I made Nagoya no promises about myself.'

'Ronin,' Hiro said, shaking his head. 'We are one, not

five.' The big man's eyes were so pained with compassion that Miles had to smile.

'Look, I'm not trying to be a martyr,' Miles said. 'It's just that . . . it's hard to explain, because you've all had lives worth living. I haven't. Not until now. Everything that's happened to me in the past five months has been pointing toward this day, this night. Before it I had no reason to stay alive. And afterward that reason will be gone. On this night my life ends, whether I live or die. But yours will go on.' He stroked the hook absently. 'That is why I must go alone.'

'I do not fear death,' Yoshio said proudly.

'Nor I,' Koji said. 'After serving you, my ancestors would receive me with honor.'

'You have been my brother, and more,' Hiro said. 'If death takes you, I wish to meet it with you.'

Sato touched his arm. 'Kyodai, you have been the leader I should have been but never was. You have given us pride and unity. All of us would follow you gladly into eternity.'

Miles's eyes welled with tears. 'Then obey me now,' he said softly. He took off his kimono. The clothes he wore beneath it were simple and black. From his pocket he took one more envelope and handed it to Sato. 'Give this to Tomiko,' he said.

Then he faced his men and bowed formally to them.

Sato clenched his fists, fighting with his emotions. When he finally spoke, his voice was scratchy but strong:

'May your ka live forever, Ronin, son of the wave.'

The four men bowed to their master. They kept their heads lowered as he left.

He parked his car on the far side of the woods bordering the DeSanto house. After a few hundred yards he came to a chain-link fence. The night was cloudy and he could not see anything beyond the woods on the far side of the fence, but he assumed that the DeSanto house lay straight ahead. With Sato's grappling hook stuck into the back of his trousers, he scaled the fence, then crawled on his belly until he could make out the dark outline of the mansion.

That's odd, he thought.

There were no lights on in the house and none on the grounds. He listened for the sound of dogs, but all he heard was the soft whine of insects and the distant roar of traffic from the city.

He moved more slowly now, inching his way along the ground, feeling with his fingers ahead of him. A sliver of moonlight came out. In it he saw the first trip wire.

Using a wire cutter, he snipped it, then continued on to the second and cut it.

He had a good view of the house from where he was now. He waited on the damp grass for a full ten minutes, then moved to different points in the woods to study the place from different vantage points. But wherever he went, he still saw no lights in any rooms and no sign of the dogs or the guards who were supposed to be patrolling the house.

It was possible, he supposed, that they were all congregated at the front of the house, the one side he had been unable to see from the woods. It was also possible that they would all appear just as he was making his way across the lawn. He took a length of thin wire from his pocket and wound it around the knuckles of his hand. If he could kill the first guard before the others saw him, he might still have a chance.

He had never killed a man before, he thought, feeling his palm sweat around the wire. The idea repelled him, even though killing had been the central focus of his life for the past five months. How would it feel when the man's life passed out of him in Miles's hands, a man he had never even seen before?

He was a lawyer. He had been raised in a family of

lawyers, in a house filled with books about law. And here he was, crawling in the woods, preparing to garotte a man.

How will it feel, Miles Haverford?

He smiled sadly. There was no more Miles Haverford. That had been a man with a future – not a very distinguished one perhaps, but one all the same. He would have had a family in time, a mistress or two, some ordinary problems, a comfortable home, a lot of dinner invitations, an eventual vice presidency in his father's firm, a membership in a golf club, a winter condo in the Caribbean, some children who would have grown up to become lawyers or to marry them, a respectable and leisurely old age, and a crypt in the family mausoleum.

That was all gone now. After tonight he would have no more home. If he lived, he could never return to his family. Too much had changed.

But he would probably not live.

He squeezed the wire in his hand until it cut through his skin. How would it feel? It would feel like *giri*, the duty owed his sister and the man he had known as his grandfather.

It would feel like justice.

He moved ahead. There was an open space between the woods and the house. Miles took it in a crouching run, moving silently, the way Sato had taught him.

No dogs.

Staying close to the wall, he peered around the corner to the side of the house he would have to climb to reach Joey DeSanto's window.

No guards.

Were Koji and Yoshiro mistaken? They had seen two dogs and three men, yet the place seemed to be deserted.

He unfastened Sato's hook and tossed it up to the roof. On the third try it caught. Then he shinnied up to the window and knelt on the stone sill, checking the ground below him.

Still no guards. Nothing but dark, utter silence.

394

He had planned to break open the window and run with Joey as a hostage, but he saw that that would be unnecessary. The window was unlocked, and open a crack at the bottom. He pulled it up slowly, not making a sound. Then carefully, silently, he stepped through the closed curtains into the room.

Suddenly his eyes were blinded by a flood of bright light. When they opened he saw five men, including Fat Frank Lupone and Nick DeSanto, grinning and pointing guns directly at him.

'Surprise, Miles,' Nick said.

They muscled him down the stairs into the kitchen and tied him onto a straight-backed chair with a rope around his chest and upper arms. While the three guards – the guards Koji and Yoshio had seen patrolling the house, Miles realized – kept their weapons trained on him, Fat Frank went to the stove and, strangely, put a huge pot of water on to boil.

Miles tested his arms pressing against the ropes, but they were fastened tight and there was no give. His legs were untied. He might be able to stand, he thought wildly, and maybe swing around using the chair as a weapon –

'Forget it, jerk,' Nick DeSanto said, kicking him in the knee. 'You ain't going nowhere.'

He pulled up another chair in front of Miles and straddled it, a cigarette dangling from his lips. Then he pulled a long folding knife from his pocket and held it closed in front of him, as if examining it. 'That *is* your name, isn't it – Miles Haverford?' he asked, squinting through the smoke.

There was no answer.

'I asked you a question, slope!' He popped open the knife and thrust it forward.

Miles raised his hands protectively over his face. As he

did, Nick stuck the knife into his sleeve at the wrist and ripped through the fabric up to the elbow.

There was the Crested Wave tattoo on the inside of his forearm.

Nick slapped him backhanded across the face. The pain of the blow rang in Miles's ears. 'Why'd you go to Joey's room?' he demanded. 'What'd you want with Joey?'

Again Miles was silent.

'Why Joey?' Nick shouted.

When there was still no answer, Nick took his cigarette and ground it out on Miles's cheek.

The pain was terrible. Miles could smell his flesh burning, but he would not cry out. He had made his peace with himself. If he had to die this night, he was prepared. But he would not give this killer the satisfaction of showing his suffering.

'Have it your way,' Nick said finally. 'Frank, that water hot yet?'

'It's boiling good.'

'All right.' Nick gave Miles a lopsided grin. 'Feel like talking yet?'

Miles said nothing.

'Get up.' He threw his chair aside, then jerked Miles to his feet by the ropes bound around his chest. 'You got a dirty face, Jap. Frank's going to wash it for you.'

He kicked him toward the stove. Miles moved awkwardly, hunched over with the chair tied on his back. Then Fat Frank grabbed him by the hair on the back of his head.

'He's all yours, Fatso,' Nick said, walking away in disgust.

'How you want him, boss? *Al dente*?' The fat man wheezed and laughed as he began to push Miles's face slowly toward the boiling pot of water. The small droplets that splashed onto his face through the suffocating steam were scalding hot. 'Look, you better do what Nicky says,'

Frank said in a low grumble. 'You ain't going to last long in this.'

Miles closed his eyes and thought of Tomiko. And he saw her, nude in the silver moonlight, with tears in her eyes.

There is only tonight, she had said.

That had been all the gods had granted them.

Yet I would have climbed a thousand mountains to see your face once again.

But he *was* seeing it, he realized. Tomiko was there, in front of him, as real as she had been that night on the forest floor, and she was looking at him with the perfect understanding her soul.

> *I walk as a stranger*
> *Seeking your face,*
> *Stopping only when the gods still my breath.*
> *Yet even then I will look for you.*

The words of the poem he had written with the priests' brush in the shrine came rushing back to him. That poem had been burned in the prayer dish; the gods had received those words.

Thank you, he thought. *Thank you for showing me her face once more.*

Then he let his spirit go to her, oblivious to the heat of the water that boiled inches from his face. Death no longer mattered to him. Tomiko's face would accompany him to eternity. Whatever punishment awaited him there, her memory would go with him.

'I am ready,' he said softly.

At that moment the windows in the kitchen burst in a spray of glass as Sato vaulted inside, kicking the weapons out of the hands of two of the guards and bashing their heads together. Yoshio slithered in like a snake through another window, somersaulting over the sink.

The remaining guard looked around frantically. In the split second it took him to get his bearings before he could fire, Yoshio disarmed him and snapped his neck.

Sato turned to Frank Lupone, who was staring stupidly at him while still clutching Miles's hair. 'It's the gook from the restaurant,' he said numbly.

'That's right, Fatso,' Sato answered. He jammed two fists into Frank's kidneys. 'Or should I say, "Yessir, Mista Boss"?'

The fat man released Miles and fell to his knees, his blubbery back arching.

While Yoshio was untying Miles, one of the two unconscious guards came to. He shook his head, then spotted Sato, who was standing with his back to him. The guard looked at Nick DeSanto.

Nick nodded, slowly taking his gun from his shoulder holster and aiming it at Yoshio. The guard carefully picked his own gun off the floor and pointed it at the back of Sato's head.

Then something shrieked through the air, and both guns clattered to the floor.

Nick screamed. Stuck through his right hand so neatly that not even one bone was broken was a six-inch knife with a red silk tassel dangling from its hilt.

The other man did not scream. An identical knife was lodged in his temple.

Koji walked over to him, pulled out the knife, and used it to snap the ropes around Miles.

Nick removed the knife from his hand and looked around frantically. No one seemed to be paying any attention to him. In a desperate lunge he threw himself on the floor, reaching for his gun, but he was stopped by a slam to his body that felt as if a truck had run over him.

'You stay here, yes?' a voice above him said cheerfully as he felt an enormous weight bearing down on his back.

Someone kicked the gun away. Slowly Nick DeSanto looked over his shoulder. A Japanese man the size of a building smiled down at him.

'I think I seen you before,' Nick grunted.

Hiro tapped him on the back of the head. Nick's face bounced once against the kitchen floor. When it came down again, he was out cold.

Miles extricated himself from the last of the ropes around his body. 'Why did you follow me?' he asked angrily.

'We could not allow you to come here alone,' Sato said. 'Forgive us, Ronin.'

Miles looked at each of his men in turn, then sighed. 'I should have expected as much,' he said. 'Have you seen the boy?'

'No, Ronin,' Hiro said.

'Wait for me here. I'll see if he's in the house.' He walked away.

'Ronin –' Sato started to run after him, but something grabbed at his leg.

Frank Lupone was clawing his way up Sato's body.

Yoshio and Koji both moved to stop him, but Sato gestured for them to stop. 'No,' he said softly. 'This one's mine.'

He reached down and pulled the fat man up by his shirt. 'Fight me, you swine,' he said in English.

He had green eyes. For the first time Frank noticed that the gook kitchen boy had green eyes. They were the eyes of a killer.

With a growl Frank reached for Sato's throat, but before his hands could connect, the Oriental ducked and wheeled away. In another instant the side of his shoe skidded across the fat man's face into the side of his nose with an audible crack. Frank reeled backward, bellowing, his hand cupped around his bleeding nose. He hit the sink the way a wrestler hits the ropes in the ring, bouncing off to race forward in a leap.

This time his arms closed around Sato and lifted him off the ground. For several seconds the tall Japanese did nothing. Then, moving almost in slow motion, Sato lowered his head. When he brought it up, it was with the speed of a train, hammering against Frank's jaw. In another instant he was out of the man's grasp and charging him with his head like a bull. While Frank was still groaning from the blow to his jaw, Sato slammed his skull into his solar plexus.

Blood dribbled from the fat man's mouth. 'Dirty . . . gook . . .' he whispered. But he said no more, because a backhand slap from Sato spun his head to the left and then another snapped his head back to the right and then a forearm smashed into the center of Fat Frank's face and he felt the rest of the nose bone break into chips and he opened his mouth to howl, but he had no chance, because suddenly he was grabbed by the hair at the back of his head and spun around and then . . . *oh, no, oh, Jesus freaking God, no* . . . his head was being forced down into the pot of boiling water and there was a giant scream inside his throat.

But only bubbles came out.

Sato held him face-first into the boiling water until the fat man stopped struggling, and then tossed him onto the floor with contempt.

Frank Lupone's face was a horrible peeling red mask of ruptured flesh and torn skin. His eyes had bulged out of his head and were clouded over like those of a dead shark. He had bitten his lips so badly that his teeth protruded through his skin from the agony of his death.

Yoshio and Koji blanched; Hiro turned his face away. But Sato looked at the corpse with no more emotion than he would have spent on a dead fly.

'He's not here,' Miles said at the doorway. 'What was –' He stopped when he saw the body.

Sato looked up at him with cold defiance. 'I will not atone for this, Ronin,' he said softly.

They stared at one another for a moment. Finally Miles said, 'I understand, kyodai. This man's death was your giri, too.'

He turned to the others. 'The boy is not here. This was for nothing. We must –'

The front door slammed. All the men in the kitchen tensed. Koji wiped the blades of his knives on his trousers, waiting.

'Nicky!' It was Joey DeSanto's voice, shouting exuberantly as he ran toward the light in the kitchen. 'Don't be mad, okay? I came to help you with those Japs. Pop's still at the house on the . . .' He nearly skidded to a halt as he entered the kitchen and saw the bodies littering the floor.

'. . . shore,' he finished weakly, looking at the faces of the Orientals.

In a panic he turned and ran. Miles sprang after him, bringing Joey down in the middle of the living room. 'Bring the rope!' he shouted.

Sato came running with the length of rope that had tied Miles to the chair, and the two of them tied Joey's hands behind his back and gagged him. Then Miles forced the young man to walk back to the kitchen.

'Take him,' he said to Hiro.

The big man got off Nick DeSanto's prone body and held Joey. Miles walked to the kitchen sink, filled a glass of water from the tap, and poured it over Nick's head. He came to slowly, groaning, pushing himself onto his hands and knees before looking up to see his brother bound and in the hands of the Japanese giant.

'Why, you –' he said, scrambling to his feet.

Miles punched him in the jaw, an old-fashioned roundhouse right. Nick danced backward, slamming against the kitchen door with such force that the frosted panes of glass in the door shattered. Then Miles came after him again and grabbed him by his collar.

'Get your father back here and wait for my call, both of you. If he's not here by then, your brother's dead. Do you understand?'

Nick's slack, bleeding mouth hung open. His eyes rolled in his head, unfocused.

'*Do you understand?*'

Nick managed a feeble nod.

Miles dumped him on the floor, then gestured to the others and led them out of the house.

Joey kicked and tried to scream through the gag in his mouth, but his brother only stared, insensate, as the five ronin dragged him away.

40

It was Lieutenant Vincent Halloran's firm belief that it was only in crime novels that things were complicated, with plots and sub-plots and tricky conspiracies that people used to mask their real intentions. In the real world the things a cop handled were pretty straightforward: murder for money, murder for passion, murder just because it seemed the right thing to do at the moment.

But this time, Halloran had to admit, he was stumped.

He looked at his red-eyed, unshaven reflection in the mirror, thinking that if his mind were in as bad shape as his face, it was no wonder he wasn't coming up with anything.

He stripped to his shorts and lay down on his unmade bed with a bottle of beer. Halloran had been married once – most of his life, it seemed – until a year ago. For nineteen years he had never had to sleep in an unmade bed. But then again, tonight he hadn't had to explain his thirty-six-hour absence from it to anyone, so things evened out. Sort of.

He took a long, appreciative pull from the bottle and tried not to think about the DeSanto situation. It didn't work. He hadn't really expected it to. It hadn't worked for the nineteen years of his marriage, when he was constantly reminded that he was choosing a low-paying and dangerous job over a good wife, so he had no reason to believe he could stop thinking about his work now. But at least he could think about it in his own bed, instead of in the cot in police headquarters where he had spent four lumpy hours the night before.

Two of DeSanto's men had been killed, one by a bow and arrow and another by being crushed like a grape in a Staten Island garage. The word had gone out that the Esteban brothers were behind the killings, until Rodrigo Esteban turned up missing and presumed to be fertilizing a lime pit somewhere on the outskirts of town. Then Giovanni Andalucci was beheaded in Chinatown and his driver skewered by a knife to the eyeball.

And now the Estebans – that was a definite, since there had been enough witnesses to the scene to populate a small town – had shot up the Peyton Place and brought the killings to the scale of a full-fledged vendetta.

So far, in spite of the imaginativeness of the murders, it had all seemed to fit within the framework of a reasonably normal struggle for power between an old established criminal organization and an aggressive young one.

Except for what Tony DeSanto had said in the hospital about the Japanese.

Halloran had raced back to the station to check the file on the wedding murder at the Inn on the Park. He had never been even slightly comfortable with that investigation, if that was what that charade could be called. Thirty dubious witnesses, a crooked judge, a vanishing valet, and on top of it all, another murder. No thanks, Halloran thought. That stank from the word go.

He read every word of Matt Watterson's testimony from the notes he'd taken when the old man and his grandson had come down to the precinct. Both of them, had sworn that six Japanese men roughed up the DeSanto boys in the parking lot of the restaurant.

'*They threw them, literally* threw *them into their car*,' Watterson had said. '*I never saw anything like it in my life.*'

'*Yeah, then what did the DeSantos – that is, the alleged*

perpetrators – do?' Halloran had asked.

He could kick himself now for ignoring the subject so completely, although at the time the presence of a handful of Japanese judo buffs at a wedding reception had seemed of little importance, particularly since the bride's mother was Japanese and Watterson himself had been an importer of Japanese art.

The more the detective thought about it, the more certain he became: the murders of Hooks Aiello and Ernie Tullio and Giovanni Andalucci had to have been revenge killings. They had been committed with too much panache to have been anything else.

As for Rodrigo Esteban's disappearance, he seriously doubted that the DeSantos had anything to do with it. Tony DeSanto himself was convinced that he was being set up for a gang war he didn't want.

It was possible that the Estebans had killed their leader themselves in order to justify a war with the DeSantos, but he doubted that, too. The Esteban boys possessed all the subtlety of nine bags of wet cement.

No, Halloran thought, Esteban's body hadn't been found yet, but he was willing to bet that when it was, it would be in as interesting a condition as the others.

But the Yakuza? A syndicate of Japanese mobsters? Despite the fascinating speculation, it would take a mighty leap of faith to bridge the gap between a respectable New York lawyer's family and a group of foreign hit men bent on destroying one of the most powerful mobs in New York City.

If the Yakuza story were even the truth. He had only the word of a Mafia *capo* for that. If Halloran even mentioned the Japanese theory to his superiors, he'd be laughed off the force.

Still, something about it made sense. If it had been his own family the DeSantos had destroyed without so much as a slap on the wrist from the authorities, Halloran had no doubt that he would consider taking matters into his own hands, just as Matt Watterson obviously had on the night he died.

He tried to remember the way the old man had looked when he'd come to the station. Most of the time the families of murder victims were simply distraught. But sometimes they were mad, with the kind of smouldering, frustrated rage that ended in murder or suicide. Those were the ones you had to watch.

And then he sat upright in the chair as the faces came flooding back. It wasn't the old man's face he remembered. It was the grandson that had been with him, the brother of the slain girl. A handsome, dark-haired young man with no Oriental features. That boy had shown neither anger nor tears. To anyone without Halloran's background, he might have seemed indifferent, but Halloran had seen that look a few times before in his career, and he understood. What it showed was something beyond grief.

His name was Miles Haverford, and Halloran had just seen him days before outside the Peyton Place.

The detective looked up the phone number of the Haverford residence and called. There was no answer. He tried again. After an hour he drove over to the East Side address on his way home and left a message with the doorman to have Miles call him as soon as he got back.

'Miles Haverford, officer?' the doorman said. 'He's been gone a long time. Months.'

'Where'd he go?'

The doorman shrugged. 'Didn't tell me. But I can ask his folks to give you a call. It won't be till tomorrow, though. They said they'd be gone a week. I think they're in New England. They've been traveling a lot since that trouble they had.'

'All right.' Halloran took back the message and wrote

another number on it. 'That's my home phone. Tell them to call me, no matter what time it is, okay?'

'You got it, officer.'

As it turned out, it had been pointless for Halloran to make the ninety-minute drive back to his apartment in Queens. Almost as soon as he walked in the door, the station called with news of the massacre at the Peyton Place. Muttering a stream of low curses, he'd gone back out, driven back to the city, and spent the rest of the night and the next day sorting out the Esteban mess.

Four of the Colombians were picked up before 3 A.M., when Halloran finally retired to his cot behind the station room. Two others were nabbed in the morning.

The case was open-and-shut. In addition to the witnesses, three of the Esteban boys had already signed confessions. But two of them – the two smartest ones, Enrique and Antonio Esteban – were still on the loose. And no weapons had been found in the apartment they had been using for headquarters.

The Colombians had drawn a lot of support lately. If they wanted to continue their war against the DeSantos, they stood a chance of winning it and launching, Halloran knew, a reign of terror that would be worse than anything the city had ever seen before.

Another complication was the follow-up on the victims. Most of those left dead at the restaurant were racketeers with long records who had been tied in some way to the DeSanto organization, and almost all of them had relatives with guns.

Halloran could only hope that somehow the two gangs could arrive at a truce before the worst happened.

He had finally gotten things into a state of quasi-orderliness by seven o'clock on the evening following the Peyton Place fracas, and headed back to Queens after a general announcement that he was going immediately to

407

bed and that if anyone dared call him before morning, he was going to shoot the phone out of the wall.

With a grunt Halloran set the beer bottle on the floor beside his bed and closed his eyes. His muscles ached. His head ached. He smelled like a sewer, and he didn't give a rat's ass. In the old days his wife would have given him a massage and set an electric fan by his feet, which also ached, but to hell with her. To hell with Tony DeSanto and the creature from the black lagoon he called his son. To hell with the Estebans. He was going to sleep.

The phone rang.

'Oh, Christ, what is it?' he said miserably.

'Detective Halloran, this is Curtis Haverford.'

He sat up, immediately alert.

'I'm sorry to disturb you, but your message said –'

'It's all right.' He rubbed his eyes. 'I'm looking for your son, Miles.'

'Is he in trouble?' The voice sounded disgusted.

'No, nothing like that. Not yet, anyway. But I've got to talk to him. I thought you might be able to tell me where he is.'

'Well, I'd like to help you, but I don't know his exact address. He's been traveling around Japan for several months.'

Halloran's breath caught. 'Japan?'

'We've had a number of postcards from him, and one call saying he'd be home soon, but that was some time ago. My son isn't particularly reliable about these things. Officer, does this have anything to do with my daughter's . . . with the incident at my daughter's wedding in March?'

Halloran didn't answer right away. He was thinking of the young man he'd seen in front of the Peyton Place less than a week before. It had been Miles Haverford. He was sure of that.

'Mr Haverford, I've got to talk to you,' he said. 'It'll take

408

me a couple of hours to get there. Will you stay home?'

'Of course. But can't you tell me . . .?'

Halloran hung up.

Joey thumped his feet uselessly against the door of the closet in the small tenement apartment on Avenue D. Hiro sat in front of it, oblivious to the muffled shouts from inside, while Koji and Yoshio waited silently nearby.

Miles and Sato were in the car, driving uptown.

'I said I didn't need you,' Miles said.

'That's too damned bad.' Sato folded his arms across his chest. 'You said he called you by name?'

'Yes. And it won't take Nick DeSanto long to figure out that he can get at me through my parents. But I can get them out by myself. I expect you to wait in the car.'

'No way.'

'Sato –'

'Just drive, okay? You can punish me later. I've still got four fingers on my left hand. I'll put your name on one of them.'

Miles sped onto FDR Drive and raced north along the side of Manhattan.

First, the cold-blooded murders of her daughter and son-in-law.

Then the finding of her stepfather's beaten body.

And the disappearance of her son, broken only by an occasional postcard from Japan and just once by a phone call to his father.

He had said he would be home soon, and she had waited, watching her husband drink himself to sleep every night, struggling with her own demons.

Her psychiatrist had said she had made excellent progress since her stay at the sanitarium. The dreams weren't so bad anymore, the terrible nightmares of bombs and fire and a woman's charred face staring sightlessly up at her – a woman who looked just like her dead daughter . . .

Miles! she wanted to scream. He was the only child she had left. Now the police wanted to talk to him. What about? What had he done?

Mickey Haverford sat at her dressing table, her unpacked suitcases piled beside her, and studied her reflection in the big mirror. She traced her finger along the aqualine nose, the hollowed cheeks, the Occidental eyelids that the best plastic surgeon in New York had provided. She had once been considered a great beauty, but after the events of the past half year, her age was starting to show.

But that was not the worst of it. Something strange had been happening in the mirror lately, something that terrified her. Beneath the altered features an entirely different face was slowly beginning to emerge. It was the face of the burned woman in her dreams.

It was happening now. As she watched, horrified, her reflection blurred the round eyes and replaced them with elongated ones, Oriental eyes staring through the film of death out of a blackened face, and her clothes were burned from her body, and nearby was the charred corpse of a five-year-old girl holding a doll and a man was bending over her, weeping, weeping . . .

'Mama!' she screamed.

When Curtis Haverford ran in the bedroom, she was clutching the mirror on either side and shaking it violently.

'Mickey, Mickey,' he said soothingly, putting his hands over her own. 'It's all right. I'm here. You're all right.'

Gently he took her hands off the mirror and led her into the living room. He set her down on a sofa facing the television set. 'How's that? Do you want to watch something else?'

She shook her head, staring blankly at a pre-season football game which her husband knew she was not seeing.

With a sigh he made himself a martini.

410

Curtis Haverford had taken steps to retire from the law firm in which he was a senior partner. He had spoken to his colleagues about taking some time off – 'a chance to smell the flowers' was how he'd put it – but the truth was that he no longer trusted his wife to be left alone. He had tried to fill her life with travel and entertainment and parties and new friends, but nothing seemed to ease the awful burden of grief she carried with her, and the fear of her committing suicide was always close to the surface of his consciousness.

He wondered how a family that had been so full of promise and life could have withered to a grieving, neurotic woman, an inactive lawyer who drank too much, and a playboy son who did not even have the character to feel outrage at the senseless killings of his sister and grandfather. While his wife slowly lost her mind, he thought bitterly, Miles had spent his time traipsing around the world, living the life of a professional parasite. And now the police wanted him.

The doorbell rang.

Well, they could have him. As far as Curtis Haverford was concerned, he had no more children.

Holding his martini in his hand, he walked down the long hallway to the front door and unlocked it.

The door suddenly slammed open into him, knocking the drink from his hand and forcing him to stumble back against the wall. Two men dressed in dark suits jumped into the apartment hallway and pushed the door shut behind them.

'Where's your old lady?' one of them growled. When Haverford was slow in answering, the man slapped him across the face.

'I said, where's your wife?'

'Who are you? What do you want?'

'Al, go inside and look for her.' He gestured toward the living room with his gun.

When the other man returned, he was holding onto Mickey, who was quaking and breathing spasmodically. 'Curtis,' she said, her eyes wild. 'Curtis –'

'Don't worry,' her husband said softly, feeling helpless inside. 'We're going to be fine.'

'That's right,' the thug said. 'Long as you do what you're supposed to do.' He jammed the gun into Haverford's side. 'Now we're going to go out in the hall and take the elevator downstairs. If you see somebody you know, say hello but no more talking. And don't try anything stupid. We'll kill you if we have to. Got it?'

Haverford nodded. He took his wife's elbow as one of the men opened the door to the hallway. The other walked behind them, at Haverford's shoulder.

Then he heard a pair of rapid-fire thuds and a grunt as the man behind him pulled away and fell suddenly to the floor. At the same moment a figure stepped out of the shadows and threw the gunman in front of him into the wall.

Instinctively Haverford threw his arms around Mickey to protect her as the two strangers pummeled the kidnappers with a viciousness that seemed to border on insanity. Then he saw the face of one of the attackers. He could hardly believe his eyes.

It was his son.

'Get back inside,' Miles commanded.

His mother gasped. 'Miles? Miles, is it you?'

She stared forward, but Haverford grabbed her and took her back into the apartment. They closed the door and stood behind it, unable to speak. Then finally, after a few seconds that felt like forever, the sounds of battle from the hallway ceased.

Miles pushed open the door and came in.

'Oh, my God,' his mother said, melting into his arms.

'I've missed you, Mother.' He looked over at his father. 'And you too, Dad.'

But Curtis Haverford could not speak.

Is this my son? he thought, surveying Miles's hardened face and body. *This is someone I've never known.*

Mickey was crying. 'Who were those men? How did you know about them?'

'There's no time for that now,' Miles said. 'But I knew they'd be here. I still had my key.' He disentangled himself from his mother's arms and held her by both shoulders.

'You have to get out of here for a while. A week or two. Do you understand?'

Mickey only wept.

'A police officer named Halloran is looking for you,' his father said. 'Do you know why?'

'Yes.' Miles didn't elaborate.

Sato came in. 'They're both dead,' he said in Japanese.

'Where did you put the bodies?'

'In the stairway.'

'All right. Go downstairs and get a cab. I'll bring them down in a minute.'

'*Hai*, Ronin.'

Curtis and Mickey Haverford both stared at their son in amazement.

'Do you have a bag?' Miles asked.

'They're still packed,' Haverford said. 'We just got back from Cape Cod. Son –'

'Go back there.' Miles went for the luggage.

Within five minutes they were in the lobby of the building. A taxi was waiting outside.

'Are you coming?' his mother asked, touching Miles's arm.

'No.'

She began to cry.

'Get her inside,' he told his father.

'Now just a minute,' Curtis Haverford bristled.

413

Miles forced his mother into the cab, then reached for his father.

'That's enough!' Haverford pulled his arm away angrily. 'You can't just leave us this way. Why do we have to go like this? What do the police want with you? So help me, Miles, if you've –'

Then he looked into his son's eyes, and his wrath dissipated. The weary face in front of him did not belong to the irresponsible boy who had left home so many months ago. It was the face of a man, a man who had saved his life.

'What *have* you been doing?' he asked quietly.

'I've been repaying a debt.'

Curtis Haverford said nothing for a moment. Then suddenly the deeply etched lines in his face smoothed out into an expression of blank astonishment. 'The DeSanto mob killings,' he whispered. 'That was you.'

Miles turned away. 'There was no one else.' When he looked back, there was pain in his eyes. 'Take care of Mother,' he said.

'She needs you . . .'

'No. She needs *you*. Susi and Granddad need me.' He pushed his father gently into the taxi.

'Will you come back?' Haverford asked.

Miles stared at him and at his sobbing mother. Their son, he knew, would never come back. He had died long ago. Wordlessly he backed into the darkness of the street.

'Miles,' his father shouted out the window. 'Miles!'

But he was gone.

'Halloran, NYPD,' the detective announced as he flashed his badge. 'I'm here to talk to the Haverfords.'

The doorman looked surprised. He looked down at the registry, then up at Halloran again.

'They're expecting me,' he said impatiently.

'Oh, shit,' the doorman said, grimacing.

'What's the matter?'

'I thought you were already here. These two guys came in about a half an hour ago. The Haverfords called down before and said to send you right up when you came, so when these two guys walked in and asked for them, I said, "You Halloran?" and the one guy said, "Yeah," so I sent them up. See, I wrote your name in the registry.'

He turned the book around to show him, but Halloran was already racing for the stairs.

'Hey, they're not there anymore,' the doorman called after him. 'Mr and Mrs Haverford left a few minutes ago. With their son Miles.'

Halloran spun around on the stairs. 'Miles was here?'

'Yeah. Miles and some Chinese guy. They showed up right after the other two. I knew you were looking for him, so I figured you got hold of him after all, and you were getting everybody together. Only it wasn't you.' He shook his head. 'Well, no harm done, I guess.'

'When did the other men leave?'

He shrugged. 'Maybe while I was in the toilet. I didn't see them.'

Halloran looked up the stairway. 'I'm going to take a look up there,' he said.

'Suit yourself. Sorry about the screwup.'

As soon as he reached the landing, Halloran knew something was wrong. He could smell it. He went up to the Haverfords' apartment door and listened. There was no sound inside. Still uneasy, he rang the bell, just in case the doorman had been mistaken.

No answer.

He told himself to relax, but he knew he wouldn't be able to now. Miles Haverford had shown himself. He had taken his parents out of their apartment. Why?

It could only mean that the DeSantos were on to him.

Quickly he scribbled a note on the back of one of his

police business cards, asking the Haverfords to call him, then squatted down to slide it under the door.

That was when he saw the blood.

On the wall alongside the door was a dark red stain. He touched it. It was still fresh. He stood up and looked around. There were more stains on the wall on the other side of the door, and on the carpet as well. He followed them to the fire exit stairwell. There, at the bottom of the metal stairs, lay the bodies of two men.

Halloran recognized them. They were soldiers for the DeSantos. He had seen them hanging around the Peyton Place a few times, and down at headquarters under arrest more often than that. Their faces were bloody, and one of them had a smashed nose, but they hadn't died in a fistfight. Both their necks had been broken. The bruises across them were clean and straight. One lethal, expert blow each.

Obviously, DeSanto or his son had sent these strongarms here to do something to the Haverfords. And obviously the soldiers had met Miles.

He wiped his hands on one of the dead men's shirts, then sat down heavily on the stairs. There was enough evidence now to begin a case against Miles Haverford, although his every instinct screamed against it. The boy had accomplished something he himself had tried and failed to do for twenty years: he had cut the legs out from under the DeSantos.

Still, the law was the law, and Miles had broken it enough times to spend the rest of his life behind bars.

Funny, he thought. The guy's sister, brother-in-law, and grandfather all get whacked by a gang of organized criminals the NYPD can't touch, but he gets a life sentence for fighting back. It was a shitty deal.

He stood up. Not that it was going to make any difference, he thought. Miles Haverford was never going to live

416

long enough to go to jail. The kid was smart, but he was in way over his head. Whatever troubles Tony DeSanto was facing, he was a professional with a big organization.

Miles had picked a fight with the wrong man. It was a fight he could never hope to win.

Still, as he walked back toward his car to radio the station, a small voice inside him was whispering, *Good luck, Haverford*. And he found himself, to his surprise, hoping that maybe, just maybe, the kid might be able to pull it off.

41

After his son had called to tell him about Joey's kidnapping, Tony DeSanto had driven up from his house on the Jersey shore at ninety miles an hour most of the way. But when he arrived, the only evidence of what had happened were a few broken windows in the kitchen. The bodies of the two dead guards and Frank Lupone were nowhere in sight. Nick was sitting calmly on the living room sofa, drinking a scotch and water.

'Where is my son?' DeSanto growled.

'Relax, Pop. Al and Paulie'll be back any minute.'

DeSanto checked his watch. It was ten-fifteen. 'I told you to send them out over an hour and a half ago.'

'So I sent them. Get off my back, all right?'

DeSanto could tell by the glassy sheen in Nick's eyes that alcohol wasn't the only chemical circulating in his body. 'Then where are they?'

'How the fuck do I know?' Nick exploded. 'Maybe the Jap's parents weren't home. Hey, I didn't ask Joey to come back here.'

With a muffled roar DeSanto lunged at his son and yanked him off the sofa. 'You listen to me, Nicky. If your brother dies –'

Nick threw him off with a vicious kick that sent the old man sprawling on the floor. 'What, huh?' Nick shouted at his father. 'What are you going to do? Send the *capi* after me? They don't want to know your name. You're finished, old man.'

He straightened out his shirt, then lit a cigarette. 'And you know what? I don't give a shit about you or your precious Joey. Joey this, Joey that. Joey so smart, so good, so goddamned special. Well, if Joey gets whacked tonight by those gooks, it's his own fault.' He picked up his jacket and slung it over his shoulder. 'From now on, you better stay out of my way.' He stomped away toward the door.

The phone rang, and DeSanto looked up at it wildly. Miles Haverford's message had been for them both to wait for his call.

'Nicky,' he whispered, pleading. He got up on his knees, unconsciously posing in the classic position of a beggar. 'Please stay.'

Nick exhaled a long plume of smoke as his father answered the telephone.

'Dad, it's Joey,' the frightened voice on the other end said.

DeSanto sniffed, his heart flooding with relief. 'Are you all right?'

But before his son could answer, another voice came on the line. 'This is Miles Haverford.'

DeSanto pulled the phone toward a window and looked out, craning his neck to see down the length of the driveway. The two men he had ordered to pick up Miles Haverford's parents should have arrived with them by now. *Hurry up, you bastards*, he thought, swallowing. 'Look – look,' he stammered, trying to keep his voice calm. 'You don't have to do this. We can make a deal. We can work things out.'

'If you're waiting for my parents to arrive, you can forget it,' Miles said coldly. 'Your men are dead.'

There was a long silence.

'How much?' DeSanto said at last.

'Not everything comes down to money, Mr DeSanto,' the voice said. 'I'll meet you at midnight to discuss my terms. Your other son, Nick, must be present. If he's not there, Joey dies.'

'Where?' DeSanto asked.

'I'll let you know.'

The phone went dead. DeSanto dialed a series of numbers, reaching out again for the dons who ran the city with their powerful organizations. Again they would not speak to him, even after he had explained that he was calling about a dire emergency. Finally he reached Luciano Avalone, who had led the others in refusing to support DeSanto.

'Thank you for speaking with me, Don Avalone,' he said, almost in tears as he forced himself to pay respect to a man who had been his inferior only a week before.

'Your troubles have pained me,' the older man said in his sonorous voice. 'But I have had no choice. Just as I have no choice tonight.'

His words felt like a weight suddenly falling inside DeSanto's belly. 'You know?'

'A stranger called me. He said that to help you tonight would bring on my organization the same fate that has befallen yours. He said that his quarrel is with you alone, Antonio, and that after it is settled, he will leave in peace.'

'They've got my son,' DeSanto rasped.

'I am deeply sorry.'

DeSanto replaced the receiver slowly. 'Nicky,' he whispered. 'Come with me tonight. You are all I have now.'

'Why should I?'

'Tomorrow I will turn over everything I have to you.' He spoke in a low monotone. 'I will not fight you for control. You will be *capo*. Perhaps you will do a better job than I have done.'

Nick stared at him for a moment, then cocked his head, and smiled. 'You got a deal,' he said.

* * *

Lieutenant Halloran also got a call. He was back at head-quarters, having resigned himself to spending another night on the cot in the back room, and even work was better than that. He was typing up a report on the night's findings at the Haverfords' apartment building, tying the first knots in the rope that would eventually hang Miles Haverford, when the phone rang.

'Halloran here.'

'I think you know who this is.'

He looked down at the sheet of paper in his typewriter. 'Yeah, Miles.'

'If you want the DeSantos, be in your office tonight at twelve-fifteen. You'll get further instructions then by phone.'

'Wait. I –'

'I'm done waiting, Lieutenant.'

Five minutes later, a telephone in New Haven, Connecticut, rang in Miles's former apartment. When it was picked up, there were the sounds of loud music and laughter in the background.

'Mark, it's Miles.'

He heard a whoop. 'Where you been, buddy? The party factory just hasn't been the same without you.'

'This is important,' Miles said. 'I need a favor. No questions asked.'

'You got it.'

'Listen carefully. At twelve-fifteen tonight, I want you to call New York City police headquarters.' Miles gave him the number and waited for the other man to write it down. 'Ask for Lieutenant Vincent Halloran. Write the name down. Right. Tell him just this. "Sheep's Meadow. Immediately. No sirens." Read that back to me.'

'Sheep's Meadow. Immediately. No sirens. Miles –'

'Exactly at twelve-fifteen.'

'I know. I've got that. But what's going on? Are you in some kind of trouble?'

'I said no questions.'

'Okay, okay, buddy.'

Miles hung up.

Hiro braced the short end of Yoshio's ten-man bow against the side of his foot, grabbed the top end in his hands, and pressed it downward, curling it into its shooting shape while Yoshio slid the bowstring into place.

Koji was oiling the blades of four throwing knives. His sword was in its scabbard hanging at his side.

Sato opened a black silk handkerchief on the table. Inside were a half-dozen black metal star-shaped objects.

'What are those?' Miles asked.

'*Shuriken*,' Sato said, examining their razor-sharp edges. 'Ninja stars.' He folded the cloth back over them. 'Don't even think about going alone tonight,' he added without looking at Miles.

'That's right, Ronin,' Hiro said. 'This is our decision, not yours. We will accept the consequences from the Oyabun.'

Miles knew when he was beaten. He could never get away with Joey DeSanto in tow without being followed by his men.

'You may not live to face any consequences,' he said angrily.

'That's fine with me,' Yoshio said. 'Compared with Nagoya, death will be an easy master.'

Koji only smiled.

Miles looked at each of them. 'Arigato,' he said. 'Thank you.'

Miles sat in a parked car with Sato in the driver's seat. Joey DeSanto was bound and gagged on the floor in the rear. Before them spread the eight hundred acres of New York

City's Central Park. Some areas of the park were floodlit like a baseball stadium for a night game, while other parts were pitch dark, shaded by tall trees even from the occasional light from the moon.

They had been watching for nearly a half hour now. Only one police patrol car had driven by. There had not been any other traffic.

'This will do,' Miles said, and got out.

He called Tony DeSanto from a pay phone nearby. 'Sheep's Meadow in Central Park. Midnight,' was all he said.

Then he whistled a signal. There was no sound in response, not even the rustling of leaves, but he knew that his men had gone into hiding in the trees and bushes, waiting for the final confrontation with Tony DeSanto and what was left of his organization.

At eleven forty-five, when the first car arrived, Miles was crouched behind an outcropping of rock, his elbow crooked around Joey DeSanto's neck. He had chosen this spot because it was a natural fortification against the guns DeSanto was sure to bring. The rock was long and curved, affording protection on two sides. Behind it, some five hundred yards away, was a stand of tall oak trees where he could run if that became necessary.

The car, a dark Chrysler sedan, pulled up and parked on the road running alongside the meadow. Four men got out and darted across the grass into the bushes. Miles knew they had been sent to set up an ambush. He could hear the men spreading out, moving through the darkness.

He hunkered back into the shadows, waited, and listened intently. He heard a thud. A muffled groan. Another thud. He did not hear the fourth sound, but he knew, even without hearing it, that Hiro and Sato had taken out all four of the men. They would not be a factor in what was to come.

At exactly midnight the main DeSanto caravan arrived.

Six cars were headed by DeSanto's brown Lincoln limousine. They parked on the road, then waited for a few minutes before DeSanto got out, with Nick following behind. Under the soft streetlight Miles could see that Nick's face was puffy and bruised from the beating he had given him.

The hate again welled up inside him as he saw the two men walking into the meadow, surrounded by some two dozen of their soldiers, who had poured out of the other cars and formed a human barricade around them.

The DeSantos had always had a wall of men to protect them, he thought bitterly. A wall that had included lawyers and judges and police, so that no matter what they did, no matter how many innocent people they slaughtered, they would never have to pay for their crimes. In their corrupt little world, they had lived like despotic gods.

That was over now. Miles watched the progress of the armed entourage with satisfaction. No matter what happened to him tonight, the temple the DeSantos had built to shield them from justice would crumble to the last stone.

As the group moved into an open area beside some tall hedges, Miles released the ropes around Joey's feet and then removed the blindfold and gag.

'Over here!' Joey screamed.

All of the weapons swiveled toward the rock ledge where Miles waited. He stood up and pulled Joey to his feet. The young man's wrists were still bound behind his back and Miles held onto the rope to keep him from trying to bolt across the greensward.

When DeSanto saw his son, he called out across the twenty-five feet that separated them, 'Are you all right, Joey?'

'I'm okay,' Joey said.

DeSanto nodded almost imperceptibly, and a man in the rear of the group peeled away, crouching, into the darkness of the hedges. As he neared the rock where Joey and Miles

Haverford stood, he dropped to one knee, looking through the infrared sight on his rifle.

He had barely seen Miles's head in the sight when suddenly the rifle fell from his hands and he tumbled backwards onto the ground. He clapped his hands around his neck, appearing for a moment as if he were trying to strangle himself. Then his arms slowly dropped to his side.

Jutting from his throat was a bloody black star.

'Anybody else want to try?' Miles called as the other men with the DeSantos looked around, spooked.

After some murmuring their ranks opened and Tony DeSanto stepped out into the open. 'What do you want?' he asked softly.

Miles's answer was equally quiet. 'A trade,' he said. 'Nick DeSanto murdered my sister and grandfather in cold blood. The law won't punish him, but you can. I offer you a life for a life. The innocent for the guilty. Kill Nick, and I will release Joey.'

There was a terrible silence that seemed to cover the park like a giant wad of cotton.

'*What?*' DeSanto said finally.

'I want you to execute your son.'

Joey turned to stare at him, horrified.

'Those are my terms, DeSanto.'

'He's crazy,' Nick muttered, taking out a nickel-plated .38. 'I say blow the bastard away, then shoot up everything in sight.'

'Including your brother –' DeSanto started to say, but he was interrupted by low hissing behind him. As he turned around to look, two men at the back of the group fell forward silently. Their necks both had long red lines drawn across them. Then, as if on signal, their heads detached and rolled away on the grass. The sound was the hiss of spurting blood.

This time the frightened men ran for cover. Nick pumped

six rounds into the hedges behind the two corpses, but hit nothing. Koji had already disappeared into the trees.

'How many guys they got?' someone whispered.

'Even if it's one, it's too friggin' many,' someone else answered.

The men were finally assembled again, but their nervousness was evident.

'Put down your guns,' Miles called to them. 'Or are you all ready to die for the DeSantos?'

With rage in his voice, one man at the far end of the group shouted, 'I am, you motherfucking Jap, and I'm going to take you with me!' as he raised a machine gun into position.

Miles heard the sound before he saw the result. Something whooshed overhead. Then the man flung his arms wide, throwing the machine gun a full twenty feet as the center of his body buckled. As if by magic, he seemed to fly backward until he smashed into a tree trunk and stuck there.

There was a grimace on the man's face. It looked like an idiot's grin, wide and unchanging. Then the man's head snapped forward in death, and the others saw the weapon that had killed him. He was pinned to the tree like a bug on a piece of cork by an arrow five feet long.

'I'm getting the fuck out of here,' one of the men said, running. Two others joined him. Nick whirled around, his gun raised, and fired at the deserters. One of the bullets hit. The man's back arched, and then he fell face first to the ground while Nick continued to fire.

'Scumbags!' he screamed. 'I'll teach you to run out on *me*, you fucking yellowbellies!'

The remaining men looked at one another in disbelief. Even Tony DeSanto realized what was happening: unable to vent his rage on his enemies, Nick was shooting his own men for sport. DeSanto stepped back from his son. 'Take him,' he said quietly.

The men pounced on Nick like a human net, disarming

him, grabbing both his arms and legs and lifting him off the ground while he screamed in wild fury.

During the confusion Sato moved up behind them and picked up the machine gun from the ground. Ducking back behind the hedge, he worked his way slowly toward Miles.

Someone tossed Nick's gun to DeSanto. He caught it and checked the barrel. There was one shot left.

It would be enough.

The men held Nick on the open ground, looking back at DeSanto for guidance, but the don did not speak or move for several minutes. He only stood holding the shiny, nickel-plated gun in the palms of his open hands, staring at it.

Finally, his mouth a thin white line, he stepped forward, his arm outstretched, the barrel of the gun pointing at Nick's head. The men moved away slowly in a widening circle.

Nick started to get up, then saw his father, and froze in his sprawled position. 'You're not going to shoot me,' he said. His voice was almost seductive. There was the hint of a smile on his face.

'I have to,' DeSanto said softly. 'You're too dangerous.'

'*I'm your son, you gutless son of a bitch!*' Nick roared, his face suddenly contorting into a mask of rage.

At Miles's command, Sato threw the machine gun at Nick's feet. Nick reached for it instinctively, but stopped, his hands raised, looking around in suspicion and astonishment.

'It's for you,' Miles said. 'If you can kill your father before he kills you, we'll let you go free. Of course, we'll kill your brother in your place.' He paused to let his words sink in.

Beneath the ropes he could feel Joey trembling. 'Take their bodies to the Estebans as a peace offering. The war will end, and you will be don. Interested?'

Nick DeSanto looked at his father.

'Nicky, no!' Joey screamed.

Moving like a commando, Nick rolled into the old man's

legs, knocking him over while he picked up the machine gun at the same time. DeSanto's gun flew out of his hand. He tried to reach for it, but in another second Nick was on top of him, pressing the long barrel of the weapon up under his rib cage. He fired without hesitation.

Nothing happened.

As father and son stared at one another in silence, something dropped on the ground near them.

'There's the ammunition clip,' Miles said. 'I just wanted Joey to see what you would do.' He unbound Joey's wrists.

Nick scrambled for the clip. Tony DeSanto sat up slowly. The nickel-plated revolver was within reach.

'Take a good look at your family, Joey,' Miles said. 'At the honor of the DeSantos.'

He shoved him onto the grass.

'Pop!' Joey called, running toward them. 'Nicky!' It's all right. They let me go!'

He stopped short when he heard the report of a gun firing a single bullet.

Nick slumped to the ground.

His brother ran over to him. 'Nicky!' he screamed. 'Nicky, don't die.'

But he was already dead. His father had executed him with a single shot in the middle of the forehead.

'You killed him,' Joey said, looking up at his father incredulously. 'You killed your own son.'

'Get him out of the way,' DeSanto said. He picked the machine gun off the ground, snapped in the ammunition clip, and took cover behind a tree. 'Level this place to the ground,' he said, and fired a burst at the rock where Miles had held Joey.

The others opened fire, shooting in all directions, as if their guns could exorcise the demons they had seen this night in the men they served.

'Are our men gone?' Miles asked.

Sato nodded. 'I gave them the signal a few minutes ago.'

'Good. Let's get out of here. Keep low.' He crawled out from behind the outcropping of rock, sprinting toward the stand of trees. When he reached them, he ducked behind a tall oak, panting for breath as Sato made the run. The Japanese had almost reached him when a bullet caught him in the back and he spun, his arms windmilling as he fell backward onto the rocky hill.

'Sato!' Miles shouted, but his voice was lost in the din of gunfire.

He ran over to him, weaving in a zigzag pattern while bullets pinged off the ground on either side of him, and dragged him back behind the shelter of the rock.

The wound was bleeding badly. It had entered Sato's back, through his ribs, and punctured one of his lungs. With every breath, blood frothed out from between his lips.

'Hang on to me,' Miles said. 'I can carry you out.'

'No.' Sato struggled to keep his eyes open. 'You go, Ronin. I'm not going to make it.'

'Yes, you will, goddammit,' Miles said fiercely, tying the wound with strips of cloth torn from his shirt.

'It's all right.' Sato smiled weakly. 'Don't you see? I was the one who wasn't supposed to make it back, not you. It was part of my ka. I am the old way, you are the new. You have to take the ronin back. They're yours. They've been yours from the beginning.' He wheezed noisily. A trickle of blood oozed from the corners of his lips. 'Go.'

Miles settled back and shook his head. 'I can't. If you die, I must die, too. It was my vow to the Oyabun.' He wiped the sweat off Sato's face. 'I'll wait here with you.'

Sato's green eyes flashed through his pain. 'You promised him *that*?'

'It is a small price to pay, kyodai.'

Just then they heard the wail of a siren close by. 'This is the police,' a voice over a loudspeaker announced. 'Put down your weapons. Your are surrounded. Repeat, drop your weapons.'

'You were always more trouble than you were worth,' Sato said. With a grimace he slowly raised his arms to Miles. 'Get me out of here.' He sighed. 'Five of us are going home.'

Miles smiled. He lifted the tall man as gently as if he were a baby in his arms.

As he carried Sato toward the stand of trees, a young uniformed officer ran up to Halloran.

'Lieutenant,' he said, 'there's two guys over there by that rock. I'm a sharpshooter, if you want them.'

Halloran looked where the young officer was pointing. Two men dressed in black were slowly climbing the hill toward a stand of trees. No, that wasn't it. It was one man carrying another. A body, maybe.

As he watched, the moon drifted out from behind the clouds and momentarily covered the meadow with silver light. The man carrying the body must have sensed Halloran watching him, because he turned his head to look back over his shoulder. For a moment, even at this far distance, their eyes seemed to lock.

'Sir?' the sharpshooter asked, lifting his rifle.

'Naah,' the detective said. 'They're probably just a couple of fags. Do you know what kind of trouble you can get into shooting at bystanders?' He slapped the patrolman's chest with the back of his hand. 'Well, do you?'

'Yes, sir. My mistake, sir.' He turned back to the police van, where the DeSanto men were being methodically herded. Tony DeSanto stood ashen-faced while police fitted him with a pair of handcuffs. Nick DeSanto lay isolated on the open ground of the meadow, the bullet hole in his head staring upward like a third eye. Joey DeSanto crouched on the grass, his face hidden in his hands.

After a word with the officer handcuffing him, DeSanto

walked over to Joey and touched his hair with his two bound hands. Joey jerked away from him. 'Get away from me,' he said through clenched teeth.

His father walked back to the van and climbed inside slowly, looking like an old, old man.

And then the moon disappeared behind the clouds again, and the hillside was dark.

Halloran smiled.

42

The kobun were seated around the low table in the teahouse as Nagoya poured a bowl of sake and set it down in front of him. Then he sat back on his knees, his back still as straight as a boy's.

'This is the last time you will gather here with me,' he said quietly. 'And you are the last of my kobun.'

The men were not surprised. The preparations for the passing of the cup from the old Oyabun to the new had been going on for weeks, while Sato recuperated from his injury.

During that time no one had left the house while it was ritually purified, and no one from the outside had been permitted to enter it. A great covered palanquin had been built, carved from teak-wood and painted with gold, to carry the new Oyabun through the streets of the city. A ceremonial kimono heavy with embroidery and precious metals was brought out to clothe him during his triumphant ride.

Now Sato was well. Today he would step into the palanquin, robed like a god. Today he would take the cup from the old master and, with it, assume his destiny.

Nagoya raised the bowl before him. 'I pass this to him who will guide you into the dawn,' he said in the old tongue. 'Take it and rule well.'

For the first time any of the men could remember, he bowed his head lower than theirs, offering the bowl to Sato in his out-stretched hands.

Sato took it, but he did not drink its contents.

The men looked at one another in silence as he sat immobile, the precious antique bowl in his hands.

'I cannot accept this,' he said finally.

There was a rustle as the kobun stiffened in their seats, shock on their faces. Nagoya blinked in astonishment.

'I have been chosen to be Oyabun, but that choice is the wrong one.' He stared straight ahead as he spoke, and his face was expressionless. 'I could not lead you into the future, but only back into the past, into the shadows where we would not thrive. Under my hand the Onami would die, as the great Yakuza houses everywhere are dying.'

His face flickered with emotion. 'Japan is no longer a ruined island of chaos and despair, but an emerging world power. The Onami can languish with the rest of the Yakuza in the twilight world of crime and death, or it can become part of the new era. We can use the power and wealth of this house to build banks, to develop businesses, to make a solid foundation for our children and theirs, to bring security to the thousands of families that depend on us. We can come out of hiding forever, if we are prepared to adapt.'

The stunned silence of the men at the table gave way to the din of agitated talk. Only Miles and Nagoya said nothing.

Miles was staring intently at Sato. *How this man has changed*, he thought. *How we all have.*

Nagoya's brow furrowed as he appraised the young man he had chosen to be his successor. He had not expected such humility from the arrogant street fighter who had come to him so long ago. But Sato would accept the cup. He had to. Nagoya would not live forever.

The room quieted as Sato began to speak again. 'You can make this change,' he said, 'but not with a leader who is a common criminal. I am not the man to take you into the dawn. For that you will need someone special. Someone whom the gods have sent from across the sea to lead you to tomorrow.'

He bowed his head low. Then he held the bowl out to Miles.

There was an audible gasp from every man at the table as the American looked up at Sato in disbelief.

Then Koji said in a quiet voice, '*Hai*, Ronin.'

'Ronin,' Yoshio affirmed, scowling, daring anyone to object.

'Ronin,' Hiro repeated. A big grin grew across his face.

'Ronin,' the others said, first softly, and then in a resounding cheer. 'Ronin! Ronin! Ronin!'

Miles turned to Nagoya. The deep creases on the old man's face smoothed.

Once he had used all his resources to break his grandson's will, to knock him down so that he would crawl back to the safe cocoon of a sheltered life. But he had not crawled. Like the legless red doll on the windowsill, he had sprung back upright to try again.

Yes, he would make a worthy leader.

'Ronin,' the old man said softly.

Miles accepted the bowl. Then he bowed to the others, each of them in turn, and drank.

Epilogue

The gilded palanquin majestically made its way up the four hundred steps of the shrine of Kumano-michi. It was carried on the shoulders of four men: a swordsman, a wrestler, an archer, and a karate fighter, the strange companions of the powerful man who had sent them.

At the top of the stone steps, high above the waterfall that painted a permanent rainbow in the sky, the temple nuns waited like yellow-robed statues. In front of them stood a woman, resplendent in the ancient white costume and headdress of a bride.

The men set the palanquin down and bowed to her. One of them, the fighter, took her hand somberly and led her to the gold-embroidered curtain of the litter.

'*Hontoni arigato gozaimashita, Sato,*' she said. Thank you for everything, from the bottom of my heart. There were tears in her eyes. 'Thank you for not letting him fight alone.'

'He was never alone, my lady,' he said. 'You were with him, in his heart.'

She bowed and blinked the moisture from her eyes. 'A thousand blessings upon you and your dear wife, old friend. I hope she has brought you the happiness I could not.'

'You were meant for one greater than I, Lady Tomiko,' he said hoarsely. 'And he for you. I only regret –'

She touched her fingers to his face. 'Regret nothing,' she

whispered. 'That is the way of the Onami.'

He bowed deeply to her. 'Come. The Oyabun awaits you.'

She stepped into the palanquin and the men carried it away, down the long steps, toward their master who lived far beyond the city, in a house with a bamboo flume and a sand garden, where warriors once walked.

MAFIA BULLETS ARE THE
GAMBLING CHIPS IN *RICOCHET*

OVID DEMARIS

RICOCHET

**Frank Conti is a successful banker, a cop's son
and a Vietnam Green Beret. Nothing wrong
with that, except that life hasn't been too hot
since the tragic death of his young son in a
bicycle accident, an accident that Frank will
never forget. His beautiful wife, Nancy, is trapped
by her grief and takes solace in gambling, an
addiction that the nearby halls in Atlantic City
can service 'til Kingdom come. And to top it all,
Conti's lifelong enemy, a big crime boss, is out to
destroy him. For the local Mob, retribution is
always sweet — especially when it takes its form
in the kidnap of red-headed Nancy and the
fuelling of her little habit . . .**

**Hard-hitting, fast-paced and with an authentic
reek of corruption, *Ricochet* is a powerful novel
infused with all the glitz and sleaze of organized
crime — avarice, high-stakes and a never-ending
desire for revenge.**

**'A fast-moving novel that pulls no punches . . .
readers will keep turning the pages'** *Publishers
Weekly*

**'Emerald City glitz in the midst of poverty and
sleaze . . . priceless'** *Kirkus Reviews*

FICTION/THRILLER   0 7472 3269 5   £3.50

PETER WATSON

CRUSADE

'The most compelling thriller of its kind to come my way since THE DAY OF THE JACKAL'

Harold Harris*

Behind the scenes at the Vatican, the Pope offers David Colwyn, chief executive of the international auctioneering house of Hamilton's, a spectacular deal. In an audacious and provocative scheme to raise money for a crusade against poverty and injustice, the Pope wants David to organise a series of worldwide auctions to sell the fabled treasures of the Vatican: Michelangelo's sculpture, Leonardo da Vinci's painting, Giotto's altarpiece – all will go.

Despite protests, the Pope's plan proceeds and the world watches as David, in the glare of publicity, raises millions of pounds. But now powerful forces range in fierce and treacherous opposition – and the Pope's plans go disastrously wrong, perverted by revolutionaries and international criminals. Soon a furious battle of power politics rages, a battle that can end only in a bloody and shocking climax...

"Crusade's real edge is that it could be next week's news."
Daily Mail

"Peter Watson's imaginative near-future thriller stands out... classy entertainment."
The Evening Standard

"Non-stop action, an incredible vortex of fights and frauds."
The Guardian

* original publisher of Frederick Forsyth

FICTION/THRILLER   0 7472 3143 5   £3.99

HERBERT BURKHOLZ
THE
SENSITIVES

'CRAMMED WITH THE ESSENTIALS OF ANY GOOD THRILLER' *BOOKS*

'Compulsive reading . . . an excellent
~~thriller~~

Born with the ability to read minds the way ordinary people read newspapers, the sensitives are literally one in a million. Zealously sought and guarded by the world's Intelligence agencies, the sensitives are doomed – not one has ever reached his thirty-fifth birthday.

For all his adult life Ben Slade has used his gift on behalf of the Centre, and given his loyalty to Pop, who watches protectively over the American sensitives. But when Ben and his Russian counterpart, Nadia Petrovna, decide to risk everything to be together, their decision has terrifying and far-reaching consequences both for themselves and for every other sensitive for whom time is running out.

For not even their strange ability can penetrate the dark heart of the Intelligence underworld – a realm where, for the good of the state, any treachery is permissible and where prey and predator become impossible to tell apart . . .

FICTION/THRILLER   0 7472 3094 3   £2.99

A selection of bestsellers from Headline

FICTION

TALENT	Nigel Rees	£3.99 ☐
A BLOODY FIELD BY SHREWSBURY	Edith Pargeter	£3.99 ☐
GUESTS OF THE EMPEROR	Janice Young Brooks	£3.99 ☐
THE LAND IS BRIGHT	Elizabeth Murphy	£3.99 ☐
THE FACE OF FEAR	Dean R Koontz	£3.50 ☐

NON-FICTION

CHILD STAR	Shirley Temple Black	£4.99 ☐
BLIND IN ONE EAR	Patrick Macnee and Marie Cameron	£3.99 ☐
TWICE LUCKY	John Francome	£4.99 ☐
HEARTS AND SHOWERS	Su Pollard	£2.99 ☐

SCIENCE FICTION AND FANTASY

WITH FATE CONSPIRE The Destiny Makers 1	Mike Shupp	£3.99 ☐
A DISAGREEMENT WITH DEATH	Craig Shaw Gardner	£2.99 ☐
SWORD & SORCERESS 4	Marion Zimmer Bradley	£3.50 ☐

All Headline books are available at your local bookshop or newsagent, or can be ordered direct from the publisher. Just tick the titles you want and fill in the form below. Prices and availability subject to change without notice.

Headline Book Publishing PLC, Cash Sales Department, PO Box 11, Falmouth, Cornwall TR10 9EN, England.

Please enclose a cheque or postal order to the value of the cover price and allow the following for postage and packing:
UK: 60p for the first book, 25p for the second book and 15p for each additional book ordered up to a maximum charge of £1.90
BFPO: 60p for the first book, 25p for the second book and 15p per copy for the next seven books, thereafter 9p per book
OVERSEAS & EIRE: £1.25 for the first book, 75p for the second book and 28p for each subsequent book.

Name ....

Address ....

....

....